D1190794

ASCENDANT

BOOK ONE OF THE ASCENDANT TRILOGY

REBECCA TAYLOR

OPHELIA
HOUSE

Denver Colorado USA
www.opheliahouse.com

Ophelia House

13490 Lafayette Street
Thornton, Colorado 80241 USA
www.opheliahouse.com

This book is a work of fiction. The names, characters, places and incidents are products of the writer's imagination or have been used fictitiously and are not to be construed as real. Any resemblance to persons, living or dead, actual events, locale or organizations is entirely coincidental.

Ascendant
Rebecca Taylor
ISBN-13: 978-0-979-73531-8

Cover Art
Holly Ollivander

For librarians and teachers everywhere.

The keepers of the secret and the torchbearers who light the way.

Contents

1.	A Bloody Failure	7
2.	Treasure House	19
3.	A Mother's Room	39
4.	Out of Darkness	44
5.	Center Jewel	57
6.	Her Words	71
7.	Little World	89
8.	Lost Mother	105
9.	Stolen	117
10.	Pieces	129
11.	Promises	142
12.	Symbols	162
13.	Fever	173
14.	Stay	193
15.	Eight Swords	205
16.	They Know	225
17.	In Control	236
18.	Door in the Floor	253
19.	Francis Bacon	261
20.	Uncle	269
21.	Underground	278
22.	Caught	291
23.	Gilded Borders	298
24.	Shame	327
25.	Rage	330
26.	Hurting You, Hurting Me	342
27.	Run	350
28.	Hiding	357
29.	Before	360
30.	The Gift of Truth	377
31.	In the Deep	396
32.	Going Through	404
33.	Blinded by the Light	411
34.	Keeping Secrets	423

CHAPTER ONE

A BLOODY FAILURE

As I watched my father sadly packing a meager number of necessities into his nylon gym bag, I thought I might scream. Hunched over the bag with his back to me, he attempted to covertly wipe his tears—my head almost exploded.

This was all my fault.

I left the room as quietly as I could and even though I hadn't eaten all day I was pretty sure I should go kneel in front of the toilet. My stomach clenched and churned and my own tears started again. I needed to go back, just one day, and do just one thing differently. One thing.

Yesterday, I was failing my sophomore English Lit class. Yesterday, during lunch, I went to West Christian Academy's state of the art computer lab and downloaded a paper on Shakespeare's *Richard II* twenty minutes before my English final was due.

Two hours later, I was sitting in Vice Principal Carney's

office waiting for my father.

As I leaned over the toilet waiting to get sick, I remembered Ms. Carney's perplexed face and the way she slowly shook her head as she examined the evidence in her hands.

We waited for my father together. The sound of the wall clock loudly tracked the seconds. I could tell by her nervous shuffling she expected him any moment, had maybe even prepared herself to, once again, do battle with another of West Christian's powerful and influential helicopter parents. But I knew from experience he would not be there soon or armed for any kind of battle. I knew, from experience, that there was a pretty good chance he would barely be conscious.

Turns out, I was right on all counts.

As we waited she looked at the stapled pages she held limply in her hands. The pages I had printed, the pages I had turned in as my final for English Lit, the pages that were worth fifty percent of our total grade—the pages that Mr. Meyer had carefully written across, in bold red ink, PLAGIARISM!!! Along with the web address as proof.

"Why?" she had asked.

I didn't have an answer, at least not one I could say out loud. "I don't know," I whispered.

"Was the work *that* hard for you?"

"No!" I was almost insulted. I had read *Richard II* at least three times before it was even assigned by the moronic Mr. Meyer.

She hesitated, "Have you been depressed?"

"No," I lied.

Ms. Carney took a deep breath and looked for a minute like she had found something to say but then, she just let her breath go. I felt bad, for what I'd done, sure, but more so for letting her down. Ms. Carney was one of those administrators who actually cared about kids.

She really had tried with me, and was the only adult who had ever been willing to ask me the *MOM* question. Last year, right after I failed my freshman midterms, she called me into her office to discuss my, "academic plan." After I shrugged my way through most of her questions she took a deep breath.

"How much do you think you are affected by the...*loss*, of your mother?"

The word '*loss*' was not quite right, *missing* might have been better. *Loss* was an uncomfortable word and somehow left a shadow of death. *Loss* had stuck in her throat and gave away her reluctance to pursue this uncomfortable topic.

"A lot," was all I said and that seemed to be enough for her—until now.

"I need to know why."

"I don't know why."

"You are incredibly smart, Charlotte."

I didn't say anything and watched as she flipped through my files. "Do you even know what you are capable of?" she asked exasperated. "Charlotte, even if your father wasn't Simon Stevens..." she trailed off and I guessed she was about to say something she shouldn't—as if it were some big secret that most of the kids attending West Christian Academy were here because they were the offspring of some of California's most famous and socially powerful people.

My father was Simon Stevens, author of the Devin Kruger mysteries. Seventeen consecutive bestsellers since he began writing them in the eighties. My father practically typed his own money. Although no one would ever know it to look at him, our house that Jack built, or the rusty Ford pickup he refused to get rid of.

"Charlotte, I know you've struggled, but this," she fingered the evidence sitting on the desk between us, "this doesn't seem like you," she pleaded. Her brown frizzy curls looked even more unruly than usual, fried under the stress of this confounding case.

"This takes it out of my hands," she had whispered sounding sad.

I had wanted to shrug, put on a smug smile and tell her *I don't care. This doesn't even matter to me—NOTHING MATTERS TO ME.*

But it did.

When my father finally did arrive, I wasn't able to even look at him. He miscalculated the location of the chair set out for him and tripped. His timing was all wrong when Ms. Carney introduced herself and his speech was overly careful as he labored to provide his own slurred name. I stared at my shoes for as long as I could while my father rambled on and on, digging our hole deeper. When I finally looked up, Ms.

Carney wasn't even looking at my father—whose inability to enunciate was the equivalent of a flashing neon sign "I'M A DRUNK!" The full force of her pity was aimed directly at me.

That's when I started to cry. I wanted to shout at her *YOU DON'T UNDERSTAND! HE'S A GOOD MAN!* I wanted to shout all the things I had told myself for the last four years, all the excuses that had become my existence since my mother had vanished. Because if Ms. Carney suspected that I was depressed, surely she could see that my father had fallen into the abyss.

She had picked up her phone and started to dial when I managed to whisper, "Please...don't."

She stopped for a second and bit her lip, as if considering my request, but then she continued to dial. "I'm sorry Charlotte, I absolutely have to."

Yesterday I was failing and facing expulsion. Today my father is sending me to stay with the only other relative I have—an uncle I don't know in England—while he spends ninety days trying to dry out at the Oasis Drug and Alcohol Treatment Center.

It was all my fault.

I got up off the floor and looked at myself in the mirror. My face looked swollen and blotchy from crying and my hair hung in limp strings around my head. It would only upset my father more to see me this way. I turned on the cold water and soaked a washcloth before pressing it against my puffy eyes and hot cheeks. How was it even possible that I would be on a flight heading to London in less than three hours?

I dried my face and considered my reflection again. My hair was still everywhere so I grabbed my brush and raked it back into a sloppy bun that I secured with a hair tie I found in the drawer. I took my toothbrush and left to go shove it into the duffel bag I would be living out of for the next three months.

In the hall, I paused outside her door. Closing my eyes I let my fingers trail lightly across the long, slender door handle. How many times had her hand been here? I waited a moment before entering and listened for the sounds of my father. Over the past four years, since her disappearance, he had too often found me in this room curled up on her chaise lost in my own grief. He didn't like me to be in here.

From his room, there was only the sound of his closet door rolling in its track and then the jostling of metal hangers as he pulled clothes to pack. I turned the handle quickly, opened the door enough to fit through, and gently shut it behind me.

When we first realized she was missing, there had been a constant commotion. Police, private investigators, and the media crawled all over the neighborhood. *Simon Steven's Wife: Missing Without a Trace.* Her disappearance fueled tabloid sales for months after my twelfth birthday. Each week brought new speculations and theories. *Murder! Abduction! Extensive Plastic Surgery!*

The police were at a loss—there was no break-in, no ransom, no note, no suspects, no evidence of any kind.

"Mr. Stevens, is it possible your wife left of her own accord?" one investigator asked.

"But," my father had wept openly. "If that's the case, she's taken nothing with her," he shook her purse strap as evidence. "Not even a dime."

I was convinced they would find her. Every day, every phone call, every knock at the door, I expected it to be her, or word about her.

It never was. Tabloid headlines melted into eighth page blurbs until eventually, her name wasn't in the papers at all. Everyone forgot about the strange disappearance of Elizabeth Stevens.

Everyone except my father and me.

I closed my eyes—this was the easiest place to imagine my mother. Curled and quiet on the chaise, she wore her soft blue cardigan with the lavender afghan across her legs. Her eyes were focused on the book in her lap but, as always, when I opened my eyes she was gone. Her shadow evaporated in the harsh glare of reality. She was always just beyond my reach.

I moved carefully around her small library. It was only a spare room that would have been occupied by a brother or sister if I had one. But in every house we moved to, my mother had constructed bookshelves that filled all four walls of one room from floor to ceiling, her book collection filled every space. I knew exactly what I was looking for and moved to the far side of the room, closest to my mother's chaise. This is where she kept them, within arms reach of where she sat; her complete collection of Shakespeare.

My mother read widely and exhaustively. There wasn't any author, subject, or genre she wouldn't try, but she kept her most beloved nearest. I sat on her chaise and trailed my fingers along the leather spines. Four of the books were rare editions, gifted to her from her family's library in Somerset, England.

I sat down and lay against the back of the elaborate brocade, pulling her afghan up to my chest. I considered her favorites for a moment before I freed my hand from the blanket and reached for her small edition of *Richard II*. The cloth binding was heavily worn around the edges and beginning to fray. I reached up and held the sapphire cross at my neck, her very last gift to me before she disappeared, and pressed the book to my stomach. This was all I had to help me say goodbye.

I sat up and inspected the small antique clock surrounded by dust on the shelf in front of my mother's Dostoevsky's— the impossibly slender hands pointed to ten thirty-seven. If I was going to make my flight we would need to get going.

In his room, my father had finished packing and was now slouched at the end of his bed with a gin and tonic. He looked up as I entered and when his eyes met mine he started to cry again. "I'm so sorry Tot," he shook his head. "I'm the worst father ever," he added and took a long drink from his glass.

I took a deep breath and went to sit beside him. "No you're not."

He put his arm around my shoulders and hugged me while

he finished off his drink. "You deserve so much better."

I didn't say anything and shook my head.

"If your mother knew--"

"Don't," I begged.

He stopped and swirled the remaining ice in his glass.

"We should get going or I'm going to miss my flight."

He nodded.

"Are you all packed?" I asked.

He nodded again.

"Did you call Susan?" Susan Richards was my father's editor and the only real person in our lives that would care that he would not be reachable for three months.

"Yes," he smiled briefly.

"What did she say?"

"She said of course I'm a drunk, she's been telling me that since nineteen ninety-five. She said that my biggest problem is that I've become ridiculously sloppy about it. She's more upset with you for the plagiarism and wants to know how the hell she is supposed to live with the fact that Simon Steven's only daughter plagiarized some college hack. She said it would have been better if you had stabbed some girl in the locker room."

This made me smile a little. Since my mother's disappearance, Susan offered what support she could. She loved us—in her own way. "Are you all right to drive?"

He nodded again, "I only had three."

"Right, so I'll drive," I said and stood up to go.

He didn't get up and I could tell he was hesitating, "Tot."

"Hmm," I turned to face him and saw the sadness and sincerity in his eyes when he looked up at me.

"I'm going to get better. When you come back at the end of the summer, everything will be better."

I smiled weakly and said, "I know dad."

But I didn't believe him. Neither of us would get better without her.

After we both tossed our packs into the back of my dad's pickup, I took his keys from him and slid behind the worn steering wheel. His truck smelled like old fast food. While I waited for him to get in the passenger seat, I sighed and collected the remnants of the old Double Deluxe he had absently tossed onto the squat backseat of the cab. Before he could get all the way in, I handed him the mess and silently pointed to the rolling trash bins at the back of the garage. He heaved a huge sigh, but didn't dare argue. After I saw him close the lid, I cranked the starter and pumped the gas pedal attempting to, once again, resurrect his decrepit beast of a truck. The engine turned over but I didn't shift into reverse until I revved the engine numerous times and witnessed the large gray puff of diesel smoke rising behind us.

With my dad back on the bench seat beside me, I pushed the clutch, shifted the stick into reverse, and slowly backed out of our Venice Beach condo garage. "Isn't it bad enough that this thing reeks on the outside?"

"I meant to throw it out. I just forgot."

This meant he was drunk and couldn't bother to throw it out.

We only lived about fifteen minutes from LAX, but I had to stop at our corner coffee shop to get my dad a tall black coffee. I could get us to the airport, but he was going to have to drive himself to Oasis and I couldn't be sure he'd, 'only had three' today.

We pulled into the departure drop off lane and he asked, "Do you want me to walk you to security?"

I shifted the stick into neutral and set the brake before saying, "I'm okay."

He handed me my printed itinerary, "I couldn't get a direct flight this late," he apologized.

I glanced briefly at the paper and saw that there was a layover in Amsterdam. I shrugged, "It's only an hour."

I had never been away from my father, at least not since my mother disappeared. I hesitated in the seat. "Are you sure you're all right to drive?"

He raised his hand in a mock oath, "I swear."

I took a deep breath. "Will you try your best?"

His face turned serious and he gazed absently out the windshield in front of us. A large man in a business suit struggled to pull his rolling suitcase out of the backseat of a blue compact. When he finally turned towards me, he looked so intently into my eyes that I shifted my gaze to the seat.

"Charlotte," he started but then seemed to lose his words. He took a deep breath and began again. "Charlotte, I love you more than anything on this earth," his voice cracked and I could tell he was going to cry again. "I don't know how we got here. It's all such a mess and I feel...it's so big. Like life is this giant boot that keeps stomping down on us ants and all we can do is try to figure out where to run next. But it doesn't even matter because that boot keeps finding us anyway," his shoulders slumped. "There is so much I don't control. So much that I don't have any power to change. I don't know how to fix things Charlotte. I'm sorry...so sorry."

I didn't look at his face, "It's going to be okay." I leaned quickly to hug him. "I love you dad."

I felt him sob against my ear before I turned from our embrace and got out of the truck. In one movement, I grabbed my bag from the back of the truck and pulled it over the edge of the open bed. On the sidewalk, I turned and waved to my father, blew him a childish kiss, and hurried past the automatic doors and into the air-conditioned airport. As I approached the long check-in line, I took one last backwards look through the tinted glass entrance. It worried me to see him still sitting in the passenger seat.

I didn't look back again.

CHAPTER TWO

TREASURE HOUSE

My eyes were on fire. When my final flight arrived in London, I figured I'd left my house about twenty-seven hours ago. With the time change and a twelve-hour delay at the Schiphol airport in Amsterdam—five of those hours devoted to a serious attempt to sleep with my head against a wall—I felt sick and like I could cry from exhaustion. When the line of passengers in front of me finally filtered off the plane, I ducked into the first restroom I saw in the bright terminal.

I ran my hands under the automatic faucet and looked at my reflection. My eyes were so bloodshot they looked demonic. I tightened up my sagging ponytail and filled my hands with water. The cool water felt good on my face but my eyes burned like I'd used acid. I wanted a bed.

As I exited customs and approached a group of people scanning for individual passengers I looked for my Uncle Nigel, although I had no real idea exactly what he looked like.

The picture my father had pulled from one of our photo albums was at least fifteen years old and I didn't see anyone here who I thought might even possibly pass for the pinched, uptight man who was photographed giving my mother away at her wedding.

I decided to just look for a man who looked like he couldn't find the person he was searching for.

I continued my scan until my eyes fell upon my name spelled across a piece of blue paper held by a skinny guy, probably my age, in khakis and a button down blue oxford shirt. Standing next to him was a younger girl with bubble gum pink stripes dyed into her cropped blond hair. She wore an eighties style pop princess outfit complete with white fingerless lace gloves.

I stopped and bit my lip before heading towards them. The guy was tall and his lanky arms held his sign as if he were formally hired to advertise for me. When I walked closer, his eyes met mine and lit up. He somehow managed to stand up even straighter while he brushed his disheveled black hair from his face. This guy recognized me.

But I had no idea who they were.

When I was only a few feet away, the girl started bouncing excitedly in her high-heeled boots. "Are you waiting for Charlotte Stevens?" I asked.

The guy gave me a meek smile and nodded but the girl, she squealed and rushed into hug me like I was an American pop star. "Charlotte!" she yelled while I stood awkwardly with her attached to me. I looked to the guy for help and saw that he was scowling at the girl who didn't seem to plan on letting me go any time soon.

"Sophie!" he said and grabbed the girl's arm to pull her off me.

Sophie withdrew and covered her mouth with her hands, only partially hiding her maniacal smile.

The guy gave Sophie another angry look before turning to me. "Sorry about her. It's good to see you Charlotte." But he didn't tell me his name, or who either of them were.

"Yes," I returned a confused smile. I was missing something. "I'm sorry, do we know each other?"

His face fell and I watched uncomfortably as he realized I didn't know who he was. God, I was too tired to feel guilty as well.

"I'm sorry, I just--"

"No," he shook his head. "It's been a long time." He forced a wilted smile. "I'm Caleb?" he shrugged. "You and your mom stayed at the house once," he shrugged again. "We played together as kids."

My father's last European book tour. I had caught the chicken pox while we were in Germany. My mother had taken me to the family home, Gaersum Aern in Somerset, while my dad finished out the last three weeks of the tour.

"Right," I said as a very vivid memory assaulted me that involved a seven year-old me, and an eight year-old Caleb, kissing behind the sea of ornate draperies that hung from the ceiling of the dining hall. "Caleb, right." Caleb was the son of my uncle's housekeeper, who I remembered as an incredibly tall woman with large but kind hands.

My uncle had been absent during our stay.

"My God, how are you?" I asked lamely.

He had a strange look on his face that I was too tired to try and figure out. Surely he could forgive me not making the mental leap from the guy standing in front of me to the boy who—besides kissing me nine years ago—had also tricked me into eating dirt.

"Here," he snapped out of it. "Let me get your bag."

I handed it to him, "Thanks."

Sophie grabbed my hand, "I love your father's books," she gushed.

A fan.

"Me too," I smiled indulgently at her, but I was truly exhausted and hoped to God she didn't want to ask me a million questions.

Sophie must have sensed my apprehension because, even though she looked like she was about ready to burst from the effort of silence, she did not utter a single word all the way to the parking garage and only clutched my right hand between both of hers while we walked. Some people stared as we exited the airport—I didn't care, just so long as Sophie was leading me in the direction of a bed.

At the beginning of the ninety minute drive to Somerset I tried to make a real effort to stay awake when Sophie, unable to contain herself any longer, broke her silence and started in on her seemingly never ending stream of questions about me, California, famous people I've seen, and my father. I was amazed at how much of my personal history we covered before we even got off the airport property. From the friends I didn't have, to my favorite hobby—reading—the only question Sophie didn't ask was the one she likely wanted to the most.

Caleb, who drove us in silence, had likely threatened his sister with loss of life and limb if she even dared mention my mother.

Sophie was recapping my father's latest installment of his Devin Kruger series *Terror Time* for me—then I felt someone gently rocking my shoulder.

"Charlotte."

My brain was deep and far away.

"Charlotte," someone whispered. "We're here."

The corner of my mouth felt wet. With great effort I forced my eyes to open and saw a door handle in my face. I was in a car, my seat was reclined, I rolled over and came face to face with Sophie grinning down at me from the backseat. Wiping the wet from my face I sat up and saw Caleb looking at me.

"I think you were out before we left the airport."

"Oh." My God, had I been drooling the whole time?

"I'll get your things and carry them in," he said.

"No, I'll--" he got out and closed the door on my words. "...get them myself. Or you can get them," I said sarcastically.

"Oh, let him get them," Sophie said as she opened her door. "I think he fancies you," she added in a whisper before she hopped out of her brother's car and slammed the door. When I went to unfasten the seatbelt I noticed the canvas jacket spread across my lap. Obviously it was his. I hung it over the back of the seat and stepped out onto the gravel drive.

I hadn't been to Gaersum Aern since I was six but the brick manor looked exactly like the picture in my memory.

I could remember my mother sitting curled in the enormous library, *"Why does this house have a name?"* I'd asked.

She looked up from her book. *"I don't know. Many of the homes in England do—maybe because the house is part of the family."*

"Like a person?"

"Sort of."

"What does Gaersum Aern mean?"

"It's a very old name. It means treasure house."

"There's treasure?"

"Oh yes."

"Where?"

My mother had her look that told me she was playing. She put her book down on the arm of her chair, *"Come here."* I followed her across the library to the enormous ornamental mirror standing in the corner. She stood behind me as we looked at our reflection. *"There...see?"*

"Where?"

"You. You're here so this house is filled with treasure."

"Mooommm," I complained.

She smiled, *"I know. Your granddad used to tell me and Uncle Nigel the same thing."* But then, I remember, she had shut herself in her room for the rest of the day.

I hadn't known then, not at six. For obvious reasons, my mother had not shared with me what had happened in this house so many years ago. I only knew the preexisting fact-- my grandparents were dead. Dead before I was even born. At seven, there was no emotion attached to that statement. I had never known those people and so did not miss them.

But my mother did.

It wasn't until I was almost twelve that I realized why my mother grew so sad and shut herself away at even the most innocent mention of her parents. My eyes scanned the multitude of windows that lined the third floor. Which one had been theirs?

My grandparents were killed in this house. Murdered while they slept. Their attacker was never found or captured and the grief it caused my mother never seemed to lessen. When I was eleven and the letter had arrived at the house informing her that the case was being reinvestigated utilizing, "the latest advances in forensic science," my mother had shut herself up in her library for nearly a week.

My father kept shooing me away from her door and then finally told me why I had to leave her alone.

Caleb closed the trunk of his rusty compact and shouldered my large duffel.

"You don't have to do that," I said.

"I don't mind," Caleb said.

Sophie, who was trying to navigate the loose gravel drive in her high-heeled boots, turned and raised her eyebrows knowingly—*I told you so.* She hobbled ahead of us, her ankles rolling and twisting as she headed toward the garages.

Caleb came and stood next to me on the drive, leaning against the weight of my bag. "Where is she going?" I asked.

"To change."

"What, her clothes? In the garage?"

Caleb nodded, "If our mother sees her dressed like that, she's dead."

I laughed.

"She has an entire wardrobe in there stashed away." His English accent gave his words a rhythm that reminded me of my mother. As I watched him smile after Sophie who was now struggling to open an ancient looking side door into the garage, I wondered if what Sophie had said was true. Did Caleb 'fancy' me?

"Do you remember much?" he asked suddenly, pulling me from my thoughts.

I turned to the house, the elaborate rose garden looked beautiful in full bloom and the giant poplars lining the property swayed in the gentle breeze. "I remember walking with my mother through the gardens...and the sound of the trees when it rained."

Caleb only nodded. I could guess he didn't know what to

say about my mother.

I didn't want to mention our childhood curtain kissing so I said, "I also remember playing lots of checkers."

He smiled, "You had the chicken pox."

"And you never let me win."

His face changed into a mock of seriousness that reminded me of my sophomore civics teacher. "I don't believe in special treatment for girls or the invalid."

"Obviously," I said with sarcasm. I liked this playful side of him.

He laughed and hitched my duffel's strap over a bit. "Let's get inside before this bag disables me for life. What do you have in here—rocks?"

I followed him towards the large front entrance, "My father asked the same thing."

We walked up the flagstone steps and under the thick mass of creeping ivy covering the archway.

"You should have listened," he said. "I'm going to need traction."

Caleb opened one side of the elaborately carved double doors. As I followed him through the entrance I looked up. There was an engraving in the brick directly above us, a snake, made into a circle with the tail in its mouth.

I stopped and stared, "What's that?" I asked.

Caleb, already in the middle of the grand entrance, dumped my bag in the middle of the floor before coming back to see what I was gawking at. The engraving was huge, at least three feet in diameter, and the detail of the snake's marking were amazingly intricate.

Caleb stood beside me. When he saw what I was looking at he smiled, "It's an ouroboros."

"A what?"

"Ouroboros," he looked at me. "It's a symbol...ancient Egypt."

"It's beautiful," I said.

Caleb nodded in agreement, "This one is exceptionally done."

I looked at him, "You've seen others?"

"Lots. In books mostly...but," he added suddenly. "I've also seen in the Louvre an amazing lapis-lazuli intaglio necklace from the fourth century with a brilliant ouroboros engraving." He used both his hands and shaped his fingers into an oval, "About this big," he shook his head. "Amazingly done and..."

I watched Caleb, lost in his own excited fascination, while he described the necklace in every intricate detail. "You see, the ouroboros means," his hands flew punctuating his important points, "All is one." He made a big circle with his arms to help his point but when I only continued to stare he began, "life and death," circling his one arm around and around, "the end *is* the beginning," like a mad windmill.

He went on and on and I wondered if he was ever going to stop. My short car nap had hardly been enough to counter an entire sleepless night of international travel. I was about to politely interrupt but when his right hand started chomping his left fist like a crazed Muppet, I couldn't help myself. I laughed so hard tears ran down my face.

Caleb stopped immediately.

Unfortunately, I couldn't. Every time I tried to stop laughing an uncontrollable fit—fueled by exhaustion and the image of Caleb chomping himself with the seriousness of a university professor—would start all over.

I kept wiping my tears, the laughter erupting over and over. Caleb stood watching me looking somewhat shocked. Obviously I was hurting his feelings. "I'm sorry," I shook my head. "I'm just so tired," but another fit of laughter erased all sincerity from my words.

"No I'm sorry," he sounded irritated. He glanced back at the stone engraving. "I guess it's just my thing."

"Necklaces?" I asked almost hysterical.

Caleb stared at me. "No. Egypt."

"Oh," I wiped what I hoped was the last of my tears. "Right, that makes sense."

Caleb didn't say anything else and stoically led the way back inside. As I followed, and slowly regained some control, I mentally forbade myself any images of a rabid Kermit devouring a plate of frog legs.

The entrance hall was beyond impressive. I walked in silence across the pink marble floors and my eyes were drawn immediately to the enormous crystal chandelier that hung high above me. The crystals twinkled, catching the sunlight from the large windows halfway up the grand staircase. The rose-papered walls supported gold-framed oil portraits of people from another age dressed in lace collars and blue velvets.

I didn't remember any of this.

In the center of the hall was a red and yellow rose inlaid within the marble floor. I stood in the center and, with a closer look, could see the small slivers of cut marble that, carefully arranged, gave the stone rose a delicate look. I looked up and could see that the enormous chandelier hung exactly over my head.

A loud stumble echoed behind me and I turned to see Caleb recovering from a trip on the rug in the next room. He continued into the room, opening drapes and shutters, and pretending like he hadn't almost fallen on his face. Pretending not to have noticed, I continued to admire the hall. I still felt horrible for laughing at him.

Caleb returned to the doorway, "If you want to wait in the morning room, I'll go get my mum," he said coolly.

"Okay," I tried to sound cheerful—maybe I should apologize again. "Isn't my uncle here?" I asked.

Caleb stopped just outside the doors and shook his head, "He's away on business."

"Oh," this surprised me, my father had only spoken with him yesterday. Or at least what I thought was yesterday with the travel delays and time changes.

Without any more explanation Caleb walked away across

the hall—towards the kitchen? I couldn't remember where anything was. My memory of the mansion consisted more of whole rooms and the people in them, not how those rooms were connected to each other.

I turned back through the doors into the morning room and sat, or rather, perched on the edge of a pinched little settee that made me nervous. It looked more like the period furniture in a history museum than something I should actually be sitting on.

Here was another room that I would have sworn I'd never been in. Long floral drapes hung from near the ceiling and the fabric ended in a pool on the floor. Delicate china figurines were frozen in a lovely dance on top of a spindly three-legged end table. When I turned slightly to inspect the curio cabinet behind me, the wood in the tiny settee creaked and shifted beneath my weight. Looking around, I realized I probably never had been in here. I would never have been allowed to play in this fragile room.

The silence was broken by the loud slap of someone's shoes running across the marble hall. "Charlotte!" Sophie yelled.

I turned to see what the emergency was, but hardly recognized the girl bolting towards me. Sophie had been transformed.

"He's here!" she cried.

"What? Who?" I asked as Sophie grabbed both my hands and began jumping up and down excitedly. "My uncle?"

Sophie stopped jumping, "Ew, no." She smiled and started

jumping again, "Hayden!"

"Who?"

"Hayden!" She suddenly stopped jumping. "But look at me," she said miserably. "I'm wretched," she pulled at her tucked in oxford and knee length skirt. "Ugh," Sophie lightly stomped one of her tiny black flats. "I hate these clothes."

Her face was freshly washed of all makeup and I noticed that even her pink hair stripes were missing from the careful low ponytail she had fashioned. She did look young, but she was beautiful. I hadn't noticed before how delicate Sophie's almond eyes were beneath the coal black eyeliner and electric blue shadow.

"I think you look good," I offered.

Sophie gave me a disgusted look. "Its my mum's fault," she whined. "I can't believe he's here."

Soft bells could be heard in the hall and Sophie started fanning her herself with both her hands. "Oooo, I'm all flushed. I can feel it."

"Well it might help if you stop jumping and flipping out." I held her arms at her side. "Take a deep breath."

She inhaled quickly and blew it out fast.

"Slower," I said.

I could hear the clomp of sturdy heels approaching from across the hall and then a large woman appeared in the doorway.

"Charlotte!" the woman exclaimed. "I'll be right back love." Before she left to answer the door the woman gave Sophie a hard look and said, "Oh do be still, you've got yourself all in a state."

I looked to Sophie questioningly.

"My mum."

We could hear voices at the door and Sophie started biting her thumbnail. "Who is Hayden anyway?" I asked sarcastically. "The king of England?"

"No, his cousin," Sophie said flatly.

"What?" surely she was kidding. People were approaching with Sophie's mom.

"Well, second cousin actually," she whispered. "But besides that, he is absolutely gorgeous."

I turned just in time to smile and greet Sophie's mom, who looked perturbed, and two men as they entered the morning room. The men were both quite tall, over six feet, and ducked their heads in a precautionary measure as they negotiated the doorway that was constructed in an era when men rarely surpassed five foot five.

My breath caught in my chest and I understood immediately why Sophie was so flustered. The younger man was one of the most handsome I had ever seen—including all the Hollywood royalty whose children attended West Christian Academy. His eyes were the deepest blue and appeared to quickly take in the room, myself, Sophie, and determine the measure of everything. His broad shoulders filled space, especially in this delicate room, and I could easily imagine him breezing through countless strenuous activities—rugby, wood chopping, home construction—with ease and the same self-satisfied grin he now wore.

"Charlotte," Sophie's mom couldn't keep the irritation from her voice. "Mister Emerick Wriothesley," the older gentleman inclined his head towards me, "and his son, Hayden Wriothesley. Gentlemen, this is Mister Spencer's niece, Miss Charlotte Stevens."

Hayden's eyes turned on me and I felt the full force of his scrutiny.

I didn't know exactly what to do. Surely there was some etiquette involved. At the very least I probably shouldn't be standing greeting cousins of the *King of England* in dirty jeans and a wrinkled t-shirt. "Um, it's nice to meet you." Why were they here and where on earth was my uncle? I tried to focus my gaze at Mr. Wriothesley but my eyes kept pulling back to Hayden's brazen stare.

Hayden quickly glanced at my appearance and I would have sworn his grin grew, "My pleasure," he said.

Self-consciously, I ran my hands down my shirt. I couldn't help thinking about how greasy my hair must look, especially since it was falling out of the knot at the top of my head. I resisted the urge to fix it.

Mr. Wriothesley seemed to read my discomfort as much as his son appeared to relish it. He cleared his throat, "We know you've just arrived so we won't keep you," he smiled kindly. "I was just in the area and hoping to catch your uncle on some pressing business," he waved his hand slightly as if now dismissing this agenda altogether. "But unfortunately Ms. Steward has informed me that we've only missed him by minutes."

Minutes? Was my uncle here just before I arrived? Was whatever he was doing so important that he couldn't wait a few *minutes* to say hello?

Mr. Wriothesley hesitated. Was I supposed to invite them to something—tea, lunch? I didn't even know what time it was.

"I must confess," he continued sheepishly. "When Ms. Steward told us of your recent arrival...well I practically insisted on being allowed to meet you."

Ms. Steward's mouth twitched beneath her frown and her brow released some of its deep furrow. She was only partially appeased by Mr. Wriothesley's acknowledgment of putting her out.

"Well I..." My eyes fluttered back to Hayden who was still staring. "I'm glad you did," I managed.

Hayden's smug expression was gone but he continued to stare. What was he looking at? I dared to meet his eyes directly, force him to look away—but he didn't. He actually looked a little confused, like he was going to ask me something.

I looked away. It was strange but I felt like I'd met him before. Maybe we had met when we were kids? Heat spread across my neck and up my cheeks and I realized I wanted to cross the room and touch his face, hold his cheeks in my hands, feel his lips.

What?

What a stupid, ridiculous impulse. But I couldn't help it, like I was falling towards him. Did he feel this?

Hayden took a step.

"Your mother," Mr. Wriothesley added suddenly.

My eyes riveted onto Mr. Wriothesley and my breath stopped in my chest.

"She was one of my dearest childhood friends."

I didn't move. With this small statement, he had captured my complete attention. I only wished Sophie would stop fidgeting with her shirt beside me.

"She and your uncle," he nodded in remembrance. "Actually...your mother and I were even a bit more then friends," he smiled. "But that was a long time ago," he shook his head. "Long before your famous father came and swept her off to the California beaches anyway." For a moment, Mr. Wriothesley seemed to get lost in his own memories.

I dared a glance at Hayden who was now busy inspecting the room. When his eyes caught me looking he smirked and gave his father a sidelong look and rolled his eyes. Hayden had no way of knowing how much I actually wished his father would go on—I was suddenly very alert.

Sophie pulled absently at her shirt again and Mr. Wriothesley came to. "I dare say, you look very much the way I remember your mother. Except...darker."

I wondered if Mr. Wriothesley didn't know about my mother's disappearance. Surely my uncle would have told him.

"But obviously you must be exhausted. We won't keep you

any longer." Mr. Wriothesley moved towards me in a gesture that I thought was to shake my hand. When he bowed instead, and kissed my knuckle, I was surprised. He stood back up and his eyes halted, fixed at my throat.

My hand moved instinctively to my necklace. For a second, there was a look in his eyes very unlike the whole rest of the meeting. It had felt almost like he recoiled.

But when he stood, he was completely composed again with not a trace of the distaste that flashed across his face only a second ago.

"What a beautiful necklace," he said.

"Thank you," I fingered it nervously. "My mother gave it to me for my twelfth birthday."

He raised his eyebrows and silently stared at the sapphire cross around my neck. "Well that is interesting," he said with a smile that did not match his eyes. His gaze met and held mine, "But I suppose, people do change."

What did he mean? But before I could ask, Mr. Wriothesley and Hayden were both saying goodbye to Ms. Steward and Sophie and heading back across the marble hall. As soon as her mother left the room to open the front door for the departing guests, Sophie collapsed into the plush chair behind her.

"Oh, he is too stunning for words," she breathlessly whispered. "And did you see him give you that private look about his obnoxious father? He didn't even know *I* was in the room," she pouted. "I hate these clothes."

I stood at the front windows overlooking the circular gravel drive and watched as Mr. Wriothesley and Hayden climbed into a midnight blue sedan and closed their doors soundlessly behind them. The car windows were tinted black and hid its passengers completely from view but as the car started up and began to roll slowly away, I had the strangest feeling Hayden was staring back at me from the other side. An electric shiver ran up my spine.

Who were these people?

And how had my mother changed since her childhood?

CHAPTER THREE

A MOTHER'S ROOM

Ms. Steward came into the room so suddenly that I turned almost immediately from the window and the Wriothesley's departing car into her thick embrace. Ms. Steward was tall and plump, nothing at all like my mother but when she pulled away and looked into my face, I collapsed into tears. I hadn't expected this, but I had not been comforted by a mother since my own mother's disappearance. Over her shoulder, I caught sight of Caleb who had suddenly reappeared near the door but he dropped back when he noticed my tears.

"Dear," Ms. Steward hugged me close as I sobbed against her neck. "There, there," she rubbed my back with vigor. "You are absolutely exhausted. So much travel for one girl all alone. Let's get you off to bed."

She kept one arm around my shoulders as she guided me through the doors.

"Caleb," she whispered. "Be a dear, would you?"

Sophie pushed herself up out of her chair to follow.

"Not you," Ms. Steward said to her. "You stay right here. We are going to have a word when I get back."

Sophie sulked but obeyed by flouncing herself back into her chair.

Caleb picked up my bag still sitting abandoned in the center of the expansive hall and followed us up the large staircase. Wiping my face, I started to feel embarrassed. To have completely lost it so suddenly—especially in front of Caleb. What could he be thinking? Probably that I was a slobbering emotional wreck.

We reached the top of the staircase and started down the dark hallway. This I remembered, my feet thundering up and down the ornate carpet runner, the sound of my voice echoing through the maze of rooms and connecting hallways. Seven year-old Caleb searching while I hid in a large armoire among my deceased grandmother's collection of fur coats, the door cracked enough to let the light in and keep my panic back. He always knew where I was long before he pretended to find me.

Ms. Steward led me left down another hall—I would have to relearn my way around—and at the second to last room she stopped and turned the crystal doorknob.

"Here we go," she soothed as I entered the enormous room. She pointed to an ocean liner sized bed with a massive canopy that nearly reached the ceiling. "What you need is some rest."

I stared disbelieving at the mountains of pillows piled on top of the "bed" that apparently—because there was one leading from the floor to the top of the mattress—required a step-stool to get into it. While Ms. Steward crossed the room and began pulling drapes across the first of the four large windows, I found myself looking for something more reasonable to sleep on—like a chair.

Caleb came in behind me and unloaded my bag at the base of the bed. "Thanks," I said.

He nodded but didn't say anything and seemed to be avoiding looking at me directly. I thought maybe he would just leave, but he hung by the door and looked as if he were inspecting the room, his shoes, the ceiling, anything but look at me.

Ms. Steward pulled the last curtain and turned her attention back to me, "You're still on your feet." She waddled back to me on her thick heels and shooed me up the steps and onto the massive brocade bedspread. "No shoes on the bed," she added and before I could do it myself, she'd reached down and slipped my tennis shoes over my heels. She motioned me back further into the mass of pillows and I felt myself sinking in as she pulled a knitted afghan from the bottom of the bed up over my legs. I caught Caleb smiling at the sight of me drowning in a sea of chintz and down bedding, but he quickly frowned and looked away when I noticed him.

What was his problem anyway? I said I was sorry for laughing at him.

Ms. Steward headed towards the door shooing Caleb out of her way. "Now sleep," she commanded as she reached for the ancient electric switch on the wall and I heard a loud crack as the overhead chandelier went black. She was closing the door and pushing Caleb down the hall, the room was getting darker.

I am terrified of the dark.

I sat up, ready to leap—or swim—out of the bed and quickly crack the drapes to let in some light, but as the door shut I could see enough daylight leaking around the drapes to chase off my personal boogie men.

If I have an addiction, it is to light. Bright overheads, warm incandescent, night lights, the sun—only these have the power to chase back the terrors that have haunted my closet, the space under my bed, and every unlit room since I was four and a child's game of hide-and-seek left me locked and alone in a neighbor's basement. By the time my mother came to pick me up I had stopped screaming. I think Mrs. Grayden had tried to explain why she didn't know where I was, but when they found me in the basement I was clutching my knees and smelled of pee. It was the only time I ever saw my mother hysterical and it was the last time anyone ever babysat me.

I've tried to get over it by forcing myself into dark spaces, the bathroom at night, a closet, our garage with all the doors shut. I've read that in order to get over your fear, you need to experience the flood of panic and not allow yourself to escape. But after only a few seconds my heart thunders and I start to sweat. My throat tightens and my mind races, I'm trapped, I can't breathe. I never even make it a minute before lunging for the nearest electric relief. Some things you just never get over.

The drapes in the room were heavy purple velvet—made explicitly to keep the sun from this south facing room. But the room was still bright enough for me to see so I relaxed back against the pillows and let my body go limp. Just a couple hours sleep and I'd be good.

The room was massive, probably the same size as the entire first floor of our Venice Beach condo. All the furniture was like the bed, antique, heavy, and amazingly elaborate in design. The chairs wore thick fabrics in brocade and crushed velvets and their carved legs ended in curled lions feet. At the far end of the room there was actually a small library equipped with a sliding ladder and at least a couple thousand ancient titles climbing the walls. A worn red leather sofa and floor lamp sat in the middle of the room and I could imagine my mother as a child spending many late nights curled under the warm glow of that light, a copy of Loves Labours Lost and an afghan across her legs. I could easily imagine this because, just as my exhaustion was finally carrying me away into sleep, I realized I had seen my mother in that very position in this very room. This was the room we had stayed in when I was a child, this was the very bed I had shared with my mother over ten years ago.

Ms. Steward had given me my mother's childhood room.

CHAPTER FOUR

OUT OF DARKNESS

My heart is racing. I am searching, desperate for light. There is nothing, nothing. Not a spark or spot, no distant glow that promised to lift this blackness if only I would run towards it. I force my legs to move, some activity, some blind investigation even though my throat is swelling and my mind is fleeing, desperate for escape, I cannot keep the panic back. I am terrified of the dark. I open my mouth and scream, but there is no sound.

I feel a brush of fabric against my leg, a skirt's twirl. But there is nothing until, again, I can feel but not see, it is my mother's white summer dress. She is here but she is not. I stumble forward and call silently to her. I think I see her but fear it may only be a trick, collaboration between my desperate mind and starving eyes, the glow of her skirt. It is moving away but I am too terrified to follow. Frozen in the black, I have an instinctual fear of where she is leading. I soundlessly call again to her. Mom, don't leave me. But she twirls ever away until again the darkness sur-

rounds me and, in the end, I am blind and alone.

I opened my eyes. It is always the same, even after I realize I am awake the dread and fear linger. There is small relief in realizing, *it's only a dream*, because wherever I am, it's still dark.

I lunged for my bedside lamp but fell into pillows and more bed. I was sweating, buried under an enormous weight. Kicking and pushing—this was not my bed—I heaved the heavy blankets off myself, found the edge of the bed and jumped out. The floor wasn't where it should be. I landed in a heap on the hard wood floor. Quickly, I got to my hands and knees and stood, pain tore through my ankle. I limped and hobbled my way forward, hands in front of me, looking for the door, a wall with a switch—light. I kept groping but the room was endless.

My chest seized, I couldn't breathe. I limped faster.

Out. I need to get out.

Where was the edge of this room? My arms flailed frantically through the dark and a scream threatened to tear away my last thread of reason. I pushed forward faster but my foot hit something hard, something caught me. I stumbled and fell, blind, powerless to stop. The thing reached out, tangled my limbs and sharp pain shot through my shin. My forehead hit the floor—I screamed.

A bright angle of light shot across the floor above my head and I heard a loud crack, suddenly the whole room illuminated in a warm blinding light that brought relief, then tears. I heard footsteps fast and hard thundering towards me and I could see that I'd been attacked by a rocking chair that lay on its side still clutching most of my leg.

"Charlotte!" In one swift movement, Caleb untangled my leg and helped me up off the floor. My head pressed against his chest and my body trembled as he helped support my weight. I could hear his heart beat loud in my ear. In a few steps he had crutched me to the red sofa and lowered me onto its worn cushions.

He knelt in front of me and searched my face, "What happened? Are you okay?"

My tears still hadn't stopped and they only became worse with his staring. I was so stupid, such a stupid idiot.

"I was in the library and heard a massive thud up here," he said. "I ran up as fast as I could. What happened?"

I shook my head. I couldn't look him in the eye.

"Are you all right?"

I nodded.

"Did you fall out the bed?"

I bit my lip and a fresh wave of tears rolled out. I wished he would leave. "Yes," I managed.

He began scanning my body, "Well are you hurt? That bloody bed is ridiculously high." He picked up my hand and held it while he looked at my head. "How did you manage to get way over in the corner?"

His hand holding mine had my attention. Caleb was very close. He touched a tender spot on my forehead and I winced.

"Well that's going to leave a mark."

This close, I could smell his cologne. It was faint, remnants from the morning, but the scent was rich and warm.

He sat back and considered my face. When his eyes found mine and he smiled. His free hand moved towards my face, as if to wipe my tears and I suddenly realized Sophie was right. Caleb did like me.

I looked away.

His hand stopped awkwardly in the air between us. I stared at my ankle to avoid looking at him directly, but still, I could tell his smile was gone. Caleb took a breath and sat back as his hand slipped slowly away from mine.

I wiped my own face.

"Does anything hurt?" he asked quietly.

"My ankle." I whispered still recovering from the rocking chair attack.

He looked at my ankle but was careful to not touch. "It looks a bit swollen."

"It hurts to walk on."

He nodded. "I'll get you some ice."

The pain in my ankle was turning into a dull, throbbing ache and I could see that it was noticeably larger than my other ankle now. When Caleb left to get the ice, I shook my head at my own idiocy. *So stupid.* I imagined how I must have looked, sprawled in the dark, panicking and freaking out like a baby.

I vowed to myself for the hundredth time, *I will get over the dark.*

Sitting back against the ancient cushions, my hand moved to finger the sapphire cross against my chest, but it wasn't where it should be. My hand flattened in alarm, searched across the whole of my chest. I sat straight up and looked down my shirt then around the couch. Forgetting my swollen ankle I stood up and immediately regretted it, "Ooooww," I cried and sat back down just long enough to make sure I positioned all my weight on my good leg before I started flying around the room in a mad search.

I couldn't have lost it, it meant too much to me.

I pulled the cushions from the sofa and searched under its pleated skirt. I scoured the rug and the hardwood floors, patted my clothes and searched my bra. Nothing. I moved in the direction I had come, heading back towards the evil rocker—it must have been torn off during our battle. The chain would be broken but I didn't care. It was the cross I was worried about.

I didn't see it anywhere.

Maybe it had flown across the room. I looked and considered the whole room, every chair, throw pillow, rug, and afghan—my current method of flailing about in a panic would likely only drive the cross deeper into the many layered fabrics of this room.

I would stay calm. After all, it had to be here somewhere.

My cross was not near the rocker or the tea table poised with its two dainty chair partners. I explored the large armoire littered with lace and more of the poised figurines—thank

God my freaking out hadn't broken any of them. I scanned carpets and moved pillows. *I have to find it.* Frustration filled my head and I felt my calm approach begin to give way to anger. I turned too fast and forgot to limp. All my weight landed on my swollen ankle.

"Oohh," I cried and fell back into a large chaise lounger.

Shards of fire shot up my leg. I threw myself back against the long cushion and stared at the ceiling. I squeezed my ankle between my hands and tried to press the pain down into a dull ache. My cross was gone. It was no use, I would never find it.

When the pain finally began to subside, I pushed myself up—there was something weird about the chaise I was sitting on. It took me a few moments of staring before I realized it was exactly the same as the one in my mother's library back home.

Obviously she had brought ours with her when she moved with my dad to the States. But it was still strange to see its twin here. Ours had a tea stain on the single arm, but this one was perfectly unblemished.

My necklace might have slid underneath the upholstered mammoth. Hopping and using the chaise for support, I managed to lower myself to my knees. I lifted the fringe skirting along the bottom edge but there was nothing but dust and bushels of lint, at least as far as I could see. The farthest side was only darkness.

I tried to pull the chaise away from the shelves it was

shoved up against but it wouldn't budge.

"Ugh!"

I climbed back on top and pushed my hand down between the cushions and the shelf. Dust collected under the pads of my fingers as they swept the floor and the empty bottom shelf.

Something sliced my finger.

"Ow," I snatched my hand back. A thin line of blood ran across the pad of my middle finger.

What was that?

Gently, I pushed my hand back down. Whatever it was, it was at the back of the shelf pushed into the farthest corner, cold and hard, like stone. Carefully, I felt around its sharp edges and rough sides.

A box?

I pulled it closer and pushed my other arm down so I could lift and squeeze the box between the shelf and cushion. The rough edges scraped across the wood shelves and I cringed when I heard the chaise fabric catch and tear.

"Sorry," I whispered.

But the bottom of the box wasn't rough and once it was up, the stone slid easily across the brocade fabric.

It was beautiful. The box was rectangular and made from a forest green stone. The top and all four sides were covered in rough edged engravings, hence my cut, that didn't make any sense to me. Some looked like Egyptian hieroglyphs but there was also writing in other foreign scripts. The center of the lid had the largest single engraving, a snake made into a circle with its tail in its mouth.

The ouroboros.

There didn't appear to be a way to open it, no latch or hinges. I looked closer but couldn't find any edge to indicate that the top had a lid or that the thing was anything more than solid stone. But it wasn't heavy enough to be completely solid. I ran my hands carefully over the sharp engravings, my fingers trailed around the snake. I lifted the box from the back and inspected the bottom. Nothing. I turned it right side up again and stared first from one angle, then another. It was like it had been shaped from a larger stone. A single, seamless piece— but I knew it wasn't.

I slid my hands down the sides of the box but nothing happened.

For my twelfth birthday my mother gave me a box. She had placed the unwrapped present in my hands, "Happy Birthday." It was a small, perfect cube. The dark wood was smooth, almost soft, except for where the sides met in razor edged precision. "What is it?" I asked. She brushed my bangs from my eyes and smiled, but only for a moment. She held my face in both her hands, "It's a puzzle," she kissed my forehead, "and your gift." I turned the cube in my hands, "A puzzle? But how..." My mother shook her head, "Knowledge is sweeter found than given," she said and left to get my cake.

I stared at the stone box in front of me. Was it possible? The wooden cube had taken me weeks to solve. When I discovered the first slide I loved it, but after many hours and then days of nothing else, I became annoyed, and then mad. In frustration I tossed it aside more than once and then complained to my mother, "Just tell me." But she never did, "You'll figure it out."

There were secret slide moves and whole cube rotations, twisting the cube in half and then sliding the two halves apart—every move had to occur in order. The wooden cube had eight moves to reveal the key, the discovery of which left me jumping on my bed, and another four to find the lock. After a month of slides, turns, and rotations, I took the tiny key and inserted it into the miniature lock. I half expected another puzzle, but the lid popped on the secret compartment and inside I found my mother's present, a silver chain and sapphire cross.

I absently moved to finger the cross around my neck in remembrance when my hand, once again, realized the cross was not where it should be.

I considered the unintelligible inscriptions engraved in the stone. If it was a puzzle, did the writings offer clues? Touching the edge of some letters, I considered solving the wooden cube, all that sliding and rotation would be next to impossible without cutting my hands to shreds—never mind the weight of the box. The snake was the largest engraving and so it seemed too obvious, but I traced its body from tail to head with my finger just in case. Nothing happened. I sat back and absently chewed my thumbnail. The tail was in the mouth—the snake was eating its tail. I leaned forward and placed my finger in the mouth, there seemed to be a tiny indentation.

Starting to trace the snake, something moved and I heard a click.

Surprised, I snatched my hand back. Looking closely, I could see the bottom of the engraving was separate from the stone, a metal slide. With the thrill of discovery I started again and listened to the satisfying series of clicks as the metal dial rotated beneath my finger like an old phone. When I reached the end of the tail the final click was actually the clunk of the mechanism shifting beneath the stone.

Something had unlocked.

It wasn't that simple—was it? The box looked exactly the same, no compartment had popped, no key revealed. Given the detail of the rest of the box, I suspected the snake was only the first of many, many secrets. What next? I reached for the center circle of the snake. Like a thief cracking a combination lock, I began to turn the dial that produced another series of clicks—my heart kept pace with every one. The dial stopped turning and I heard a latch release. The center circle opened up and revealed a small compartment in the top of the box. I didn't breathe.

The space was not large, a few inches in diameter, but there was something inside. I removed a folded swatch of black silk and what looked like a note. I opened the note first, it was my mother's handwriting.

What is the above is from the below and the below is from the above.

I read the passage twice but had no idea what it meant.

Was it my mother's work—or some quote? I put the note aside and picked up the silk, pulling back each of the folds like a new bud. When the last fold revealed what was inside, I froze. Disbelieving, I stared for half a second longer before I dropped it to the chaise. There, illuminated against the black silk was an encircled five-pointed star—the pentagram.

The images in my head were from movies—demons, ritualistic killings, people summoning beasts from hell. All the terrifying images that kept me away from dark spaces. The five pointed star, the sign of Satan.

I stared at the black silk and pentagram on the chaise in front of me. Fear crept in around my abdomen and fluttered up through my chest. I didn't want to touch it again and felt like I had already been stained by some evil. As if the highly polished star had the power to draw the dark over me completely.

Why would she have this? I tried to think of reasons.

Maybe it wasn't hers. It had been years since this bedroom officially belonged to her, anyone could have hidden the box in here.

Of course.

But my eyes were drawn to the note. I knew my mother's writing, her distinctively small, backward slanting print.

"I got the ice!" Caleb suddenly announced as he strode through the door.

"Oh God," I gasped. My heart accelerated so fast I could feel adrenaline flood my body and then the tingling in my fingers and feet. It only took a second to realize it was Caleb, but I grabbed one of the chaise pillows from behind me and threw it across the room at him. "You scared me to death!"

He watched the pillow fall lamely only half the distance between us. "Sorry," he offered unconvincingly, his eyes already riveted on the items before me. "What's that?" Caleb crossed the room quickly to inspect what I'd found.

"I'm not sure." I didn't know how I felt about Caleb seeing all this. Were these my mother's secrets? I glanced again at the pentagram brightly illuminated by the crystal chandelier. Were they secrets I didn't want to know?

Caleb hadn't noticed the pentagram yet, he was enthralled with the box and its many markings. "This is amazing, where did you find it?"

"On the shelf behind the chaise."

He gave me a strange look.

"I was looking for my cross," I touched my chest briefly. "I lost it."

Caleb gave a half-interested glance to his immediate area, "Sorry. I'm sure we'll find it," but his attention immediately returned to the box. "These are Egyptian."

I nodded.

Then his eyes caught the pentagram and he was still. "What's that?"

"A pentagram."

"I know it's a pentagram. What's it for?" He looked as nervous as I felt.

I hesitated. It was impossible to ignore the clasped chain attached to the silver symbol. I envisioned this necklace hanging around her slender neck. "I don't know," I answered.

Caleb picked the note up off the chaise and read the words my mother had left long ago. His brow furrowed in concentration.

"What?" I asked.

"I've seen this before."

"The note?"

"Yes. Well no," he shook his head. "Not this exact note," he held up the paper to clarify. "This phrase...I know I've read it before. Or at least, something very like it."

"Where?"

"I don't remember."

"What?"

"Well, I don't remember exactly. It's in one of the books in the library."

I crumpled the silk back around the necklace and stuffed it, along with the note, back into the small compartment. While Caleb watched in wonder, I closed the lid, reversed the ouroboros mechanism, and shoved the box back between the chaise and bookcase to the bottom shelf.

"What are you doing?" he asked.

"Going to the library," I got up off the chaise and took one hobbled step before I remembered my ankle.

I grabbed Caleb's arm for support, "And so are you."

CHAPTER FIVE

CENTER JEWEL

The manor was dark. Caleb flipped a series of switches to light our way to the library. "What time is it?" I asked.

Caleb checked his watch, "Three thirty."

"a.m.?"

He nodded.

I felt a surge of guilt that my jet lag should be keeping him awake as well. "Sorry, I didn't realize it was so early," I offered as he helped me down the grand staircase.

Caleb shrugged, "I was mostly up anyway."

When we got to the library doors, it was the collective scent of thousands of titles, from the rare to the recently released, that captured my senses first. The unique mixture of paper, leather, and aging glue always made me feel calm. Whether I was entering my mother's sanctuary back in Venice Beach or the public library down the street, the scent of books always relaxed me. That scent was my mother and it was how I remembered her. Buried in her books, outwardly peaceful—internally unreachable. All of her most rare and treasured titles at home were gifts from this larger library.

When I was little, I believed I could hear my mother's thoughts. Believed I could hear the words running through her mind as clearly as the ones she spoke out loud. I imagined every silent word she read floating like a thread through my own mind.

By the time I was seven I realized it was impossible. I had only pretended to hear her to fill the silence. *Don't be dumb, you can't hear her thoughts, you just wish you could.* I stopped pretending and found another way.

I could not know her, could not touch that inner life she led in her books—until she put them down. Then I could pick them up and follow in her footsteps across time and history, space and myth, become the character she had been hardly hours before. I always followed her.

I waited near the light from the hall while Caleb moved throughout the room lighting one lamp and then the next. There was no overhead switch for this room. All I could see was a small table lamp illuminating a wingback and an overturned book, evidence of Caleb being, 'mostly up.' When he was about halfway through the room, I began to hobble and hop after him and caught sight of the title he had been reading before he heard me fall out of bed in the room above. It was my father's first book, *Trinities Tyrant.*

The whole of Gaersum Aern was expansive and magnificent but if the entire house were a setting, then the library was the center jewel. The lamps only created puddles of light throughout the massive room. Every wall was covered in row after row of books, beginning at the floor and extending up to meet the copper tiled ceiling high over my head.

Across the room, I could see the mirror my mother had stood in front of with me and near that, her reading chair. I could almost feel my mother in this room, like she might walk up behind me at any moment and put her hand on my shoulder.

While Caleb climbed one of the many rolling ladders in search of books that may contain the phrase from the box, I approached my mother's chair and sat in her place. I smiled when I saw that the nearest shelves contained all the Shakespeare.

"So what is it about Egypt anyway?" I asked elevating my sore ankle up over the arm of the chair.

"Hmm? What was that?" Caleb replied absently.

I turned and saw Caleb was flipping through an enormous volume while still twenty feet up the ladder. "Egypt," I said louder. "You said you're really into it. Why?"

He looked down at me for a second as if considering the question for the first time. Finally, he shrugged, "I don't know." He continued searching the book. "Because it's amazing I suppose. I mean, think about it. They were a civilization that came about over five thousand years ago and yet they had the technology to construct enormous monuments that are still standing today. There is still so much we don't know, so much left to discover." Caleb replaced the book he had and slid another off the shelf. "It's the only thing I can imagine ever wanting to do with my life."

"What will you do?"

"How do you mean?" he asked from behind another book.

"I mean, how will you get to do Egypt with your life?"

"Oh. Well, I'm planning on applying to Cambridge University. They have an Egyptology department." Caleb looked at me from over the top of his book, "Your uncle is helping me apply." He disappeared behind the large tome he was holding. "No one in my family has ever attended university."

Caleb continued to flip a few more pages before he replaced the book and grabbed another off the shelf. He thought Egypt was, 'amazing.' I watched as he kept looking, engrossed in every volume he pulled down—I had no doubt he would find what he was looking for. I somehow knew he had read every one of those large books cover to cover. I imagined he spent hours in this library.

My mother had her Shakespeare.

Caleb had Egypt.

Even my father had a passion. Actually he had two and was hopefully on his way to breaking up with gin, but he also had his writing.

I turned back around in my mother's chair and looked out across the expanse of library—what did I have? What was my thing? My passion, *my gift?*

Suddenly, I felt a great emptiness in my chest, like a cold ocean wind. A thought swept into my mind so clearly, it might have been whispered in my ear. *Not everyone has gifts Charlotte. Not everyone is special.*

I realized I was jealous of Caleb's *amazement.* Only one subject occupied most of my waking thoughts, and my compulsive mental spinning about my mother probably classified as more of an obsession than a passion. A life preserver that kept me afloat from one day to the next.

"It's got to be this one," Caleb called out as he began to climb down. He had the book in one hand while the other navigated the ladder rungs. His face practically beamed as he jumped down the last few feet and spread the giant book open on a nearby worktable. He turned on the desk lamp and began scanning the back of the book and then flipping to pages, followed by more scanning then flipping, scan, flip. Suddenly he stopped and looked at me still sitting in my chair, his brow furrowed, "What are you doing?"

What was I doing?

"Aren't you coming?"

I nodded and got out of the chair slowly, using the furniture in the room as my crutch. Satisfied, he returned to his scanning and flipping. I didn't rush. In the bedroom, with the box and the note—the pentagram—in that moment, my first impulse was to look for answers. Now Caleb was potentially on the verge of finding an answer, I realized I maybe didn't want to know what that note meant. Did I really want to know why my mother had owned a pentagram necklace? Wasn't the box better shoved back onto its secret shelf and forgotten altogether? Because now, I saw the risk. I was in real danger of losing the only piece of my mother I had left.

"Aha! I found it!"

My memory of her.

I stopped five feet from where Caleb stood triumphantly over his information treasure. Whatever was in that book could rip away my only support. The hole my mother left was still so big, without those memories, I would fall in.

When I didn't say anything, Caleb looked up. "What are you doing?" he looked back to the book, "It's right here."

His lips moved silently while he read.

"What is it?" I asked cautiously.

He heard the reluctance in my voice and stopped reading. When he looked up this time, I saw understanding for my fear flash across his face. The realization that this wasn't, for me, just a search for information—it was about my mom. He looked down at the book and back at me, his shoulders dropped and I could see the sympathy in his eyes. "It's nothing bad," he said. "If you're worried..." he shook his head to assure me, "it's not bad."

I took a hop closer, and then another.

"It's actually not really that clear. See here," he pointed to the book. "It's the larger text that I recognized the note from. But honestly," he shrugged, "I don't understand what it means."

I stood next to Caleb and looked over his shoulder at the section of text his finger was pointing to. The wording wasn't exactly the same as what my mother had written, but it was very similar. The phrase was actually a part of a larger block of numbered text. I started at the beginning.

Tis true without lying, certain most true.

That which is below is like that which is above and that which is above is like that which is below to do the miracles of one only thing.

And as all things have been arose from one by the mediation of one: so all things have their birth from this one thing by adaptation.

The Sun is its father, the moon its mother, the wind hath carried it in its belly, the earth its nurse.

The father of all perfection in the whole world is here.

Its force or power is entire if it be converted into earth. Separate thou the earth from the fire, the subtle from the gross sweetly with great industry.

It ascends from the earth to the heaven again it descends to the earth and receives the force of things superior and inferior.

By this means ye shall have the glory of the whole world thereby all obscurity shall fly from you.

Its force is above all force. For it vanquishes every subtle thing and penetrates every solid thing.

So was the world created.

I read it again, my eyes lingering on the second line, *that which is below is like that which is above*—it was almost exactly what was scribbled on the note in the box. I lifted up the front of the book and read the title, *The Alchemical Writings of Sir Isaac Newton.*

Newton? I was surprised. "Like under the tree, discovered gravity, apple hitting his head?" I asked.

Caleb rolled his eyes at me and sighed, "You know that's not true, don't you?"

Actually I didn't know it wasn't true, but I wasn't about to let Caleb know that. "What, gravity?" I asked sarcastically.

"Funny," he shot back. Caleb opened the book all the way again and began rereading the text.

He was right about what he found not being bad, but it wasn't anything else either. Like Caleb, I didn't understand what it meant. It did occur to me though, that this wasn't a book I had expected Caleb to pull off the shelf. I lifted up the front cover again to see the title. "Alchemical? Isn't that trying to turn lead into gold?"

Caleb tilted his head so he could continue reading at the weird angle I had created. "Yes," he said curtly.

"I thought you were looking for a book about Egyptology?"

Caleb kept reading and nodded his head.

"Well what does alchemy have to do with Egypt?"

He held his index finger up to me, signaling for me to either wait or be quiet. Whatever he meant by the gesture, it made me mad. I let the front of the book fall from my hand and the loud slap it created on the desktop made Caleb jump.

He took a deep breath and looked annoyed, "I thought I was looking for one of the books about Egypt, but then I remembered that I had been on one of my research trails and it started at Egypt and ended at Newton."

"Research trail?"

"Yes. You know one question leads to an answer that is actually another question, so you have to start down that path in order to link the first idea to the explanation of the second."

"What?"

He sighed again and pointed to the high shelf where he had pulled down the alchemical writings book. "About six months ago, I was reading *Newton's Revised History of Ancient Kingdoms—A Complete Chronology,*" he let his arm drop. "Specifically the parts about ancient Egypt. Something I read in that book led me to search out all Newton's books here in the library. That's when I came across this." He pointed to the text neither of us understood. "I only briefly flipped through it before, but some of the wording obviously stuck with me. Especially the part that is similar to the note in the box upstairs, the above and below. I remember thinking I knew it from somewhere," he shook his head. "But I think I must have just gone on with what I was originally looking for."

He didn't say anything else. "Which was what?" I asked.

Caleb looked at me puzzled. "What was what?"

My eyes grew wide in exasperation, "What you were originally looking for."

"Oh! Right." His eyebrows raised and he shrugged. "I don't

remember now. That was six months ago."

"Well what about the above and below, any ideas now?"

He pursed his lips for a second before shaking his head slowly, "No, but it is still very familiar. I just can't place it." He seemed to be thinking for a moment more before he said, "Well, I'm sure it will turn up eventually. Things like that always happen. A year from now it will pop up when I least expect it."

I didn't have a year. For me it wasn't just a curious bit of research. My mother wrote that phrase and concealed it in an elaborate puzzle box hidden in her room.

With a pentagram.

I needed to know, but I didn't want to tell Caleb why. My mother was my own business. But I would need Caleb's help.

Caleb closed the book and was carrying it back to the shelves.

"I want to figure this out," I blurted.

He stopped and turned to look at me.

"I want to know what that note upstairs means, now. I want to know how that stone box works and," I hesitated with my last demand. I still wasn't certain on this last point. "I want to know about the pentagram necklace."

Caleb's lips pursed. I expected him to ask why, or what was the big deal. So when his mouth opened up into a huge grin and he began to nod his head, I was relieved.

"Yeah. I mean, why not? We have the summer," he said. "This is actually a great idea! I haven't been on a trail for weeks.

Granted, this is not my usual, but that box did have quite a few Egyptian symbols." When he looked at me, his eyes were almost wild with excitement. "This could be brilliant."

"What could be brilliant?" another voice asked.

Caleb and I both jumped and spun towards the sound. Sophie, who looked like she had just crawled out of bed, was curling onto one of the sofas and pulling an afghan over herself.

"Sophie." Caleb chastised. "You're like a slinking cat."

She yawned and lay her head on the sofa's plush arm. "What? Am I supposed to come in blowing a trumpet? I saw the light and walked in. It's hardly my fault if you're completely absorbed in Charlotte."

Caleb didn't say a word and I was too embarrassed to turn and see his expression. I imagined he was strangling Sophie with his eyes.

Sophie smiled sweetly and closed her own. "You had a call last night Charlotte but Mum wouldn't let me wake you. She said her name was...Susan?"

"Richards," I finished. "She's my dad's editor."

"She said for you to call her tomorrow, well today, and you should make *sure* to calculate the time change. She said if you call her in the middle of the night you better be dead."

I smiled. Dad wasn't supposed to have any outside contact during his first couple weeks of treatment, but Susan had her ways. I wondered if she had somehow gotten in touch with him.

Sophie yawned again before she asked, "So how come you're here for the whole summer anyway? No one will tell us."

"Sophie!" Caleb scolded.

"She doesn't have to say if she doesn't want." She opened one eye and peeked at me, "But maybe she does want to say and just needed someone to ask."

I didn't mind telling them but I suddenly found myself looking at the floor. I took a deep breath and couldn't help but notice the sense of shame that crept into my chest. "I downloaded a paper for class."

Sophie bolted upright, "And they sent you away for that!"

I couldn't help smiling at her indignation, "No," I shook my head. "When my dad showed up to the impromptu discipline meeting, he didn't have any time to...prepare himself."

Sophie gave me a questioning look.

I sighed, "He was really drunk. The vice principal called Susan, who is the only person we have for emergencies, and now he is spending three months at the Oasis Drug and Alcohol Treatment Center in Malibu."

"Do you think it will make it into the gossip mags?" Sophie asked excitedly.

"If it does, it will be a small blurb hiding under the large pictures of more famous tragedies. Simon Stevens is more likely to be gossiped about in the *New York Times*."

"So official," Sophie punctuated my thought exactly.

Caleb had been quiet throughout my confession. When I

turned to look at him, he was staring thoughtfully into space. "What paper was it?" he asked.

"Well, I mean I can only guess the *New Yor*—"

"No, I mean what paper did you download?"

"Oh. It was on *Richard II,*" I said and felt the shame creep back.

"Shakespeare is difficult for you?"

"No! I've read almost all of Shakespeare's work, and *Richard II* at least three times."

Caleb looked confused, "Well why..."

Good question. I had been asking myself that for the past two days. "I don't know. I guess I just kept putting it off and couldn't get it done. I had practically the whole semester to work on it—and then it was due. I panicked."

Sophie rolled her eyes and stood up, "I hate that feeling. I swear they think up ways to make school as bloody boring as possible."

I didn't say anything because Sophie was trying to be supportive—but she somehow made me feel worse. It wasn't ever that I hated school, or was bored. I just couldn't get the work done. Reading, that I would do until my eyes were clamping shut from exhaustion. I just never produced any tangible evidence of what was rolling around in my head. I had sat down to write that paper at least a hundred times and every time, my mind would wander, or dad would come to see what I was doing, or I would get up to go read something else. I probably knew more about *Richard II* than any other kid in my class—I just hadn't proved it.

"Did you make tea?" Sophie asked Caleb.

"Not yet."

She flung her head back against the cushions, "I'm going to die being up this early." She looked at me, "I hope this isn't your habit because you'll be knocking about the house by yourself. Even Mum doesn't get up this early." She got up off the couch and started for the doors. "Although, if you must, I suppose we could show you where all the bits are for tea." She waited at the door for us with a sly smile. "It might be nice to wake up to tea in bed."

"Sophie!" Caleb chastised.

"I'm only kidding," she said.

Caleb took my arm and helped me towards the door.

"Oou," Sophie exclaimed when she saw me limping. "What's happened to you?"

CHAPTER SIX

HER WORDS

The cup of tea Sophie made me, sweetened with milk and sugar, warmed my hands while I waited for the shower to do something more powerful than dribble water from its ancient looking head. It eventually managed a few spits, and I did hear some encouraging rumblings erupt from the pipes behind the tile, but when the water stopped altogether, I figured I should leave the poor thing alone. Turning off the faucet I directed my attentions, and prayers, towards the shower's neighbor, a claw-foot cast iron tub.

To my relief, the tub faucet produced a slow, but steady, stream of water and the massive beast was soon half full. I lowered myself into the steamy waters and started to feel less greasy with every passing minute.

Sophie had agreed to help me and Caleb investigate the meaning of my mother's note and the stone puzzle box. I had thought she would have been practically vibrating with excitement over the mystery, but she had actually been fairly underwhelmed by the whole thing.

"Does this mean we're going to be spending the entire summer in dusty stacks of books?" she asked while inspecting her pink polish for chips. "Because, honestly, I can think of nearly a million other, more exciting, prospects. I mean, we might as well still be trapped in school."

"No one's forcing you," Caleb reminded her.

"I'm just saying, let's figure it out quick. It is summer after all."

"The quicker the better," I offered, but not for the reasons Sophie suggested. The sooner we discovered the meaning of that note, and the reason my mother had a pentagram necklace, the sooner I could get back to not doubting my own most precious possession—my memory of her.

I propped my leg with the sore ankle up over the edge of the tub. The swelling had gone down quite a bit since last night, but I still couldn't put all my weight on it. At least I was now able to get around by limping on my own without Caleb's constant support.

I thought about the way he had rushed into the room and helped me up off the floor. I thought about his fingers on my bruised forehead—the worry on his face. His worry over me.

Caleb was smart and handsome, in a lanky, bookish sort of way. I let my head rest against the back of the tub and wondered, if things were different, if I were different, could Caleb be something more than a friend? If I wasn't so damaged, so obsessed with loss, fear, would I have let Caleb believe I was actually capable of normal emotions?

It was impossible to know how my heart would feel if it were whole. I had never had any of the normal crushes or first love, but I suspected Caleb would be the type of guy I would want to spend time with. In fact Caleb was the only boy I had ever kissed—I just happened to be six at the time.

I held my breath and slid all the way under the water.

After I had soaped, scrubbed, and washed the smell of stale airplane from my hair, I pulled the drain plug with my toes and listened to the sucking and slurping of water swirling into the ancient pipes. A chill quickly overtook my wet skin. Since I had been here, I had noticed that all the rooms seemed a few degrees below comfortable. This was probably why it seemed every room came equipped with a fireplace and was littered with throws and afghans draped over the arms and backs of sofas and chairs.

Holding a towel tight around my body, attempting to keep warm, I dug a clean t-shirt and my favorite jeans out of my duffel bag. I pulled on the clothes—ugh—they smelled like airplane. I wasn't really one for perfume, but I wouldn't mind a few spritz of something right now. I would need to wash everything to get the smell out.

Wrapping my dripping hair in the towel, I scanned the room hoping to see a shot of light, or a twinkle of blue. I still hadn't found my necklace. The thought of it actually being lost lost, as in forever gone, was a weight on my heart.

I *would* find it.

Bending closer to the floor, I looked again. I avoided the large chaise and bookshelf—I already knew what was back there. That box would occupy hours of my time when I eventually got into trying to solve the puzzle, but right now, I wanted to find my necklace. My large sweeps across the room weren't turning up anything except more worry that I would never find it. On my hands and knees, I carefully inspected one of the many oriental rugs hopeful that my necklace was only camouflaged amongst the elaborate designs.

Even dressed, my bare arms prickled with goose bumps. My bag was filled mostly with shorts and short sleeve shirts. When I had packed, it hadn't really occurred to me that summer in England was vastly different from summer in Venice Beach. I hadn't even brought a sweatshirt.

Still searching, I considered the massive stone fireplace on the other side of the room. I could tell by the black stains and ash swept interior that this was not the flip-the-switch-instant-flame kind of fireplace we had in the condo. When I saw the wood stacked neatly in the corner along with a canister of long wooden matches, I gave up on this potential heat source. I had never started a real fire and would likely end up burning the whole house down.

Freezing, I stopped looking for my necklace and considered the large armoire in the corner. Maybe there was something I could borrow. I got up off the floor and limped over to the massive structure. Its girth was intimidating and I felt a bit like a character from one of my mother's many books—what world might lie beyond those heavy carved doors? I smiled at my own stupidity. Growing up in books, it was easy to be drawn into and lost within the impossible.

When I pulled open the doors, the old hinges stuck for a moment and I thought I wouldn't be able to get in, but when I tugged a little harder, they began to move, stiff and creaking from disuse. What I saw made me gasp.

"Oh."

Dresses. Probably thirty hung carefully, each in their own plastic shell of protection. Sequins and silk, taffeta and velvet—in every color imaginable.

Were these my mothers?

Back home, her closet didn't contain anything even remotely like these. Jeans, t-shirts and cardigans, I couldn't remember her in anything else. I reached out slowly and lifted a rich indigo colored dress from its place—the weight of it surprised me and when I looked closer I could see the thousands of intricately placed beads that made it so heavy. Unzipping the plastic shell, I could better see the full color of the dress and the scrolling design of the beadwork—it was stunning. Without thinking I held the dress up to myself and caught sight of my image in the mirror mounted inside the armoire's door.

My eyes—they looked the exact color of the dress. I imagined having the occasion to wear such a thing. It was far too much for even a West Christian Academy prom.

I hung the dress back in the armoire and carefully zipped up the plastic shell. My mother must have worn all these dresses at one time or another. What was her life like before she met dad?

I shut the doors and remembered that I was looking for a sweater—maybe the dresser.

I turned and bright light from the window caught my attention. Moving to one of the large windows I saw that it was the sun reflecting off the highly polished chrome wheel of an expensive looking black sports car parked on the circular drive out front.

Was my uncle home? The idea made me nervous—I had never met him as far as I knew.

I crossed the room quickly and started pulling drawers on the heavy dresser. The first two were empty but when I pulled open the third I was shocked by what I saw. It was filled with books, and not like the ones on the shelves of the small library. I picked up one from the top and felt that it was bound in soft leather. The cover had a raised design and, looking closer, I could see that it was two snakes, each positioned in a figure eight. Their tails were in their mouths. When I opened the book, I flipped only a few pages before I stopped and stared. It was handwritten and it was my mother's.

Her diary?

I picked up another of the many books in the drawer and saw that it too was filled with her words. I flipped through five others, they were all the same, filled cover to cover in my mother's handwriting. I ran my hand over the covers, each had its own unique design, snakes and dragons, trees, and one that looked like a wagon wheel. They were beautiful but left me feeling lost with all I didn't know. Like the stone puzzle box, these journals had symbols I did not understand—and they all belonged to a woman who, I realized more and more, I did not understand.

What keys to her would I find in her words? An excitement ran through me, here was the possibility to hear her again. Opening the journal with the dual snakes, a folded notebook page slipped from the book and onto my lap.

I never imagined feeling so whole, so utterly complete and perfect. In his arms time stops and it is enough to only be with him. I can no longer conceive of a life without him, we are bound mind and body. I see in his eyes, feel in his touch, it is evident in the press of his lips, he is who my soul forever seeks and I his. We are complete, whole, together at last. We are one.

Again.

I refolded the page and slipped it back into the journal. There were no dates anywhere. How would I ever tell where to begin? I flipped back towards the middle and read.

Emerick is taking me to one of his secret meetings tonight—I can hardly believe it. I must admit, even though I am forever teasing him and rolling my eyes about his "order" I can bare-

ly wait to find out what goes on. I have begun to suspect that many of our friends already belong, and that this is what they whisper about in the corners of our summer parties and evening outings. I swear Emma and Adam already attended; they are always conspiring and then changing the conversation whenever I approach. And I'm practically certain that Margot goes. She may have even been one of the very first that Emerick recruited, but since he's cloaked the whole thing in veils of secrecy, he will never answer any of my questions. And so, I've never been sure if being jealous of Margot sharing his confidences was something even fair to accuse him of. Never mind that he's never invited ME. In the end I ended up asking if I could go.

She and I have grown apart so much since Emerick and I have been together, I almost feel now as if I don't even know her anymore. Would she try to steal Emerick away? Does she even care for him anymore? All these questions, doubts. And still, I miss her. Maybe, once I'm a part of that circle, she and I can again be the friends we once were.

I laid the journal in my lap and thought of Mr. Wriothesley's words, *Actually...your mother and I were even a bit more then friends. Long before your famous father came and swept her off to the California beaches.* Emerick Wriothesley, how weird to meet a man your mother loved before your father. The cousin of the king no less. I imagined her laughing and lounging during lazy summer garden parties. A smiling Emerick, a much younger version than the one I had met, bringing her a tall, cold lemonade. For some reason, I imaged everyone dressed in white and violin music wafting through a warm breeze. I closed the journal and smiled at myself, *a person can read too much Jane Austen.*

I laid that journal aside and considered all the others still in the drawer. How many were there? Moving some to the side so I could see and estimate, there were about fifteen. The excitement this gave me felt electric. Fifteen books. Not only words she had read, but words she had written about her own life. It was a gift so big, so unexpected. A gift I never would have thought to ask for. I ran my hand gently over the journal covers. I would read every one start to finish, but where to start? I shifted the books back from where I had moved them, considering each one briefly when my eye fell on one in particular. Near the bottom of the drawer there was a plain black journal. I touched the leather cover and lifted it out. It was the same as the others in every way, size, shape, and texture. The only exception was that this journal didn't have any raised symbols decorating its cover. But there was something else different about this journal. What? I held the book in my hands and stared, trying to figure it out. I opened the cover and then I knew.

I was different about this book, the way I felt. The excitement of discovery had left me completely.

I read my mother's name, Elizabeth Spencer written in her careful, backward slanting hand on the first page. It was still hers but a nauseating sense of dread was growing inside me.

I had a strong urge to close the book and put it back at the bottom of the drawer and that urge kept me from turning the first page. As I sat there, only staring at her name, my body began to tune to a sickening vibration. I didn't want to read this book.

"It's only a journal. You're being stupid Charlotte," I whispered to myself. But I didn't believe it.

To prove it I turned the page, and immediately wished I hadn't. What was this? I turned another page, and another. They were all the same. I turned to the end and, grasping all the pages, watched them flip rapidly past my thumb. They were so different from the pages in the other journal, if not for her unmistakable writing, I wouldn't have believed it was hers.

Every page, front and back, was filled with an erratic violence of words.

They were irregular, written in every direction. Swirling, circular, heavy handed gashes of ink and lead. Her words were chunks of thought, expressions and questions that mashed into each other. I rotated the book in various angles to decipher the scripts.

I feel it, growing, coming. I SEE YOU
Shadows shadows shadows shadows shadows of a self
Where have I gone?
I know of power, it courses through my every fiber. Bends to my smallest thought, shapes the whole world at my feet.

I ran my fingers lightly over the words that didn't seem

anything like my mother and felt how her pressing hand had pushed the letters into the paper. Pages and pages...

My mind is shoved in a corner

I can not dig from a hell so deep

The kindle of rage licks at my breast

turn turn turn

What is opened will not close

The invited will not leave me

Lost Help

Help

Please help me

God please don't leave me here

Towards the end of the journal, the writing grew more and more erratic. Her words made even less sense and the handwriting looked as if it were scratched onto the page with great difficulty, like a child just learning to write for the first time.

God has forsaken us all

There is no God BITCH

Burn burn burn burn melted gore from sinners flesh

Fire erupts from within and the power radiates like a beacon of invincibility igniting all who dare step into my path

I AM GOD

I closed it and held the book shut between both my palms. How was it possible that these words flowed from my mother's mind. A pressure built in my brain until I realized I had been holding my breath. I opened my mouth and filled my lungs with air. My eyes wandered to the chaise where the puzzle box and pentagram necklace was hidden. It had something to do with this. I knew it. But whatever that was, I didn't want to read anymore. With shaking hands, I shoved books to the side and replaced the black journal at the bottom of the drawer covering it with the others.

I didn't want to understand this.

I kept out the one I had started with dual snakes on the cover and closed the drawer. I had given up on the idea of finding a sweater, but when I pulled the last drawer, it was filled with cardigans. I grabbed one that looked the least dated and slipped my arms into the soft cable knit. I suddenly felt in a hurry to share my find with Caleb and Sophie, snuggle into my mother's chair in the large library and begin reading.

When I turned to leave, something on the floor sparkled in the early morning sun streaming through the windows. I stopped and stared, but I couldn't see what had caught my eye. I moved my head a few inches, *there!* A bright beam of sunlight reflected from a spot next to one of the bed's foot posts. Hurrying to the spot, I bent down and saw it wedged under the post's carved edge.

"Thank you, thank you, thank you," I pried my cross from between the floor and the post, relief rushed through my body and I pressed the cross to my heart. "God, thank you." The chain was nowhere, but I could easily get another. If I had lost the last gift my mother had ever given me, I never would have forgiven myself.

I placed it in the center of the lace runner draping over the dresser, I didn't want to chance losing it again before I found a new chain.

I moved quickly down the hall and towards the staircase. I could hear voices drifting towards me as I approached the entrance and I remembered the black sports car—my uncle. I made a silent wish that he wouldn't have the time or inclination to get to know me right now. Never had I wanted to start any book as much as the one I held right now.

At the stairs I slowed my pace, hoping that whoever was there would move to some other place in the house and I would be able to slip past them and into the library. Caleb and Sophie were probably already in the library searching for clues to the stone box and the message it contained. I needed to share what I had found with them.

I rounded the corner slowly and saw Ms. Steward talking with a man who's back was to me. Her eyes caught my movement and she turned her attentions to me. When the man turned to follow her gaze, I was surprised to see not my uncle, but Hayden Wriothesley.

"Here she is," Ms. Steward said.

Hayden turned slowly and his eyes found mine, a small smile spread across his lips.

I stopped and watched them for a moment. They were waiting for me. Why was Hayden here?

I came down the rest of the way, highly aware that they were both watching my every move—*don't trip*.

"Charlotte," Ms. Steward began. "Hayden Wriothesley has

come to call."

I was confused. *Come to call?*

His smile grew even bigger.

I glanced towards the library and could see Sophie staring from one of the couches while Caleb sat at a desk and pretended to not notice what was happening in the entrance. His face was buried in a book. For a second, he raised his eyes to meet mine, then quickly returned them to his book.

I found my voice, "Hello."

"I hope you don't mind me dropping by?" I could tell by his confident air that Hayden assumed there was not a chance I actually did mind.

"Charlotte," Ms. Steward continued. "Before you go,"

Go?

"You'll need to call Susan Richards. That woman has called twice this morning and is quite insistent that she speak to you."

This got my attention. "Is my father all right?"

Ms. Steward waved her hand as if to dismiss the very idea, "Oh yes. It's nothing to do with him. She just seems to feel that my own assurances about your being well are not to her *satisfaction.*" Ms. Steward shook her head and added under her breath, "Cheeky American."

I paused, not sure what I was supposed to do next. "I'm sorry, did you say *go?*"

Hayden spoke up. "I've come to steal you away for the day."

I looked at him unable to hide my surprise. This seemed

to please him. I looked to Ms. Steward who didn't appear to register my distress—I didn't want to go anywhere, I wanted to get into the library with my mother's journal.

"Call that woman first," she said.

"But, where are we going? I mean, I should wait here. What if my uncle arrives?"

"Your uncle called and will be meeting you at the Wriothesley's later today. He has some business with Mr. Wriothesley and will be flying out again later tonight."

What?

"There's a phone in the morning room dear," she pointed towards the French doors. "Now, do you have any washing that needs doing?" she added in a whisper that Hayden clearly heard.

I only shook my head.

"All right, well I have a million things to get ready for your uncle," she said and waddled off across the marble floor towards the kitchen.

I looked into the morning room and then at Hayden.

"Do you need help dialing America?" he asked smartly.

I opened my mouth with a sharp *no thanks* ready—but then I realized, I did need help. I closed my mouth and nodded.

Hayden dialed in the necessary codes and Susan's cell number that I recited to him and handed me the phone. "Don't worry, I'll write it all down."

"Thanks."

After I convinced Susan that I was alive, and promised to check in with her every other day, I slipped my mother's journal into my shoulder bag and followed Hayden out the front door. He aimed his key fob at the sleek black machine parked on the drive and I heard it roar to life. *Of course this is his.* I moved to get in the car and found that Hayden was following closely behind me. *Was he going to open the door for me?* I stood back for a moment waiting to see what he was going to do. He moved past me and opened the door, I assumed for me.

"Thank you," I said and went to get in.

Hayden stopped and looked at me. Then he smiled, "Oh, I'm sorry," he stepped to the side, holding his keys out and revealing the interior of the car, "Did you want to drive?"

I saw the steering wheel—*opposite side.*

"No," I said trying to cover my embarrassment. I huffed to the other side and opened my own door. Right before I slipped onto the taut black leather seat, I caught movement, near the garden, in my peripheral vision. I stopped and stared, certain that I saw something black, like the tail of a coat, disappear behind the towering hedge. I strained to see, but whatever, or whomever it was, had disappeared.

"Are you coming today?" Hayden asked.

I took one more look toward the hedge before sliding into the belly of Hayden's purring car. Once in, Hayden finished selecting music from the touch screen on the dash and looked at me.

"You'll want this," he said and reached across me. Before I knew what he was doing, he had stretched the seatbelt across my lap and fastened me in—as if I were some small child.

I was about to protest when he announced, "Let's go." He shifted the car into first gear and I felt the world move as my body pressed into the seat. I gripped the door handle for support and felt the car fishtail on the loose gravel drive before Hayden had us shooting up the road leading away from Gaersum Aern. The trees lining the road blurred into a mass of green and brown and I could see the manor shrinking at an alarming speed in the side view mirror.

Then I saw what had caught my eye near the garden. In the mirror, I saw a man in a long black coat suddenly run onto the drive. I turned in my seat to look out the small back window. We were too far away for me to make out his features aside from a long trench coat and black hair.

He stood staring after us.

"Who was that?"

Hayden was concentrating on the road in front of us. "Who's who?"

"The man that came chasing after us." I looked back out the window to see him still standing there. "Right there."

Hayden checked his rearview mirror and shrugged. "I don't know. Probably the groundskeeper wanting to give me hell for disturbing the drive."

A groundskeeper in a trench coat? "I don't think so."

"Who cares who it is? It's nobody." He pushed play on the

touch screen and gave me a serious look, "Nobody to us."

Then I felt my body begin to pulse from the deep rhythmic boom that began pumping through the car's expensive sound system.

I had no idea where he was taking me.

CHAPTER SEVEN

LITTLE WORLD

Fifteen minutes into our drive, I began to wonder if Hayden was ever going to slow down. I easily imagined us careening off these isolated roads into an embankment, wheels spinning, bodies crushed and mangled. Somehow Hayden's music would still be blaring from the Aston Martin's speakers, eerily contrasting these normally serene rolling English hills.

"Are you going to slow down?" I tried. My yelling barely registered in my own ears.

Hayden looked over to me, pointed to the radio, pointed to his ears, and then smiled while shaking his head.

Normally, I hated guys like him. The brash overconfidence, their reckless sense of invincibility—obviously he wasn't worried about any potential harm to me, or himself.

But I didn't care enough to hate Hayden, not yet anyway.

I stared out the passenger window and watched the world

blaring past us. I didn't really want to slow down. Hayden was being ridiculously irresponsible and, for some reason, being along for this ride felt good. It felt a lot like sitting in the computer lab of West Christian Academy downloading a paper on *Richard II*.

My fingers traced the outline of the journal hidden in my thin shoulder bag. I considered pulling it out, starting to read in spite of the noise and speed. I could tune out practically anything with a book and I figured this small act would likely annoy Hayden enormously. *I am so unimpressed that I would rather read my book.* Then, as if he could read my thought, Hayden pushed the clutch, shifted higher, and my back pressed even deeper into the passenger seat. We were flying.

Clutching the journal, I closed my eyes and let my head rest against the seat. The thump, thump of the music vibrated through the interior and was, very likely, causing permanent damage to my hearing. But for this moment, I didn't care. I let everything—my mother's disappearance, my father's alcoholism, the puzzle box, the strange message, all my many questions—they rolled away with every passing mile towards wherever Hayden was taking me. I knew they would all return, but for right now, I pretended to be just like any teenage girl who was just picked up in a ridiculously expensive sports car driven by an amazingly handsome, probably illegally, older guy.

The car decelerated and I opened my eyes. Hayden pushed the clutch and downshifted in one graceful movement. I couldn't helping thinking of the physical effort it took to perform the same function with my father's rusting Ford and the accompanying mechanical complaints that eschewed from deep within that metal beast. Not even with all the financial ability of the parents at West, did even a single kid there drive a car remotely like this. Hayden wasn't from a world of simple wealth. I imagined Hayden was the most recent incarnation of his family's legacy and all the entitlement that went along with it, a modern day Mr. Darcy, with all the pride and prejudice to match. He was from a very different world.

I thought of all the dresses that hung in my mother's old room—this had been her world as well. My hands pressed the journal in my lap as I thought of her words, *I can no longer conceive of a life without him, we are bound mind and body.* Life without Emerick Wriothesley? Did she regret it?

All those books. I loved to read, but my mother, she buried herself in books. No, she escaped into them. She was always so far away, as if self ejected from her life.

Hayden slowed further and made a sharp right that threw me against the passenger door. We drove for several more minutes before the expansive lawns and gardens began. We had entered the Wriothesley Estate. Could this have been hers? I wondered for the first time if my mother hated her choice to come to America with Simon Stevens. They had always seemed an odd match. It was true, my father worshiped my mother, but from a distance. She was careful, quiet, kind, but certainly I never saw the passion of *we are bound mind and body.* I couldn't really imagine her professing an undying love for my father. There were no memories of my mother holding his hand, or kissing his cheek. All my memories were of her and a book.

Was I a mistake? Did she regret me?

I shook my head slightly at my own stupidity. Whatever she did or didn't feel for my father I did know this, my mother loved me. It was always there, every time she looked at me I could see it, her love. But there was something else. Something unspoken, something secret.

As Hayden slowed the Aston Martin to a stop in front of what could only be described as a modern day mansion, an image of my mother came to me so clearly my breath stopped. When she found me, in the neighbor's basement clutching myself and rocking hysterically, she was not simply worried and then relieved to find me. Kids go missing. But I could remember the crash of her footsteps as she flew down the wooden stairs, the brightness of the one swinging bulb suddenly illuminated, and the violence in her eyes when she finally located me and locked me in her stare. I couldn't even remember her moving towards me, just her viscously sweeping me into her arms and running back up the stairs. My mother had not been worried—she was terrified.

Of what?

My mother loved me...but she was haunted.

Hayden switched off the car and the music stopped abruptly only to be replaced by the low hum of my inner ear that continued to vibrate.

"Welcome home," he said and slipped out his door.

I stared out the windshield at the grand columned entrance leading into the Wriothesley *home.* It was at least twice the size of Gaersum Aern. Pressing my mother's journal to my stomach, I suddenly felt like running. I wished I could go back to Gaersum Aern, or better, back to the beach condo where I would be surrounded by our personal, but familiar, emptiness.

Hayden opened my door, "Madam," he said with a sarcastic grin.

When I didn't move Hayden made a gracious bow and a ridiculous flourish of his arm as if to usher me onward. I bit my lip and stared at my lap. I wanted to go home.

Hayden held his awkward position for a moment longer before looking up to see why I wasn't moving. When he stood up, I expected him to say something cutting and sharp, but he didn't say anything at all. When I finally dared to look at him I was surprised. He didn't seem like the overbearing jerk filled with snide and condescension I had come to expect, there was actually a hint of concern around his eyes. Without the act, he didn't look as old as I had first assumed. He was tall, and his thin polo shirt hinted at the chiseled muscles that were underneath, but it was the uncertainty now on his face that made me realize he was probably closer to my age.

"How old are you?" I blurted.

His back stiffened and defensiveness clouded his features,

"Old enough," he shot back.

I looked at him for a second longer before I closed my eyes and sighed, "Fine, whatever."

"Your uncle should be here soon," he said and headed for the front door.

I nodded and took a deep breath as I unbuckled the seatbelt and got out. I wasn't going to get home by sitting here.

The sun reflected brightly off the Aston Martin's highly polished chrome and I shielded my eyes until I was able to move into another angle. The driveway was broad and entirely tiled in a deep blue stone that swept around the side of the mansion to, where I assumed, the garages would be. As I followed Hayden towards the entrance, we passed the perfectly maintained tiered landscapes filled with various decorative trees and flowers, low growing hedges, and topiary artfully shaped into geometric and animal designs. Off to my left I saw two gloved gardeners shaping and pruning what appeared to be an eagle with outstretched wings.

At the top of the wide stairs leading to the entrance I stopped and stared at the circular mosaic inlaid at my feet. The bottom half was a right-angled ruler and the top was a compass like the one I had used for creating and bisecting angles in geometry. The two parts were open to each other creating a diamond shaped figure.

It was a weird design to have decorating your front porch. But then again, was it any weirder than a self-eating snake etched above your door?

Hayden pushed one of the massive doors and, to my surprise, moved to the side so I could enter first.

"Thank you."

"Sixteen," he said.

"What?" I stopped.

"I'm sixteen." A small smile appeared on his lips that made him look almost sheepish. "I'll be seventeen next month."

It was nothing short of amazing. If Hayden should ever grace the halls of West Christian with his regal presence it would be an all out female war. The thought of Hayden inciting an actual stabbing in the girls' locker room made me smile.

Hayden's face brightened and I worried he was interpreting my smile as interest—and I was definitely not interested in Hayden Wriothesley.

Dropping the smile, I shrugged, "So am I." Maybe now he would give up the pompous pretense for good. I hated when people tried to act older. Kids at West Christian Academy did it all the time, as if being sixteen were a disease they needed to hide. I just always thought it seemed so weird especially when their parents were often trying to be younger than they actually were.

"Master Wriothesley," a very austere, English gentleman suddenly appeared as if from nowhere and proceeded to take Hayden's keys. "Miss Stevens," he inclined his head towards me. "Welcome to the Wriothesley Estate. May I take your things?"

Only it wasn't a question. Before I knew it, my shoulder

bag was clutched in his skeletal hands along with my mother's old cardigan.

"If there is anything you require, do not hesitate to make a request. Camilla is also on staff today, you need only ring the kitchen." He pointed to an intercom system mounted into the nearest wall. "You'll find one in every room." The man returned his attentions to Hayden, "If there is nothing else sir?"

"No, that's all Charles."

Charles nodded, took two backward steps, turned, and proceeded down one of the many hallways leading away from the vaulted main entry. Only after he disappeared did it occur to me that my mother's diary was out of my immediate keeping. "Where is he taking my bag?"

"The cloakroom. Do you want to watch TV?"

I stared down the hall where Charles had just vanished. "Um...sure, I guess." I didn't really watch much TV, but I wasn't sure what else we would do. I had hoped my uncle would already be here, we could meet, say a few kind things, and then he could get back to his "business" with Emerick Wriothesley and I could get back to Gaersum Aern and start reading my mother's old diaries. Hopefully Caleb and Sophie had made some headway in figuring out the meaning of her 'above and below' note.

I sighed and followed Hayden down a different hall than Charles had taken. Maybe TV would make the time go by faster.

Hayden's TV room was actually a small theater complete

with red velvet stadium seating. *Who lives like this?*

After two episodes of a British teen drama called *Masks,* a voice called through the intercom system on the wall behind us.

"Master Wriothesley?" a woman asked.

"Bloody hell!" Hayden said. "Pause!" he commanded and the scene projected onto the large screen froze in place. "What?"

"Um...I was, was just—" she stammered

"What Camilla? Spit it out we're in the middle of *Masks.*"

"I'm sorry sir. I only wondered if the Miss was hungry."

Actually, the Miss was bored. "I am hungry," I said.

Hayden looked annoyed, one of the title characters was just about to get caught having an affair with his chemistry teacher.

"I can just go. I'm sure I can find the kitchen," I offered and got up.

"You're going to miss the climax," Hayden looked flabbergasted.

"It's okay, really. Don't wait for me." I waved my hand at the screen.

Hayden shook his head. "Camilla, Miss Stevens is on her way."

"Yes sir."

As I slipped out of the theater, Hayden called, "Play!" and the screen jumped to life.

I stood outside the door for a moment. Even though I knew

the episode's background music was thundering through the sound system on the other side, I couldn't hear even a whisper through the super soundproof walls. I was beginning to see that the Wriothesley's had only the best—of everything.

I wondered again if my mother had regrets. Would all of this have meant something to her? I thought of the gowns hanging in her childhood closet, did she miss this life? The more I learned about my mother's past, the more I felt like I didn't know her at all. Ever since I had arrived in England, I had started harboring a secret unspoken dread. He had never spoken the words, but it was the same worm of doubt that I knew had haunted my father for the last four years. We never found her, not even a trace of her. There were no ransoms, no body; nothing had been missing except her. There was no evidence of anything at all. She had simply vanished.

Did my mother leave us?

Why had my mother followed Simon Stevens to America?

I headed down the hall that I thought lead back to the entrance figuring I could attempt to find the kitchen from there.

My father was also ridiculously wealthy. Not like the Wriothesleys, but still, she could have had almost anything. I had always assumed my parents' less audacious lifestyle was a choice.

Unless it had nothing to do with money. Nothing to do with money and everything to do with being bound *mind and body* to someone you loved. Even money wouldn't buy back a lost soul mate. *What happened between my mother and*

Emerick Wriothesley? God, I just wanted to get back to the manor so I could read her diaries. Every minute here was like torture.

I found the entrance and considered the halls along with the sweeping circular staircase that led upstairs. Well the kitchen was probably not up there but I still had no idea which way to go.

The intercom. I found the small box on the wall and pressed KITCHEN, "Um Camilla? This is Charlotte." I waited a few seconds but didn't hear anything.

"Camilla?" I tried again but still no reply.

"I'm in the entrance and I'm not really sure which way the kitchen is."

Silence.

"Okay," I said lamely. "Well in case you can hear me I'm going to try and find it," I felt like an idiot. I imagined Camilla and Charles both laughing themselves stupid.

The hall Charles had taken earlier seemed like a good place to start. Maybe I would stumble across the cloakroom and I could get my bag back—it made me uncomfortable to think my mother's diary was somewhere else. If I ever found the kitchen, I would ask Camilla to take me to it.

The Wriothesleys' mansion was incredibly bright inside. With high vaulted ceilings and a multitude of skylights, even in the halls, the all white walls glowed with natural light. It took me a minute to realize that the various pieces of artwork lining the hall were by artists I was familiar with. Monet, Van

Gogh, I stopped to stare at one of Salvador Dali's melting clocks...surely these were reproductions. Looking closer I noticed the signature and gasped. They might still be fakes, but somehow I doubted it. If these were in their halls, what on earth did they have displayed in the formal living areas?

A door further down the hall was ajar. I went up and knocked gently, "Hello? Excuse me." I pushed harder and the door swung open into a dark room. I felt along the inside wall until I found the light switch—well, at least now I knew where one of the bathrooms was. I stared for a moment at the toilet and bidet before shutting off the light and moving onto the next room.

I entered several rooms before thinking I should try to find my way back to the entrance. One room looked like someone's office, there were a number of spare bedrooms, and an atrium with a glass ceiling, tropical foliage and the sound of rushing water pulsing from somewhere deep within the jungle like room.

With every room it was becoming more difficult to remain unimpressed.

They should pass out maps at the front door, like a tourist attraction.

Someone grabbed my arm.

I gasped and turned into the terrified gaze of a young woman. Her wide dark eyes held mine as she quickly pressed the tips of her fingers to her lips.

"I'm sor—"

Like lightening, she placed her hand over my mouth. When I moved to pull away, she roughly grabbed the back of my head. Her strength surprised and frightened me.

She leaned in close and whispered, "You are in danger." Her accent sounded German. I recognized it from the theater intercom.

I met her eyes and made myself relax. When she took her hand away from my mouth, I asked, "Camilla?" keeping my voice low.

She nodded and then tilted her head to the left. She pulled her shirt collar to the side and showed me a tattoo. Just below her left collarbone was an inverted pentagram bordering a five-pointed star. Each arm of the star was a different color: green, red, blue, yellow, and white. There was something in the center of each arm as well as within the center of the star, but it was too small to make out before Camilla quickly covered herself.

I stared blankly at her. It was like she was trying to communicate some secret meaning or code, but I had no idea what the tattoo could mean.

"Charlotte, you must leave here. You are endangering everything your mother has worked for. Everything she has sacrificed for."

"I'm sorry, what? You know my mother?'

"I know *of* her."

"What do you mean? Have you seen her? Do you know where she is?"

We both turned our heads when the sound of a door closing echoed down the hall.

"There is no time. Charlotte, trust no one. No one. Never return here, there are ears and eyes all over this house."

"Charlotte?" Hayden called from up the hall.

Camilla quickly backed away. She looked terrified.

"Wait," I begged.

Camilla shook her head silently. She pressed her fingers to her lips in a final gesture of silence and then disappeared through the atrium.

"There you are," Hayden called.

I was still staring at the door Camilla had only just slipped through.

"You're nowhere near the kitchen. What's the matter? Did you get yourself lost?" He asked with a smirk.

Camilla's warning and words were still ringing through my head. I wanted to chase after her, make her tell me how she knew my mother and what on *earth* she was talking about. What had my mother done? Sacrificed? Did she know where my mother was?

"Helllloo. Come in Charlotte. Earth to Charlotte."

I turned to Hayden and resisted the amazing urge to drill him about Camilla. Who was she? Was she crazy? Why was I in danger?

Charlotte, trust no one.

"I got lost," I said.

"Obviously," he laughed. "The kitchen's this way." He motioned for me to follow.

I walked a few steps and stopped. "Actually, I'm not really hungry any more."

Hayden stopped and looked at me like I was insane. "You're not hungry? The kitchen's not *that* far off," he scoffed.

I shook my head. I wanted to get my bag and go back to the manor, I needed to think about what Camilla had said, find a way to figure out what it meant. And if Camilla's warning was valid, wasn't Hayden one of the *no ones* I shouldn't be trusting.

I didn't even really care about meeting my uncle. If he was that busy, fine. He'd never been a part of my family's life as far as I knew. My mother certainly never spoke of him, and he was her brother. Just because he was suddenly saddled with me this summer didn't mean we needed to pretend there was any great relationship. He didn't mean anything to me. What I wanted was to talk to Caleb and Sophie.

I decided to ask Hayden to take me home. That's where I was closest to learning about my mother.

"Hayden?"

"Hmm? Oh, hang on." He felt his jean's pocket and pulled out his cell phone. Hayden touched the screen, "Hello? Yeah...yes," he corrected. "We'll be right there." He pocketed his phone. "Your uncle's here, I'm supposed to take you to my dad's office."

Of course. "All right," I sighed. At least it meant I could probably go back to Gaersum Aern somewhat soon.

"You don't seem happy to see him."

"Don't I?"

Camilla's warning continued to spin through my head.

No one.

CHAPTER EIGHT

LOST MOTHER

Hayden and I had been waiting in the study outside his father's office for twenty minutes. "I thought they were waiting for us."

Lounging on the sofa, Hayden continued to throw a small marble ball high into the air over his head and catch it right before it hit his face. "They are never waiting for us. *We* are expected to be immediately available. *They* will get to us when they have time."

"But he called you."

"Correction, Charles called me. We, or rather you, are on the schedule."

"So why are you here."

"I am your entertainment."

"I don't need *entertaining*."

Hayden shrugged, "Those are me orders, me lady," he said and threw the ball again snatching it out of the air with one hand right before it could hit him on the forehead.

"What orders? What are you talking about?"

"Dad. He said I am to, and I quote, keep Charlotte entertained this summer, end quote."

"Why?"

"I don't know. Probably he is trying to lay some foundation with your uncle. He rarely does anything unless it will have some positive impact on business relations."

"Well you can just forget your orders. I am perfectly capable of entertaining myself."

"Sorry, that's not possible."

"Excuse me?"

Hayden stopped throwing the ball and sat up straight. "That little black beauty you rode in on today, she's my paycheck for this summer job." He placed the ball back into the decorative bowl on the table in front of him. "And I very much want to keep that stallion, so I'm afraid you're stuck with me all summer."

I stared at him disbelieving. "You can't force me—"

"Watch me."

My mouth dropped. The arrogance! No words would come so I turned and stormed to the farthest end of the room near the fireplace. The urge to grab that marble ball and throw it right at his face was overwhelming. With my back to him, I shut my eyes and clenched my fists instead.

"Now, don't be angry. Who knows, you might fall madly in love with me. Summer romance being what it is."

That was it. I spun around, "You are unbelievable! I have met some real jerks in my life, but you," I was practically sputtering.

Hayden continued to lounge with his self-satisfied smirk. "See, you're already half mad with passion."

Furious, I grabbed the closest thing I could find.

Hayden's face went white and bolted up. "Wait!" His eyes were riveted on the object held behind my head. "Not that," he pointed.

My arm froze mid-swing.

"Please, I'm sorry," he said.

I brought my arm down to see what could possibly hold such sway over him.

"You can clobber me with anything else, I swear. Just not that."

It was a small black and white photo in a battered wooden frame. The picture was square and yellowed with age. In it, a young woman stood next to a small boy.

Once he was sure I wasn't going to hurl the photo at him, Hayden got up off the couch, took the picture from me and carefully placed it back on the mantle.

"What is it?"

Hayden took breath. "The only picture my dad has of his biological mother. That's him," he pointed to the serious looking boy in the picture, "when he was five."

I looked more closely. The boy looked like a little Hayden, except with none of the cockiness. The woman's expression was blank and she appeared to be staring through the camera, not at it. What was most noticeable was the distance between them, as if they were strangers asked to stand for a picture.

"Why is it the only one?"

"She died six months after that was taken."

"She looks so young."

"Twenty-one."

I was shocked. "And he was five?" I did the math. "She was sixteen when she had him? How did she die?"

"Tuberculosis."

I couldn't help thinking of my own lost mother. "He must have been devastated losing her so young."

"Maybe," he said as he stared at the photo.

What an odd thing to say. "Maybe?"

"That picture was taken at the asylum where she lived. She had schizophrenia. The family had her committed just before my father was born. In truth, he hardly knew her."

I watched Hayden a moment longer, when he was sincere and not acting like a total pig, it was hard to look away. Sophie was right, Hayden was breathtaking. "How horrible," I offered. "For your whole family."

Hayden turned his eyes on me. Like before, on the driveway when I wouldn't get out of the car, his whole act was gone. "She was a maid. When my grandfather got her pregnant, my family, my Wriothesley family, hated her. They made her disappear."

"But your father, how...?"

"My grandfather, he loved her—or so I've been told. But he was a weak man. Without giving up everything, the best he could offer her was convincing his family to at least provide for my father. My grandmother was left to the animals at Our Mother Mary's Asylum. My father was taken to visit her, once a year at Christmas."

"What happened to her?"

"When he was seventeen, my father hunted down the truth. He never told me what exactly they had done to his mother. But when I was little, he had Our Mother Mary's shut down. Many of the priests, nuns, and orderlies are still in prison."

I thought of the way Emerick had recoiled from my sapphire cross yesterday in the morning room and the look in his eye made perfect sense. How he must hate anything to do with Christianity and the institution that had tortured his own mother.

Hayden stared at the mantle, as if he had forgotten I was even in the room. "He has decimated certain members of our family. Anyone who had anything to do with his mother's suffering—he crushed them."

The power of his words made my breath catch in my chest. Hayden once again seemed much older than sixteen. When he turned to me with his brow still furrowed, I took a step back. A moment later, he seemed to realize I was there and his features softened.

"I don't know you," he said shaking his head. "Why did I

tell you all that?"

"I don't know," I whispered. "Maybe you needed to tell someone. Maybe it's easier to tell someone you don't know."

He thought about that for a moment. "Maybe." He took a step closer to me and I stopped breathing. His hand reached towards me and tucked a loose strand of hair behind my ear. His touch was electric down the side of my face and my heart thundered involuntarily in my chest. My God, what was happening? I couldn't move.

Hayden moved even closer, his hand cupped my face and turned it up towards his. His lips felt like a soft fire pressed to mine. My eyes closed and I felt his other hand press into the small of my back. It felt as if waves were rolling through my body.

When he let me go, my face flushed with embarrassment.

The expression on his face was almost smug. He didn't seem embarrassed at all. I imagined Hayden did this sort of thing on a fairly regular basis.

"Don't do that again," I stammered.

He looked at me with curiosity, like he couldn't quite figure something out. "Who are you Charlotte Stevens?"

My anger from earlier returned, "Nobody," I said. "And certainly not one of your idiotic, lovesick girls."

A look of amusement crossed his face. "No?"

I swung to hit his chest but he easily caught my arm in the air. In one gentle movement, Hayden brought my wrist to his mouth. As he kissed the base of my palm, his eyes met and held mine, daring me to make him stop.

And I couldn't.

The office door opened suddenly. I snatched my hand away from Hayden but not before Emerick Wriothesley saw us. His raised eyebrows quickly turned into a gentle smile—he was not at all shocked to see his son seducing some girl he hardly knew.

As my blood rushed to my head the tips of my ears burned. I was practically a scarlet flag of shame.

Hayden, on the other hand, appeared completely unfazed as he turned casually to the door. "Father," he greeted as if what had just happened was nothing at all.

"Hayden," Emerick acknowledged. "And Miss Stevens. You must be anxious to meet your uncle. So sorry to keep you waiting. Please do join us."

"Anything else?" Hayden asked.

"Not just now. You will need to drive Miss Stevens home however so don't leave the estate."

"Of course." Hayden turned to me and smiled. "Until later then."

I was still too overwhelmed with embarrassment. All I could do was continue to bite my lip and nod like an idiot. I hated him for making me feel so stupid.

Emerick turned and headed back to his office, "This way Miss Stevens."

As he left, Hayden paused and made sure his father's back was turned before raising his eyebrows and giving me a private wink.

When I gave him my dirtiest scowl, his face crumpled into silent laughter.

"Miss Stevens?" Emerick called.

"Yes, I'm coming."

I followed Emerick down a dimly lit hall connecting the study to his private offices. The narrow hall was lined with oil portraits illuminated with individual brass art lamps. A few of the portraits I recognized right away: Einstein, Beethoven, and George Washington, *an odd portrait to be hanging in an English gentleman's home.* Others I recognized when I caught sight of their nameplates: Emerson, Thoreau, and Henry Ford. Hanging just outside his office door was a strange portrait that caught my attention more than any of the others. A man sat on a throne with his face obscured by a dramatic mask, half comic, half tragic. The nameplate read *Sir Francis Bacon aka Shake-Sphere.*

I stopped and starred at the portrait. "Mr. Wriothesley?"

Emerick was just opening the door. He stopped and turned, "Yes?"

I pointed to the nameplate, "What does this mean?"

He looked to the plate and then back to me. "What does it mean to you?" Emerick gazed at me. Like in the morning room the day before, his expression was confusing—his mouth was smiling but his eyes were scrutinizing. Measuring me. Teachers had the same look when they were waiting for you to disappoint them with the wrong answer.

It didn't mean anything especially to me, but it had struck me. The aka Shake-Sphere reminded me of Shakespeare. And anything even remotely related to Shakespeare grabbed my attention.

"Um..." being asked outright, I felt foolish for the association I had made. I shook my head and shrugged. "I guess it just made me think of William Shakespeare. I'm sure that's not what it meant."

He stared a moment longer before turning on his heels. "I am sure you are correct either way." He entered the office ahead of me.

He didn't answer my question. Either he thought I was too stupid or, like most adults, he was trying to inspire me to figure it out for myself. Nearly every time I had tried to get an easy answer from my mother she would reply, *Knowledge is sweeter found than given Charlotte.* From spelling words to math facts she would answer, *Knowledge is sweeter found than given Charlotte.* And then I would stomp off to either the computer or the reference section of her private library depending on what I needed. Even though I had come to automatically expect it, my mother's stock answer to my every question always irritated me to no end. It seemed such a normal way to be with your mother, irritated with her for not giving you what you want when you want it.

I wish I had known I would lose her.

I glanced at the portrait once more and memorized the inscription on the brass plate. *Francis Bacon aka Shake-Sphere.*

Emerick Wriothesley didn't know me. If he thought I was even remotely like his own son he might be surprised to know I wasn't stupid or lazy. I would figure out for myself what it meant.

In the office, Emerick moved around his desk and sat in the high backed chair. One of the two chairs positioned in front of the desk was occupied. The man's back was to me, but I could see the elbow of his dark suit coat resting on the arm of the green wingback chair.

I moved around to sit in the other chair and my uncle leaned forward. Seeing me he stood up, "Charlotte," he nodded more in acknowledgment than greeting. He looked exactly the same as he had in my parent's wedding photo. It was like he hadn't aged at all in the last seventeen years. His movements and expression were more than formal, Mr. Wriothesley was formal, but my uncle seemed cold as well.

"Mr. Spencer," I said without thinking. There was just no way I could call this man Uncle to his face.

He sat in his chair and I followed by sitting in mine. "It's good to see you are well Charlotte. My apologies for not being able to attend to you, this is a very busy time of year for me. With your father's sudden...illness, well unforeseen *personal* circumstances can be difficult to schedule."

I sat listening to him politely explain how he couldn't just drop all his important business responsibilities just because my alcoholic father dropped the ball and now he was saddled with the kid for the summer. I felt like reminding him that I was now sixteen, not six.

"You will, of course, make yourself at home at Gaersum Aern. Ms. Steward is more than capable of seeing to your needs." He looked across the desk to Emerick, "And I believe Mr. Wriothesley has made arrangements with Hayden..." Emerick gave a silent nod, "for you to be included in some of the local events this summer."

Yes, Hayden had already explained that he was my *entertainment* for the summer.

"I am afraid Mr. Wriothesley and I have a number of matters still to discuss—I believe Hayden will be driving you home?"

"Yes, of course," Emerick said.

"Well then," my uncle stood.

I was dismissed and I followed his cue by standing as well.

"I have a flight to Paris this evening and won't be back until sometime next week. It was a pleasure seeing you Charlotte."

"Thank you," was all I could manage.

"Charlotte," Emerick said. "Hayden will be waiting for you back in the study. You can find your way?"

"Yes," I nodded and wondered if Emerick knew about my earlier lost wanderings through the hallways of the estate. I thought of Camilla's warning, *there are ears and eyes all over this house.* Yes, I could manage to walk down a straight hall from one room to the other. When I opened the office door to leave, Emerick called out.

"Oh Charlotte, I almost forgot."

I stopped and looked back.

"My wife Margot, she has a midsummer ball and bonfire every year. She would love for you to come."

Ball? "Thank you."

"Margot will be delighted. We will have the invitation sent over."

My scheduled meeting with my uncle was done. As both men sat back down, I quietly closed the door behind me and went to find Hayden.

All I wanted was to get back to Gaersum Aern as soon as possible. I needed some space to sort through everything. Camilla had shown me her tattoo like it was supposed to mean something to me. Who was she and what did she know about my mother? What had my mother sacrificed?

I stared again at the strange portrait of a man sitting on a purple throne holding a tragic-comic mask to his face. It was a curiosity, but nothing more. If I was expected to be spending time with the Wriothesleys this summer I needed to figure out who Camilla was first. She had warned me to trust no one and to never come back to the Wriothesley estate.

But how? And more importantly, why?

CHAPTER NINE

STOLEN

"You're going to kill us," I said.

Hayden smiled and shifted the Aston Martin into a higher gear.

I sighed and watched the countryside fly past us. It was no use chastising him any further. When I had rejoined him in his father's study, he had bent over and kissed my cheek before I could shove him away. I was quickly learning that Hayden loved to annoy me.

Before we left the estate, Charles returned my bag and cardigan. I felt the outline of my mother's diary through the fabric and was relieved to have it back in my possession. As soon as I got back to Gaersum Aern I would head straight to my room and the battered red sofa in my bedroom library. I would read all night if I had to. I needed to learn as much about my mother's past as I could.

Hayden reached across the center console and put his hand

on my knee.

I slapped his hand and pulled my knee away, "What is wrong with you?"

He pretended my slap had hurt by shaking his hand. "I like you Charlotte."

"No you don't, you don't even know me. And even if you did, I don't like you. So you can just stop."

"Yes you do."

"No. I don't!" But I remembered the feel of his hand on my face and his lips pressed firmly against mine and my stomach did a little flip. I didn't like guys like Hayden—so sure, so cocky. And certainly there were many, *many* girls who fell over left and right for him, but there was no way I was going to be one of them.

Hayden put his hand back on the steering wheel and focused on the road. We drove the last mile in silence and I was beginning to think he'd finally gotten the message. We pulled around the circular drive and Hayden put the Aston in neutral, he turned his amazing deep blue eyes on me. "You will though," he said.

I shook my head. "You're impossible," I sighed reaching for the door handle.

"I know," he said and gave me a wicked smile. I suddenly thought about kissing the crooked corner of his mouth. Leaning against his chest while his hand pressed into the small of my back like earlier in Emerick's study, the feel of his open lips at the base of my palm.

I got out of the car as fast as I could and slammed his expensive door behind me. The gravel crunched under my tennis shoes as I tried to get to the front doors as quickly as possible. There was no trusting myself; he was too handsome, too good at seduction. Not that I would ever tell him, but I hadn't even kissed a guy before today—except for Caleb when I was six. Hayden affected the senses and even if I didn't like him, it was still almost impossible to think straight under his influence.

His electric window opened behind me and I heard his voice, smooth and confident, "I have plans tomorrow so I'll call you in a few days."

I spun around and glared at him. "I told you, I don't need entertaining."

He still had his crooked smile that I had envisioned kissing. "I know." He pushed the clutch and shifted the Aston into gear. "But I'll see you in a couple days anyway." He hit the gas and accelerated out of the drive—the back wheels sliding slightly on the loose gravel. The engine practically roared as he shot back up the road and out of sight at an amazing speed.

My stomach churned and my head felt hot. I had the childish urge to grab a handful of gravel and throw it after him. Instead, I turned and stormed towards the manor. As I swept through the massive stone entry, my eyes caught sight of the intricate ouroboros chiseled into the stone and I was reminded of the emerald puzzle box stashed away behind the chaise upstairs. I had plenty on my plate already. There was certainly no need to waste even a second thought on Hayden Wriothesley. He could call all he wanted—it's not like he could *force* me to do anything with him. Entering the marble foyer I recalled his veiled threat when I had pointed this fact out to him earlier, *watch me*, he'd warned. I huffed—did he think I was one of his wilting lilies? Did he honestly think I would bend just because his eyes had the power to make my stomach drop? Physical attraction was one small part, I told myself. Compared to the whole person? And Hayden's whole was mostly jerk.

There was a dim light coming from the direction of the library so I headed that way. I would not be swayed by Hayden's physical prowess I promised myself. No, I won't—but my mind betrayed me not even a moment later with the remembrance of his hand on my face. There was something about the way he hadn't even asked to kiss me, he just did it. It was infuriating. The audacity. For him to assume that it was even remotely okay to, what? *Invade* my person that's what. But it was something else as well.

Dizzying. Like being shot through with electric current.

It would not be enough to swear off of Hayden—when he was in my presence, I would need to be on guard against him. It was a game to him, this much I knew. And he'd obviously had a lot more practice.

When I entered the library I didn't see anyone, which was just as well. I would catch up with Sophie and Caleb later and find out if they'd had any success in deciphering the meaning of my mother's cryptic note. Right now I could use some quiet time alone. Not to mention Sophie would no doubt have an endless array of questions about Hayden—and I wasn't sure I was stable enough to discuss anything that had happened while I was there, like the Wriothesley's crazy confusing estate and Camilla's strange warning—meeting my uncle, without her picking up on and making guesses about the reasons for my current distress. One thing was for sure, I didn't want Sophie or Caleb to know anything about what had happened between Hayden and me today.

The light next to my mother's chair was on as if it were an invitation into her world. There was still a bit of the fading daylight streaming through the gauze sheers coving the large windows but it wouldn't last long. As I crossed the room, I reached under the shades of two other lamps and created two more pools of light. I had no idea what time it was but as I flopped into the chair it occurred to me that I hadn't had anything to eat since the tea and toast Caleb had made me this morning. I would just start my mother's diary and then find something for dinner.

When I reached into my bag, I immediately knew something was wrong. I pulled out her diary, only it wasn't her diary. Her book was leather bound with two raised snakes in figure eights. The book in my hands had a cloth cover and when I opened it, the pages were empty.

I could only stare, disbelieving. It felt like someone had knocked the wind out of me.

Where was my mother's diary? I sat staring at the blank

pages before me.

The Wriothesley's of course. My bag had been out of my possession all day, completely available for anyone at the estate to rifle through. Camilla's warning suddenly seemed more pressing and I thought about the panic on her face. Did she have something to do with this?

Having only read a few pages, I didn't even know what was in the diary. From what I'd seen, it was about my mother's childhood friends and Emerick. Her private thoughts about Emerick.

Someone was reading them. The thought made me feel ill—like I had betrayed her confidence.

Who would have taken it? Why?

Looking around the empty library—I didn't know what to do. Should I call Mr. Wriothesley, outraged, demanding that they scour the estate? What if it was him? I had no way of proving that the diary had been stolen— as far I knew, no one but me even knew it existed. A lump formed in my throat promising tears. It was all too much, everything. I couldn't hang on to my mother—she slipped through my fingers over and over again and every time was like losing her all over. These *things*, they were all I had. I needed them.

Curling my legs sideways up into the chair, my head fell back against one of the high back wings and I cried.

The light from the windows changed from the soft orange of sunset to a pale blue. When Sophie entered the room, I had no idea how much time I'd spent feeling completely lost and now, after Camilla's strange warning which I still didn't know if I should believe or not, more alone than ever.

As Sophie neared, I wiped my face with the sleeve of my mother's cardigan.

"Charlotte?" she asked softly.

The concern in her voice brought on a fresh wave of tears. I nodded and wiped my face again.

Sophie knelt in front of the chair and placed her hands on my legs. "Ooo, you're a right mess."

I couldn't help the blurt of laughter that escaped through my tears.

"What's happened? Was it Hayden? He has a horrible reputation," she said almost wistfully.

I shook my head, even though yes, it was partially Hayden. "No. I mean, don't get me wrong, he is horrible. But mostly I just don't know what to do." I proceeded to relay the entire day—minus Hayden and me kissing—and every bizarre and horrible circumstance from getting lost, and Camilla's warning, to meeting my frigid uncle.

"He is completely tight," she interjected.

And I finally finished with my mother's stolen diary.

"Oh, Charlotte!" she sympathized. But her face quickly clouded with anger and she stood up and started marching towards the door. "Let's go," she commanded.

"What? Where?"

"Caleb is going to drive us straight over to the Wriothesley estate and we will demand that they find it and return it. I mean, for God's sake, obviously someone there took it!"

"We can't!" I breathed.

Sophie stopped dead. "Why not!"

I shook my head as I stood up. Sophie watched and waited while I crossed the room to her and then held each of her hands in mine. "Because I don't know what is going on Sophie. But something is. Something to do with my mom. And until I figure it out, I have no choice but to believe Camilla. I have no idea where my mother is, if she is even still alive after all these years. If there is a chance..." *of finding her* I didn't finish. Camilla's words had me wondering about a number of things, at the very least there was her reliability and mental stability—or lack there of—but a thought had been growing since this afternoon, and a particularly dangerous one at that. If I could piece it all together, her past, and connect that with the image I clung to of the woman I had known—maybe, maybe this time.

"A chance of what?" Sophie insisted.

"Of finding her," I pleaded.

"Your mother?"

I nodded.

For once, Sophie was silent and only bit her lip with a worried expression on her face.

"What?" I asked fearing she would say exactly what I didn't want to hear. That I was crazy and this Camilla lady probably was too.

Sophie shook her head and her eyes darted quickly away.

"It's just, I mean hasn't she been gone for four years?"

"Yes."

"I guess I just don't see how. What if it's all nothing? What if you read every one of those other diaries upstairs and it's nothing other than she thought she loved Emerick and then he broke her heart so she dumped him and ran off to America with your dad? What if it's no mystery, what if she just..." she stopped.

I glared at Sophie, "What, why don't you say it? What if she just left? That's what you were going to say, right? What if she's just left us and is living some other life with some other people? People that make her happy."

"Charlotte, I didn't mean..."

"No. It's true. It's not like I don't think that every day Sophie. I think it every day because it is entirely possible."

"I'm sure..."

"But maybe it's something else. That's why I have to try. Does that make sense? Believe me I know I could just be setting myself up for a huge fall—but I *have* to try to learn as much as I can."

Her lovely arched brows furrowed over her apologetic eyes, "Of course. I'm sorry Charlotte."

I took a deep breath and sighed. "Don't be sorry. Just help me."

"Anything," she vowed.

Leaning in, I gave her a huge hug. "You're fantastic, Sophie."

"What do you need me to do?" she asked over my shoulder.

I pulled out of our hug but continued to hold her shoulders in my hands. She wasn't going to like what I had to say. "Read?" I asked waiting for her tantrum.

Her face fell. "What, like Caleb's great tomes of death?"

I suppressed a smile—even I didn't want to read those. "No, the diaries. I figure the faster I can get through them, the better."

Sophie brightened somewhat. "You said she wrote about her and Mr. Wriothesley?"

I nodded. "From what little I saw of that first one." *The stolen one*, I thought to myself.

"There's probably some steamy stuff in there," she seemed to be convincing herself.

"Probably." Although the very thought made me somewhat nauseous. Emerick was certainly handsome—in a middle-aged way. But obviously, if Hayden's looks were any indication, he must have been extremely handsome when my mother had known him. It was almost impossible to imagine my somewhat distant mother writing anything 'steamy' about a man. Certainly she'd never even appeared lukewarm with my father.

"All right then." She conceded. "But I'm not going to get stuck in the library all summer. We can read and lie out by the pool."

"I promise." We started walking towards the library doors

together. "Wait," I stopped and narrowed my eyes. "There's a pool?"

"Yes," she looked at me like I was crazy. "Out back. There's a photo somewhere of you and Caleb swimming in it when you were little."

"Oh?" Yet another thing I had no memory of. It occurred to me that I hadn't seen him since this morning. "Where is Caleb?"

She waited at the door for me. "Sulking somewhere."

"Why?"

"Are you kidding? Hayden Wriothesley swept in with no warning and whisked you away in his *amazing car* for an entire day." Her voice softened. "I actually felt really sorry for him. I thought he was going to lose his mind."

Guilt flooded through me as we started up the grand staircase towards my room. It's not like Caleb was my boyfriend—but still, I didn't want him to be hurt either. It would be better if he didn't ever find out about Hayden kissing me. Especially since I was now aware of exactly what kind of games Hayden could play. It wasn't like it had meant anything to me anyway.

When we reached the top of the stairs I asked, "Have you seen him lately?"

"Last I saw of him he was reading in the garden. But that was just after supper."

With the mention of food I was reminded of my now mutinous stomach. The climb up the stairs had actually left me lightheaded. I would grab another one of the diaries for myself, assign one to Sophie and then find something to eat in the kitchen. I also wanted to track down Caleb—I didn't like the idea of him worrying about Hayden and would somehow try to reassure him while at the same time maintaining our status of 'just friends.' How I would do that I had no idea.

As we entered my room, I reached for the switch and heard the resounding crack of the ancient electric wiring as the chandelier illuminated above our heads. "Thank you Sophie. You are truly wonderful to help me." I saw my cross still sitting on top of the large armoire—*Don't forget to get a chain* I reminded myself.

"I'm bloody brilliant is what I am," Sophie corrected.

I knelt down and pulled the handles of the drawer with the diaries stashed inside.

The shock of it made all the air rush out of me. My weight shifted back and I went limp. Completely defeated, I could only stare at the now empty drawer in front of me.

"Charlotte?" Sophie questioned. "What's happened?"

"They're gone," I cried. "All of them."

The next thing I felt was Sophie pushing me gently aside while she proceeded to open every other drawer, checking to make sure of what I already knew.

They were gone, every one of them.

"Are you sure it was this armoire?"

"Yes," I answered weakly.

"But how? Who?"

I didn't know.

CHAPTER TEN

PIECES

I sat with my head propped in my hand at the thick butcher-block table in the kitchen. The shepherds pie Sophie had reheated for me had gone cold again while I picked and stirred the potatoes into the gravy heavy beef. Even though I was starving, I only managed a few forkfuls into my mouth—the sight of the empty drawer was too depressing.

Sophie sat across from me sipping a can of Coke while she scrutinized my every move.

"Charlotte, you have to eat," she had already pleaded more than once.

And so I would fork in another bite of cold mashed potatoes.

When Caleb wandered into the kitchen, I had finally convinced Sophie that I was full, "Really, I swear I am," full on the mere five bites I'd eaten and she was scraping my plate into the disposal.

"Hey! Where have you been?" Sophie asked him.

His eyes met mine but looked quickly away. "Around," he said sounding somewhat defiant.

"Well Charlotte's had a horrible day—go on," she urged. "Tell him."

I didn't feel like it but I dredged through all the details again, carefully avoiding the parts about Hayden's lips, except that this time I finished with not one stolen diary, but an entire drawer of missing books.

While I spoke, Caleb's expression changed from sullen defiance to intense interest, "Wait, the books were your mum's diaries?"

"Yes," I said miserably.

He placed his head in his hands while I finished my story and only when I mentioned Hayden's name, "Then Hayden brought me home," did he lift his head and furrow his brow.

When I had finished, Sophie asked, "Well, what are you thinking?"

Caleb sat a moment longer looking worried before getting up from his chair and opening a drawer near the fridge. I realized he actually cared about the missing books, he understood how much they meant to me and he didn't like to see me so upset. When he returned, he had a skinny pad of paper and a stub of a pencil, both of which he shoved in front of me before taking the chair right next to mine.

"From what you did read in that first diary, write down as much as you can remember. Every detail."

What did I remember? Certainly that she had been in love with Emerick. I didn't want to write down the exact words she had used—they were her private thoughts and feelings. She had probably never imagined that almost twenty years later people would be sifting through the intimate details she'd hidden in her journals. I wrote what I could remember as a list.

1. *Dating Emerick (very much in love)*

2. *Summer parties with her friends: Emerick, Margot (best friend?) Emma, Adam? Emerick's order or something about she was going to a meeting/ she thought all the others already went to these meetings.*

3. *She hoped to become close with Margot again.*

Caleb sat close and leaned over my shoulder while I wrote. He smelled fresh, like the outdoors. I noticed that his hand that rested on the table had dirty fingernails, like he'd been digging in the dirt.

When I finished writing, he leaned back, "Is that it?" he balked.

His tone irritated me. "Yes, that's it. I only had a chance to read a few pages."

He looked at what I'd written, "She was in love with Emerick Wriothesley?" he asked incredulous.

"Apparently."

He pointed to number two on my list. "This is interesting. Did she happen to give a name for the order, like Templar, or Mason? He paused. "Although, if she was invited to attend it couldn't have been those."

"Why?" Sophie and I both asked.

Caleb shrugged and raised his brows matter-of-factly. "They're fraternal. No girls allowed," he smirked.

"How would you know?" Sophie mocked.

"Because I *read*," he shot back. "And as it happens, I just read that today."

"That's weird," I said.

"Not really. I was looking up everything I could find on pentagrams and their use. Like the necklace in the puzzle box."

Like I would have forgotten. I suppressed the snide remark that flew to mind only because I wanted to hear him out. But I wouldn't be able to tolerate much more of his assumed intellectual superiority. I wished I'd never told him about cheating at West Christian. Susan had been right—a locker room stabbing would have garnered more respect.

"Yes?" I pressed.

"Well it's actually used by all sorts of organizations, governments, and religions."

"I thought pentagrams were supposed to be Satanic?" Sophie asked.

Caleb shrugged, "Apparently it matters which way the pentagram is pointing." He took the short pencil from my hand and flipped my piece of paper over. He drew two five pointed stars, one with one point straight up and another inverted star with the single point down and two points up. "This," he circled the first star. "Is the pentagram that is most commonly used and is supposedly *good*. It means all kinds of things—it's believed by some to have magic properties and, if you believe in that sort of thing, is used in magic by Wiccans and other pagan religions."

This was exactly what I didn't want to hear. "Aren't Wiccans like witches?"

"Honestly I didn't go down that trail. I mean, I think so—but that's just a guess."

"Yes Einstein," Sophie said. "Let's not muddy the waters."

He gave her a dirty look. "But it's also used in more mainstream religions," Caleb continued. "Christians have used the pentagram to represent the five wounds of Christ and Taoist use it to reflect the five elements. It's supposed to have some amazing mathematical properties. There was something about the Golden Ratio, which is some equation that is found over and over again throughout art and nature. But that was over my head. I'd need to spend more time on that one."

"So what's this?" I asked pointing to the second inverted star.

"That," he said raising his brows. "Is a sign for black magic or Satanic magic...depending on who you ask. In the right way up star, the top point represents the spiritual world presiding over the four elements, earth, fire, air, and water. This way, with the two points up, has something to do with the head of the goat of black magic?" Caleb started sketching inside the inverted pentagram, two horns in the top two points, two floppy goat ears in the side points, and a long goat beard extending down into the bottom point. When he finished the result looked more like a sad bunny.

Sophie started laughing. "That's supposed to be evil?"

"Well obviously not the way I've drawn it. It's just a rough idea."

I ignored their bickering. "But earlier you said something about five elements."

He nodded. "Taoism has the usual four, earth, fire, air, and water but also metal."

My head was swimming. I was trying to figure out how all of this was going to help me when Sophie suddenly asked.

"Wait a minute. You got all of this from the library...today?"

Caleb put the pencil down and seemed to be thinking about her question. "I didn't say that," he corrected. "I said I *read* it today. I never said where I got the information from."

"Mum is going to kill you if she finds out."

"Well she isn't going to find out," he said.

"Find out what?" I asked.

Sophie turned to me with her hands on her hips. "That he's been in your uncle private office using the computer. His *locked* private office."

"Wait. You guys don't have a computer?"

"We did." Caleb looked accusingly at Sophie who was now having her turn looking guilty.

"I got into a bit of trouble on my FaceSpace account," she

explained.

"A bit?"

"Okay! Massive. I got into a massive amount of trouble."

"How?" I dared to ask.

Sophie sighed. "It wasn't even my fault. I'm mean, as far as I knew the guy was fifteen."

"Only he was forty-five!" Caleb said exasperated.

"What?"

"How was I supposed to know?" she asked. "How am I supposed to know that some pervy lech is using his step-son's picture and trying to hook up with younger girls?"

"Oh my God Sophie!"

"I know. So horrible, right? When Mum found out she came absolutely unglued.'

"And unhooked everything," Caleb added.

"Everything!" Sophie emphasized. "We used to have a cell..."

"Not that I ever got to use it," Caleb interjected.

"Not that you ever had any cause to use it. You need to have someone to pick up the other end," she pointed out before continuing. "That was also when she went on the rampage through my closet that resulted in these." She pulled on her polo shirt and khaki capris.

I remembered her pop princess outfit at the airport and realized that her mother really had instituted a one-eighty for them. I couldn't help wondering what that would be like, someone hovering over your every move. Worrying, watching you like a hawk. Doing things that made you crazy but also for your own good. Dad loved me—but he could hardly negotiate his own life without Susan managing the professional and me taking charge of the day to day. The memory of my father stumbling into my discipline meeting still brought on a wave of embarrassment. In my world, I was definitely the one making the better choices.

I smiled sympathetically—Sophie would likely never understand just why I was actually envious of her. "So how do I get into his office?" I asked.

They both turned to me with shocked expressions and said, "You don't!"

"What? Why not? You did!"

"Yeah but only because mum was insanely busy getting everything together for your uncle's trip to Paris tonight."

"Sorry to say but your uncle is a complete nutter about anyone going into his office. He keeps it locked and mum only ever goes in there to empty his trash and dust. The only reason mum went in today was because he needed some book off his shelf and wanted it sent to the airport with his suitcase." Sophie explained.

"The only reason I managed to sneak in there was because mum didn't think to lock it back up right away."

"I wish I'd thought of that," Sophie mumbled.

"Why?" Caleb asked. "So you could email your lech?"

"Shut up!" Sophie yelled.

I took a deep breath and tried to think while they fought.

I took the piece of paper and pencil from Caleb. Under the two stars he had drawn, I drew one of my own. Mine also had five points, but instead of being constructed from five straight lines, it had five isosceles triangles and I wrote the corresponding color names, red, green, blue, yellow, and white in each triangle. In the center of the radiating triangles I drew a pentagon rotated so that it's five corners lined up with the midpoints of each triangle's base. "I need to figure out what this symbol means."

They both looked at the picture I had drawn.

"That's the tattoo Camilla showed me today—or what I can remember of it anyway. There were also some pictures in each triangle and in the center of the pentagon but I couldn't make those out."

"Cool tattoo," Sophie said.

"But what does it mean?" I asked. "She showed it to me like I would know, like it was some sort of secret code I would understand."

"There's a few books on symbols in the library. We could start there," Caleb said.

I nodded, hopeful that we would find something.

"There is Cyberzone," Sophie said. "But it costs money."

"What's Cyberzone?" I asked.

"An internet café in town," Caleb explained. "But you need an account or a credit card."

I actually smiled. Like most of the kids at West Christian I was well equipped in this area. It was just that instead of buying five hundred dollar purses, I generally used mine to buy groceries. "I have a credit card," I said sheepishly.

Sophie looked at me with pure envy. "Really? Charlotte you are like the luckiest girl in the world."

"Not really," I shook my head.

But I didn't want to wait. I had never in my life not been able to just look up anything I needed to know right away. *No Computer?* "It's ridiculous," I blurted. "Surely if I just call my uncle and ask him, he would let me use his computer."

Sophie shrugged. "You can try," she said looking skeptical.

"Where does your mom keep the keys?" I asked.

Sophie nodded towards a slim cabinet mounted on the wall in the pantry.

I got up and opened the cabinet door, hundreds of keys hung from perfectly spaced tiny hooks. Each one meticulously labeled with tiny white tags.

"Charlotte," Caleb said sounding worried. "You can't."

I scanned the tags until I found the one labeled *Office*. It slipped over the hook and into my pocket with hardly any effort at all, "Watch me."

My uncle's office was rich, highly polished wood and books. One entire wall was floor to ceiling bookshelves. The rest of the room was sparsely furnished with his desk anchoring the room and, in the corner, a single wingback chair coupled with a floor lamp for reading. It was a room designed to handle the presence of one person, he clearly did not entertain anyone other than himself in here.

His monitor sat on the desktop. I moved around the desk, grabbed the mouse and tried to shake and click the monitor to life. Nothing happened. I pressed the monitor power button and shook and clicked some more, still nothing.

Caleb came over and scanned the desk before he lifted up an unconnected cable like it was important evidence. "Mum must of sent his laptop with his other things. This is just a docking station."

I sighed and my shoulders slumped with defeat. "Well let's go then before we get caught and into trouble for nothing."

Sophie stood near the enormous picture windows that overlooked the grounds leading the woods. Something on the small table in front of her held her attention. "Come on Sophie, let's go."

"You need to see this," she said looking over her shoulder.

Caleb and I both walked over, it was a book, a scrapbook filled with newspaper clippings. Someone had pasted a recent article about the reinvestigation of my grandparents' murder. Sophie reached out and flipped back a page, I was stunned by recognition. I leaned over and flipped the next page, and the next. They were filled with articles about my mother's disappearance. There were newspapers from England and the States.

"Some of these are from tabloids," Caleb said incredulous, the glossy paper and sensational headlines giving them away. "Why would anyone want to save that trash?"

I turned more and more pages, the clippings growing increasingly yellow from age, to a time before my mother vanished. There were several clippings about a hospital fire, "Hundreds Killed in Fiery Inferno" and then the original stories that ran about my grandparents' murder. "Spencers Stabbed to Death while Sleeping." The beginning of the book held a collection of small articles, "Eaton Wins Match Against Revel" "Spencer Meets with Indian Ambassador" "Eaton Student, Young Hero" there was a picture of a very young uncle Nigel who had "rescued a toddler from a busy London street." A second picture showed the ecstatic mother kissing him on the cheek.

I grabbed the front of the book and closed it. "Come on," I warned. "We should go before your mother finds us."

That night, sinking deep into the folds of her childhood bed, I again dreamt of my mother. Only this time, she didn't deafly twirl farther and farther away from my pleas until I was left alone in the dark. This time, she lay right beside me. The other side of the bed felt heavy with her presence and her breath was deep and rhythmic while we slept. I heard her voice so close to my ear that her breath tickled the fine hairs on the side of my face. *Charlotte, I love you.* And the voice I hadn't heard in over four years reverberated through my mind like a gift. It was her exact pitch and cadence. *I love you so much.*

She was so close. I reached across the bed groping for her

arm or the spill of her hair on the pillow.

The bed felt cold.

I knew before I even opened my eyes it was only a dream. The side of my face and pillow were wet from my tears and my chest was so heavy I couldn't take a full breath. Rolling onto my back, the tears slid down the sides of my face and pooled in my ears. The pain was unbearable, as if someone had cut out my lungs and then commanded me to keep breathing without them. I was never going to get over her.

Never.

The light from the bedside lamp I had left on stretched far enough across the room for me to see the chaise lounge shoved into the corner of the bedroom bookcase. I crawled out from under the heavy covers and dragged the top duvet over to the lounge. I didn't want to go right back to sleep. I wanted to remember, for as long as I could, the clear sound of her voice in my ear, the feel of her safely asleep beside me— even if it wasn't real.

I wrapped the duvet around me and reached down the far side of the upholstered beast into the dark. Suppressing a shiver, I forced myself to not think about scary things like rabid rats or dead eyed zombies while I grabbed the stone box and pulled it into the light.

If I couldn't have her, then I would have her secrets.

CHAPTER ELEVEN

PROMISES

There was a sound, like a continuous low roar. *What was that?* When I opened my eyes it took my mind a moment to adjust to the still unfamiliar room. Right, Mom's old room, I thought. I propped myself up and turned towards the windows. I had left the curtains open but the morning light in the room seemed wrong. It was too dark.

The low roar was coming from the windows and a torrent of water was running down the glass like tiny rivers. I could barely see the driveway below through the rain smeared glass and the heavy showers outside blocked the view of anything beyond that.

The cold wood floor chilled my bare feet and sent a shiver running down my back. I grabbed my mother's borrowed cardigan from the chair I'd left it on last night and dug a pair of socks from my duffel bag before heading downstairs.

Caleb was in the kitchen making tea, picking up the electric kettle and pouring it into the floral pot.

"Morning," I said softly.

He startled and boiling water splashed all over. "Damn it!" he yelled violently shaking his burned hand.

"Oh!" I rushed in to inspect his hand. "God Caleb, I'm so sorry," I said grabbing his hand and trying to see how bad the burn was. "Here, quick." I pulled him to the sink and turned the cold water on.

I felt horrible.

"It's freezing," he complained trying to pull his hand free.

"It'll cool the burn," I insisted holding his hand under the water.

He stopping fighting me and stood still. I held him in place watching his whole hand turn red from the cold. When I pulled it from the water, the skin where he'd been burned was beginning to rise into a welt. "It might blister," I mumbled putting his hand back under the stream. Feeling awful I turned my head to apologize again.

Caleb was staring at my face. When my eyes met his he quickly looked away and stared at our hands in the water. "It's okay," he said softly. "It'll be fine."

We were so close, I suddenly realized his chest was pressed against my back, his face only inches from mine. If he wanted, he could easily reach his other hand around the front of my body, bend his mouth to my neck. My mind reeled from the feel of his body and the intensity of his green eyes.

"Well now," Sophie exclaimed entering the kitchen. "What

have we here? Have I missed something?"

I let go of his hand and stepped away while he shut off the water.

"A bit of *hello*," she teased sitting down at the table. "*Good morning* to ya."

Caleb handed me a tea towel hung under the sink and used a second to gently dry his hand. "Shut up Sophie."

"And so defensive," she grinned.

I couldn't look at him or her so I sat at the table next to Sophie and continued to dry my already dry hand.

While Caleb returned to the teapot and poured the rest of the water into the pot, Sophie crossed her arms on the table and rested her head, still smiling at her own wit.

It felt like a thunderstorm was wreaking havoc through my body and I realized I was a little more than embarrassed that Sophie had walked in on us. I was actually disappointed. What was wrong with me? Back home there had never been a single guy I had even the vaguest interest in—but here?

Hayden hardly counted, he was a pig dressed in wolf's clothing. *But you didn't exactly hate how it felt*, I chastised myself.

Caleb poured the milk and scooped the sugar and I listened to the light tinkling of the teaspoon stirring three china mugs. When he returned to the table he placed steaming cups in front of his sister and me before taking the chair across from us.

"Thank you," I whispered.

"Umm," Sophie acknowledged.

Caleb raised his cup to his mouth. *What if Sophie hadn't barged into the kitchen? What would his mouth feel like on my neck? On my lips? Would it take my breath away like Hayden had? Only better because it wasn't Hayden?*

The mug was hot against the palms of my hands but I welcomed the sensation, anything to get my mind off what I was thinking. I tried to concentrate on the milky tea swirling in my cup.

"Charlotte?" The teasing was gone from Sophie's voice. "You look all flushed."

Caleb's head shot up, the full force of his concern aimed at me was palpable.

I took a deep breath. "I'm fine. I'm just a bit hot." I explained shrugging off the cardigan.

"Are you kidding?" she asked. "It's freezing in here."

"I'm fine," I mumbled growing more and more embarrassed, my traitorous face was betraying the thoughts that were racing through my head.

They both continued to stare at me with worried looks,

"Fine, I swear. Maybe just some fresh air after breakfast."

"It's pissing with rain," Sophie said.

I had forgotten. "Right." I shook my head at my own stupidity.

"You could sit on the porch out back," Caleb offered. "It's covered."

"Yes," I nodded. The porch sounded perfect because my

body suddenly felt like it was on fire.

"I found one of the books on symbols this morning," he explained. "So you can go through it and see if there's anything like Camilla's tattoo. I'd rather wait on Cyberzone until the rain stops. My car's not that amazing in bad weather."

"Okay." I took a drink and was surprised by how much the hot liquid burned my throat. The mug didn't feel that hot in my hands.

When we'd finished our tea and I refused the toast Caleb made, "I'm just not feeling all that hungry." Sophie showed me the way to the back porch. On our way, we passed through the drawing room with a blue billiard table and then what I took to be a family room, complete with a large cabinet that I assumed enclosed a television. There were several family photos on the walls, end tables, and arranged across the mantle.

Walking past the overstuffed couch, my eyes fell onto a faded photo of a young girl, maybe twelve, making a strong-arm pose while leaping into a shimmering pool. I had to stop. Except for the blonde hair, she looked exactly like me.

Sophie came and looked over my shoulder. "That's the pool," she said.

"That's my mom."

Sophie looked closer. "Oh, she's your image. Except for the hair of course." Sophie stepped back and gave me a puzzled look.

"What?"

"Oh, nothing," she shrugged. "I was just thinking how

strange you should end up with jet black hair when your mother was so fair." She took the picture from my hands and replaced it on the end table. "Your dad's hair doesn't look that dark in his book jacket photos."

I followed her towards the door. "He's kind of light brown. Or was anyway...he's mostly gray now."

"Huh," she said sliding glass door open. "You've just ruined his author picture for me."

"That picture is ten years old."

"Yes, but *I* didn't need to know that. He looks so adventuresome in that photo. Like he's just come down from Everest to crack out another great read. Now I'll always imagine him craggy and gray."

I didn't bother to tell her that my dad was a far cry from Everest. He had always drank when he wrote but since my mother disappeared, he was practically flammable while writing.

"Genes are weird," Sophie said. "All that recessive and dominant business."

I stepped into the cool, wet day. The sound of the heavy rain hitting the flagstone reminded me of a waterfall.

"Here," Sophie offered me one of the cushioned patio chairs.

Sitting down, I could just see beyond the sheet of rain cascading over the roof we were under. There, just like I'd seen in the photo in the family room was the pool. Its surface jumping and splattering from the multitude of falling drops.

I heard the sliding glass door open behind us and I turned to see Caleb, holding a small book, stepping out onto the patio.

"Here," he said handing me the slim volume.

I took the book from him and read the title. *The Ultimate Guide to Symbols Across Time.*

"It seems kind of small."

Caleb smiled. "I figured it would be a good place to start."

"I'm going to head in," Sophie said slipping through the door. "You guys don't need me *hanging* around, being the *third wheel.*" She raised her eyebrows in case we could have possibly missed her meaning.

"Shut up," Caleb snapped.

"See you," I said ignoring her innuendo.

I narrowed my eyes at the simple text. It felt like an insult. I imaged Caleb sorting through the library's collection, trying to find the most easily digestible book on symbols. Opening the book, I saw the glossy pages with brightly colored photographs and simple descriptions for each symbol.

"I've read *Richard II* at least four times," I blurted.

Caleb was pulling a chair next to mine. "Wow," he said giving me a confused look. "You must really like that play." He sat down in his chair and took the *Ultimate Guide* from me.

"It's about the duality of a king," I continued staring out into the rain. "His mortal body and his spiritual or kingly body." I looked at Caleb who was staring down at the small book in his hands. "Throughout the play, Richard's two bodies are separating. He is losing his kingship and becoming more and more mortal."

"It sounds interesting."

"That paper I turned in…it didn't have any of that in it. It was basically a simple plot synopsis."

"Are you mad about something?" he asked.

"I'm not stupid, Caleb."

He looked stunned and shook his head.

"I don't know why I cheated, but it's not because I didn't know what *Richard II* was about."

"I…I don't think…"

"Well I do think! That's the point!" I wasn't hot anymore—I was freezing. My head was swimming and my back and arms were starting to ache from shivering.

Caleb looked confused. He sat staring quietly while I yelled.

"I don't need you to over simplify…" My stomach churned and my mouth watered—I was going to be sick. I rushed out of my chair to the edge of the patio and threw up the two cups of tea I'd had this morning into a beautiful planter of begonias.

"Charlotte?" Caleb was behind me in an instant his hand on my back, I could see his face hovering in my peripheral.

The ice-cold rain was pelting my head and back soaking my hair and shirt. I tried to shove him away as best I could but he barely budged.

He moved his hand to my forehead then down the sides

of my face.

"Stop," I pleaded trying to turn away. I turned my face up into the rain hoping to wash away any vomit that might be there. The smell from the planter was unbearable.

"You're burning up," he said exasperated. "Let me help you."

"No! I'll do it myself." I turned to head inside but in my rush to get away, I missed the step up onto the patio and fell sprawling across the flagstones. I sat up and pulled my stinging knees to my chest. They were both grazed and bloodied. Caleb knelt beside me and pulled a handkerchief from his pocket.

"Your chin," he said holding the linen to my face.

I felt terrible and my body was practically vibrating with chills. I took the handkerchief from him and groaned when I saw that my blood had stained the white cloth. *Wonderful, now I'll have a facial scar.*

There was no point trying to hide my shame now—I was a mess. This time, when Caleb offered me his hand I took it. "Let's get you inside and I'll call mum."

Once in the house, he deposited me onto the plush couch in the family room. My teeth chattered and my wet t-shirt was not helping with the violent chills racking my entire body. Caleb grabbed one of the afghans off the arm of the couch and carefully pulled it over me up to my chin.

"I'll be right back," he promised and left to get Ms. Steward.

I clutched the afghan to my chest and tried to control my shaking. Rolling onto my side, I made a conscious effort to relax the muscles in my back and stomach but it didn't help, my body felt like it was seizing up. I closed my eyes and waited for Ms. Steward.

When she finally burst through the family room door a few minutes latter, she was equipped with an arsenal of home medical supplies and Caleb trailing behind her.

"Look at you," she exclaimed. "I let you out of my sight for a minute and look at you." Ms. Steward propped a pillow behind my neck and stuck a quick-read thermometer in my mouth. After a few seconds the device in my mouth beeped and she slipped it from between my clenched lips.

"Oh my! Is that right?"

Before I knew it she was putting the thermometer back in my mouth to double check the first reading. When it beeped she pulled it out.

"Thirty-nine degrees! Caleb," she commanded. "Get a glass of water quick."

I watched as she rummaged through her kit of band-aids, cough syrup, ointments, and God knew what else until she found a bottle of pills, alcohol swabs, and a handful of band-aids. She popped the cap and shook out two ibuprofen. She started to hand them to me but then snatched them back.

"Are you allergic?" she quickly verified.

"No," I croaked.

This seemed to relieve her and she gave them to me. When

Caleb arrived with the water I swallowed the pills while Ms. Steward swiped both my knees and my chin with the astringent wipes. In a few swift movements, she pulled apart the band-aids and covered my grazes. The one on my chin didn't quite lay right and I was sure made me look like a complete idiot. I felt like I was seven.

"It'll take a few minutes. We should get you up to bed."

"Is it okay," I asked in a whisper. "if I just stay here?"

Ms. Steward looked as if she were weighing the pros and cons of my dying on the couch as opposed to the bed upstairs. "It would be easier," she finally said. "Do you want me to stay with you love?"

I only shook my head.

"All right then. We'll need to get you a dry shirt—Caleb!" she ordered.

"I'll get one from your bag," he said and got up to leave.

"And after that," Ms. Steward added. "Stay with her and come and get me if she gets any worse."

I couldn't possibly imagine feeling any worse. Certainly I looked terrible, I only hoped that there wasn't any lingering traces of sick glomming in my hair.

"I'll be back in twenty minutes to check your temp again," Ms. Steward explained while she heaved herself up from the edge of the couch. "If you need anything, send Caleb to come fetch me."

She continued to stare at me until I nodded indicating that I understood her instructions. When she left, I let my head drop back against the rolled arm of the couch and closed my eyes. Shivers continued to seize my body despite the thick wool of the afghan. I almost never got sick. The last time I could remember was when I was thirteen and my father had brought me regular intervals of cinnamon apple cider and read to me until I fell asleep. Another violent shiver ran through me and made the muscles in my back hurt. I rolled onto my side and pulled my knees to my chest. I wished I could go home, I wished for my own bed and my father's familiar hand on my face.

I missed him. He was probably miserable too. Sleeping on a single bed in a shared room with some other addict. The situation was so horrible I couldn't help the tears that filled my eyes and eventually dropped onto the couch pillow under my head. He must feel so lonely right now.

"Charlotte?" Caleb whispered.

I sat up the best I could and wiped my face. "Yes."

"Oh, sorry. I wasn't sure if you'd fallen asleep."

I shook my head and he handed me one of my clean T-shirts. "Is this one okay?"

"Yes, thanks," I said taking the shirt and looking for somewhere to change.

Caleb turned his back, "No, don't get up." He walked to the other side of the room and occupied himself with the TV cabinet. "I got a movie from the library."

While he put a disc into the DVD player I pulled my wet shirt over my head and put on the dry one. It was somewhat comforting to have the wet fabric off my skin. "Okay," I said so he knew he could turn back around. When he came back, I noticed the sweater he held in his hand.

"I didn't see anything with long sleeves in your bag," he said bringing me the large blue sweater. "I thought you might want this." He held it out and I took it, slipping the soft cable knit over my head. It was huge and I felt like I could probably camp inside the tent it created around my body. But it felt good.

"Thanks. Is it yours?"

"Yes," he said looking embarrassed before he sat on the couch next to me and pointed several different remotes at the TV to start the movie he'd brought. "My mother made it," he shrugged.

I pulled the end of the sleeves up past my hands and snuggled back into the downy cushions behind us. It felt like the ibuprofen was starting to help, my shivers were becoming less and less intense.

When we had come inside, Caleb had tossed *The Ultimate Guide to Symbols Across Time* onto the coffee table. While he was starting the movie, I leaned forward and grabbed it from the table. I felt more than a little stupid for getting so angry. Caleb was only trying to help. It wasn't exactly his fault that I continually gave the impression of being incapable. It was my problem with school and why I was always on the brink of failure. Knowing information was never enough. You had to be able to show you knew it. And I hadn't felt like I could do anything since I was twelve. I tucked the slim volume under the pillow—I would read the whole thing after the movie.

The storm must have been getting worse because the gray light coming from the windows seemed to become even less. Caleb had finally pointed and pressed enough buttons at the TV because a soft blue screen suddenly appeared and added a dim glow to the ever darkening room.

"What are we watching," my voice failed and came out a hoarse croak.

Caleb gave me a worried sideways look. "You sound terrible, maybe you shouldn't try to speak." He turned his attention back to the TV and pressed one final button before sitting back against the couch. I could see his face clearly enough and the sly smile that played on his lips. "I grabbed this from the library when I went to get your shirt."

I watched the screen waiting for some hint of what we may be watching. I could only hope it wasn't something loud and fast like Hayden had chosen. I doubted I could handle screeching tires and rapid scene shifts right now.

Caleb shifted his weight next to me and got comfortable. He wasn't exactly sitting on the opposite side of the couch but I still had enough room to lie on my side with my legs curled up. It seemed like if I moved my leg even an inch, my foot would touch his leg.

The colors on the TV changed and the DVD's opening menu surprised me. I pushed myself up off the cushion and looked at Caleb. "*Richard II*?" my voice was barely audible now.

He was trying to look casual but it was obvious that he was pleased with my reaction. "You said you liked it," he shrugged.

I nodded and laid back down while Caleb pushed play.

I had never seen *Richard II* performed, which seemed strange given how many times I'd read it. *Richard II* wasn't exactly the first Shakespeare play English Lit teachers thought to show high school kids. *Romeo and Juliet* was the standard, and that play I had seen in both my freshman and sophomore lit classes.

But I had never seen my mother read *Romeo and Juliet*. Not even once. And so it held little interest for me.

Richard II she had read again and again and so, so did I. The characters were so clearly defined in my head, I wondered if the actors would live up to the images I had created. Movies based on books were almost never as good. Books had more time than a movie, more layers. Movies were like the backbone of a book, the single most obvious structural story. They ended up feeling like a naked skeleton in comparison.

But Shakespeare plays were meant to be seen, and you always got the whole story. You don't pare down Shakespeare; word for word would be exactly as I had read.

We watched Richard's slow decay. The plots, intrigue, and eventual end of Richard's reign until he is finally transformed from the regal God-like king, to a fragile and broken man, assassinated on orders from the new king.

When the movie ended, I realized the bottom of my foot

was pressed against Caleb's thigh. He reached awkwardly for the remote on the coffee table without altering the placement of his leg making me suddenly self-conscious. He knew we were touching but didn't make any movements that would cause his leg to move.

The memory of how close we had been to each other at the sink, the press of his chest against my back made another shiver run down my spine.

"You're cold," Caleb worried. He moved his hand and I could feel its warmth and weight through the afghan, resting on my calf.

"No, I'm fine." My voice was still weak and not at all reassuring. His hand was distracting me. "I think the ibuprofen did the trick."

He got up and moved closer, sitting where my body curved away from the edge of the couch. He looked doubtful. His hand reached and felt my forehead and then the side of my face. It should have only taken a second, maybe two, to determine that I was telling the truth. My fever was being held back by the medicine. But Caleb kept his hand on the side of my face.

"Well," I whispered.

"You don't feel feverish," he looked right at me and I was again amazed at how green his eyes were, even in the dull gray light that was barely creeping in the windows.

"You see." My gazed shifted away. "I said I was fine," I attempted lightly but my heart was picking up the pace in my chest. He was so close, I worried he would hear it.

He could sense my apprehension and sat back. His hand slid from my face but I was surprised when, instead of retreating altogether, he rested it casually on my arm. As if this were the sort of intimacy we had had our whole lives. I was torn between the comfort of his physical closeness and the anxiety of what it meant.

"So why exactly do you like that play so much?" he asked airily, as if this closeness between us was nothing.

I took a breath and tried to collect my thoughts around something other than the feel of each and every one of his fingers against my forearm. "It was my mother's favorite," I croaked.

He frowned, "I shouldn't be asking you questions. I forgot about your voice."

"It's okay," I whispered.

His gaze shifted away and he seemed to be thinking about something. "Do you remember much about when you visited before?"

"When I was six?"

"Yes," he said still not looking at my face.

"Sort of," my memory of our time here was sporadic bursts. Bright spotlights on specific events, but there was no general stream of connection between them. For all I knew we could have been here for five days or five weeks. "I was pretty little."

Caleb sat quietly. He had more to say but was working up to it. He took a deep breath. "Do you remember me at all?"

I felt his hand on my arm tighten ever so slightly. I did remember Caleb, but how could I tell him that what I most remembered was sneaking behind the drapes and kissing him. "Yes," I offered hoping that would be enough of an answer.

His thumb absently brushed the inside of my elbow making me shiver again and get goose bumps all along both my arms.

"What? What do you remember about me? About us?"

Us? I sighed not wanting to say it out loud but feeling more and more like I would just have to blurt it out. We were only little. It's not like laughing about it now would be any big deal. I hesitated a moment longer before deciding that it would have to be handled like leaping into a cold ocean. Just do it. "We kissed," I said casually. "Behind the curtains in the dining room."

He looked directly at me. "Our honeymoon," he said.

I couldn't hide my shock. "What?"

"That was our honeymoon," he repeated as if hearing it a second time could possibly make it any more sensible.

I smiled, certain he was joking with me. "Our honeymoon?" my tone was incredulous, waiting for the punch line.

Only Caleb wasn't smiling. "We were inseparable...I had already had the chicken pox," he explained. "We married each other in the garden," he added quietly, like he was unsure he should.

I opened my mouth to both laugh and object but then snapped it shut. *And I promise to love you forever and ever and ever and be your wife forever and ever until I die Amen.* I had on my purple bathing suit with the orange tulip embroidered on the front. A wreath of yellow roses Caleb had helped me string together was in my hair. I looked at him now. The vividness of the memory left me feeling dumbfounded. "We ate dirt."

He smiled at me. "That was our wedding cake."

"And then we went on our honeymoon."

Caleb nodded. "In the dining room."

"And we said that we would wait..." but this memory was too embarrassing to repeat out loud. We would wait to have our baby until he was old enough to get a job. I could tell from his expression that he knew what I didn't want to say. "Oh my God! I completely forgot," my voice was really raspy now.

Caleb couldn't hide the disappointment that flashed across his face. He smiled quickly and shook his head. "Kids. I *was* older. It makes sense that I would remember."

"Yes," I agreed still astounded.

He squeezed my arm lightly and then stood up. "Hey," he said brightly. "Where's that book, we should get cracking on that. If you're up to it."

The abrupt change in subject caught me off guard and it took me a minute to remember I'd put the book under my pillow. I reached under and pulled out the book. "Um, here it is."

Caleb nodded. "Good. That's good." He looked from me to the book and back again like he didn't know quite what to do next. "No, we can't both read it," he said seemingly to himself. "You start that, I'll go grab a couple more." He left in a hurry without another word.

"Okay?" I whispered to the room. The memory of that day in the garden still running through my head.

Forever and ever until I die Amen.

CHAPTER TWELVE

SYMBOLS

There wasn't anything in the small brightly illustrated volume that looked like the tattoo I'd seen on Camilla. But still, I found myself studying the other symbols and getting caught up in learning about what each of them meant. It was fascinating. My fever was held off by the pills, but I still didn't feel like I could have focused on any of the three, academic type books Caleb had found in the library. I was secretly glad to have ended up with the small volume—it was basically a beginner's crash course in symbols.

At the other end of the couch, Caleb flipped through a larger leather bound volume with dense text and small, hand drawn illustrations. It was an older publication and the explanations for each symbol went deep into origins, variations, uses, and cultural significance. Caleb was basically flipping past everything and only looking for a replica of the drawing I'd made in the kitchen.

I kept pointing out interesting ones I came across in my volume and reading their descriptions out loud. "Here is the ouroboros!" I croaked with as much excitement as I could. "The Ouroboros often represents self-reflexivity," I whispered aloud the text below the photo. "Or cyclicality, especially in the sense of something constantly re-creating itself, the eternal return, and other things perceived as cycles that begin anew as soon as they end, compare with phoenix."

Caleb got up from his spot on the couch and moved closer.

"It can also represent the idea of primordial unity," I continued. "Related to something existing in or persisting from the beginning with such force or qualities it cannot be extinguished."

"That's what I told you!" he interrupted.

I looked up from my reading. "What? You didn't tell me this."

"I certainly did! The very first day you arrived and you asked me about the ouroboros chiseled over the manor's entrance."

I thought of the hand puppet show he had performed and his wild pin wheeling arms. "You never told me *this*."

"Well...maybe not word for word...exactly the same. But what I said was basically this," he pointed to the book.

"Okay." I rolled my eyes at him and kept reading. "The ouroboros has been important in religious and mythological symbolism. It is frequently used in alchemical illustrations and symbolizes the circular nature of the alchemist's opus. It is also often associated with Gnosticism, and Hermeticism."

"That is pretty much what I told you," Caleb claimed.

I ignored him. One word in the last passage distracted me. "Alchemical." I looked up at him. "We've read something recently about this."

Caleb nodded. "The Alchemical Writings of Sir Isaac Newton. The book from the library with the 'above and below' message."

It felt like a click in my head. There was some connection. Something about this symbol, the ouroboros, the note in my mother's puzzle box, and alchemy. But I didn't understand what the connection meant. "What is alchemy?" I whispered more to myself than to Caleb.

Caleb shrugged and returned to his side and his book. "We could look it up," he said flopping onto the cushion.

"Yes, we should do that," I said absently. But I couldn't help feeling like every time I went looking for one answer, I only ended up with many more questions.

I dog-eared the page with the ouroboros so I would remember to do some more digging later and continued my slow browse though the symbol book. Every so often Caleb looked over jealously from behind his dense academic book that he was only scanning. After awhile he put his down and said something.

I nodded absently but didn't look up from my reading.

"Charlotte!"

"Huh? What's wrong?"

"I said it's not in here."

"Oh...okay."

"I thought we were looking for a five pointed star like Camilla's tattoo."

"I am. But there are some really neat ones in here." I scanned the next few pages. I was amazed by what I saw and read not because the symbols listed were things I had never seen before, but because they were shapes and signs that I saw almost everyday. It never occurred to me that a picture of a tree would have a deeper meaning beyond just being a tree. That colors actually elicited emotions. Or even simple geometric shapes like a circle or a square were anything but preschool curriculum.

"Did you know that shapes can actually make you feel a certain way?"

"No," Caleb said flatly picking up the next heavy text on symbols. He was obviously still annoyed that my little book was so interesting.

"Symbols with a circular shape represent wholeness, or something that is complete. Triangles are power or strength and squares give you the feeling of order or organization." I looked up from my book, "There's all kinds of cool stuff in here."

"Great! You slog through this and I'll read that one."

I held my copy to my chest, "No way. Besides, you're the one who doled out the reading assignments."

I turned the page and stopped abruptly. The photo looked

almost like the cross you'd find in any Christian church. This one was gold, heavily jeweled in what looked like rubies and sapphires, but the top of the cross was different. Instead of being shaped like a T, this one had a loop at the top.

"I've seen this," I turned the book around and pointed to the picture.

Caleb's eyes lit up. "The ankh." His eyes met mine. "That's the cross of the Egyptians."

I read the description out loud while Caleb tossed his book on the couch and came over to sit next to me. "Ancient Egyptian ankh, Also known as the Egyptian Cross, the Key of the Nile, the Looped Tau Cross, and the Ansate Cross. It was an Ancient Egyptian symbol of life and fertility, predating the modern cross. Sometimes given a Latin name if it appears in specifically Christian contexts, such as the crux ansata, or the handled cross."

"I've read about that before."

"This is carved into the stone box upstairs."

"Yeah, I remember. It was one of the symbols I recognized as Egyptian."

I needed to think. What was the connection? Being sick was making my brain feel clouded and I couldn't focus. It was frustrating, staring at a puzzle and trying to solve it but too many pieces were missing.

Or stolen.

I looked up suddenly. Caleb was sitting very close and staring at me again. When he realized I'd caught him, he cleared his throat and glanced away.

Forever and ever I thought. It was confusing, wanting to pull someone closer and at the same time shove them away. The only thing I could do was just pretend there was nothing between us.

"I need to find my mother's diaries," I said.

"How? I mean, we don't have any idea who could have taken them."

I bit my lip and played with a thought. I did have some idea. "The one in my bag was obviously taken at the Wriothesley's estate. And, Emerick Wriothesley had a relationship with my mother, it was in her diary and he said at much himself."

"You can't very well just march up to their front gate and accuse Emerick Wriothesley of being a thief!"

I gave him a dirty look, "You really do think I'm stupid, don't you."

Caleb flinched but regrouped quickly. "I don't think you're stupid but I think messing around with the Wriothesley family is incredible dense. Charlotte, you don't have any idea who those people are, what their capable of. Emerick Wriothesley may seem like just a smooth, charming business man...but I've heard stories about things he's done to people who've crossed him...his own family Charlotte."

I remembered what Hayden said about his father and how he handled anyone who had had anything to do with his mother being committed. "Hayden told me," I said absently.

Caleb stiffened and sat back. I hadn't considered how this

simple statement would affect him.

"He's no better," he said icily. "Your friend, Hayden," Caleb said, his voice was full of hatred. "He's dangerous Charlotte. He uses people like their disposable. And girls..." he trailed off looking pointedly at me. Implying that I was nothing more than a piece of tissue in Hayden's eyes.

I knew this from experience. Hayden had a toxic combination of stunning good looks and a rampant sense of entitlement that made him bold beyond belief. It wasn't hard to imagine his history with girls. But Caleb's possessive, superior tone irritated me.

"Thanks for the warning," I said coolly. "I'll keep that in mind when I'm with him."

Caleb looked like I'd slapped him. When he didn't offer a sharp reply I realized I'd wounded him more than I'd intended. Obviously he thought I meant *with* Hayden.

I sighed. "I will need him to get back onto their estate," I explained. "The diaries are there...somewhere. I need to find them." I knew that everything I needed to know about her and her past was contained in those books. All this other stuff, the symbols, the messages, and the puzzle box would make sense if only I could get her words back. Her memories—her life.

If only I could get her back.

What if I could find a clue, an answer? I realized that the secret I was keeping from myself was this growing hope that in her words, I would find a trail to her.

This thought, this glimmer of hope settled in my stomach

right next to a small stone of dread. Hope like this, hope for a far-fetched possibility—it could crush me.

"How?" he asked, his worry still making him angry. "You plan on ransacking the whole place? It's enormous!"

"I don't care," I whispered. Without thinking, I reached across the sofa and took Caleb's hand. It was warm and his long fingers curled automatically around my pale hand. I looked into his eyes, he couldn't possibly understand how important this was to me. "I have to Caleb." I bit my lip and paused, reluctant to say my secret wish out loud. Saying it might make it ridiculous, or worse—impossible. I squeezed his hand slightly and watched him take a deep breath. "I need to try...try and find her."

The anger had left his face but not the worry. I waited for him to say it. He would say it with kindness, the concern still all over his face. But he would say it nevertheless. *I'm sorry Charlotte...but your mother is gone. There is no getting her back.*

Caleb reached out, his fingers cupped my face while his thumb gently brushed my cheek. I didn't stop him and I felt the smear of wetness across my face, I hadn't realized I was crying. I waited for his words, the clear explanation about why what I wanted was not going to happen, why it was not reasonable.

But he was silent, hesitating, he didn't *want* to hurt me. His other hand still held mine and I felt his thumb brush the inside of my palm and then let go.

I dared to look up and meet his eyes, questioning.

169

Without warning he moved closer and I felt my body being folded into his arms. I didn't resist, I rode the pull into him, into whatever this moment was starting. Pressed to his chest, I wrapped my arms around him, felt the heat of his back through his shirt with the palms of my hands.

What was I doing? I didn't know, I didn't care. Right now felt right, it felt good to be held—protected. Maybe it was the fever, or being so far from everything I knew, but I was tired of feeling so alone.

Caleb wanted me. It was in his every glance, his every gesture.

Was it wrong? It felt good to be wanted like this. To be so close. But...

"I don't want to hurt you," I whispered.

"Why would you?" I could hear the disbelief behind his words. They were too light, too trusting.

"I don't know."

"This is right Charlotte." He moved and lifted my legs up and across his lap so he cradled me.

"What's right?"

"Us, you and me, this moment." I felt his hand trail down my arm. When it reached my hand, he laced his fingers with mine. "I've thought of this...so much."

"Us." I whispered the word against his shirt. The word both comforted and terrified me. The sweet relief of another person, their touch, their love. My finger traced the buttonhole near his neck. The possibility of losing it all. I lifted my head and ran my finger across his chin, up his cheek, over his lips that parted slightly from my touch.

I felt him tremble.

Don't hurt him Charlotte.

My lips brushed his jaw line and gently kissed the corner of his mouth. My hand pressed his cheek and guided his face to mine.

He kissed me. Gently, carefully.

"I'm sick," I whispered.

"I don't care," he mouthed against my lips. He kissed me harder, our lips parted and I felt the soft swell of his tongue with mine. Electric currents ran down my spine and left my limbs feeling heavy and numb with shock. I reached my hands up and buried my fingers in his thick hair. If only I could get lost in him.

He pulled away and his hand held my face while he kissed my cheeks, my nose, each of my eyes. "Charlotte," he murmured.

"Yes," I tried to catch his mouth again but he only brushed my lips with his.

He sighed and shut his eyes. "I love you, Charlotte." He opened his eyes and looked straight into mine, there was no questioning that he meant it. "I have loved you since I was seven," he smiled. "There has never been anyone...anyone but you."

I didn't know what to say. There were a hundred reasons why this couldn't be true, *you didn't even know me, it was only how you imagined me that you loved, it doesn't count when you get married at seven*—does it? But I didn't say any of this.

I kissed him again and then let the side of my face rest against his chest, the sound of his heart thundered next to my ear. I didn't know what we had done, what *I* had done. It felt like a promise—a promise to be his.

I could only hope there was something of me left to give.

His lips pressed the top of my head and I could feel his warm breath next to my scalp as he spoke into my hair. "I promise you," his arms tightened around me, "We will find her Charlotte." He turned and rested his cheek against my hair. "We'll find her and I'll help you."

I didn't pull away—I didn't want to.

CHAPTER THIRTEEN

FEVER

My fever lasted for days. Ms. Steward routinely dosed me with ibuprofen to keep my temperature down and the aches and shaking from infiltrating my body but she staunchly refused to let me leave Gaersum Aern.

"You can roam as far as the gardens, some fresh air would do you good. But there is no going anywhere else. You hear me?"

"Yes ma'am."

She gave me a discerning look, making sure I understood her instructions completely. "All right then," she gave me a thick hug. "You'll be well before you know it. I'll not have that Richards woman barking that I didn't mind you when you were ill."

Ms. Steward released me and waddled off down the hall towards the kitchen. I sighed, it was nice having a mother fretting over me, but being penned up was preventing me from getting the information I needed.

I needed to get back to the Wriothesley estate and start searching for the diaries. I knew Emerick had them. Hayden had called the house four times asking to come and pick me up. Each time I'd spoken to him explaining that I was still quarantined, Caleb had hovered, listening to my side of the conversation. While I spoke, Caleb paced and fidgeted with the delicate figurines in the morning room. When Hayden would insist that he come and get me, Caleb's face crumpled in anger. He slammed one of the figurines down so hard I worried the legs had shattered.

The last time Hayden called and I managed to put him off again, Caleb rushed to my side as soon as the phone was on the cradle.

"Who does that guy think he is?" he asked nearly hysterical.

I reached out and touched his face trying to reassure him. "He thinks he's *Hayden Wriothesley*. That's the problem." Caleb had become increasing agitated with Hayden's every call. I started to worry about how he was going to react when Hayden actually showed up at the door to pick me up.

"Come on," I said taking his hand and pulling him towards the French doors. "Let's get back to the library."

When our arms had stretched as far as they could between us, he didn't budge. He pulled back on me until I spiraled into his arms. "Don't," he pleaded.

"Don't what?" I asked as he held me to his chest. But I already knew what he was going to ask.

He looked into my eyes, "Don't go over there Charlotte. Please, I'm begging you. It's not safe."

I tried to kiss him, but he pulled his mouth away. "No, I need you to promise me."

I hesitated, biting both my lips and avoiding his gaze. "I can't. I know the diaries are there."

"We'll think of another way."

"What? Break in? You know there isn't any other way."

He let go of me and ran both his hands through his hair in frustration. "This is killing me. That guy's a viper."

"I will be careful. I swear. Besides, I'm not going anywhere until your mother gives me the all clear anyway."

He looked at me hopefully. "Maybe you won't get better," he tried a halfhearted smile but it quickly faded.

I hit him playfully, trying to get him to stop worrying about Hayden Wriothesley. "Yes, wouldn't that be wonderful. Maybe I have the plague."

"Or tuberculosis."

"Consumption," I volleyed.

"Wrong century," he corrected.

I rolled my eyes, relived that he wasn't obsessing any-more—at least not out loud. "Come on," I said pulling him out the door. "We'd better get back to Sophie or she's going to accuse us of sneaking off and leaving her with all the work." Since she'd realized that Caleb and I were not *just friends*, her teasing had been relentless.

We strode through the library doors holding hands, Sophie was at the far end hunched over one of the worktables. As we moved closer to her, I waited for her to notice us and braced myself for one of her embarrassing taunts.

But she didn't look up. "Hey guys," she called still intently studying whatever was in front of her.

"What have you got?" Caleb asked letting go of my hand and moving next to his sister for a better look.

Sophie stood up and looked at me. "It's the Spencer family tree."

"Really?" I asked and walked around to Sophie's other side so I could see too.

"Yes."

"I've never seen this," Caleb protested. "Where was it?"

"Hidden." Sophie pointed to a shelf across from us. "Behind those books."

It was the shelf with all the Shakespeare, the shelf next to my mother's chair.

"Hidden?" Caleb asked. "What do you mean, hidden?"

"The shelf behind those books is hollow. This was rolled up inside."

Caleb went to the shelf to inspect it for himself. Sophie had removed many of the books and a small door to the secret compartment stood open. Caleb moved the door back and forth as if he were testing it. "How on earth did you discover it?"

"I didn't. When I came in all those books were all over the

floor." She pointed to the pile of rare editions flung onto the floor.

I could see from where I stood that some of the pages were bent, the bindings cracked back too far like broken wings. I was about to rescue them from the floor when an entry on the Spencer tree caught my attention.

"I thought the two of you had done it and discovered the compartment," Sophie continued.

I stared at the paper in front of me.

"I didn't have anything to do with *this*," Caleb exclaimed looking at the broken books. "Oh my God," he said picking up one of the books like it was a wounded bird. Three of the pages hung limply away from the rest, ripped nearly all the way out.

The last entries on the Spencer tree, someone had altered it. There was my mother, Elizabeth Spencer next to my uncle, Nigel Spencer. There was the line connecting my mother to my father and then my name below theirs, Charlotte Stevens.

But someone had blackened out my father's name and birth.

"Well I knew Mum would have a fit if she saw them all over the floor," Sophie continued while she helped Caleb pick up the rest of the books. "I was putting them back when I saw the door in the shelf, it was only cracked open, but when I pulled it I could see that there was a whole compartment behind the shelves. The Spencer tree was rolled up and all the way at the back."

I touched the black ink that blotted out Simon Stevens. Why would someone do such a thing? Seeing his name erased in such a violent way made my chest feel heavy. My father was all I had left in the world. The black ink made me feel alone.

I knew he was suffering right now. Guilt for our current situation swept over me. He wouldn't be stuck in some treatment facility if it wasn't for me and my stupidity. I felt alone and I had Caleb and Sophie, how must he be feeling. I imagined his body racked in agony, suffering while his body tried to get used to functioning without the alcohol he craved. The alcohol that helped him forget.

"I need to call my father," I said. Suddenly, I wanted nothing more than to hear his voice.

Caleb and Sophie were placing the last few damaged books back onto the shelf. Caleb gave me a puzzled look while he worried over the state of one of the smaller books. "Okay," he said not understanding why I would make such a request when clearly the most pressing concern was the books and figuring out who had done this.

"Yeah, I thought that was strange too," Sophie said to me.

"What's strange?" Caleb asked.

"Someone crossed out her dad's name on the family tree."

Caleb put the book down and focused his attention on me. "What?"

"Yes, but that's not all," Sophie added. "Did you notice some of the dates? They can't be right."

I hadn't noticed anything except the growing dread that

had been growing in my stomach. All that black ink blotting my father out, it was like looking at a curse.

Caleb stood next to me looking over my shoulder. I scanned the rest of the document with him.

"There," he said pointing to Charles Spencer. "According to this he lived to be one hundred and eight!"

I saw the date under Amanda Ryan and did the math in my head. "One hundred and five," I said pointing her out.

"Lots of people live to be that old," Sophie said.

"Not in sixteen ninety-three," Caleb said.

"Yeah but look at this one," she said coming around to where we stood staring. "According to this," Sophie pointed to a name near the top of the page. "he lived to be one hundred and eighty-seven."

"That's one hundred and eighty-*nine*," Caleb corrected.

Sophie gave him a sour look. "Okay, one hundred and eighty-*nine*! Like it matters!"

"It does matter. You should pay more attention..."

I ignored them. Reading the name over the astonishing dates I realized I had seen it before.

"I've seen this," I whispered but they didn't hear me over their bickering. "In the hallway," I said louder so they would stop fighting over math. "Leading into Emerick's office from his sitting room. This name was engraved into one of the small brass plaques beneath an oil portrait."

Caleb read the name, "Francis Bacon?"

"Yes," I nodded.

179

I had seen this name before.

"Well, according to this he's your great, great, great, great something," Sophie said.

"And there was something engraved about shaking a sphere. But it was weird because the way it was written made me think about Shakespeare. When I asked Emerick about it he just gave me this really blank look and some non-answer."

"It's obviously a mistake," Caleb said running his hand over the date span. "But it seems weird that no one would have caught it and corrected it."

"Yes, but how long's it been stuffed back in that hole? It hasn't exactly been on display for lots of people to notice." Sophie asked.

"But it has been updated, at least since Charlotte."

I looked back to the blackened smudge that was my father's name. They both seemed to be forgetting something. "Who's doing this?" I reminded them. "*Someone* has been coming into the house."

Sophie and Caleb looked to me and then back to the shelf behind my mother's chair. As if some clue would jump out at us.

Someone had thrown those books all over the floor and vandalized the Spencer tree, and someone had taken all my mother's diaries.

"Should we call the police?" Sophie asked.

I nodded absently. "But tell them what?" I asked. "That someone broke in and threw some books on the ground?

Blacked out a name on the family tree?"

"Your mother's diaries were stolen," Sophie pointed out.

"They won't even come out here for that," Caleb said. "There is no sign of a break in. All they will do is make a report over the phone."

"We should tell your mother," I said. "She should know that someone has been getting in."

"She's in town grocery shopping," Sophie said.

"As soon as she gets back," I said.

Caleb nodded. "She'll want to call your uncle."

I remembered his coldness from our meeting at the Wriothesley's and wondered if he would bother to come home for such a thing. Certainly the damaged Shakespeares would upset him, he could probably get the police out here to make a report on those for insurance purposes. Although there was no proof that we hadn't damaged them ourselves. I stared at the family tree still spread open in front of me, the ridiculous date span under Francis Bacon looming out at me. "Wait," I said as a thought occurred to me.

I looked up and saw Caleb and Sophie were looking at me, waiting for me to finish. What was my uncle's business with Emerick Wriothesley? Growing up, my mother had almost never spoken of her brother. Why? There were never birthday cards or Christmas presents. Aside from our one visit when I was six, we never had anything to do with my uncle—and he hadn't even been home during those two weeks. Had something happened between my mother and uncle?

"What if my uncle has something to do with this," I blurted.

They were both silent, wondering over the possibility of it.

"Think about it. I know Emerick Wriothesley took my mother's diaries and my uncle obviously has some special *business* relationship with him."

"But how," Sophie had asked more than once. "How do you know he took them? I mean, how could he manage to get all those books from your room upstairs?"

"I'm sure he didn't do it *himself*, he would have hired someone."

"But how would none of us have seen it? It's not possible Charlotte."

"Of course it's possible. The diaries are gone so obviously it is possible. I was out of the house the whole day and your mother was busy rushing around getting things together for my uncle's trip to Paris. That leaves you and Caleb and he was busy sneaking into my uncle's office to use the computer. The house is enormous, it wouldn't be hard for someone to sneak in undetected. Especially someone who has been given access."

"Oh brilliant, now I have the creeps. How am I supposed to sleep now?"

Caleb who had been silently listening to my theory spoke up. "I don't think so Charlotte. I mean your uncle is stern I suppose. But I've never had the feeling he would do anyone any harm. I mean, he's helping me get into Cambridge. If he was like the Wriothesleys he certainly wouldn't bother trying to help out his housekeeper's son."

"Just because he's pulling strings for you to get into school doesn't mean there isn't potentially bad blood between him and my mother." I suddenly realized a very obvious fact. "I mean, how come he seems to have inherited the entire Spencer estate?"

"He's not pulling any strings!" Caleb said defensively. "He's helping with the applications and paperwork."

I rolled my eyes, "Fine, just because he's helping you fill out paperwork doesn't mean he didn't have something against my mother." I remembered how he spoke of my father's, 'sudden... illness' and 'unforeseen *personal* circumstances' with clear disdain. "And against my father for that matter."

Caleb and Sophie exchanged a look.

"What?" I asked.

Caleb shook his head and Sophie looked out the window.

"No, tell me. What do you know?"

"It's nothing, really," Caleb said.

"Well tell me then."

Sophie sighed. "Your uncle doesn't keep any of your father's books here in the library."

My eyes narrowed while I looked from Caleb to Sophie. For some reason they both looked uncomfortable. "What?"

"We noticed it a couple of years ago," Caleb explained.

"*I* noticed it," Sophie interjected. "I was just getting into thrillers and when mum pointed out that your mum had off and married Simon Stevens, well I tried to find copies of his books here in the library."

"Except there wasn't any," Caleb said.

"Not one," Sophie said. "When I asked mum about it, she just sort of shook her head and said she would pick one up for me next time she was in town."

"But she didn't say why he doesn't have any?"

"No. But you could kind of tell by the way she acted that maybe your uncle had something against him," Sophie said.

"You don't know that!" Caleb protested.

"Why else then?" she shot back.

"Look around Sophie. This library isn't exactly filled with genre novels. It's a collection."

I leveled a glare at Caleb. He needed to be careful about what he said next. It was no secret that my father churned out popular fiction. And certainly, judging by my own mother's reading habits, the Spencers were raised on more literary texts. But Simon Stevens was still my father.

Caleb raised his hands at me in surrender. "I like your father's stuff. I've read every one." He shrugged. "Your uncle just doesn't keep them here. Whatever the reason."

I took a deep breath. What was the reason? Was my uncle just a literary snob, or did he, and Emerick Wriothesley, have something against my family? I looked again at the ink spot that should be my father's name. Did my uncle hate my mother's choice in marrying my father?

Could my uncle possibly have something to do with my

mother's disappearance?

I needed to get back to the Wriothesley's. "When your mother gets home," I gave them both a serious look. "You tell her I am one hundred percent better."

Caleb gave me a worried look that told me he knew exactly what I had in mind. "No Charlotte."

"Yes. I am calling Hayden Wriothesley tomorrow and finding those journals."

Caleb's brow furrowed but he didn't say anything else. Sophie, on the other hand, looked excited by the prospect of seeing Hayden again. "Okay, but what do we do until then."

I looked at the Spencer tree and all the freakishly long life spans. "I don't know...is there some way to try to verify these dates. They're sort of bugging me."

The corner of Sophie's mouth turned up in a mischievous half smile, "We could try to break into your uncle's office. He probably has all kinds of stuff in there."

"No!" Caleb said. "We don't know anything for sure. If he found out we'd been snooping around in his private office he'd hate us."

"And not help you," Sophie added.

"Yes! And not help me. Besides, if we're just checking dates why not go look in the Spencer cemetery."

Surprised, my head shot up, "There's a cemetery?"

"Yes," Sophie answered, "there is. And you can count me out—it is beyond creepy. The cemetery is where my help ends."

My tennis shoes were getting damp from the tall wet grass. The Spencer family cemetery was within walking distance from the main house, but the gravel path leading to the garden curved around the garden's exterior and wove in and throughout the many blooming summer plants and flowers. The cemetery was past the well-manicured lawns and beyond a grassy hill. Standing at the cemetery gates, I looked back but only Gaersum Aern's rooftop and chimneys were visible over the hill. Behind the cemetery was the edge of the Spencer's densely wooded forest.

"I don't remember ever coming down here before."

"You probably didn't," Caleb said coming to stand beside me and taking my hand.

The simple gesture still took me by surprise. Apparently it was going to take me awhile to get used to having a boyfriend.

"I was terrified of this place when I was younger. There's no way I would have led you here when I was seven."

We stood silently surveying the grounds from the gates. It was quiet except for the breeze that rustled the forest's trees. The headstones were close together without any of the symmetry and straight lines I had seen driving past any of the large burial grounds in California. The oldest headstones were cracked and crooked. A few had fallen completely over, pushed inch by inch by the maze of tree roots that had grown in around them over the years. All of them had various stages of moss creeping, only the newest one near the far corner was still a shiny gray marble.

"It's actually quite beautiful," Caleb said breaking the silence.

"Yes," I whispered either out of respect or fear, it was hard to tell what I was feeling. The place felt like it had a presence and I could understand why Caleb was afraid of it as a child. I definitely wouldn't want to be here alone after dark.

"Come on," Caleb said pulling me past the gates and onto the ivy covered grounds. "Let's see if we can find any." The Spencer family tree was rolled up in his other hand so we could look up names and dates.

We threaded our way through the massive stones as we checked. The ground was soft from the thick layer of ivy and broken twigs—my shoes were now soaking wet. The sun was far below the tree line, every time the breeze touched my bare arms they prickled into goose bumps.

"Here's one," Caleb called crouching in front of one of the smaller stones.

He referenced the family tree and checked the stone, "Margaret Spencer, seventeen twelve to seventeen thirty-three. She was only twenty-one."

I made my way across to where he was, cognizant of the fact that we were stepping all over the gravesites of my ancestors. I hadn't spent any time in graveyards but it seemed like there should be pathways or something. It didn't feel right walking on top of the graves.

I stood next to him and read the inscription with her name

and dates—*Beloved*, was all that it said. Next to her site was a tiny cross—*Boy Spencer, Born 1733 Died 1733.*

"Oh," I gasped. "She died giving birth."

Caleb stood up and read the family tree. "She was married to Herbert Spencer and then he remarried a woman named Eleanor, they had five children."

I looked to the left of Margaret's grave and read the crooked stone, *Herbert Spencer Born 1705, Died 1802.* "Herbert lived to be ninety-seven," I said. On his other side, his second wife, Eleanor was buried. "What were the names of the children?"

"Edgar, James, Mary, Ruth, and Richard."

"I can only find Edgar," I said checking the nearby stones.

"He was the oldest and probably inherited the estate. The others could be here or wherever their lives carried them I suppose."

I imagined the other four children buried in other grave-yards across England, the girls married off to other families. "It doesn't seem fair that only the oldest had any inheritance."

"The oldest male," Caleb corrected.

"That's even worse."

Caleb nodded, "Women didn't have any rights to property, for the longest time they were considered property themselves."

I knew this from history lessons. Women were basically powerless and unless they had a father or older male relative who looked out for their wellbeing, they could end up in horrible circumstances, abusive husbands or penniless with no recourse to better their lot in life. I couldn't imagine floating through life at the mercy of others' good graces.

Caleb came up behind me so quietly I jumped.

"Sorry," he said. "So far any dates I have found seem to be accurate."

"But what about Francis Bacon...that can't be right."

Caleb checked the family tree. "According to this he was born in fifteen sixty-one and died in seventeen fifty. Look for one of the older headstones."

We split up and scanned names and dates. The sun was setting and the temperature was dropping fast. I hadn't had any ibuprofen in hours and I could feel my fever creeping back up. If I was going to convince Ms. Steward that I was well enough to leave the estate tomorrow I needed to get back soon and take some more medicine without her noticing. "Have you found anything?"

"Not yet," he called from across the cemetery near the gates.

I was at the back near the forest. The newest headstone was back here in the corner. It was like a beacon compared to the others and I wondered how old it could be. Maybe it was one of my grandparents who had both passed away when my mother was eighteen.

I made my way towards it checking the other headstones as I walked. Something moved in the forest.

Startled, I froze and my heart began racing immediately. My eyes scanned the edge of the forest—it was probably some animal, like a squirrel. *So stupid and jumpy, getting creeped out by old graves.*

But then I saw him.

Deeper into the forest, shielded by the dark and shadows—there was a man. He was walking away, he seemed to be wearing a long black coat that concealed his form and was making it difficult to track his movements as he receded farther and farther into the dark forest.

Who was it? The groundskeeper? But why wouldn't he have spoken to us?

My mind raced and I remembered movement in the gardens the day Hayden had taken me to his house, the vision of the man in a long black coat in the rearview mirror as we sped away.

Fear began seeping through my veins making my feet and fingers tingle. Was this man the person who had broken into the house, stolen my mother's diaries, and vandalized the library?

My heart was thundering and felt like it was going to exploded in my chest. I couldn't speak or move, fear paralyzed me. Who was he? How long had he been watching us?

"Caleb," I cried. But my voice was too weak and didn't carry over the sound of the breeze in the trees. The man's movement slowed—as if he'd heard me.

He stopped walking. I watched, frozen in place while he turned around. He was too far to make out his features but I knew he was staring at me.

I couldn't breathe. *Run!* But my legs were like water beneath me. *Caleb*, I tried to shout but my throat was constricted and wouldn't form the word. Any minute the man was going to take a step towards me, he would start running after me.

I forced my head to turn, find Caleb, call to him with my eyes.

He was already walking towards me.

"Charlotte?" I could hear the concern in his voice and when he saw the terror on my face he started running through the graves to get to me.

I looked back into the woods and saw the man still staring. Caleb was almost at my side. He reached for me and I raised my arm to point out the man.

But he was gone.

"Charlotte! What is it? You're white as a sheet."

"A man," I said finding my voice. "In the woods."

Caleb's gaze followed to where my arm pointed but I knew it was useless—the man had vanished into the dark. "Where?" he shook his head. "I don't see anyone."

"He was just there, walking away into the woods."

Caleb let me go and started running towards the forest.

"Caleb, stop! What are you doing?"

"What if it is the person who's been breaking in?"

"Exactly!" I ran the few steps to where he had stopped and grabbed his arm. "You can't just go thundering after him. What if he has a weapon?"

"We can't just let him go Charlotte."

"We need to call the police, we need to tell your mother."

Caleb looked into my eyes and took a breath. What I was saying seemed to make sense. "Come on," I pulled his hand. "Let's get back inside and call right away."

Caleb took one more look into the woods and then let me drag him away. We were just about to leave and I realized we were standing right next to the newest grave, the only one still not covered in moss. I caught sight of the inscription.

That's not right. I looked carefully this time. I read the name before me very slowly. I checked the dates.

Caleb was three graves away, "Charlotte I thought we were calling the police." He turned and saw me staring.

"That's not right," I said, my voice cracking.

"Charlotte?" He came back to me and put his arm around me. "What's not—"

He saw it too.

Elizabeth Stevens

I was standing on my mother's grave.

CHAPTER FOURTEEN

STAY

Depression crept over me. It slid over me like a gray shroud, slowly as my understanding for what I'd seen grew. Elizabeth Stevens, as far as my uncle was concerned, died four years ago. As far as the Spencer family, what was left of it, was concerned, Elizabeth Spencer Stevens was dead.

Ms. Steward had held me tight against her until my hysteria had stopped.

"Love, I don't know what you're talking about," she swore.

Caleb explained what we had seen, the headstone and the strange man, as well as the damaged books and the missing journals from my room while I sat comatose at the kitchen table.

Did my uncle know something my father and I didn't? Was her body out there—out there all this time? Beneath the earth, cold, far from where I could ever reach her.

"I'm calling the police...and your uncle."

"Wait," I managed. I needed to think. "Wait."

Ms. Steward stopped at the kitchen door.

I shook my head slowly and met her eyes. "Not my uncle."

"Love, I can't call the police to Mr. Spencer's home and not report it to him. I'm only a housekeeper and I don't especially want to lose this position."

I wasn't convinced my uncle didn't have something to do with all of this. What if who we saw in the woods was working for my uncle and Mr. Wriothesley. Calling him now might tip him off. What if they destroyed my mother's diaries?

But whatever was going on, I didn't want Ms. Steward, Caleb, and Sophie affected. "Don't ask him about the headstone. Not over the phone. I want to ask him myself when he gets back."

Ms. Steward considered my request for a moment. "Are you sure? What if it's a simple explanation?" She grimaced at her own words.

There could be no simple explanation. Either he knew she was dead and never told me or my father, or he didn't know anything and had just written her off.

"All right," she agreed. "I'll only tell him about the strange man you saw on the property and the missing items." She started to walk away. "I wish I didn't have to tell him about the damaged Shakespeares, he's going to be fit to be tied," she continued to herself.

I sat and stared blankly out the kitchen window. It was getting darker. Soon the window would only reflect the bright electric light streaming from the kitchen's overhead. Caleb came and sat next to me.

When he put his arm around me I shoved it off.

"What's the matter with you?" he asked defensively.

"What a stupid question," I said flatly. It felt good, lashing out like this, even though I knew Caleb didn't deserve it. Still, I didn't feel like being touched. I wanted to be alone.

He looked hurt.

I sighed. I didn't have the energy to try to help him feel better. "I just don't feel like having you hang on me right now."

He pushed his chair away from me. "Fine," he said. "I wouldn't want to *hang* on you. I was only trying to help you feel better."

I looked blankly at him. The idea that he thought a hug might help me now almost made me laugh in his face. There was no way he understood even remotely what I felt like. "Don't try," I looked back out the window. "It's impossible."

A plain-clothes officer showed up an hour later and questioned Caleb, Sophie and me in the kitchen while Ms. Steward sat in the corner listening.

"But you didn't get a look at him?" the officer asked me for the third time.

"Not his face. It was dark and he was far away," I said. "But he had dark hair and wore a dark coat, like a trench coat. I also saw him three days ago as I was leaving."

"You were leaving?"

"In a car, I saw his reflection in the rearview mirror of the car."

The officer wrote something down but I could tell from his bored expression that he was doing me a courtesy. The information I was giving him was useless.

"And you didn't see him at all," he asked Caleb.

Caleb sighed, "No sir. But we think this may be the person who's broken into the house."

"Uh huh...yes, I got that. Now, just to clarify, there wasn't any sign of break in, correct?"

"No," we both answered.

"And the only things that have come up missing are some personal journals?"

"Yes," I said.

"But these were not a part of Mr. Spencer's insured collection?"

The officer completed his report and left. "Call if you see the man trespassing again. They're only reports, but they can be used as evidence if he does try something more substantial in the future."

Ms. Steward closed the door as the officer made his way down the dark drive.

"So basically we have to wait until this wacko kills one of us before they can do anything?" Sophie asked.

"There's no evidence of anything," Caleb sighed.

"Well we'll just have to make sure we keep all the doors and windows locked from now on," Ms. Steward said. "Your uncle said we shouldn't worry. He suspects it's only a poacher using the woods. He'll deal with it when he gets home in two days," she added absently. I could tell the thought of a strange man prowling the property was frightening her.

I didn't point out that poachers don't generally steal from *inside* the house. She was worried enough already.

"Well I'm off to bed," she said. "You lot should do the same. It's gotten late and Charlotte's not been well."

This reminded me. "Actually, I'm completely better," I lied. I had taken two ibuprofen while she called the police. "I should be fine for going out tomorrow."

She gave me a skeptical look. "You've had quite a shock today, we'll see how you are tomorrow. Good night—lock your windows."

The three of us sat for a moment longer in silence and then Sophie got up and headed for the stairs. Caleb and I followed her up the grand staircase towards our own rooms. My legs felt heavy as I climbed and I held the handrail for support. I didn't want to think anymore tonight.

Sophie's room was first. At her door she stopped and turned, her eyes were full of sympathy. She leaned in and hugged me. I heard her whisper in my ear, "I'm so sorry Charlotte." She squeezed me once more and then disappeared into her room, closing the door gently behind her.

Caleb walked me to my door. Now that we were alone, I remembered my mean words earlier in the kitchen. "I'm sorry I bit your head off earlier," I mumbled.

"It's okay."

"It was mean, you were only trying to help."

Caleb shook his head, "Really, forget it. It's a lot to try and deal with."

He was again trying to make me feel better but I noticed he was keeping his distance. I could hardly blame him if he wasn't rushing to hold me, *I just don't feel like having you hang on me right now.* "I didn't mean it," I said.

"...I know."

I didn't know how to make this better. I was afraid that if I tried to touch him he'd recoil.

"Do you want to hang out for a while," I asked opening my door. "I was going to work the puzzle box until I fell asleep."

He hesitated and I thought for sure he was going to shake his head. "Okay," he whispered.

I took his fingers, pulled him slowly past the door and shut it quietly behind us. I wasn't sure how Ms. Steward would feel about us being in my room together at night and I didn't want to find out.

Caleb stood in the middle of the floor while I got the box from behind the chaise. I carried it over to the bed and heaved it into the middle of all the down and chintz.

When I climbed up the stairs onto the bed, Caleb lingered where he stood until I looked at him, "Are you coming?"

He avoided my gaze and seemed nervous. When he started up the step stool I could hear the sound of his leather soles on the wood.

"No shoes on the bed," I reminded him of his mother's words.

He smiled, pushed each of his shoes off with the other foot, I heard them thud onto the wood floor, and he climbed onto my mammoth bed. When I started sliding the ouroboros in the center of the box, he seemed to relax a little more, relived that there was someplace to put his attention besides the fact that we were both sitting on my bed.

Being alone with Caleb didn't make me nervous, I trusted him. Somehow I knew he would never do anything to hurt me. At least, not on purpose.

I finished opening the top circular section and removed the pentagram necklace and my mother's note. We both stared at the box and took intermittent turns pushing an engraving or attempting to slide an edge. Nothing either of us tried had any effect.

We sat silently working with the box between us. The house felt still, like it had fallen asleep around us.

"I think this is Hebrew writing," Caleb pointed after a while.

"This is different over here," I said. "Arabic?"

Caleb shrugged, "I'm not sure. Languages I don't know."

He traced an inscription with his finger. "You know... there's a good chance your mother isn't buried there. I've heard of families doing that, like soldiers who've gone missing during war and are never found. They bury something that belonged to the person, something significant. Just so the family can move on."

I thought about what he said, I wanted it to be true. But I was terrified of letting this hope in. "Do you think she's buried there?"

"Honestly Charlotte...I don't know. I never saw anything and your uncle never mentioned it. But he is a very private person. I do think that if she is or was seriously involved with Emerick Wriothesley...anything is possible.

"Do you know my uncle well?"

Caleb thought about my question before he answered. "No. I don't think your uncle is probably close with anyone. At least not as far as I know. But I don't think he's a bad person. I don't think he would do something without a good reason."

"You think he had a reason for putting up a headstone with my mother's name on it and not telling me or my dad?" I was trying to keep the accusation out of my voice. I didn't want Caleb to leave just yet.

Caleb took a breath. "I do. I don't have any idea what it could be and maybe you wouldn't agree with it, but I'm sure he had a reason. You uncle is someone I respect Charlotte. If you knew him..." he trailed off.

But I didn't know him.

Absently, I reached into the circular compartment in the top of the box and felt around.

More importantly, my mother never took steps to ensure that I would know him. Why?

I pushed the interior wall of the hole, it moved. I snatched my hand out and gasped.

"What?" Caleb asked.

"It moved." I reached back in and continued rotating the inside. Like when I dialed the ouroboros I could hear a series of clicks and then it stopped. I took my hand out wondering what could be next.

Caleb leaned forward to get a better look at the inside. "I don't see anything."

What could be next? "These puzzles can be so irritating. You spend forever looking for one in, you finally find one and practically shoot through the roof with excitement, except it could take you a month to find the next thing."

"Maybe..." Caleb reached back into the hole. I heard something move.

"What did you do?" I asked excitedly.

"The bottom pushed down a few centimeters."

I looked inside and could see where the floor of the compartment had separated from the circular wall. When I reached in, I felt the gap and explored all around the edge with my finger. "I don't feel anything else."

"Let me see."

I removed my hand so Caleb could try poking around. We hunched over the box taking turns again trying to discover what else may have changed.

When I finally looked at the antique clock on my bedside table I was shocked. "It's after twelve."

Caleb sat up surprised. "Wow," he said looking for himself. "I didn't even realize." He started to get up and make his way through all the fluff to the edge of the bed.

"Caleb?"

"What?" he paused at the step stool.

I hesitated, not sure how he would interpret what I was about to ask. "Would you...stay? Just a bit longer. Just until I fall asleep."

His eyes met mine and then he nodded. He climbed back over to where I was while I slipped beneath the sheets and coverings.

The bedside lamp clicked off. The room was dark all around us. I felt my heart start to thunder in my ears but then Caleb laid down beside me, the weight of his body on top of the covers pulling the blankets tight across my body.

He put his arm around me and I could feel his breath on the back of my neck. My heartbeat slowed, I wasn't afraid of the dark as long as I wasn't alone.

"Caleb?"

"Hmm?"

"Before you leave...turn the bedside lamp back on, okay?"

He didn't say anything for a while, then he brushed my hair away from my ear and I felt his lips brush my neck. "I will."

I expected him to ask why but he only lay silent and still beside me. After a few minutes, I relaxed and my mind wandered. Caleb's breathing was deep and even, I hoped he had fallen asleep. It would be comforting to have him with me all night.

"Charlotte?" he asked.

"I thought you were asleep," I whispered.

"I want you to do me a favor."

"What?"

"Tomorrow, let's go to Cyberzone."

He was trying to keep me from calling Hayden and going to the Wriothesley's. "I'm going to have to go eventually. If it's not tomorrow it'll be the next day, or the day after." I rolled over under the tight blankets so I could face him. "I am going to find them. I'm sorry if me spending time there worries you."

He looked into my eyes. His hand rose up and held my face as he lowered his lips to mine. After a moment he pulled away enough to whisper, "I know. But please, just one day. A nice day, you and me in town."

"Why? What will one day matter?"

He didn't say anything, his hand swept over my shoulder and down my arm. He kissed me again. "I don't want to lose you Charlotte. I can't shake this dread, this sense that Hayden is going to do something."

"Don't worry about Hayden."

"You keep saying that."

"And you keep not listening. Hayden is not the type of guy I would ever fall for. His charm may work on a lot of girls but I don't happen to be one of them."

Except, the memory of Hayden's breathless kiss reminded me that my assurances to Caleb weren't exactly true. *That's never going to happen again,* I reminded myself. *No, I'll see him coming next time.*

Next time.

"One day," I said, suddenly nervous myself about the potential of seeing Hayden tomorrow. "I've been wanting to buy a new chain for my cross anyway."

Caleb smiled in the dark and kissed me again. "Thank you Charlotte. We'll have fun. I mean, we'll get some stuff done too, but I want to show you around."

A date. "It will be nice to get out of the house." I rolled over and Caleb buried his face in my hair.

I didn't remember Caleb leaving but I slept all night without a single nightmare. When I woke up the sun was creeping around the edge of the heavy drapes. I checked the clock, seven thirty-three.

I reached over and switched off the bedside lamp—he'd left it on for me.

CHAPTER FIFTEEN

EIGHT SWORDS

Sophie was taking forever.

"What about this?" she asked considering herself from every angle.

We had been in the garage staring at her secret wardrobe for over an hour and she had tried on at least ten different outfits.

"It's cute, the best one for sure. Now let's go."

"I don't know..."

She pulled on the hem of the miniskirt wedding dress and twirled around in her black stiletto ankle boots. When she stopped she peered at her reflection from over her shoulder. "It might be a bit too much."

As far as I could tell, every outfit she'd had on so far was *too much*. If she tried on one more thing my head was going to explode. "No. No that one's the best. It's perfect."

But she wrinkled her face at her reflection.

I stood up, "Okay, I'll get Caleb and we'll meet you around back." I hoped that she would take the hint.

"I'm not sure..."

"Five minutes," I interrupted and bolted for the door. I pulled the crooked door behind me forcing it back into the warped frame. Turning back towards the house I stopped, Caleb was crossing the gravel drive looking annoyed.

"What's taking her so long?"

I shrugged and forced a protective smile. I had never understood the fascination with clothes and makeup, but I suddenly felt a sisterly compassion for Sophie. "She's almost ready," I said sounding unconvinced.

Caleb rolled his eyes and unlocked his car. He was already not thrilled that she was intruding on our *date* day. We sat waiting for another ten minutes before Sophie finally emerged, still in the shrunken wedding dress but she'd used the time to draw a black arrow around her left eye.

"Oh my God," Caleb groaned when he saw her.

"Stop," I whispered.

"It's embarrassing," he said as she opened the back door.

"All right, let's go," she said sliding across the seat.

I smiled at her. "You look good."

Sophie's face lit up from the compliment.

"Mum'd kill you," Caleb said looking at her in the rearview mirror.

Sophie stuck her tongue at him. "Mum's not here."

When we got to Glastonbury, Cyberzone was closed. Sophie read the sign and checked her chunky digital watch, "Two hours," she said.

"What should we do?" Caleb asked.

I thought for a second. I hadn't been to England since I was six. "You could show me the sights."

"There's the Tor," Sophie said.

"And the Chalice Well," Caleb added.

"Sounds good to me."

We headed back up High street. We were almost back to the car when Sophie cried out.

"Ooo, I've always wanted to do that," she pointed to one of the shops ahead of us. There was a pink neon sign in the shape of a hand in the window.

"A psychic?" Caleb scoffed.

She clutched my hand. "It'll be fun. Please Charlotte, let's go."

I read the sign in the window.

Psychic Readings

Tarot

Birth Charts

Palm Reading

"Pleeeeaaase," she begged. "I want to have my palm read."

I looked at Caleb and shrugged. "Why not?"

"Because it's a waste of money, that's why not."

"It's my money," Sophie said stomping to the door.

I couldn't help but smile while Caleb scowled and reluctantly followed his sister through the heavily tinted door.

Inside, a musky incense burned my nostrils and I could see the thin tendrils of smoke swirling into the air from the stick burning near the front door. Dim light danced on the walls from the candles that burned all around the small room. There was no one here.

"Hello?" Sophie called out.

A moment later, a curtain at the back of the room brushed to the side and a young woman emerged from another room. She smiled wide.

"Hello,"

"Hi," we all said at once.

She wasn't what I expected. I had imagined a wizened old women in a flowing gown and crystal necklaces. This woman was much younger and she wore jeans and a t-shirt. The most eccentric thing about her was her dreaded hair that she had pulled up into a ponytail.

"What can I do for you today?"

None of us said anything until Caleb nudged Sophie.

"I'd like my palm read?"

The woman smiled warmly and nodded, like she was used to people being unsure in her presence. "Okay." She looked at Caleb and me. "Are you two just the moral support?"

Caleb shook his head, he looked nervous.

"I'll do it," I said.

The woman suddenly focused on me. Her eyes squinted and her mouth opened slightly, as if she were listening to something or deep in thought. I was starting to feel a little uncomfortable but then she shook her head once to the side, as if clearing away a thought and her smile returned. "Yes, okay." She turned away from me and pointed at Sophie, "But we'll do you first." Her smile was warm and infectious, Sophie smiled back and the two disappeared behind the curtain into the back room.

"You didn't ask how much it cost," Caleb hissed.

"So I'll ask when she comes back."

"But what if Sophie doesn't have enough? I doubt she's even considered it."

"I'll pay for both of us. This is fun."

Caleb's face flushed red.

"What?" I asked.

He turned from me and sat down on a rickety looking wicker chair.

"What?" I asked again.

Caleb picked up a magazine from the table in front of him. "Nothing," he said sounding annoyed.

I sighed and decided to ignore him. What would it hurt to let Sophie have a little fun? After all the restrictions put on her this summer, not to mention all the time she'd put in for me in the library, it seemed like the least I could do was pay to have her palm read.

While we waited for Sophie, I browsed the bookshelf in the waiting room. I didn't recognize any of the titles. *Metaphysics and Your Mind, Riddles of Existence, Your Soul's Plan,*

The Oxford Handbook of Metaphysics, Journey of Souls. Then one caught my attention, *The Modern Alchemist: A Guide to Personal Transformation.*

Alchemist, alchemy. I remembered the book from Gaersum Aern's library—*The Alchemical Writings of Sir Isaac Newton.* The book that contained the phrase my mother had scribbled and hidden in the emerald box. I pulled *The Modern Alchemist* from the shelf, flipped to the table of contents and sat down.

Chapter One: Persona................................*23*
Chapter Two: Shadow..............................*35*
Chapter Three: Anima..............................*45*
Chapter Four: Animus..............................*55*

There were sixteen chapters all together. Each one labeled with a strange title: *The Adversary, Great Mother, Wise Old Man.* The final chapter, chapter sixteen, was titled: *The Master or God-Man.* I turned to the introduction and read the fist few lines.

In our modern culture, traditional religion has not been able to meet the spiritual needs of many individuals. Still, these seekers yearn for a greater understanding of self and the Higher Power, however one conceives that force.

I turned the book over and read the back cover...*a first-hand, experiential guide to the process which medieval alchemist represented as the transformation of "lead into gold," or lower substance into higher ones...we can find a more intimate connection with the guiding, nurturing powers of the universe and the "lost" parts of ourselves.*

I reread the last line, the *lost* parts of ourselves.

I had lost so much.

I turned the book over and stared at the cover, I needed this book. Somehow I knew it had answers, glue for the scraps of clues that I hoped would lead me to my mother.

I sat down and began reading the book's forward. Ten minutes later, Sophie emerged from the back room looking disappointed. Obviously, whatever she had been expecting, or hoping to hear, she hadn't.

"Your turn Charlotte," she said flatly. When I passed her at the entrance to the back room she leaned towards my ear and whispered, "Don't get your hopes up."

I leaned back and gave her a questioning look. She rolled her eyes and shook her head.

"See," Caleb whispered triumphantly. "I said it was a waste of money."

Sophie made a nasty face at him and flopped into the chair I had been sitting in across from her brother.

"Let's just pay her and go," he added. "There's no need to dig deeper."

"I'll just be a second," I said waving him off. I didn't care about the palm reading. I wanted to try and buy the book.

I pushed the curtain to the side and stepped into what looked like a living room. Like the front room, there were many candles burning and casting shadows that danced across the walls, but there was no circular table topped with a crystal ball, no skulls or vials. I knew why Sophie had been disappointed, it looked like any other home.

"Hi Charlotte."

Despite the normalcy of the place, hearing my name called out made me jump.

"Sorry," she smiled emerging from what looked like a small kitchen on the right. "I didn't mean to startle you."

I started to protest but stopped. How had she known my name?

She laughed again and placed two Cokes on the coffee table. "Sophie told me your name," she said sitting down. "Here, come have a seat."

But then how did she know that I was wondering how she knew my name. I felt like I was half a step behind what was happening. "Can you...?"

"Read your mind?" She paused, popped the top of her can and took a foamy sip. "Ooo, that's good. No. I can't read your mind."

"Then how did you know what I was thinking?"

"Because it was all over your face," she smiled. "It always surprises me that most people don't realize how much information they pass out without even opening their mouth. But then again, I am very, very good at reading people."

"So that's all there is to it? It's not really psychic ability, you just read body language."

"Now I didn't say that. Reading body language it a small part of what I can do. But to be quite frank, anyone can do what I do. To some degree or another. I just have a natural inclination and have practiced a ton." She tilted her head to the side in the same strange way she'd done earlier, like she was listening to a far off sound. She smiled and leveled her gaze at me. "Just like reading Shakespeare. Some people find it difficult but when you have a natural proclivity for language and you've also practiced a lot, reading the complete works of Shakespeare can be no harder than breezing through a Devin Kruger thriller." She took another sip from her can and placed it back on the table. "For someone like you anyway."

I stared stupidly at her.

"See, now I can tell from your body language I've struck a chord."

I couldn't believe it. I walked around the coffee table and sat down, never taking my eyes off her. "Two things actually," I whispered.

"Shakespeare and Devin Kruger. That's what was shown to me. I'm Eve by the way."

"Charlotte," I touched my chest reflexively. She already knew my name.

"But I don't know how they relate to you," Eve continued. "It's sort of a back and forth process. But sit back, relax. This is going to take a while."

"What is?"

"There's about twenty people trying to push in all at once to speak. I'm having a hard time sorting them out."

"I'm sorry. Twenty people?"

"Well, not people like you think. They were people, now it's their souls. Who are you anyway? I've never had this many trying to contact one person still manifest in this plane." She narrowed her eyes at me and tilted her head again.

Souls? Trying to contact me? Fear started a slow creep over my skin and my heart sped up. What souls? I thought of the shiny headstone planted in Gaersum Aern's cemetery inscribed with my mother's name. The thought of her being buried, lifeless, underground—I didn't want confirmation of that. While this strange woman listened to whatever she was hearing, I braced myself.

She sat that way for what seemed like an eternity, but I didn't interrupt.

"One at a time," she murmured sounding a little annoyed.

Finally, after another few minutes she took a deep breath and shook her head. She reached for her Coke and looked at me. She took a drink and wiped her mouth.

"Well?" I asked not able to wait any longer. If she was going to tell me my mother was dead then I'd just as soon her spit it out. I would choose to believe it or write her off as a quack later. But this silence was unbearable.

"I'm sorry. It's just...with some people, the messages that come through are so clear, simple even. Messages about a passed relative being fine or that the living should move on with their lives. Stuff about forgiveness and the release of guilt for the living to take away. At most I've seen five, maybe six immediate family members offering communication." She leveled her eyes at me and took another sip from her Coke. "It is difficult for me to hear the message for you Charlotte because there are so many."

"You said twenty."

She shook her head, "At first, when you first walked through the door there were immediately about twenty. The Shakespeare and Devin Kruger were offered up quickly to connect you to the process. But the longer I tried to listen, the more I tuned in to your frequency...there were so many," she breathed. "It was like they multiplied again and again, if you could image stadiums full of souls, all crying out to you Charlotte. And not with answers, that was weird. It's like they wanted to ask you the questions."

"Me?"

"At first, before it was too overwhelming, that first few had clearer imagery. I believe they were direct members of your soul family. There was a crown, that was clear. It was larger than anything that could possibly fit on a person's head. It was in a desert. It began to spin, slowly at first and then faster and faster, sand kicking up everywhere, a dust storm. The crown lifted up off the ground, above the dust until it hung high in the sky, spinning. There was a deep vibration that emanated from it...I could feel it. It was wonderful Charlotte, like it hummed in tune with the center of my being. The air around the crown pulsed or throbbed in waves." Her eyes met mine, "It was amazing. Does it mean anything to you."

I shook my head slowly.

"The next image was a stand, like a lectern. A large room full of people were sitting in front of it...like they were waiting for class to begin. But the last thing I saw was a small girl, so tiny and alone. She was wandering in a forest, terrified. In her hand was a scrap of something. Thicker than paper. It was old, what was it called that they used to write on before paper?"

I shrugged and shook my head.

"But this wasn't even that, it was like it was animal hide and what she held was a tiny piece of a map that had been shredded into a thousand pieces. She kept looking at the scrap and wandering but she was lost. She started to cry, but there was no sound. The trees grew taller, darker all around her. She stopped wandering and fell to the ground, curling herself into a small ball. The forest grew even faster. But it was strange because there were other scraps all around her, in a bush, nailed to a tree, one was stuck to the back of her shirt. But for some reason, she couldn't see them."

"This is supposed to relate to me?"

Eve shrugged and took a drink. "Yes."

"But I don't understand any of this. It's like you're describing a bad dream."

"That's exactly what it felt like," she said, her face illuminated like we'd made some sort of breakthrough.

"I'm sorry, but this is all very weird."

She nodded and looked sympathetic. Eve turned and reached for something on the small table beside the sofa. "They usually feel that way at first." It was a deck of cards and

216

she began shuffling them on the table in front of us. "Often times the images shown to a person don't make any sense for years and then it's like, click, all the pieces fall exactly into place. The image can be read and understood only when we've learned to speak our own language."

She stopped shuffling and began laying cards on the table in front of us. On the first card was the image of a woman, bound and blindfolded, she was surrounded by swords in a desolate landscape.

Eve finished laying the cards and considered the entire spread before placing her finger on that first card. "The eight of swords. You, or some aspect of your life, feels powerless. Boxed in by the circumstances of fate. Tied and blind, waiting for a rescue that is not on the horizon."

"That's depressing."

Eve smiled, "But look at our lady here. She is surround-ed by swords she could use to free herself. If only she would move. Her feet are not bound and nothing blocks her way, step forward. She needs to rescue herself."

I suddenly realized why Sophie had been so disappointed. "You said something earlier about a soul family.

She sat back against the cushions, "Well, now that I *can* ex-plain. That's universal stuff. A soul family are soul mates. Most people, if they believe in them at all, think they only have one soul mate and they spend most of their lives trying to find them or determine if the person they've chosen as a mate is *the one*. When, in actual fact, everyone has many soul mates and these are the souls that you planned and agreed with before your experiences here on earth. A soul mate could be your best friend, they almost certainly are, or your husband, teacher, your next door neighbor. Souls create groups that are learning towards the same or similar goals."

"So there's no such things as a soul mate in the *true love* sense."

Eve smiled wryly and seemed to be thinking about her answer. "No, I didn't say that. It's just that many people have and learn from relationships that pull from their soul family. Soul families often have lived many lifetimes together. They are familiar with one another and working towards common goals, even though they rarely know this in their present material lives." Eve leaned forward and opened a small wooden box on the coffee table, she pulled out a thin brown cigar and a lighter. "Do you mind?"

I shook my head and watched as she lit one end while taking a series of small puffs until the tip burned bright red. She blew a plump cloud of rich scented smoke into the air and sat back again. "We all have many soul mates and our relationships with them, whatever form they may take, can be happy or sad, challenging or easy, they can last a lifetime or only a season and regardless of all this, we are always learning from that relationship, attempting to achieve the goals we set for ourselves before beginning this life." She took a long drag from her cigar, blue smoke rushed in a thin stream from her mouth. "But we only have one twin flame."

"Twin flame?"

"When a soul decides to be created out of the singular universal energy, it splits in two." Eve held up one hand, "Yin," and then the one with the cigar, "and yang."

"One true love."

"No. We can have many true and real loves with our different soul mates, or souls from our soul families, across lifetimes. Always these relationships are set up in the infinite before we are born, or reborn, into this world. Your twin flame is out in existence collecting information at the same time. Living another life, having it's own relationships, growing and learning as a soul so that when the two can finally be reunited, they have between the two of them, built up to the heights of ultimate understanding. They come together and are whole again."

"How do you find your twin flame?"

She laughed, leaned forward and picked up her Coke. "You don't. Twin flame relationships are rarely actualized here on earth. It would mean that a soul had reached its full height of knowledge concerning the universe, God...the meaning of existence. Being reunited with the twin flame would mean that a soul was nearly done with the cycle of life and death. They could merge again with universal energy, become one with the universe."

I thought of Caleb sitting in the waiting room, could he be my twin flame? I didn't want to ask Eve this though, it felt like too personal of a question for someone I'd just met, psychic or not. "What does this have to do with me?"

Eve rolled her cigar between her thumb and two fingers, "Everything," she said. "But then, it pertains to everyone," she swept her arms wide looking around. She passed her tongue between her lips and teeth and settled her eyes on me again. "You though..." she stopped.

"What?"

"I'm sorry, it's just the whole time we've been talking, it's not like the multitude of souls that have been trying to speak to you have gone away. I've been trying very hard to ignore it but it's like trying to ignore a rock concert happening in your brain. I'm getting conflicting messages about sharing some information with you."

"What information?" This was it, this was where she told me my mother was dead. That she loved me and missed me but that it was time to move on.

Eve's lips parted slightly, hesitating.

"It's about my mother, isn't it."

Eve nodded.

I held my breath. Already I could feel my throat tightening and the tears forming. My temples felt tight. "I thought so," I whispered.

"Do you already know?" she asked. "She told you?"

"I didn't," the tears started and fell down my face. "But I suppose I do now. I found her grave yesterday...they never even told us," I cried.

Eve narrowed her eyes at me. "What are you talking

about?"

"My mother of course. She's dead, right? That's what you see."

Eve shook her head slowly staring at me. "That's not what I see. I mean, I can't guarantee it, there isn't some certificate I can offer you. But I didn't see your mother coming through in the way dead loved ones generally do."

I stopped crying. "What?"

"She never told you?"

"Told me what?"

"Or your father?"

"What?"

"Charlotte, if I'm understanding the imagery right...you are the daughter of twin flames. Twin flames that actually found each other in the same space and time, on the same dimension...it's so rare! And they had you. I've never heard of that happening."

I tried to process what she was saying. My mother and father were *twin flames*? It seemed more like a one sided case of infatuation to me. I could believe that my father was deeply and truly in love with my mother—the loss of her had practically broken him. But had she loved him? It was difficult to think of her polite mannerisms as all encompassing universal connection.

"You don't believe me," Eve stated.

"It's just, if you knew my parents. It's hard to imagine them like you describe. They always seemed more like, I don't know...partners."

Eve thought about what I said. After a moment, her head tilted to the side, "A straw man, or, maybe a scarecrow. Does that mean anything to you."

"No," I shook my head.

"Hmm," she pressed the center of her forehead right between her eyebrows. "We're going to have to stop here." She squeezed her eyes tight and stood up.

"What's the matter?"

"I've got a massive migraine beginning to bloom," she opened one eye and peeked at me. "It happens sometimes. But it hasn't happened in a long while."

"I'm sorry," I apologized feeling like it was my fault.

She waved her hand at me, "I'll live, but I better get to bed. I'll just lock up after you."

I stood and suddenly remembered the book in my hands, *The Modern Alchemist*. "Can I borrow this?"

"Yes, yes, of course," she didn't even look at what I had. "Just bring it with you next time." She stopped at the dividing curtain. "You are coming back, right?"

I nodded even though I had no idea. Of course I would return her book, but that wasn't what she was asking. Eve wanted to know if I was coming back for another session. "What do we owe you?"

"Don't worry about it, I work from donations. Just drop something in the bottle by the door."

I dug through my wallet as fast as I could while she herded

me through the curtains, past the front room and to the door. Sophie and Caleb stood up as soon and we entered and joined me. I barely had time to grab a twenty pound note and shove it through the narrow opening of the large water bottle she kept near the door before the door was closing behind us and we heard the deadbolt sliding into place.

The three of us stood staring for a moment, not sure what had just happened.

"What'd she tell you Charlotte?" Sophie asked. "You were back there forever."

I looked at my watch, *an hour*?

"Well," Caleb scoffed. "Did she tell you your *future*?" he rolled his eyes.

I thought about what she had told me. "No," I answered. "I'm not sure what she told me."

"See, that's exactly how it was for me too. Lot's of *imagery*, but no bloody explanation."

"Sophie!" Caleb chastised.

She rolled her eyes. "What it end up costing," she asked sheepishly. Caleb must have lectured her while I was in the back.

"Nothing, a donation."

Her face relaxed. "Well, at least we didn't have to pay much for it."

"Yes," I whispered.

Sophie and I followed Caleb down the street. I looked back to the blinking neon sign illuminating her window and thought of Eve, suffering in a darkened room, her head exploding in pain. I wasn't sure what she had told me, but I knew in my heart of hearts, it was all true.

CHAPTER SIXTEEN

THEY KNOW

Caleb led me down High Street's bricked sidewalk. We were surrounded by tourists strolling in and out of the tiny shops lining both sides of the street. Mothers pushed strollers. Older couples—who for some reason all seemed to be dressed alike in khakis and windbreakers—held hands and admired the overflowing baskets of flowers hung from the lamp posts running up and down the street.

Caleb held my hand. It was strange and a little scary, being part of a couple. Especially since we were right out in public. Not that I knew anyone here besides him and Sophie, but still. It felt like everyone was staring at us, as if we were our own couple parade marching down between the shops, even though I knew logically nobody was giving us a second glance.

We passed a group of kids sitting and hanging out on a low stonewall, I felt Caleb's hand tighten slightly on mine and Sophie draw closer—I wondered if they knew them. Caleb had never mentioned any friends. We passed them and a couple of the girls looked up from their phones but Caleb didn't even break stride. Based on Sophie's comments and Caleb's intense interest in everything Egypt, it wasn't hard to figure out that he probably didn't have many friends—if any. Not that it mattered to me, I wasn't exactly the homecoming queen at West Christian.

"Here Charlotte!" Sophie pointed to a shop window a few yards ahead. "They'll have a decent chain here."

Caleb and I followed her in and I browsed the jewelry cases looking for a new silver chain. "This one," I pointed.

The sales person pulled the chain from the case. I tried it on to check the length. "What about this one?" When I turned, Caleb jumped away from the case he was bent over, and walked quickly to me. "It's nice," he offered.

Sophie considered a pair of long earring dangling from her own ears in a mirror, "Yes, that's perfect Charlotte."

"You didn't even look."

"I did," she glanced at me. "It's perfect," she repeated turning back to her own reflection.

"I'll take it," I handed the necklace back to the sales girl. "What were you looking at?" I asked Caleb as I moved towards the case he'd just been hovering over.

"What?" his voice cracked. "Me? I wasn't looking at anything..."

I saw the rows of rings in the case he'd been next to.

"I was just roaming around," he added unconvincingly.

226

I nodded my head and moved quickly past the rings choosing to believe him.

The lady rang up my purchase and I paid cash.

"Cyberzone is just the next block," Caleb said pulling me from my thoughts. "After, I thought we could see some of the sights." He shrugged. "It's funny, living here I never come to see them but with you it gives me a good excuse. There's the Tor, and Glastonbury Abby, and the Chalice Well. People come from all over the world for the festival at the end of June. It's kind of crazy, lots of hippies and healers, but we could come if you want. There's hundreds of bands."

I was anxious to get online. It was strange not having computer access for so long. "Sure, maybe." I wanted to send Susan an email and see if she'd spoken to my dad. I was also going to let her know about my lack of communication ability—she would probably FedEx me an international phone by tomorrow complete with Internet and texting ability. I had my doubts that my uncle would be super receptive to my complaints.

Cyberzone was packed with people. When we finally got to the counter to put our name on the list, the roundish man slumping on his stool gave us a suspicious look.

"It's five quid for twenty minutes, one hour maximum." He pointed to the sign hanging over his head without bothering to look himself. "Accounts and *major* credit cards only."

He obviously expected us to leave after hearing all this. Instead, I opened my bag and pulled out my wallet.

"One hour," I placed my platinum American Express on the counter. "Do we order food here as well?"

He picked up my card, looked at me and then flipped it over to check the signature strip. "You have identification for this?"

I reached into my bag to get my passport. It wasn't in the side pocket. I pushed aside keys, my wallet, a pack of gum and old receipts, my passport wasn't in my bag.

Where was my passport?

I could tell from his darkening expression that all my shuffling was making the guy suspicious. Quickly, I opened my wallet back up and slid my California driver's license from its sleeve and pushed it across the counter.

He picked it up and eyed it a long time before scrutinizing my face, I gave him the fakest smile I could muster. "Do you prefer Visa?"

When he turned away and ran the card through the machine behind him I whispered to Caleb, "My passport's gone."

"What?"

I opened my purse again and rifled around some more. "It's not here."

"Did you leave it in your room?"

"I don't know…maybe. But I don't think I ever took it out of here."

"It's probably back at the house."

I nodded but wasn't reassured. I had no memory of doing anything with my passport since going through customs in

Heathrow.

The man turned back around and handed me my American Express.

"What about food?" I reminded him.

He nodded his head towards a section of the café that had open seats but no computers. "No food near the computers. Order over there while you're waiting or wait till after. But the queue moves pretty quick. If you're not ready when your name comes up I just roll you to the end of the list."

We had rushed out the house this morning with only cups of tea in travel mugs. I was starving but I wanted to get on the computer faster. "Never mind then," I said signing the charge strip he had laid out.

"Suit yourself. Adams!" he called out. "Adams! I'll give you your code when I call your name."

A couple was sitting in the café, sausage rolls and steaming cups had just been delivered to their table. The man jumped up, rocking the flimsy table and sloshed liquid all over the top. "Here! Adams here!" He said waving his hand at the unfriendly attendant. "We're just going to finish this—"

"Sorry, no waiting, no food. Caron!" he called. "I'll put you back on. Caron!"

The man sat back down looking irritated while the woman tried to soak up the mess with a handful of napkins."

"Wow," I said quietly to Caleb and Sophie. "Such amazing service here."

"He's a fat prig," Sophie said loud enough for the guy to

hear.

"They're notoriously rude," Caleb whispered. We stood awkwardly waiting our turn. I watched both sides of the café with envy, maybe we should have eaten first.

"Stevens!"

I jumped and Caleb started towards the counter.

"Stevens!" The man shouted right at Caleb.

"Here," Caleb said.

Our computer was in the row facing the front pane window. As we positioned our stools I noticed a man walking by talking into his cell, he glanced through the window and made eye contact with me before continuing on. It felt like being an advertisement for the café. While Caleb logged us on I pulled the list I'd made from my bag.

"What's first?" he asked.

"Camilla's tattoo."

"How do we search on that?"

"I don't know, describe it I guess."

He positioned the keyboard towards me so I could type.

I thought for a second before I typed in—five pointed star red yellow white blue green. The search engine produced any related pages it found. The first was for Lucky Charms cereal. "Pink hearts, orange stars, yellow moons, green clovers," I chanted from memory. "That's helpful," I mumbled. There were links for world flags, clip art, and positional colors for military officials.

"There," Caleb pointed to the second to last entry. "Try

that one."

It was an encyclopedia entry for five pointed stars. I clicked it and Caleb sat close so we could both read.

A five-pointed star is a very common ideogram throughout the world. If drawn with lines of equal length and angles of 36° at each point, it is sometimes termed a golden five pointed star. If the colinear edges are joined together a pentagram is produced, which is the simplest of the unicursal star polygon, and a symbol of mystical and magical significance. The golden five-pointed star has particularly strong associations with military power and war.

We scanned the other headings. Some of them I recognized: Flags, Socialism and Communism. Other headings I didn't recognize: The Druze, Ottomans, Bahai Faith, but none of the pictures looked like Camilla's tattoo. I scrolled down and read more. Other Uses, Brigate Rose, Sigma Kappa.

Then I read, *The Order of the Eastern Star, an organization associated with Freemasonry, employs a downward-pointing star as its symbol, with the five points colored blue, yellow, white, green, and red. This emblem sometimes appears in the form of a pentagram.*

I clicked the link and saw the passage described.

"That's it!"

Caleb looked closely. "Are you sure?"

"Absolutely."

We sat close with out heads together and read the page.

Caleb sat back, "It's Masonic."

"What does that mean?"

He shook his head, "I don't know much about it. They're like a society or private club. Every so often I'll read something about some historical figure and their ties to Freemasonry. But I've never read anything that described what it was about."

"A secret society?"

"Maybe."

I scrolled down the page further and saw in the sidebar index a link to Freemasonry. Below the link was a symbol.

"I've seen this," I breathed.

"What?"

"This," I pointed. "I've seen this symbol before. Carved into the entrance of the Wriothesley's estate."

Caleb read the description beneath the symbol. "The square and compass is the single most identifiable symbol of Freemasonry. Both the square and compass are architect's tools, and are used in Masonic ritual as emblems to teach symbolic lessons."

I sat back remembering what little I had read from my mother's diary, about Emerick and his meetings. Was my mother a member of this society? "That's why Camilla showed me her tattoo. She thought I knew, that I would understand she was a member of Eastern Star." I turned to Caleb. "Can we print this?"

"They'll charge us."

I gave him an exasperated look, "I don't care!"

"Sorry." He took the mouse and started scrolling through the menus trying to figure out how to print the page. When he left to collect the pages from the printer, I scrolled down the page and read, See Also—*Bilderbergs, Bilderberg Conference, Bilderberg Club.* I clicked each link but they all led to blank white pages that said *Error: Page not found.*

"Well that's annoying," I said.

"Try it in the search window," Sophie said.

I typed Bilderberg into the window. One result came back, *Bilderberg Conference,* I clicked on the link. Sophie and I leaned our heads together and read.

The Bilderberg Conference is an unofficial, annual, conference that is invitation only. It is speculated that approximately 130 guests attend every year. Attendees are thought to be people of influence in the fields of politics, business, banking, media, and military from all over the world. The conferences are closed to the public and the media and no press releases are issued.

Caleb returned with the pages. "Here we go."

"Wait," I highlighted the section Sophie and I just found and sent it to the printer. "One more thing."

Something through the glass window caught my attention. I looked out past the glare from the café's interior lights. Tourists and shoppers still wandered the brick sidewalk in and out of the small shops, a blue compact car and a couple on a motorcycle drove slowly past.

A woman stood on the other side of the street staring at me.

When the traffic passed, she started running across the street. She waved her arms in the air and yelled something I couldn't hear.

It was Camilla.

Too fast, I thought. Something black and heavy was moving too fast.

"Okay," Caleb said. "That should..."

I grabbed his arm.

Camilla's body was hit, she spiraled up and over the hood of the Land Rover racing down the street.

People stopped, stared.

Camilla bounced, like a doll over the vehicle's hood and landed crumpled, broken in the middle of the street.

The Land Rover was gone.

"Caleb!"

A second ticked, like a heartbeat. No one moved.

Blood pooled around Camilla's head.

"Oh my God!" a woman from inside the café screamed.

A man rushed to Camilla, a woman pulled her cell phone from her purse.

I stared at Camilla's broken legs, her twisted, lifeless form for a moment, then she disappeared behind a crowd, surrounded by onlookers and others trying to help her.

"What's happened?" Caleb stood and stared out the window.

People began shouting and talking.

"A woman's just been run over!"

"Call the police!"

"Is anyone a doctor?"

People from the café began getting their things and rushing out the door.

"Charlotte? I can't believe it, how horrible," Caleb said.

And my mind replayed, trying to make sense of what it couldn't. I saw her running as if in slow motion. Her eyes focused only on me, her face worried, afraid. She was shouting something I couldn't hear, but I saw the words form on her lips.

Charlotte. They know.

CHAPTER SEVENTEEN

IN CONTROL

I was scared.

I tried to call Susan but I only got her voice mail. When I called Oasis they wouldn't let me speak to my father.

"Please," I begged. "I need to speak with him."

"I'm sorry Miss. There are no exceptions. We can't allow Mr. Steven's healing process to be compromised."

"I'm his daughter!"

"I'm sorry but you need to talk to whomever is taking care of you while your father is in rehab."

That may *be* the problem I felt like screaming.

Ms. Steward was sympathetic, "Oh, how awful. And you knew her?"

How could I explain? Yes I knew her, sort of. "I met her when I was at their house."

"Well it's a dreadful thing to witness. Why don't you get some rest. I'll make tea."

I didn't want to rest. There was no way I could. I left Ms. Steward standing over the kettle and went to my room. My small shopping bag from the jewelry store was on the bed. I opened it, pulled the silver chain from the tiny brown box and turned to get my cross off the dresser.

I didn't see it. The figurines twirled and posed across the white lace runner, but my sapphire cross was not where I'd left it. My breath caught in my chest, "No," I whispered. I checked under the lace and behind the dresser, the floor all around the dresser but it was no use—it was gone.

When? When did I last see it? Had it been there last night? While Caleb and I were working the puzzle box had I looked and seen it still laying there? I didn't know for sure but I didn't think so. We had been so transfixed by the box. *Stupid, stupid, stupid,* "Why didn't I put it somewhere safer?" Because it never occurred to me I should have to. *The library.* When the house was broken into and the library vandalized, the man in the woods—he had been in here, he must have taken my cross.

Why? I closed my eyes and touched the bare space at my throat, how could it possibly be of value to anyone but me. The loss of her last gift settled like a weight in my chest—I would likely never see it again.

My hand brushed the tears off my cheeks and I left to find Sophie and Caleb in the library.

Sophie was lying on one of the sofas staring at the ceiling while Caleb pressed out a limp tune on the piano.

I stood at the entrance for a moment, not sure what to do next. "My cross was stolen," I stated.

They both turned their heads to look at me, but I could tell from their expressions they were still in as much shock from witnessing the accident as I was.

"Are you sure?" Caleb asked.

I nodded my head, "It's not anywhere. I'm sure it was the man who took the diaries and wrecked the library...and killed Camilla."

They both stared at me.

"I'm responsible for her death," I said suddenly. "She was trying to warn me about something. Someone."

"That's ridiculous," Sophie tried to console me. "It's not even remotely your fault. Were you driving that car?"

"No, but I'm the reason she was there."

"You don't know that for sure," Caleb stopped playing. "It could have been a horrible coincidence."

"I saw what she was yelling."

"You think you saw."

"I did see Caleb! She was shouting, Charlotte, they know, Charlotte they know."

"Who knows what though?" Sophie asked.

I didn't know. "Whatever she had been trying to warn me about that day at the Wriothesleys' has something to do with her death. I know it."

I heard Ms. Steward's thick heels on the marble floor behind me. "Charlotte."

I turned and saw her pinched expression. "Yes?"

She closed the distance between us and peeked into the library before she told me in a low tone. "Hayden Wriothesley is here to see you." She glanced at Caleb who was watching us. "He said his father sent him to fetch you."

Caleb got up from the piano. "What's up?"

I sighed. It was impossible to hide my nervousness. One because I knew Caleb was going to have a fit when he found out Hayden was here and two, Hayden was here and he was taking me to see his father.

"Mum?"

Ms. Steward didn't answer. She hadn't asked any questions about Caleb and me, but I could tell by the expression on her face that she knew there was something between us. And Hayden Wriothesley's presence here wouldn't likely leave her son jumping for joy.

"Charlotte?" he asked apprehensive.

He was going to hate this. "Caleb..."

He looked shocked, his eyes locked on something over my shoulder. His face blazed with hatred.

Oh no. I could guess why.

"Charlotte," Hayden voice reveled behind me.

I turned in a flash and saw him coming fast across the floor. As soon as he registered my distress he beamed.

"Sweetums," he smiled. "We really must be going." He gave his watch an exaggerated tap.

I could feel Caleb's fury radiate through the room.

"Hayden," I begged. "Please wait out front. I'll be there in a minute."

I could see from the wicked look on his face that he had no intention of doing anything I asked.

What should I do? Hayden was almost at my side—he was absolutely about to do something that would drive Caleb insane. I could only watch, paralyzed by Hayden's raw audacity and my own angst.

Hayden's eyes darted into the library and then quickly back to me. He couldn't hide his amusement, the smirk on his lips was meant only to goad Caleb further.

A game. Hayden practically crouched and sprang at me and I felt myself being swept up into his arms and then he actually twirled me around burying his face in my neck.

"Stop it!" I thumped his back lamely.

He put my feet back on the floor as I tried to regain my balance and straighten my shirt.

Sophie was sitting up now, her eyes wide and her mouth hung slightly open.

Caleb was very still. His hands and jaw were clenched but he seemed to be keeping it together.

I brushed my hair back off my face and started to fix my ponytail, "Hayden," I started in on him. If he thought I would allow this, he was crazy. "Don't ever..." the look on his face stopped me.

He was staring at Caleb, his smug expression openly mocking him. Daring Caleb—the son of a housekeeper who worked for his father's business associate. Hayden's eyes said everything but the words. *I dare you to do anything.*

Hayden turned to me, his face suddenly light again, "Don't ever what?" he teased.

I opened my mouth to yell at him, but nothing came out.

Hayden smiled indulgently. "Never mind then." He picked up my hand and pulled me towards the entrance like an errant child. "You tell me when you think of it. But you're to come with me now. Daddy said."

I followed clumsily while he pulled me along. When I looked back, I could see Ms. Steward going to Caleb, trying to calm him. He ignored her and continued to stare after us, his eyes locking with mine, his body burning with hate.

When Hayden and I crossed the entrance and slipped from Caleb's sight, I could hear a commotion in the library behind us. Ms. Steward and Sophie were talking excitedly and then a loud crash echoed across the marble floor, like a thousand splinters of glass.

As we passed through the entrance Hayden laughed. "Someone's not happy."

I yanked my hand from Hayden's. "You're a jerk."

"Maybe. But you're coming with me anyway." He lunged for my arm but I dodged his grasp and gave him a look that seemed to pause his ego stampede.

"Don't touch me again," I hissed.

I passed him, walked calmly to his car, opened the door and got in.

Hayden was still standing in Gaersum Aern's entrance, framed by the creeping ivy. He lingered a moment longer and then pointed his fob at the black beast and started the engine. The blare that erupted from the speakers made me jump.

"Spoiled pig," I whispered to myself.

Hayden got in, slammed his door and turned down the volume.

"Please tell me you're not in love with the unportioned pauper."

"What?"

"Steward," he jerked his head at the house. "He's your uncle's charity case. Pays for him to go to school."

"What do you care if I am?"

He shrugged and started his car, but the scowl on his face didn't match his attempt at nonchalance. "I don't care," he snapped shoving the stick shift into first. "I just don't know why you'd *want* to hurt him."

Hearing his words, my own fear spoken out loud, it felt like a punch in the chest.

We throttled up the driveway and he looked at me to register his impact.

It was taking me too long to gather my wits. "I have no intention of hurting him."

"But you will," he said with a certainty that frightened me. "You will because you belong with me."

I didn't say anything. I only stared out the window and pretended to ignore him. But my insides felt like utter confusion. I wanted to laugh in his face, cut him low with words aimed directly at his ego. But it felt like my very fiber was attuned to his every movement. As if I could feel the touch of the steering wheel under his hand, the pull of his jeans across his thighs.

The inside of the car felt like an energy chamber, both exciting and sickening.

"You don't know what you're talking about."

Now he laughed at me. "Don't I? You're going to sit there and tell me you don't feel this."

But I did feel it, wave after wave of electricity. It was everywhere.

"Do you have any idea what the last week was like for me? That fat housekeeper intercepting my every call—and you— *I'm sick*," he mocked.

"I was sick."

"You think I care? I've never experienced anything like this. I can't sleep, I never eat, other girls call and I don't even want to look at them."

"That's all this is," I said as calmly as I could. "Hayden Wriothesley finally found something he can't have."

I expected him to shoot back, but he didn't. "I thought about that," was all he said. He shook his head, "I don't think that's it."

"Caleb is my boyfriend Hayden," I said flatly.

"No, he isn't."

"Yes, he is," I insisted. "I can't believe you have the nerve—"

"It's not nerve or conceit or any other nasty word you want to fling at me. It's just fact Charlotte. Charity Case can think whatever he wants and you can pretend anything you like, but you know it's true."

"What's true," I dared him to say what I couldn't explain.

He hesitated for a moment and I thought I had him. His vanity wouldn't let him completely expose himself.

The car slowed down and I heard the crunch of the loose gravel as we pulled over to the side of the road.

"What are you doing?" I asked.

Hayden put the car in park and turned to me. "I don't know what you want to call it," he said. There wasn't even a hint of sarcasm on his face. "Soul mate, true love, other half, frankly I don't give a damn. But," he reached up and slid his hand behind my neck and my breath stopped. "all I know is that I want to be with you every moment."

He pulled me to him. His mouth was warm and soft—fire exploded through my body. I didn't stop him.

Caleb, my mind yelled. *You're hurting him.*

I was hurting him. "Stop," I said limply against Hayden lips.

"No," he kissed me harder, his other hand slipping around my waist.

Oh God. I felt drugged. I reached up and held his rough face in my hands. *Stop, stop, stop*, my mind yelled at me. But this rational thought felt far away.

I wanted Hayden.

His mouth slid away from mine and down my neck. I could feel his hand slipping up under my shirt.

Caleb's kind eyes flashed clearly in my mind. *I love you Charlotte.*

I placed both of my hands in the middle of Hayden's chest and shoved as hard as I could. He barely moved, but it was enough space between us for me to turn and open the door.

"Charlotte!" he called after me but I was already ten feet from the car.

I needed air. Air and space. I stood with my arms crossed trying to just breathe.

Hayden was getting out of the car. I worried he would come to me, hold me, confuse me more.

But he stood at his door with his hands clasped on the roof of his car. "I'm sorry," he said.

I looked up in surprise. I hadn't expected an apology.

He smirked, "I guess I'm just used to girls who move a little faster."

What? He thought I was upset because we were moving too fast? My confusion was swept away by anger. I narrowed my eyes at him. "Just take me to see your father," I snapped. "I am not doing this," I motioned to the car. "I don't care what you think it is. I am not your...anything. Got it?"

"No," he whispered. "I don't *got it.*" He slid back into the car and started the engine.

I hesitated, not sure if I was able to get back in the car. My body trembled, warring between guilt over what had already happened and fear that I wouldn't be able to stop it from happening again.

I didn't want to ever feel that out of control again.

He was waiting, watching me in the rearview mirror. I walked slowly, *you are in control Charlotte,* I silently chanted. *You are.*

By the time I slid onto the taut leather seat, I still hadn't convinced myself.

He didn't say a word. As soon as my door closed, Hayden released the clutch and the Aston Martin rocketed up the quiet country road.

I am in control.

This time, there was no waiting for Emerick Wriothesley—he had been waiting for me.

"Charlotte," he greeted me at his office door with a strained smile. "Please come in."

I took the same high backed chair I'd sat in the day I'd met my uncle.

"I'm afraid we've had a bit of an upset since your last visit," he sighed taking his seat. "Most distressing really," he opened a drawer in his desk and reached in. "My wife Margot is simply beside herself."

He pulled a blue booklet from the drawer and placed it on the desktop between us.

It took me half a second to guess what it was.

"This belongs to you?" he pushed it towards me.

I stared for a moment, and then reached out and took it. Flipping it open to the first page, I could clearly see a picture of my own face. My passport.

"I am very sorry. We were quite surprised to find it actually. One of our housekeepers was in a most unfortunate accident, hit and run." He shook his head, "Very unfortunate," he sighed. "But then, when we were gathering her things to send to her family, your passport was discovered. I don't know how it should be in her possession," he looked pointedly at me. "But then, I don't make a habit of speaking ill of the dead."

He knew exactly how she got it, Camilla had taken it from my bag the day I was here. Her words whispered through my head, *trust no one Charlotte.*

Not even her?

Emerick sighed. "Please accept my apologies. We do try to be careful about who we hire," he raised his eyebrows. "Sometimes people slip through the cracks."

"Thank you," I said placing it back in my bag.

"It would be difficult for you to get home without that little document."

"Yes," I whispered.

"One might even say Camilla's accident was fortunate, for you that is. At least we were able to retrieve that before she could do whatever she had planned. I imagine she had intentions of selling it, maybe even identity theft."

Fortunate? It wasn't a word I would have used, stolen passport or not. Suddenly, the memory of Camilla hit me, waving her arms and running towards me. *Charlotte, they know.* "I suppose."

Emerick pursed his lips and nodded. What did he know? I was expecting him to say something else but he stood up. "Thank you for coming Charlotte."

His sudden movement surprised me. I sat a moment longer before getting to my feet. "Um, thank you," I mumbled.

"Again, many apologies."

"Yes," I moved awkwardly around the chair and headed for the door.

"Oh, I almost forgot," he said reaching back into his drawer. This time he handed me a small purple envelope. "The midsummer ball," he explained.

I had forgotten about his previous invitation. I reached across his desk, the envelope felt thick and expensive.

"I told Margot how much you look like Elizabeth, she is very excited to meet you."

Margot. The name suddenly clicked. From my mother's diary, Margot had been one of her friends.

"Where is she?" I asked.

"Paris. She's vacationing with our daughter, Diana."

Daughter? "I didn't realize—"

"They'll be stopping at our London home, but should be back next week for the rest of the summer."

This was their *summer* home. I nodded. "Thank you for the invitation," I placed it inside my passport.

He picked up the phone and pushed a button. "Hayden,

please meet Miss. Stevens in my study."

Outside his door, I stopped and stared at the strange portrait of Francis Bacon. I rubbed my finger lightly over the nameplate. According to the Spencer family tree, he was an ancestor of mine. Why did Emerick have his portrait in his hall? I stared for a moment at the dramatic mask hiding Francis's face—it annoyed me. This man, Francis Bacon, had something to do with all of this. I wished I could reach back in time and rip that mask from his face. I needed to know who was behind it. Who was he? Where were my mother's diaries? What was inside the emerald puzzle box? And what was between my mother and Emerick?

Too many questions without answers. The diaries were here, I knew it. I thought of Camilla's warning, *there are eyes and ears everywhere.* Regardless of what Emerick wanted me to believe about Camilla, I knew there was more to it. She had been trying to warn me when she was run over in Glastonbury. *Trying to warn me*—all at once it occurred to me, and a chill ran through me. What if it wasn't a horrible accident? What if Camilla was killed because *they* knew, like she said, and *they* also knew she was trying to help me in someway. It was no accident. Camilla had been killed.

Emerick's hall felt tight and it was as if a thousand eyes were all focused on me at once. Were there cameras even in here? Was Emerick watching me at this very moment? I resisted the urge to turn my head up and search for cameras. If I was going to find my mother's diaries, I couldn't afford for

Emerick to know that I was on to him. I would need him to believe that I was here to see Hayden and pass the summer.

I forced myself to start walking towards the study. There had to be a way to search for them without attracting attention to the fact that I was searching. I needed Hayden, he would be my cover—access to the house and hopefully information that might help me think of where Emerick may be keeping the diaries. Goosebumps broke out up and down my arms and my legs felt sluggish with fear, I knew what I was going to have to do. I was going to have to break into Emerick's office.

Who was Emerick Wriothesley?

When I opened the door to the study, Hayden was lounging on the sofa talking on his cell phone. He knew I was there but was obviously making a point of not looking at me right away.

"Whatever you want," he said into the phone. "...I can't right now," he glanced up at me. "...Yeah, tonight. I'll come get you," he smirked. "Me too," he finished with a leer and slid his phone off.

If he thought I was going to be jealous he was insane. And to prove it, I completely ignored whatever it was I'd just heard. "Can I use your computer?"

When Hayden opened the door I groaned. His computer was in his bedroom. Just look for what you want and leave, I thought.

The room was enormous. With high ceilings and light

gray-papered walls, it was bright and open. His furniture was sparse and minimalistic, two large black leather bean bags for watching the big screen TV mounted to the wall and a king sized steel framed bed. I had expected posters of half naked models, but there was actual artwork on the walls.

Hayden sat down at his desk and started his computer. Aside from his phone call, he had been unusually quiet since we'd arrived.

"Your dad said you have a sister."

"Yes, Diana."

"How old is she?"

"Thirteen," he got up from the desk chair. "There you go."

"Thanks." I sat down and logged into my email account. Susan still hadn't returned my call from earlier. I sent her a quick email.

I don't have easy access to a computer. Can you send me an international phone with Internet capability? I know dad will take care of it when he's out. Please call the house as soon as you can. I need to talk to you. Have you been able to speak with my dad? I pressed send, pulled up the search engine and typed, Francis Bacon.

Many pages came back. I didn't want to sit here and read them all. "Can I use your printer," I asked.

"Go ahead," he shrugged.

I pulled up and printed out the first five entries. I could hear the printer somewhere under the desk. I leaned under and pulled out the first few pages. The print was faint and smeared. "I think you're out of toner."

Hayden came over and took the mouse from my hand. He stood over me and switched the printer destination. I took a deep breath. It was hard being this close to him. I couldn't understand it, there were so many things about him that I hated. But the attraction between us was raw and physical, like a living thing with its own personality. "I'll send it to my dad's workroom."

"His office?" I asked, my stomach flipped. This might be my opportunity to poke around, see if Emerick was keeping my mother's diaries in there.

Hayden finished clicking and gave me the mouse back. "No. His workroom's in the basement."

"The basement?"

I didn't much care for basements.

CHAPTER EIGHTEEN

DOOR IN THE FLOOR

Hayden led me through what seemed like a maze of hallways and rooms. When we passed it, I recognized the entrance to the atrium where Camilla had warned me.

"Your father said your housekeeper was killed in Glastonbury?"

"Hit and run...they haven't found the guy. They won't."

"How do you know?"

"No one got the license plate," he shrugged. "She was a complete nutter and a thief anyway. You wouldn't believe the crap dad found in her room. She had an alter in there complete with voodoo candles and pentagrams all over it."

Pentagrams.

"She had taken some of dad's files from his office, if she wasn't already dead he would have killed her himself," Hayden said. He stopped outside a door and looked at me. "Didn't she take something of yours?" he asked opening the door in front of us.

"My passport," I said wondering if there was a black Land Rover with a dented grill sitting in the Wriothesley's garage.

The room we walked into shocked me. It was dark until Hayden switched on a small hurricane lamp centered on a rough looking table in the middle of the room. It was like we'd traveled back in time. The floors were dirt and the walls looked like an old shack. "What is this?"

"Dad had the larger house built around this one."

"Why?" I asked following him. "Why not just tear it down?"

Hayden bent over and grasped a metal ring in the center of the floor. "Who knows? He liked it I guess." He pulled and a square wooden door opened up into the floor.

I stared into the black pit at my feet and my heart sped up. "I can't go in there," I blurted.

Hayden looked up at me with an evil smile. "Scared of the dark?"

"No," I tried to cover. But I gave myself away by instinctually taking a step back. I waited for his merciless teasing and taunts.

Feet first, Hayden slipped down the hole. A moment latter, bright florescent light radiated from inside. His head popped back out, "Better?"

I pursed my lips. Light or not, I still wasn't thrilled about going down there. I took a step forward.

"Come on, I'll protect you from the bogey we keep down

here."

"Funny," I snapped.

He disappeared with a crooked smile back into the hole.

"Okay," I sighed. There was a lot of light. *You can do this Charlotte.*

I looked down the hole and saw Hayden halfway down the ladder. I turned around and climbed down after him.

"Nice bum," he said.

"Shut up Hayden."

I was almost at the bottom when I felt something brush my arm. Hayden had stopped on the ladder and I had climbed down between his arms.

"Charlotte," he whispered near my ear.

"Cut it out," I shrugged him away. "You're going to make me fall."

"Impossible, I'm right behind you."

"Still. Quit messing around."

The lights went off.

"Hayden!"

I felt his hand press against my abdomen.

"Turn the light back on, now!"

His mouth was on my neck.

"I'm not kidding, Hayden!"

"Why? This is nice," he purred into my ear.

I could see the light from the room above me. I started to move up the ladder but Hayden's grip around my waist tightened.

I couldn't help it, panic exploded through my head. My scream echoed though the small space around us and I shoved back against him with all my weight.

Hayden let go of my waist and the light clicked back on.

I clutched the rungs in front of me and tried to slow my breathing.

"Bloody hell! I was only playing!" he barked before climbing down the last five feet.

I closed my eyes and forced myself to loosen my grip on the ladder. *Relax Charlotte, breathe.* "I *told* you to cut it out!"

"Well I didn't know you were going to completely freak out!"

I took a deep breath and lowered myself to the tiled floor below.

"You bloodied my nose," he cried.

I turned and saw his blood smeared face and hand. I wasn't sorry. "Well...that's what happens when you mess around."

"Apology accepted," he said sarcastically. Blood poured from his nostrils.

"You need to tip your head back...pinch you nose. No, like this," I showed him.

Hayden copied me and the blood flow seemed to slow.

"Now, where's the printer?"

Emerick's 'workroom' was amazing. "What is this?"

Hayden flipped a switch and the display in front of us became even more incredible as tiny little lights illuminated the entire structure. "He wanted to be an architect."

It was a sprawling miniature city constructed in such detail, I couldn't image the patience and hours it would require. There were gleaming skyscrapers and several brick churches. Row shops and apartment buildings. Tiny human figures were frozen in their artificial world, mid-step, walking a dog, pushing a child on a swing, hailing a cab, coming out of a grocer—thousands of tiny people. There was an expansive park with clumps of broccoli shaped trees sprouting near ponds, and walking paths.

I didn't recognize the city. "Where is it supposed to be?"

Hayden stared blankly at the structure not answering. He turned to me, "It's in his mind."

"It's not a real city?" I asked disbelieving. It looked so real, so intricate—I fully expected it to be a replica of somewhere.

Hayden shook his head slowly and pursed his lips. "No. It's his world, his design from start to finish. His little buildings and little people and tiny cars...he is the designer and builder."

"It must have taken ages."

"He's worked on this ever since I can remember...my whole life. He adds to it all the time. Spends hours down here."

I reached out to gently prick my finger on the largest church spire.

"No," Hayden quickly caught my hand. He sighed and let my hand go. "We mustn't touch," he said absently, parroting what was probably an often repeated instruction.

"Why didn't he become an architect?

"Because he became a banker."

"But why?"

Hayden shrugged. "It's not the kind of thing the family does." Hayden looked at me sideways. "Actually, it's interesting."

"What is?"

"You, being from...outside. It's sort of weird that you would even consider that architecture would have even been something my father would have pursued as a career. Most people are so awed by who he is, they never even think to consider he might have been something else." He returned his gaze to the perfect world before us. "I certainly never considered it," he whispered.

"Because he's the cousin of the royal family?" I asked.

Hayden seemed to be thinking about my question. "It's not that actually. The royal family has lots of extended family, being a cousin is not as prestigious as you might imagine. It certainly doesn't hurt as far as connections, girls like it." He added eying me as if he were hoping I'd have a jealous fit or something. "But I don't think my dad's influence has much to do with the royal family to be honest. In his business, he's the royal," he whispered.

"Hayden?"

"Hmm?"

"Who is your father?" It felt like a silly question and I expected him to laugh. But his brow creased and his gaze grew more intense.

"Emerick Wriothesley," he said softly. "Emerick Wriothesley is president of the world's largest international bank. He manages and controls money all over the world...the power behind powerful men." Emerick looked up into my eyes. "The prime minister once called my father at eight o'clock at night on his private cell. A real emergency," he added mysteriously.

I thought of my few brief meetings with Emerick and smiled nervously. "You're joking." But I could tell from his stoic expression that he wasn't. "Oh my God," I whispered. If Hayden was trying to impress me, it worked. "What was it?"

Hayden laughed and looked away. "He doesn't tell me anything. When the call came in he left the dinner table and closed his office door." Hayden stared out across the miniature city before us. "Honestly, I have no idea who my father is." He waved his hand over the city. "This is as close as I get." He looked me in the eye. "But don't touch."

I caught myself reaching out to him, a swell of sympathy rising in me. I knew what it was like to live with a parent you couldn't reach. To distract myself, I walked around the massive structure and studied it from other sides and angles—it was dangerous to let my guard down with Hayden. As annoying as he could be, it was safer when Hayden was acting like a jerk.

At the far end of the structure, a small square building caught my attention. It was off on its own, surrounded by tiny rolling hills and a dense forest. "What's this?"

Hayden looked to where I was pointing. "That," he explained. "Is his mother's house. His real mother. The one he would have built for her had she lived I suppose."

It was surprising. Given the size of the Wriothesley summer home, I would have imagined Emerick creating something grander. The house in the model was quaint. Simple and adequate, the four sided single story brick house looked like something from a storybook, like the house the wolf couldn't blow down.

It looked like home and, I suddenly realized, Emerick wished it was.

CHAPTER NINETEEN

FRANCIS BACON

I wasn't looking forward to facing Caleb.

Hayden was quiet and contemplative after our trip to the basement. The whole ride home he behaved, only uttering goodbye as I climbed out of the Aston Martin. It was one tantrum avoided.

But as I crossed the gravel drive and Hayden pulled slowly away, I saw the swish of an upstairs curtain closing. The real tirade was waiting for me inside. I wondered what the chances were of me sneaking inside and heading straight for my room.

Crossing into the marble entrance, I expected to see Caleb come flying down the staircase, ready with his interrogation questions fresh on his mind. Seconds passed, I knew he had seen me from the window.

Then I heard it, the distant sound of the library piano drifting through the hall. I stepped lightly across the floor, careful so my shoes wouldn't echo and give me away. At the edge of the library door, I leaned my head around and saw Caleb hunched over the keys intent on the rapid classical notes that poured from his fingers. Sophie was sprawled on one of the couches with headphones and a magazine.

Who was upstairs? Ms. Steward?

I backed slowly away from the door, I didn't want to answer any questions. I was half afraid the truth about what happened in Hayden's car would come tumbling out of me. The undeniable physical pull I felt for Hayden was hard to shrug off a second time. He hadn't exactly attacked me against my will.

There was no way to explain to Caleb. Yes I really, really *want* Hayden...but honestly I hate his guts.

I leaped the stairs two at a time, stopping at the top to catch my breath and let my heart slow. I kept an eye out for Ms. Steward, she had seen me arrive but I was hoping to have a couple hours to myself. I needed to think. I wanted to read through the pages I'd printed up about Francis Bacon, there was the book I'd borrowed from Eve, and I wanted to seriously work on the puzzle box.

I also needed time to think about where Emerick could be hiding the diaries. His workroom and his office were the two most likely places. The workroom seemed to be the easier to access, I could always use the printer as an excuse again, but I had no idea how I would get into Emerick's office undetected. And I would have to figure out a way to get Hayden to clue me in on where the cameras were without making him suspicious.

I closed my door gently behind me until I heard the click of the ancient latch catching and headed straight for the battered red sofa in the small library. Reaching up under the dusty shade, I rolled the switch between my thumb and finger until a cone of warm light flooded the cushions.

Lying back against the rolled arm, I sifted through the printed pages and began to read. Right away, the dates caught my attention.

Sir Francis Bacon, Born January 22, 1561 Died April 9 1626.

It certainly seemed more reasonable than the Spencer family tree claiming that he lived to be one hundred and eighty nine years old. I kept reading.

English statesman, philosopher, scientist, author and lawyer he is considered the father of Empiricism (the theory that knowledge is gathered from the evidence of our experiences.) He is responsible for establishing the deductive methodologies for scientific questioning referred to as the Baconian Method or, as it is better known, the scientific method.

The scientific method. Of course, I knew I had heard the name before. My physics textbook last year had a one-sentence acknowledgment about Francis Bacon and his contribution to the scientific method. The unit test had been about the process itself, which I could still remember: Conduct your observation, Form a hypothesis, Predict the outcome, and finally, Test and experiment.

I was the descendant of the guy who developed the scientific method?

I read on. Francis Bacon studied to be a lawyer and sat on counsel for Queen Elizabeth I. There were pages and pages about his philosophical works, essays, and books.

Main article: New Atlantis

In New Atlantis (1623) Bacon's ideals for a utopian society were expressed. In his fictional country of Bensalem, "generosity and enlightenment, dignity and splendor, piety and public spirit" were the most common attributes of the people living there. In New Atlantis, Bacon envisioned a future of human discovery and knowledge that was available to all people in a society, not only the privileged and elite.

Some scholars believe Bacon's ideas for improving the human condition, that he laid out in New Atlantis, were the foundational elements for the creation of the New World in North America. He envisioned a land where women would have greater rights, slavery would be abolished, debtor's prisons were eliminated, and a separation between church and state where citizens are free to express themselves religiously and politically. Francis Bacon played a leading role in creating the British colonies in America, particularly Virginia, the Carolinas, and Newfoundland.

I laid the papers against my chest. If he was so instrumental in the creation of the United States, how was it that in all my history classes, I had never heard the name Francis Bacon mentioned once?

Thomas Jefferson, the third president of the United States identified, "Francis Bacon, John Locke, and Isaac Newton," as, "the three greatest men that have ever lived, without any exception." Their works in the physical and moral sciences were instrumental in Jefferson's education and worldview.

My fingers tingled and I sat up straighter. Isaac Newton--*The Alchemical Writings of Sir Isaac Newton*. Now cited by the third president of the United States along with Francis Bacon—*who I was related to*—as one of the greatest men in all time. There was the note my mother had written and the portrait of Francis Bacon hanging in Emerick's hallway.

Along with the portrait of George Washington, I reminded myself. And I had thought, at the time, that it was odd for an English gentleman to have a portrait of the first president of the United States hanging in his home.

There was so much more, I read over scholarly studies, findings, and theories. Accusations that were made against him and treatise offered in his defense. His personal connections during his lifetime and the long reaching influence his work has had on western society. By the time I reached the last page, it had grown dark outside and my eyes were burning. I rubbed them gently, watching the flashing lights the pressure created. I was tired.

I opened my eyes and waited for the blurring to pass and the words on the page to refocus. When they did, the headline halfway down the page caught my attention.

Bacon and Shakespeare

The Baconian theory regarding the Shakespearean author-ship claims that Francis Bacon was the true creator of the Shake-speare works, not William Shakespeare, the actor from Stratford. Proponents of the theory point to the fact that the actor from Stratford was uneducated and raised in a home with illiterate parents that didn't own a single book aside from the family bible. Furthermore there was little opportunity to be exposed to the type of schooling, knowledge, and resources that would be required to create such a cannon of work. They attest that "Francis Bacon was the unacknowledged son of Queen Elizabeth I and Sir Rob-ert Dudley. Francis Bacon's extensive education was designed for a prince and future king. His experiences at both the English and French courts are what laid the foundational grounds for the work commonly attributed to an actor from Stratford who signed his last will and testament with an X."

Mainstream scholars reject all arguments supporting Bacon as the author of the Shakespearean works citing that the poetry that is attributed to Francis Bacon is too dissimilar to the work of Shakespeare.

I lay all the way down on the couch and let my arm with the pages hang over the edge. I opened my hand and let the pile fall the few inches to the Persian rug. I brought my arm back up and rested my forearm across my eyes, shielding them from the lamp's light. Did my mother know about this theo-ry? Did she know that some people thought that an ancestor of ours was the unacknowledged son of Queen Elizabeth I? That he might have written Shakespeare?

My face felt strained and I could feel my throat getting tight from the tears. *Wasn't that an amazing possibility?* My tears ran down my face. *Some people think we might be the descendants of the real Shakespeare—of Elizabeth I.* I couldn't help it, I was tired and overwhelmed and my tears came harder. "Amazing," I whispered.

Even if it wasn't true, "Isn't this the kind of thing most mothers would tell their daughter?" I whispered to myself.

Certainly my mother had known about this, hadn't she? Why didn't she tell me?

"Why didn't you tell me?"

I wished I could ask her.

It's dark. I am alone and afraid. It is silent, not a sound, not a whisper or a breath. I am going to scream. I open my mouth; feel the muscles in my jaw stretch wide in panic and loss. But I have no sound, not even the hum of existence can be heard on the air. I close my eyes, but the blackness is the same. I cannot escape the dark, even in my own mind.

There is a flash of white, far away. I know it is her and I run, towards the light, towards the twirl of her summer skirt. "Mother! Please!" But there is no sound from me, only a silent scream echoing through my brain.

I am closer, her hem flashes more and more in the light, she's spinning faster and faster. This time, this time, this time let me touch her, I pray. I can see her whole skirt now, fanning out around her. There is her waist, the curve of her breast, her white slender arm is reaching out for me. I can't keep up.

"Mom! Wait, stop. Please, stop!"

I can see her bare shoulders spinning, her slender neck. But her head is tilted, questioning. Tragic—Comic—Tragic—Comic—Tragic—Comic. The dramatic mask frowns and smiles at me faster and faster until they blur and I can no longer tell the difference. "Mother," I stop running and beg. "Please."

But the light is leaving her, already she if far away, her skirt turns, then her hem, I see only a single flash of white and she is gone.

It is dark.

I am alone.

CHAPTER TWENTY

UNCLE

Someone is shaking my shoulder. "Charlotte, wake up."

When I open my eyes, I see Caleb standing over me. I'm still lying on the red sofa in the small library connected to my bedroom.

"Your uncle came home while you were out," he said not meeting my eyes. "He wants to speak with you."

I sat up and pushed my hair from my face. The pages I printed on Francis Bacon were still splayed all over the rug near Caleb's feet. When I looked up at Caleb, I could see the confrontation with Hayden still hanging between us. "Are you angry?"

Caleb shook his head and looked into my eyes. "Not with you anyway." He sat down on the sofa next to me and stared at the floor. "I can't stand you being near him Charlotte. The way he looks at you...you might not see it, but I know he's after you." When he finally looked me in the eyes, I saw the torment this caused him. "Please, I'm begging you…"

"I can't make that promise, so please don't ask me too." I reached for his hand. "I'm sorry, but finding those diaries means more to me than anything right now and after yesterday, I know for sure that Emerick has them."

"You don't know that," Caleb said, anger edged his words.

"I do because yesterday Emerick gave me my passport, which was in my bag with the diary the day it was taken. He said Camilla took it, and maybe she did, but Emerick has the diary now. That's what Camilla was trying to warn me about in Glastonbury, Emerick knows something that's in that diary, something to do with my mother." I stopped. Caleb had closed his eyes and had his head in his hands. "Caleb, I know this sounds crazy, but I think Emerick has something to do with my mother's disappearance and Camilla's death. That was no accident."

"Charlotte, listen to yourself. You don't have any evidence. You said yourself he gave you your passport back. If he knew—"

"He conveniently blamed Camilla," I interrupted. "All he has to do is pretend he doesn't know anything about the diary that went missing at the exact same time."

"Don't go back there. Even if you're right, and you're not, but even if you are then everything you've said is exactly why you shouldn't put yourself in danger. If Emerick Wriothesley is the type of man who can make one woman disappear without a trace and then have another murdered without arousing even a breath of suspicion by the authorities, then I should think you would want to stay as far away from him as possible."

"I need the proof."

"You won't find it."

Angry, I stood up glared at him. "I'm not asking for your help Caleb and I certainly don't need your permission. I will find what I need," I said and stormed out of the room.

"Charlotte wait," he called after me. "I have to tell you something."

But I didn't want to hear any more of his argument. "Save it," I yelled and slammed the door.

Outside my uncle's office, I tried to calm down before knocking. I pressed my temples and willed my breathing to slow down. I was mad with Caleb for not supporting me in this, but I was also afraid he would find out how right he was. Hayden did want me, but what was worse, and what would kill Caleb if he knew, was my own weakness. My own irrational attraction to Hayden that felt difficult to control. When I was with him, there was the constant pull to just give in to it—even though I knew it wasn't good for me. Being in Hayden's arms felt good, his mouth on mine, running down my neck, it felt good and that made me feel guilty.

I knocked on my uncle's door.

"Come in," he called.

I opened the door and was surprised to see my uncle sitting

271

in the dark. I stood for a moment by the door waiting for my eyes to adjust. "Come in and take a seat Charlotte."

"Do you want the light on?" I offered hoping he'd ask me to flip the switch.

"No, no I like to watch the morning light come up." He swiveled in his high backed office chair away from the window he'd been looking out. "I'm sorry I haven't been available during your stay thus far. The timing was unexpected and I needed to take care of some things."

I remembered how he'd referred to my father's rehab as an, 'unexpected circumstance.' He had made it perfectly clear before what an inconvenience my staying here was.

He pointed to the chair that I hadn't yet sat in. "I need you to sit down Charlotte, I'm afraid I've had some unsettling news."

With his words, my heart began to beat loudly against my chest. I didn't sit. "What's happened?"

He took a breath. "Susan Richards phoned me late last night. Your...father, Simon is missing."

"What?"

"Apparently he checked himself out of the rehabilitation center before his treatment was complete. I'm sorry Charlotte. I see that you are quite shocked, I do wish you would sit down before you fall over."

I held onto the back of the chair until I was able to slip into the seat. "How is that possible? He promised me...why hasn't he contacted me himself?" I thought about him drinking and driving. "Oh God, was there an accident?"

My uncle rubbed his cheeks and then his eyes, he looked tired. "She doesn't know. She said she's checked the hospitals and any known acquaintances. There doesn't seem to be any trace of him."

"If he's not at home...he doesn't have anywhere else to go. There's no one, except me and Susan," I shook my head. "He doesn't have anyone."

"I'm sorry to have to tell you this. Truly Charlotte. But there is another matter as well. Ms. Steward informed me that you witnessed the accident that killed the Wriothesley's maid, a Ms. Jensen."

"Camilla," I whispered.

"You knew her?" he asked.

"Yes, well she spoke to me when I was at the house."

My uncle's eyes narrowed so slightly, I might have missed it if I hadn't been looking right at them. "And what did she say?"

"I'm sorry?"

"You said she spoke to you. What did she say to you, in particular?"

My breathing slowed, I could feel the intensity behind his question. "Nothing, in particular."

"It seems peculiar that she should have such a horrible accident right in front of you. Was she meeting you there?"

"No. It was only Caleb, Sophie, and myself. I don't know why she was there."

"You're sure?"

"Why are you asking me this? Who is she?"

"I don't know who she is. Or what she wanted. I was wondering if you knew."

"I met her once." I thought of the grave bearing my mother's name. I didn't trust my uncle and until I did, if I ever did, I wasn't telling him anything.

My uncle watched me while holding the edge of his desk. We sat in silence for a few moments, I knew he didn't believe me. "For now Charlotte, you are to inform me of your whereabouts at all times. I shall be home for the remainder of the summer and, given that your father is…missing, I am taking steps to assume guardianship of you."

I started to protest.

"Just until your father is found. While here, you are not to go to Glastonbury or anywhere else without my prior knowledge and consent. Is that understood?"

I had never in my life needed permission to do anything. This injunction of control over me irritated me. "And what about the Wriothesley's," I said not hiding my sarcasm. "Will I need your permission to go there as well?"

"Yes. I want to know where you are and who you are with at all times. I will inform Caleb that he's not to take you anywhere without my knowledge. I am sorry Charlotte, I realize you are accustomed to a more…free lifestyle. It is for your own safety. I'm only trying to look out for you."

Look out for *me*? I didn't buy it. My anger bloomed and I felt the pressure from holding it back in my head and face. I didn't know what to do so I stood up to leave. I was almost to the door when he stopped me.

"Charlotte, do you understand? You are not to—"

I spun around and shouted at him, "Were you *looking out for me* when you erected a tombstone for my mother! How is that looking out for me? Who are you anyway? I don't know you, my mother barely mentioned you. Now suddenly I am to obey you and your sanctions. You judge my father...you don't even know my father."

"I know that he couldn't take care of you, or my sister."

"So it's his fault she's missing? And you take it upon yourself to bury her. As if there isn't any hope that she'll ever come back."

"She isn't coming back," his words were flat and hit me like stones.

"You don't know that!"

His words were calm, "I do know that Charlotte. I'm sorry, she was your mother, but she's gone."

"She *is* my mother, not was."

"And she *is* my sister, Charlotte. I miss her a great deal."

"Is she buried out there," I pointed. "Is there one shred of my mother in that ground?"

He hesitated. "That grave is for me," he said finally.

"Why?" I raised my arms, "Because then you get all this to yourself."

He only stared at me, his face emotionless. "You are so very like her Charlotte," he whispered. He stood up and his chair rolled away behind him. "You will inform me of your comings and goings. If you choose to disobey me, then there will be no more coming or going anywhere. Is that clear?"

"Perfectly."

"Then that's the end of it."

"Hayden Wriothesley is picking me up today. I will be spending the day at their house," my voice dripped with forced compliance. It felt somewhat redemptive to act so childish.

My uncle closed his eyes and took a breath. "Very well."

If he was going to treat me like a child then I would act like one. "It would be easier to keep you informed if I had a cell, and a computer."

"I'll see what I can do," his patience was stretched.

"And a car to drive."

"No car."

"Fine. I suppose it does make it easier to monitor my every move."

"Susan Richards is expecting your call this morning. She is coordinating the efforts to find Simon."

"That's because Susan loves my father, and me."

He started to say something but I left his office, I didn't want to hear whatever it was.

I had never heard Susan cry. She had known he was missing for days but had hoped he would turn up or there would be some word from him. She said she was sorry she hadn't told me, but she didn't want to upset me if he was just needing to get himself together. But now she was worried and there hadn't been any word from him and none of the hospitals had taken in anyone matching his description. He had disappeared.

Just like mom.

"I'll find him Charlotte."

I had never felt so alone in my whole life.

CHAPTER TWENTY ONE

UNDERGROUND

I didn't know what I was doing. While Hayden scrolled through his digital movie selection looking for something for us to watch, I was trying to figure out how I was going to search for anything with him glued to my side.

"How about *Infernal Escape?*" he asked.

"Sure," I said pretending to be interested in a Cubist looking painting hanging in the theatre. "Your family has an amazing art collection, you must have a ton of security."

Hayden pointed remotes to start up the sound system and draw the curtains away from the gigantic screen. "All the art work's wired so alarms sound if someone tries to lift them without the code."

"And cameras, I mean, I assume," I looked up at the ceiling. "Does it make you feel like your dad is watching your every move?"

Hayden sat down and patted the seat next to him, "Come

here."

I looked at the seat next to him, we would be so close, in the dark. I walked slowly, unsure of myself and what would happen once the lights were out. When I finally sat down, I half expected him to pounce on me, but he didn't.

"You get used to it. The cameras only record and store images. Honestly, Dad only looks at them if something is missing." He lowered the lights with the remote, "Play," he commanded and the screen in front of us illuminated. "That's how he knew it was Camilla who'd taken files from his office."

The movie started and I wondered what else Emerick had seen, had he seen Camilla speaking to me in the hall outside the atrium? "What files did she take?"

Hayden kept his eyes glued to the screen and shook his head, "Bank stuff, I suppose. Dad figured she was working for someone. There's an investigation."

The movie's soundtrack began with the credits, the music was low and eerie, like it swirled from the speakers and saturated the room in suspense. It was not helping me have the courage to do what I was about to. Hayden lifted his arm and placed it on the seat behind me. His hand touched my hair and then rested between the curve of my neck and my shoulder sending shivers up my scalp.

My breath caught in my chest. Hayden would not stop at holding my neck. Already I could feel the energy between us growing.

I had not made up with Caleb before leaving the house.

My head had still been spinning with anger from our early morning fight and was only driven higher by my worry for my dad. I was trying very hard to not freak out about him being missing, trying to reassure myself that he was only panicking somewhere, in some hotel on the beach drunk beyond belief and avoiding rehab. But he had promised me he would get better. My father may be an alcoholic, but he had never promised me something and not come through. He was careful to never make promises he knew he couldn't keep.

Hayden's hand slipped over my shoulder and touched the bare skin around my short sleeved shirt. Goosebumps covered my arm.

No, as much as I was trying to calm myself with images of my father stinking and passed out on a poolside lounger in Malibu, I realized this wasn't anything but a movie I was playing for myself. A self-protective story to keep the wave of desperation back.

Whatever was hanging over my family, whatever it was about my mother's disappearance, Emerick Wriothesley, a stone puzzle box, alchemy, pentagrams, and Francis Bacon, whatever the connection was, it had drifted across the sea and taken my father as well.

I wasn't going to let that happen.

I leaned closer to Hayden and rested my hand on his stomach. When he looked down at me in surprise, I lifted my face towards his. He paused for only a moment, while the realization sunk in—I was giving myself to him. His hands collected me quickly, pressing me closer while he kissed first my lips and then my neck.

I'm sorry Caleb.

But I needed Hayden. I needed Hayden to trust me. I needed Emerick to believe I was Hayden's girlfriend, securely attached to him, a part of the family.

I felt Hayden's hand reaching under my shirt. My body tensed, but I let him.

Everything that mattered to me in this world had been taken from me.

When his hand pushed my bra aside I trembled.

"My God Charlotte," he whispered, his lips brushing my ear. "You're mine. Now you're mine."

I held his face in both my hands and kissed his mouth.

"Say it," he spoke between our kisses. "Say you're mine."

I tried to keep kissing him, but he pulled me onto his lap, cradled me in his arms.

"Say it," he insisted.

I was going to find my family, I was going to take my life back.

"I'm yours," I whispered.

His strength surprised me. In a fluid movement, as if I weighed nothing, Hayden stood and carried me out of the theater.

"What are you doing?" I protested as we rushed down the hall.

He laughed, "Carrying you."

"But where are we going?"

"My room."

Oh God. "Put me down," I kicked my legs.

"Almost there."

"I'll walk, this is ridiculous."

We reached his door and I could feel Hayden trying to reach for his door handle while still keeping me in his arms. "It's not...ridiculous." He managed to turn the handle and push the door open with his foot. "It's romantic," he grinned. Once inside, he carried me straight to his bed.

When he flopped me onto the mattress, my body bounced gently before sinking into his pillows and bedspread. Hayden quickly kicked off his shoes and laid down beside me, his body pressing against my side, he began kissing me again. His mouth ran over my ear, along my chin. I felt the warmth of his open mouth and the soft press of his tongue against my neck. Before I knew it was happening, he pulled the bottom of my shirt up and over my head.

He stopped kissing me and sat up long enough to look. It was the most naked I'd ever felt, lying there in my jeans and bra.

"You're beautiful."

I shook my head and felt his full weight press me into the bed as he lowered himself on top of me. He pushed my bra straps to the side and kissed first my shoulder and then the swell of breast pushing past the top of my bra.

I reached for his face and held it between my hands while

looking into his eyes. "I'm not going to have sex with you," I expected him to get mad and pout but he gave me a wicked smile instead.

"So presumptuous," he mocked. "What makes you think I'd want to have sex with you."

"I'm serious Hayden."

"Would I be your first?"

I hesitated but I knew he already knew the answer. "Yes."

He didn't bother to hide how much he liked the idea of me being a virgin. His smile was practically triumphant.

"Although I doubt very much that you could say the same," I shot.

"How was I supposed to know you were out in the world saving yourself for me? You should have called me when I was thirteen, I would have saved myself for you."

"You were thirteen!"

"Yes," he started kissing my chest, his hand trying to work the front clasp of my bra.

"That's disgusting."

"It's true," the clasp fell apart in his hand and he pushed my bra to the sides of me. "The whole thing was incredibly disgusting." His hand brushed across my breast and he lowered his mouth to me.

It was obvious, Hayden knew exactly what he was doing. But I had never done anything like this before, my body shook uncontrollably, from anticipation, fear—want. It was as if my body didn't know which feeling to run with. "I mean it," I stammered.

Hayden heard the tremor in my voice and looked up from what he was doing. "Mean what?" he whispered.

"I'm not having sex with you."

He nodded his head. "Not today." He kissed my breast one more time and then slid up and kissed my mouth. "But I will be your first Charlotte," he brushed a strand of hair from my cheek. "And then I'll be your only."

Hayden was sleeping next to me. Grabbing my shirt, I slipped off the bed while trying to keep the mattress from moving too much. The wood floor was cold on my bare feet and I stooped to grab my sandals. Hayden's expression was slack; his chest rose and fell in a deep even rhythm.

This was my chance.

His computer was on and it gave me an excuse. I brought up the online encyclopedia and typed in Richard II. If Hayden came looking for me, I would just tell him I was doing research for the English paper I needed to rewrite.

At the door I quickly slipped my shirt back on and made sure the latch didn't make a sound.

Scurrying through the maze of halls, I tried my best to remember the way to the strange one room shack that Emerick had his mansion built around. I backtracked twice before finding the right door. I pushed the door and hoped Hayden had been right about Emerick checking the security video only if something went missing.

Enough light from the hall spilled into the room for me to find the ancient hurricane lamp and once I had that on, I carefully closed the door behind me.

Tugging on the large metal ring, it took all my strength to open the door in the floor that led to Emerick's workroom. But once I had the door opened, I stopped.

It was a black hole.

Not one ounce of light from the weak hurricane made it's way past the lip of the entrance. And then I remembered, Hayden had descended into the dark before flipping the switch.

Instinctively, I fell a step back.

I didn't even know where the switch was. My heart pounded louder and louder as thoughts of climbing down into the dark flooded me. The freeze of fear fell over me, paralyzed me. I couldn't do it.

My breath had stopped so I forced myself to take a long deep breath, inhaling the smell of the dry wood walls. The cord of the lamp was long enough to bring a little closer to the opening.

The brass base felt cool against my sweating palm and I lowered the light to the floor, shifting the throw of the table's shadow until it stretched up the wall and hung over me like a black umbrella.

The glass shade had already grown hot from the bulb. Protecting my hand with the edge of my shirt, I lifted the glass shade from its base and hung the lamp as far into the hole as the cord would allow.

It wasn't enough. I could see the ladder and space surrounding it, but the small bulb barely illuminated the bottom rungs or the floor and I couldn't see a switch anywhere.

I sat back, gently biting the back of my tongue with my molars. I wanted to go back and get Hayden, figure a way to get him to bring me back—I needed printed pages. But I wouldn't be free to search the room. What if I did find the diaries? How would I get even one of them without Hayden noticing?

I took a breath and did not think.

The wood floor pressed my knees as I flipped myself over and descended into the room.

The switch, the switch, Hayden was still on the ladder when he had flipped the switch. The rungs slipped beneath my wet hands. Once the opening was completely over my head, I began groping behind the ladder. The wall. The light barely touched it but I could feel it and I slid my hand all over the top portion.

The switch, the switch, the switch, my mind chanted over and over but my body was not fooled. My breath was shallow and quick and my ears rushed with the sound of my own blood pushing through my veins urging me to run. *Run Charlotte, escape.*

My shaking body fumbled on the ladder, down, down. My hands swept the wall madly. *The switch, the switch, the switch.* I looked up, the small bulb felt far away. My sight stretched into the darkness around me, the darkness that surrounded me like a predator. *Run Charlotte! Run, up, up. Slam the door behind you.*

The switch...

Run. A strained cry slipped past my throat. I had to get out. My hand grabbed the rung up and then the next, my legs pushed me up. Flight flooded me, the dark clawed at my back. *Run.*

And then I saw it. Lunging, just beyond my immediate reach, my fingers brushed the switch up and bright florescent shot through the room.

I clung to the ladder and cried. My body shook too violently to move, my breath came in gasps.

Light.

Breathe Charlotte. Breathe. I gulped the air and wiped my face on my shoulders. *Breathe.* Hysteria clutched my throat. *Breathe Charlotte! Look! Light! Light everywhere.*

And I looked, light was everywhere, washing over every thing, every space, into every corner of Emerick's workroom.

My arms and legs felt like water as they strained to lower me to the floor below. Once there, my legs folded beneath me until my shins and knees pressed into the cold tile while my shaking arms acted like a kickstand for my upper body. I hung my head between my shoulders, my stomach churned and my mouth began to water.

No.

I half stood and stumbled, desperate for somewhere to be

sick. Was there a bathroom down here? Past Emerick's model city, there was a door I hadn't noticed before. I pushed myself as fast as I could, diving for the door handle I crashed into the other room searching for a toilet—a sink.

It wasn't a bathroom.

The sick heaved up my esophagus and I grabbed the first thing I could find, a half filled water pitcher. My stomach pitched, rejecting the egg salad sandwich I'd had for lunch.

When I was mostly sure it was over, I wiped my mouth on the bottom of my shirt and avoided looking at the swirling mess in the glass pitcher. I'd have to find a way to clean it, obviously.

My fingers pressed both my eyes until blue and white lights shot across my vision. When I opened them—the room blurred while my eyes struggled to focus. I raked my fingers up over my head, combing my hair away from my face. I felt thin, like a loose thread.

My sight adjusted, first close up—there was a thick book, a bible, on a gold stand right next to me—and then far away. In the center of the room stood what looked like a white stone alter. It was surrounded by three candle holders as tall as me. The floor around the altar radiated out in what looked like a blue and white sunburst while the rest of the room was tiled like a chessboard.

What was this?

I moved slowly towards the alter, the bottom half had the square and compass symbol, the same as the Wriothesley estate entrance. The Masons.

There were chairs lining the perimeter and small desks in each corner. I imagined Emerick down here, cloaked and surrounded by other men, chanting by candlelight—or whatever it was they did in their secret meetings.

Nowhere seemed like a place to hide anything and besides the bible, I didn't see any books. I backed up, grabbed the pitcher while trying to not look at the disgusting contents, and closed the door behind me. I wondered what Hayden knew about what his father did down here.

In the model room, I started pulling drawers and opening cabinets. Glue, plywood, architectural sketches, several magnifying glasses, loose keys and pens, there was a miniature refrigerator in one corner stocked with club soda and different types of cheese, a box of crackers had been left open on the counter next to it.

Walking around the large model to inspect the other side of the room, the small home surrounded by rolling hills caught my attention.

A minuscule light glowed inside.

I leaned over as far as I dared trying to see through the windows. There was something inside but it was too small and I couldn't get any closer. I grabbed one of the larger magnifiers from the counters and stretched it as far across the table as I could while keeping my balance.

Inside, a small boy sat reading on a red cotton rug while a fire burned brightly, warming the room. Nearby, a woman in a blue dress stood, her back to the boy, chopping vegetables at the kitchen counter. The light came from a single hurricane lamp, exactly like the one I'd left hanging into the hole above me. I stood up and considered the small house's exterior—it was an odd contrast to the metropolis Emerick had constructed.

When I looked up, I saw it. On a workbench near the city, lying open, exposed, surrounded by a scatter of paper and tools.

My mother's diary.

I rushed, gathered her up in my hands, closed her. I pressed it to my lips and closed my eyes. Waves of relief washed through me and I inhaled the scent of rich leather and aging paper.

"Master Wriothesley?" a man's voice called from above me.

My eyes opened. I froze.

"Sir? Are you down there?"

My eyes rose to the opening at the top of the ladder, a decrepit hand reached down and grasped the lamp I'd stupidly left and pulled it out of view.

"Master Hayden?"

It was Charles, the Wriothesley's head servant.

CHAPTER TWENTY TWO

CAUGHT

First one black trousered leg and then the other appeared on the ladder. "Who's here?" he began the decent.

I watched Charles climb down, my brain felt slow, my body wouldn't move. *Hide!* I scanned the room, there wasn't anywhere I could get to in time.

I could see the back of his thin gray hair, all he had to do was turn his head slightly and he'd see me.

Underneath.

My knees buckled and, still clutching the diary, I ducked down and crawled as quietly as I could beneath the model's platform.

I couldn't see him but I could clearly hear the sound of his leather shoes scraping across each rung. I held my breath. When he reached the bottom, I watched his lower legs pause near the ladder.

"Hello? Master Hayden?"

And then he slowly moved, a few steps and then a few more. Investigating the room. Any moment he would bend down, his pointy face would peer into my exposed hiding space. My breath sounded like a wind chamber in my ears, I covered my mouth and nose with both hands to cover the noise I was sure would give me away.

His sharply polished shoes turned away from the table and headed towards the ritual room I'd just left.

The pitcher.

I'd left the glass pitcher I'd thrown up in on the workbench where my mother's diary had been.

Charles's feet and legs disappeared into the next room.

You have to get it Charlotte.

My body wouldn't move. I was crouched into a debilitated ball. *He might not notice it.*

Yeah, and then again, he might. And if he doesn't find you five seconds after that, how many questions will he not have to ask before everyone figures out you where down here.

I hugged the diary to my chest. If they discovered me now, there would be no hope of searching for the others.

I crawled on hands and knees, my every movement radiated sound. I watched the door over my shoulder. He was going to hear me.

At the edge of the platform I paused, watching, waiting for his legs at the door.

Do it!

I peeked over the top of the platform, past a cluster of row

homes and a tiny lake surrounded by a walking path. I didn't
see him.

Crouched, I hurried the two steps, grabbed the pitcher
and turned.

His skeletal body lurched past the door.

I ducked.

I watched his legs stop on his side of the door. "Hello?"

He'd seen me.

"Is someone there?"

Or at least my movement.

His legs moved closer. His steps were slow, he was looking,
listening.

I wasn't even under the platform now but I didn't dare
move. My heart sounded like a drum in my ears. All he would
need to do was walk around this side.

And he was. His shoes were following the platform's perimeter.

A small cry rose up my throat and I pressed my hand hard
against my mouth to keep it back.

Three more steps.

I didn't think. I held the pitcher in front of me and tried to
keep the open end up while my knee, hip, then back rolled me
just under the table, inches from the edge.

Charles came around the side and I laid on my back holding the pitcher up above me. His shoe was next to my ear, I
could smell his hot feet sweating inside polyester dress socks.
I turned my head the other way.

The seconds stopped, I imagined him, eyes narrowed, feeling the air.

Please.

Eternity inched by, any moment he would stoop and see me.

His shoes turned, took a few steps and then his hand was reaching under the table. He felt along the edge. I saw what he was groping for, a small switch six inches from where his hand was.

Find it, don't look. I willed his hand to slide further up and half a moment later it did, the sound of the switch click satisfied him. He was leaving, heading back towards the ladder but still, I didn't move.

His legs disappeared as he climbed back up.

The lights went out.

No. I heard him climb the rest of the way up. I put the pitcher down and got ready to run for the ladder.

He was closing the door in the floor. As soon as I heard it shut I reached for the edge of the platform.

I could feel my eyes adjusting, straining to find any light. There was nothing. I was underground and there was nothing for my eyes to adjust to.

Moving helped, moving towards the switch. And now I knew where the switch was, exactly where it was. My throat tightened. *Breathe, breathe.*

The dark stretched, grew—I could feel its breath.

I was halfway around the platform. *Almost there*, my tears

welled up and spilled hot and wet across my cheeks. I moved faster and stumbled, but my hand was touching the ladder.

Go, up, up.

The permission to run unleashed the fear, a demon purring at my back. I pressed my body against the ladder while my hands searched wildly, flying all over the wall where I thought it was. I reached.

LIGHT.

"Where have you been?" Hayden opened one eye and propped himself up on the bed.

"The kitchen." It wasn't a lie. I'd managed to sneak the dirty pitcher through the halls to the nearest bathroom where I dumped the mess down the toilet before washing it in the kitchen sink.

"Aw," he gave me a fake sad look. "Did you get lost again?"

"A little bit," I whispered.

"Come here," he patted the bed beside him. "Let me make it better."

My mother's diary was shoved into the waistband of my jeans, my shirt hid the bulge. "I have to use the bathroom." I grabbed my bag off the floor and didn't wait for his response. After I'd stuffed the book in my bag and flushed the toilet for effect, I went back out.

"I'm not really feeling that great," also, not a lie. "I want to go home."

His face darkened but when I sat next to him and pushed

his hair away from his eyes, he relaxed. "You're not changing your mind on me," he said.

I leaned in and lightly kissed the hollow of his cheek. "No. I'm just tired."

He searched my face for a second and then grabbed his shirt off the bed and stretched it over his head and chest.

In his car, on the driveway in front of Gaersum Aern, Hayden kissed me.

"You're coming tomorrow. My mother is having a pool party."

"She's home?"

He shook his head, his eyes were soft, wanting. He was hardly paying attention to anything I said. He kissed me again. "No, tonight." His hand reached and felt the swell of my breast through my shirt.

Please, my eyes darted to the house windows as his mouth slid down my neck. *Don't let Caleb be watching this.*

When I finally managed to untangle myself from him, I slipped into the house as quietly as I could.

At the bottom of the staircase, I heard him. I closed my eyes and I could imagine him, hunched over the keys, gently pressing, swaying—creating the familiar music, Beethoven's Moonlight Sonata.

He knew I was home and I didn't go to him.

I couldn't.

The memory of Hayden's touch hung on every part of my body. Caleb would feel the stain it left. I pushed myself up the stairs and rushed to my room. I couldn't face Caleb, I couldn't look into his eyes, say the words I had to—not yet.

I closed my door, pulled the diary from my bag and headed for the red sofa. As I sat and turned on the light, I saw the pages I'd printed on Francis Bacon still splayed across the rug. I laid my head against the sofa's arm and lifted my feet onto the cushion. For a moment, I rested the diary against my knees, ran my hands across the figure eight snakes. I took a breath and opened to the first page.

CHAPTER TWENTY THREE

GILDED BORDERS

Margot hates me. Emerick stopped by this afternoon. I was surprised to see him but I'll admit, I was happy. I know Margot has always been completely in love with him, but it hardly seems fair that every other person should stay away from him, especially since he has never shown the slightest interest in her.

I feel horrible even writing this.

He stood at my door and I worried he'd hear the race of my heart. His eyes played beneath his lashes, his smile, it's a miracle I didn't throw myself at him right there. Why does Margot get to stake a claim?

He ended up coming in. What was I supposed to do? At first we only sat in the library and talked, he loves to read too. His favorite writer is Dostoevsky and his favorite book, Crime and Punishment. I told him I love Shakespeare and that my father used to read it to me until I was old enough to read it myself.

He flirts and I can't resist. Sitting next to him felt like torture, all I wanted was some excuse to touch him.

We ended up swimming, he borrowed some of Nigel's trunks. At first we just splashed each other, but when I sent a huge wave directly into his face, he came after me. He's a strong swimmer and caught me in two strokes. His hand swept across my stomach pulling me closer. We pretend to wrestle a minute but then he pressed me to him.

He kissed me!

And then I saw her. Margot had come, she was standing at the sliding glass door to the family room. She had seen everything. When I looked at her, she just turned and left.

I haven't the courage to call her.

I love her, she is my best friend.

It's not fair.

I got up. The invitation Emerick had given me for their Midsummer ball was on the dresser in the other room. I grabbed the purple envelope and pulled out the card stock.

Emerick and Margot Wriothesley cordially invite you...

He married Margot.

I carried the invitation with me to the sofa and slid it between the diary's pages near the back. It would be a good bookmark.

I read through their summer. My mother and Emerick went to movies, swam in the pool—he snuck into her room late one night and stayed over. Margot didn't speak to my mother for over a month. And then,

Emerick was strange today.... And pages later, *Emerick can-*

299

celed our date, there is some meeting he's going to.

I turned the page.

Today was awful. Emerick and I were in the library and I could tell from his restless pacing something was wrong, he was so cold and silent. When I asked him about it he turned on me and began asking me questions about mother and father, about their friends. Things like, What did I know about the parties they attended? Did I ever go? What sort of things went on at these parties? What influential people attended?

I told him I had no idea. I had never been to their private parties, mother and father both know a great many influential people.

Political? He asked.

Yes, I said.

And royal?

This question made me nervous. Yes, I answered faltering.

He turned from me then and stared out the windows. We have never discussed it but I have many times imagined how sensitive Emerick must be about his family and what they did. Mother has told me how they had turned him and his mother out in order to save face and the family's name from scandal. What a horrible thing it must have been for Emerick to be bounced from orphanage to foster homes and back again. It was only recently that his father, in a crisis of conscious mother said, was able to persuade his family to at least let him provide for Emerick's education. Margot, Emma, and I would never have even met Emerick had Adam not befriended him when he be-

gan his studies at Eton last fall.

We all knew that Emerick had grown up in radically different circumstances but we didn't care. It's true that there are some at school that have shunned and excluded him, gossiped in cruel tones. Teachers even who have taken sick pleasures in finding subtle ways to remind an entire class that Emerick was the bastard son of a domestic. But for us, it has never been more than an unspoken history. Regardless of the past, Emerick is brilliant, gorgeous, and his own person regardless of the mistakes his family made. He is one of us now, we never held to those ancient conventions of judgment.

But today, I realized just how deeply he is wounded by his past. His stormy mood filled the entire library with electricity and I sensed that, today, his past was a wall he was surrounding himself in.

Still, I had never judged him or uttered a cruel word and his barely checked anger made me feel like I was the one directly responsible for his misfortunes. His questions were more interrogation than information gathering. After a few minutes the silence made me so uncomfortable I made the mistake of laughing and telling him as much.

What happened next I can scarcely believe. When Emerick turned from the window, he erupted in rage. He accused me of keeping secrets, "Great secrets," he practically hissed at me. I have never seen Emerick angry like this, I was so surprised that it took me several moments to find my voice. When I finally did, I told him that I had no idea what he was talking about. But then he clenched his fists and stormed towards me so quickly I shrank back into the sofa certain he was going to hit or grab me. Instead he loomed over me and called me a liar, "You expect me to believe that you don't know? That your own parents never told you?" I felt frozen as my mind raced trying to figure out what he was so upset about. Having no idea, I could only shake my head. I pleaded with him, "Emerick, please, I don't know what you're talking about."

He stared at me for a long time, his brow still furrowed in anger but his eyes seemed to consider the possibility of what I claimed. I explained, honestly, that my parents have never shared any confidences with me, certainly nothing that Emerick would care about or give him cause to think I was keeping any secrets from him. Yes, my parents know a great many influential people, yes they know his father and about what happened to Emerick when he was born. They know that his mother was a domestic, that she was sent away to avoid scandal and Emerick was then left to be raised by strangers and institutions, but this was nothing we've kept from Emerick. I explained that my mother felt it was a great tragedy. She has said to me on more than one occasion that it was a blessing that his family finally gathered some sense of decency and agreed to secure Emerick a reasonable future by providing for his education.

I was doing nothing short of begging him. He couldn't possibly think I would keep anything I knew about his past or his family from him. Or, that any of that even mattered to me. How could he be judged for circumstances so far outside his ability to *control?*

He was silent and his eyes held mine for a long time, seeming to monitor my every expression for even the slightest hint of a lie. But every word I spoke was the truth and I felt sure that when he realized this, and we moved past this anger, which was very frightening and unexpected for me, the entire ordeal would serve to bring us closer. We would be bonded in understanding and shared alliance, his past completely open and acknowledged between us. I sat there believing that this episode, while enormously scary, was actually a good thing.

Imagine my surprise when he stood abruptly, looked at me with utter contempt and said, "You really don't have any idea what I'm talking about. You are even more blind than I am," and walked out.

I have been crying ever since.

I turned the page and saw more of my mother's writing and then an envelope taped to the opposite page.

I have felt so utterly alone. Emerick has refused to take my calls. Emma has been sympathetic and Adam's tried to speak with Emerick, but then he wouldn't speak with Adam either. I have never missed Margot's friendship as much as I do right now. It has been this way for almost two weeks and I was beginning to believe that Emerick's continued silence meant we were through.

But today, this letter arrived.

I opened the flap of the envelope and pulled out heavy sheets of stationary.

Dear Elizabeth,

I hardly know where to begin. I can only imagine that you are expecting an apology for my behaviour, and you very likely deserve one. But so much has happened to alter my mind and thus it's world view over the course of these last few months, I'm not entirely sure it isn't I who deserve an apology. Before I explain let me first admit that yes, it was unfortunate that you should have born the brunt of my extreme frustrations. Hopefully by the time you have finished reading this letter, my present state of mind and affairs will be clearer to you.

Again, where to begin? I can hardly expect you to understand the extreme variance that has been my existence since my natural family's decision to pluck me from obscurity and enroll me at Eton. Do you suppose everyone lives the way you do Elizabeth? I realize you've had little cause to explore the world beyond your gilded borders so allow me to enlighten you, the world is a bloody cruel and terrifying place Elizabeth. Unless, of course, you're a member of the privileged, oh so privileged few who can afford to keep that world far from your own consciousness. Do you have any, ANY idea what it's like for a child to go to bed, every night, terrified of what dark evils will likely descend upon him at any moment? What foul mood might over take the dregs of humanity that are being paid to keep him? The constant never knowing of when you might be fed, or bathed, provided a coat against the winter months? Do you know what it's like to know, now, finally after all these years, that you did have a mother?

I realize your parents have long known of my existence and circumstances. But up until last year the very idea that there was anything more in store for me than only more of what I had always known was pure fantasy. When my father's assistant came to collect me and move me to Eton, it was initially nothing short of a miracle to my eyes. My undying gratitude for my rescue was so all encompassing, there wasn't room to wonder. Wonder WHY.

WHY had I been left to suffer for so many years to begin with? I wonder that now Elizabeth.

So yes, I have been saved, so to speak. But when my family, who I have yet to ever be allowed in the presence of, opened my eyes to their world and my place in it, they also broke open a need to understand. I needed to know the truth. What happened all those years ago? Who was my mother? And why?

For the last three months I have been discovering the answers to those questions. I searched, found people willing to talk. I learned what you and your family already know. My mother, Lilith Brewster, was a domestic and my father got her pregnant. So she, like many women before her, was sent away. But this would hardly be the first time in history such a thing has happened. Have you or your family, never wondered why should I have been separated from her?

And that I suppose is where this letter should have started. Yes, I have recently discovered my mother's history. You were right the other day, my mother was sent away when my father's family found out she was with his child. I now know where and, more importantly, why.

My father's family had my mother committed. Before I was born she was diagnosed with schizophrenia and sent to Saint Mary's Asylum. I was born there, the evidence is right on my birth certificate, and after my birth I was placed in foster care.

This information alone has been quiet the shock to my system. I have gone through life never knowing anything of my past outside of what my own memories could supply. What I learned, I pieced together. Investigated, followed leads from one person to the next. Documents, records, all in an attempt to learn the truth. A truth that I was, up until very recently, beginning to accept. But then, last month, my search brought me to the home of one woman, whose identity I swore to protect. She worked with my mother at my family's estate and described herself to me as, "Lilith's dearest friend." This woman shared her personal memories of my mother with me. Images that were bright and beautiful. She spoke of Lilith's sharp mind and, "delicious wit." When I asked her about the relationship with my father, her face grew dark and she shook her head, "the worst thing to ever happen to her."

I have learned a great deal Elizabeth. Most importantly, I have learned the truth.

My mother was not a schizophrenic.

There are things in this world Elizabeth that creep beneath the surface. They go by names that encourage the unlearned, the uninitiated to dismiss them: mysteries, enlightenment, magic, higher consciousness. But they are real, just as real as you or I. And my father, because he loved her, and even though it was for-

bidden, had begun trying to teach my mother about these things in secret. He tried to give her the tools she needed to rise herself up from her lot and position in this world, to equal the material playing field between them. But he was neither sanctioned, qualified, or talented enough to take on such a task. When he realized this, too late I might add, my mother's mind was long lost from this world.

After our last meeting, I now realize that there are a great many things your parents have not yet shared with you. And thus, much of what I am telling you may not find a grounding place within your sense of reason. But let me assure you, regardless of whether or not you yet understand them, every word of what I tell you is the truth.

I have come to believe that my father was only able to take my mother so far along the path to enlightenment. He cracked open her consciousness and then left her to cut loose from the only material reality she has ever known. When my family discovered what my father had done, they took the path of least resistance. In her babbling incoherent state, my mother was easily gotten rid of with a diagnoses of schizophrenia and left caged within the walls of Saint Mary's Hospital and Asylum. Subjected to horrors, restraints, isolation, and experimental drugs. Broken beyond recognition or repair by the hands of doctors, nurses, and staff, all in the name of patient care and under the neglectful eye of "God's" church. The year I turned three, they lobotomized her. By the time I was six, she was dead.

So yes, I had a mother. A mother who did want me, a moth-

er who was stolen from me. Collected and caged. Killed by her keepers. Can you imagine, Elizabeth, being a small boy who all his life believed that it wasn't circumstance but himself that drove his mother to abandon him? Certain that he wasn't worth keeping, a detestable speck of a nothing.

Of course you don't Elizabeth. Your family has wealth and privilege. Power. They have the power to keep all that unpleasantness far from you.

If after reading this letter you still feel you require an apology for my behaviour the other day, well then, my apologies Elizabeth. Please forgive my anger, please forgive my injustice, please forgive my lack of etiquette, good grooming, and emotional control.

Unlike yourself, I have not enjoyed the benefits of a proper upbringing.

Sincerely,
Emerick

I held the pages limply and took a deep breath. The framed picture on the mantle in Emerick's waiting room, that aged image of woman and child filled my head. The distance between them, her vacant stare, his small frame. Emerick and a mother he didn't know. Lobotomy. My hands shook slightly as I folded the pages back along their creases and slid them inside the envelope. Outside the large, constructed world in his basement, he had built her a home. A home with a fire and a boy playing on a rug. Another ragged breath escaped me. I understood what it meant to lose a mother. But had she? Had my mother been able to relate? I couldn't help but feel that what Emerick had written was somewhat true, my mother had been very protected, privileged. Had she been able to understand how deeply wounded Emerick was? I turned the page.

So what am I to make of it? I'm stunned and saddened by the choices his family made. But how could his mother have been committed to an asylum if she wasn't truly mentally ill? And his father cracked open her mind? What does that even mean? I am worried that Emerick is deluding himself. Of course he would look to hang on to anything, any shred of disinformation to avoid believing his mother was sick. Whomever this woman is that he's found has surely filled his head with a false fairytale that he's now clinging to like gospel. And what of us? If anything there is nothing more than the barest hint of a back handed apology. Are we still together? Is it over? I understand he is wrestling with his past, and I'm sympathetic to it, but that doesn't give him the right to abuse me. I am more frustrated and annoyed than I have ever been in my entire life. Which, admittedly, is better than the unrelenting sadness that has been hanging over me these past weeks. Enough moping around, I will call Emerick and demand some kind of resolution. Either we are over or we will move past all this but I refuse to just dwindle in the breeze of not knowing any longer.

I read on. She did call him and after she vented her feelings to him about the way he treated her that day in the library, they made up. But, I could tell from her words, things were not the same. Between the passages about movies and car trips, pressed bodies and lips, Emerick was changing, starting something outside his existence with my mother.

Emerick believes my parents, and his, belong to some sort of fraternity. This is what he meant in the library that day when he accused me of "keeping secrets." He believes my parents will one day initiate myself and Nigel but fears, because his family still does not publicly acknowledge him, that he will be forever shut out from this underground association. It is ridiculous! And I would, this minute, share all his mistaken beliefs with my mother if only to verify the falsehood and stop his obsessing, except that I worry, given his mother's unfortunate history, they would likely begin to "encourage" me to stop seeing him. He says he's taking the matter, "into his own hands." I noticed the other day that his room is filling up with books on subjects of all sorts. Symbols, magic, consciousness, meditation, the history of Freemasonry, alchemy, God. Just yesterday I saw one with "occult" in the title, I felt so nervous I could only turn away quickly and pretend not to have noticed.

He told me on the phone last night that he realizes he will never be admitted into the "true inner circles" of this world. "So I'm going to start my own."

I don't even know what to say to this. I'm starting to become frightened. I am ashamed to say it, but I think more and more about Emerick's mother every day.

She began to complain, *Emerick is obsessed, he never has time for me anymore.* She worried about her friends, *How long will Margot continue to torture me? I'm beginning to think she will never forgive me for being with Emerick.*

And then, one day, my father showed up.

Adam and Emma have found a new friend to bring round. They met him while he was signing copies of his new book, Trinities Tyrant, at a bookstore in Bath. His name is Simon Stevens and he's AMERICAN. Emerick hates him and is forever trying to goad him into an argument. But Simon always wears his relaxed and easy expression and never jumps into a war of words with Emerick. I think this only makes Emerick hate him even more. Emerick called him, "slow and shallow," and dismissed his book (after reading nothing more than the back cover) as, "drivel, candy for the masses." He's staying at a flat in Bath for the summer while researching his next book. If you ask me, I think Emerick is just jealous of all the attention Simon has been getting. Emma and I both love just listening to him talk. He's sweet and kind, I couldn't imagine him ever losing his temper. And he's certainly better company than Emerick's been these last few weeks. I find myself looking for him whenever we all get together. With Emerick so preoccupied with his 'meetings' and the distance between Margot and me (that's not getting any better!) it's been nice to make a new friend (especially one not so wrapped up in everyone here!)

I laid the diary against my chest. Here was my father, young and funny...sober. Stealing my mother from Emerick with nothing more than his easy nature and kindness. If Emerick hated my father so much it was too bad he couldn't see that he practically gave my mother to him.

I hadn't heard back from Susan. *Dad, where are you? Not you too...please.* He was a mess. But I needed him and he needed me. I needed to take care of him, it meant something to take care of him. To try to help him get back to writing.

I closed my eyes and whispered our goodnight chant, "Be safe, be fine and know I love you all the time." *Please God, let Susan find him.*

I pulled the book back and started reading again. Halfway through, I reached the page I'd flipped to the day I first found the diaries.

Emerick is taking me to one of his secret meetings tonight—I can hardly believe it. I must admit, even though I am forever teasing him and rolling my eyes about his "order" I can barely wait to find out what goes on. I have begun to suspect that many of our friends already belong and that this is what they whisper about in the corners of our summer parties and evening outings. I swear Emma and Adam already attend; they are always conspiring and then changing the conversation whenever I approach. And I'm practically certain that Margot goes. She may have even been one of the very first that Emerick recruited but since he's cloaked the whole thing in veils of secrecy, he will never answer any of my questions. And so, I've never been sure if being jealous of Margot sharing his confidences was something even fair to accuse him of. Never mind that he's never invited

ME. In the end I ended up asking if I could go.

She and I have grown apart so much since Emerick and I have been together, I almost feel now as if I don't even know her anymore. Would she try to steal Emerick away? Does she even care for him anymore? All these questions, doubts. And still, I miss her. Maybe, once I'm a part of that circle, she and I can again be the friends we once were.

I would be meeting Margot Wriothesley and Hayden's sister, Diana, tomorrow at the pool party. It would be weird, meeting the grown-up version of Margot. Especially since she had no idea I knew all about how she dumped my mother's friendship because of Emerick. Although, I wondered if she even remembered the details of those days. It was a long time ago and, after all, she did end up with him and their colossal summer home. God knows what their London home was like.

I turned the page.

What can I say? Nothing. I am bound by silence since my last entry. Since then I have attended five of Emerick's meetings, now they are mine as well. Everyone goes, I alone had no idea. Emerick was so right, about everything.

I am learning the great secrets.

The journal entries grew shorter and I could tell from her words that there were larger gaps of time between her recordings.

I am not supposed to speak or write of our meetings. Except tonight, something happened. Every time we are all together, we try to cross into the astral plane together. In the past, many of us, myself included, have reached a deep meditative state (Adam once fell asleep!) but we've never done what Emerick describes as, "transcending out of this physical flesh into the realm of the energy plane." The books we study call it an, "out of body" experience.

But tonight, I did it.

And I was the only one. Even Emerick, who I think also practices a great deal when we are not all together, has never accomplished this.

Tonight, I left my body. I have no idea how.

Moonlight Sonata, the music we use to trigger the sessions, began to fill the room with its ghostly voice. Somehow, tonight, I managed to float away on it. Strange cannot begin to describe it. To be outside of yourself, to see yourself, your body, separate from your mind. And everyone else sitting there, meditating together without the slightest idea that I was above them, watching. The minutes moved on and I waited to see if someone else might also be with me, outside of us, but one by one I saw the others below me begin to shift from the discomfort of sitting so long. Their eyes peeking, checking to see if anyone else would be the first to get up. Eventually, every one of them looked around at the other until they saw that it was only me still quiet. Above them all, I could see Emerick again looked frustrated by failure. Time ticked and I could tell my continued silence was beginning to make them restless. I then realized that I wanted to go back, back to my body. To open my eyes and share what had happened.

But I didn't know how.

Adam and Emma began whispering to themselves. Margot

stood up and went to get a drink of water from the sink. Everyone was beginning to resume life.

Everyone except Emerick. Emerick was staring at my body.

I felt it even stronger then, the pressing need to return to myself. But nothing happened. I continued to simply hover above the room. What happened next is the reason I'm breaking my promise of silence, why I'm recording the experience hoping that, in time, I may read back over these words and make sense of what I saw, what I felt.

I didn't know how to get back to myself and I began to become afraid. What if I never got back? What if I were to end up suspended this way, outside my body, for the rest of my life?

The longer I remained outside myself, the more my fear began to edge towards a panic. I felt a desperate rush surge through my mind—and that's when I felt it. I was not alone.

I was not alone in that space. I sensed a presence, another being, their energy radiated towards me from some unknown place.

At first I wondered if it was maybe someone else from the group. But when I looked, I could clearly see everyone from our group below, eyes open, talking, whispering, stretching, awake. So who was here with me?

Emerick had moved closer to my body and was watching me intently, a few others had also noticed me, and I could tell from their glances they were beginning to wonder what I was up to.

It was then that I looked around, how to describe it? It was like looking through a veil. I was in the room with everyone else, *but I was also somewhere else. Was this the astral plane? But then I saw it, nothing more than a shadow but it had weight that I could feel in that strange dimension. Weight that pressed all around me, infiltrated my sense of self—clung to me. I was trapped in this place with another being and it felt as if it were mixed up with my own presence. As I watched, the shadow shifted, moved towards me. Terror swept through me so quickly I tried to scream but all I could hear was a muffled silence, my voice was mute.*

Then, so suddenly, like a rubber band snapping back, I was opening my eyes and the scream I couldn't form only a moment before was filling the room around me. The physical room with everyone from the group, they were all staring at me.

Emerick wants me to come back tomorrow, alone he said, so that just he and I can try to recreate the experience. I tried to explain to Emerick what I saw, how I felt. The shadow that pressed into the space with me, lurked on the fringes of my consciousness. I tried to explain to him that it frightened me. He wasn't listening. It was like he was both thrilled and frustrated by what had happened to me. "Do you realize what we've accomplished?" he asked. But the way he looked at me, it was like awe and envy struggling for space. I know he wished it were him that had crossed first.

I wish it had been him as well.

I agreed to come back, to try again. But I am frightened. I can't shake the feeling of that shadow presence. It's almost as if it were still with me, here in this very room.

A creak sounded from the bedroom and pulled my eyes and ears towards it, a chill ran across my skin. The rooms had grown darker since I'd started reading, the colossal furniture morphing into hunched and hulking beasts.

Something moved.

I saw it at the edge of my vision, something moved or shifted on the far side of the bed. I froze and stared into the dark, my eyes struggling to find a rational source.

Everything was still.

My heart thundered as my eyes continued to stare at the space, waiting for the dark to shift again.

Nothing moved.

It was nothing. I continued to stare as I reached behind me for the lamp beside the red sofa. When I found the slim chain and pulled, a soft glow radiated behind me and stretched a small distance into the bedroom. But as my eyes adjusted to the light around me, I could see that the far spaces in the room had only been tossed deeper into darkness by the contrast.

It was nothing. I looked back to my mother's journal, her words were the reason I was so jumpy. Like reading scary stories late at night. *Just keep reading.* My galloping heart was beginning to slow but I was still too nervous to ignore it. I needed more light. I placed her journal on the cushion beside me and looked toward the bedroom door and the light switch besides it. Deep breath. I gathered courage from the lamps warm glow and pushed myself up off the sofa.

I ran for the switch.

Running cut the fear loose, allowed it to take hold and race through my blood. In my imagination, hundreds of hands grabbed for my ankles, demons lunged to claw and catch me, pull me down. Unable to help myself, I practically leapt towards the wall.

The electric crack sounded and bright overhead light filled every space. Transferred every monstrous piece of furniture back into dead wood and fabric. Breathing heavy, I walked around the bed to inspect the fearful movement while safely surrounded in the light. When I saw it, I stopped and stared. An afghan lay pooled on the floor where it had slipped from the bed. That was what I had seen, this is what terrified me. A blanket sliding to the floor.

I took a breath of irritation with myself and walked back to the red sofa. When? When would I stop being afraid? I let myself fall into the sagging cushions and plucked the journal from the arm beside me.

Annoyed, I turned the page and continued.

It's happened again. And again, I felt the shadow presence in the astral space with me. It was easier to come back to myself this time but Emerick was still not successful in joining me.

I have crossed five times now, Emerick still struggles.

Emerick is angry, always angry now. I want to stop but he won't listen. I told him that I am afraid, that I feel as if the shadow moves closer with my every crossing. He said I was be-

ing stupid. Emerick has discovered the name of a man, Franzen a master alchemist, who it is said operates and practices with many fraternities throughout the world and yet belongs to none. Emerick said my parents would know him if I dared to drop the name in their presence.

Since beginning the practice with Emerick, I have come to believe that what he says about my parents and their friends is true. Amongst the thousands of books in our library, there are a great many books on alchemy. Now that I am more knowledgeable about the symbols and signs connected to the art, I can see that a great many of these have been hidden in plain sight from my mind that did not comprehend any deeper significance.

Yesterday, I asked my mother about the snake carved into the stone above our front door. She nearly beamed with pride. "You've noticed that have you?" And then proceeded to name the ouroboros and explain what I have secretly already learned through my studies with the order. I listened to her, silently, nodding my head. "This is just the beginning Elizabeth. Your father and I have a great deal to teach you, and your brother when he is ready." She then led me to the library and, from a secret panel behind a row of books, she removed a smooth wooden cube and handed it to me. When I asked her what it was she said, "A puzzle. And a gift. One that my mother received from her mother and she from hers. It is a great treasure that has been held by the women of our family for generations. Now it is yours to keep until the day your own daughter is ready to receive it."

319

I turned the box over and over but could not begin to imagine how it could be a puzzle. When I asked her what to do with it she only smiled, "Knowledge is sweeter found than given."

I remembered the day my mother passed the gift to me. But her mother, my grandmother, had said she was ready and to pass the gift when her daughter was ready.

My mother had never taught me anything about what I was now struggling to learn. She had given me the box when I was only twelve and without my grandmother's assurance that more knowledge would soon be following.

My own mother had disappeared without a sound.

Emerick was right, my parents will initiate me and Nigel. We will learn the ways, make the connections to others who enjoy the privilege of power, the luxury of wealth. All the while Emerick's family still treat him as a distant relation for which they provide the charity of a decent practical education and a pocketful of living expenses. And, seeing as how he has yet to even meet his father in person, it seems that Emerick's fear of always being an outsider are not without cause.

It's a great injustice.

Emerick has contacted Franzen and he has agreed to come and meet with our small and burgeoning group. In his letter, Franzen expressed support for "The Learning" to reach beyond the borders of the select and privileged few who are born into ready-made connections. He said, "I have long worked and waited for the time when the whole world would light up with the gift of knowledge and universal understanding."

I have never seen Emerick so excited.

Franzen has come and met with us all. He teaches us the secrets, the mysteries. I watch Emerick, he tries to emulate Franzen in every respect. Practically his every word now is about the order, the mission. I'm certain his thoughts are too. What we are learning is fascinating, but Emerick no longer has interest in anything else.

I invited Simon but he shrugged me off. I'm secretly glad of it. It has been good to have at least one friend on the outside. Simon keeps me connected to this world, the reality of this material, this here and now. My head is so filled, without him, I would likely float away.

I will not write of Franzen. He is beyond description. Any meager words I might scratch out here would be a dim shadow. He is the light.

I put the book down. It was a cult. Whoever this Franzen was, he had brainwashed them all and converted Emerick into his most ardent zealot.

Something has happened. Today, as I climbed the stairs to Emerick's, I could hear voices, angry and arguing, carrying through the hall. By the time I reached his door, I knew they were coming from inside his flat. It was Emerick and Franzen. I stood outside trying to listen, trying to make out what they were fighting about, but the walls and door muffled the sound sufficiently to keep the details from me. I stood there for several minutes unsure as to whether or not I should knock or just leave. When I'd finally decided to go, the door flew open and Franzen who had been ready to storm into the hallways stopped abruptly at the sight of me. He looked into my eyes and I would swear he breathed my name, "Elizabeth." Before I knew what was happening, he had hold of my hand and was beginning to pull me down the hall.

That's when Emerick came out.

When he saw Franzen holding my hand, pulling me away—Emerick erupted. The outburst he had that day in the library was nothing compared to what happened today and I believe that if a weapon of some sort had been readily available, Emerick would have killed Franzen. "Get your hands off of her!" he shouted. Emerick grabbed my other arm and yanked me from Franzen's grasp so roughly that I fell to the ground and banged my head on the wall. Franzen moved towards me, his eyes franticly connecting with mine, "You have to come with me, now," he said.

Emerick punched Franzen in the face so hard he fell to the floor.

I sat against the wall, I couldn't believe any of what I'd just witnessed. What had happened? Emerick worshiped Franzen.

Emerick stood seething over Franzen's limp body, he had hit him so hard it knocked him out.

When I finally found my voice it came out in a tiny croak,

"What happened?"

Emerick grabbed Franzen's foot and began dragging him down the hall. "Get inside the apartment." When I didn't immediately move he shouted, "Now Elizabeth!"

"What are you doing?"

"Franzen's not welcome here anymore," was all he said just before he started pulling Franzen's still unconscious body down the stairs.

I should have done something, shouted at Emerick to stop, gotten up off the floor and at least tried to prevent the sickening sound of Franzen's head banging against each step as Emerick dragged him down to the building's front door.

But I didn't. I sat there, frozen and scared until Emerick came back up, grabbed my arm and pulled me roughly off the floor and into his flat.

He didn't speak to me, only sat me on the floor while he scribbled a note on a piece of paper. When I asked him what it said he showed me the words, "DO NOT DISTURB!" he taped it to his front door and then slid the deadbolt.

When he came and sat next to me, I asked him what had happened. He stared into my eyes and was silent for a long time before he finally said, "Franzen is not one of us. He does not truly want to share the depth of the secrets with us. He means to hold the true powers for himself, to keep us his subjects, his underlings, his...students. I will not bow and scrape. I will not be manipulated like a puppet on a master's string."

He turned on the CD player and Moonlight Sonata began

filling the room. I said no. I remember, I said no. I didn't want to cross again. I didn't want to cross ever again. I said this to him. But the music, it wove through my brain, the connection started anyway.

"I promise," he said. "I promise this is the last time Elizabeth. I won't need you again after today."

And so, I think we did cross. I think I did go again.

But I don't remember. I don't remember crossing. I don't remember being on the astral plane. I don't remember how I even came to be here, sitting in my own rooms. It is as if I woke up, sitting on my bed, staring out my window. I have no idea how I got from Emerick's to here. The memory exists within me, I can feel it there in the depths of my mind but it feels like a great dark shroud has been thrown over those images.

Something is different. Something has happened. If we did cross, I don't remember if the shadow was still lurking there. Still watching. Still waiting.

But its breath is at my back. Here, in the physical, I feel the same slinking sickness as in the plane and when I turn to look and look and look, there is nothing, nothing that my eyes can see. Except my skin, it crawls and my nerves scream out a warning, urging me to run.

I am not alone.

I am scared.

The pages after were empty. One after the next, I pushed through the last quarter of the book finding nothing until a folded page fell from the journal and into my lap. I picked it up and opened it. I recognized the words from day I'd first found the diaries.

I never imagined feeling so whole, so utterly complete and perfect. In his arms time stops and it is enough to only be with him. I can no longer conceive of a life without him, we are bound mind, body, soul. I see in his eyes, feel in his touch, it is evident in the press of his lips, he is who my soul forever seeks and I his. We are complete, whole, together at last. We are one.

Again.

It wasn't Emerick. Emerick who I thought she felt *bound mind, body, soul.* It was my dad all along. My dad who had the sense to not get mixed up in a cult, my dad who had been her tether to the world outside, she had loved him. I refolded the page and slipped it back between the journal's last pages. When I closed the book, my eye caught the sight of something inside the back cover and so I pressed the journal back open. There were more words, quickly written onto the inside back cover.

The mistakes I have made...I can hardly bear to think. I was so utterly wrong in my thinking. I see that now. I fear Emerick becomes more powerful with every moment. If he should suspect what this is growing inside me, his jealously would roll like the ocean to consume me. Filled with the omnipotence of his new friends, I only suspect what he is capable of. That alone is enough to make me very much afraid of him.

I must run.

I leave today.

CHAPTER TWENTY FOUR

SHAME

I stared at those words. She got out. She had escaped. That was why she'd run to America with my dad.

And with me.

My eyes ran over her words, *If he should suspect what this is growing inside me, his jealously...*I was growing inside her. She was pregnant with me and I wasn't Emerick's child.

I was Simon's.

"Charlotte?"

I jumped and clutched my chest.

"Sorry," Caleb walked slowly from the bedroom to where I sat on the couch. He stopped when he saw what I was holding. "Where did you find that?"

"At the Wriothesley's," I shut the book and ran my hands possessively over the cover. "It's the one that was in my bag, I found it in Emerick's workroom."

Caleb stared at the book for several seconds before he let

out a shaky breath and sat next to me. "Then you don't have to go back there." He leaned over and kissed me gently on the lips.

It was like my spine had become an inflexible rod. I didn't move.

By the way Caleb pulled back, I could tell he sensed something was wrong. He avoided my eyes and reached for my hand, brushing his thumb nervously across my palm.

"I'm going back tomorrow, I have to find the other diaries."

His thumb moved faster, no doubt keeping speed with his spinning thoughts.

He leaned awkwardly towards me to kiss me again but when he stopped halfway between us to adjust, I took the opportunity to stand up and move away from him.

It was like Hayden was in the room, standing between us. I moved quickly to the shelf and pretended to search the stacks.

I could hear his movements behind me as he got up and stood behind me. I felt his hands rest lightly on my arms.

"Charlotte?" his worry radiated off him.

The vivid memory of lying in Hayden's bed while his hands roamed all over my body assaulted me.

"Is everything okay?"

Shame crawled through my skin.

"Did Hayden *do* something?" his voice edged into hysteria.

There was no way I could do this. I had to break up with Caleb.

My body felt limp as his hands turned me around to face him. "You're scaring me. What happened? Tell me!"

I shook my head.

"Charlotte, you have to tell me..." his voice broke.

Hayden kissed me, his hands...his hands were..."Nothing," I shook my head. "I just...finding the diary. I almost got caught."

He searched my eyes, ignoring the lie I knew he felt. Suddenly he kissed me, pressing his mouth to mine until it hurt.

I welcomed the pain.

He pulled away, "Don't go back. We'll do something...get out of this house."

My eyes fell to the diary lying on the sofa.

"You're not going," he tried.

But I was.

CHAPTER TWENTY FIVE

RAGE

I resisted the urge to pull at the bottom of my bathing suit.
Girls in bikinis and guys in swim trunks swarmed all over the
Wriothesley's pool deck. Except for the one thirty something
guy who was doing cannonballs into the deep end and trying
to talk with girls half his age, all the adults were drinking and
laughing at each other's wit around the outdoor bar.

I was the only girl under forty in a one-piece suit.

"Sexy," Hayden laughed when he saw me. "And here I
bragged to all my mates that my California girl was coming."

"I live on the beach, I don't play in it."

"Never mind," he put one arm around me and with his
other hand, pulled at the top of my suit and looked down it.
"We'll soon have you out of this all together."

"Stop it!" I swatted his hand.

"You must be Charlotte?" a woman suddenly appeared.

"Um...yes."

She extended her polished hand, "I'm Mrs. Wriothesley, Hayden's mother."

I took her hand, her grasp felt limp and was brief. "It's nice to meet you."

"You may not know this but your mother was my very best friend when we were growing up."

"No, I didn't know," I lied.

My apparent lack of information about her past with my mother seemed to comfort her. Her smile softened. "I can't tell you how wonderful," she eyed Hayden carefully, "this is for us."

"See, she's practically planning our wedding," Hayden finished whatever he was drinking, it looked like beer.

I ignored him. "Thank you for inviting me."

"You're family now Charlotte," she smiled, but her eyes looked flat, expressionless.

She left us and continued on her greeting tour, "Marjorie…"

"You want a drink?" Hayden lifted his own glass.

"What is that?"

"Beer."

"No."

"It might help," he raised his eyebrows.

"Who, you?"

"Who else?"

"I'll have a soda or something…nonalcoholic," I called after him.

Emerick was off in a corner speaking with a man who was wearing a suit. *At a pool party?* I needed to sneak away from Hayden. With everyone outside, today was my chance to search Emerick's office.

While Hayden crossed the pool deck to the bar, girls all over the pool glanced first at him and then quick, poorly veiled glares at me.

Hayden came back with Coke for me and more beer for himself. I drank mine as quickly as I could. "I think some of your girlfriends are not happy I'm here," I took another chug. The bathroom was the best excuse I could think of to get into the house and away from Hayden.

Hayden brazenly scanned the pool, he even pointed to one girl who clearly saw him, and then leaned in near my ear. "See her? She's madly jealous of your swimsuit."

I shoved him but he barely budged.

She was too far to hear anything he said, but she quickly looked away, her face beamed with embarrassment.

"Why do you do that?"

"Because it's easy."

I sighed and looked around. A few more sips and I'd make my excuse. "Where's your sister?"

Hayden took another gulp of beer. "Probably hiding in her room."

I couldn't imagine a Wriothesley hiding from anything. "Why?"

"Parties make her nervous."

332

"Really?"

"My sist—"

"Hayden!" A monstrous looking guy came and slapped him on the back. "So this is your *new* gal?"

"Charlotte," I offered. "Nice to meet you." I didn't wait for his name, this was my opportunity to slip away. I turned to Hayden. "I'm going to the restroom."

"You need help?"

I narrowed my eyes at him, *funny*.

Hayden and Monster's laughter followed me into the house.

I did stop at the bathroom, just in case Hayden decided to carry his joke in after me. I washed my hands, splashed water on my face, and fixed my ponytail. Finally, I looked at my reflection, "You're stalling," I whispered.

I nodded and bit my lip. I could feel my intestines shift. *Go now.*

I navigated the halls quickly, the house was more familiar to me now. When I reached the door to Emerick's outer study, I slipped quickly inside and leaned against the door. My hands were shaking. *Everyone is outside, just be quick.*

I pushed myself off the door, and entered the hall that led to Emerick's office. I rushed past the portraits of famous men and only glanced at Francis Bacon's strange pose. *AKA Shake Sphere.* I knew now some thought he was Shakespeare.

I paused at the office door and knocked gently, just in case. *Silence.* I turned the handle slowly, slipped in, and guided the door back into its frame as quietly as I could.

I crossed and held my arms tight across my abdomen, my whole body shook and would not stop.

I scanned the room. Where? There were a few shelves and filing cabinets. His desk, and a large armoire stood in the corner.

The bookshelf was the least nerve racking. I scanned the shelves looking for leather spines with no titles. *Crime and Punishment, The Brothers Karamazov, The Idiot, The Possessed*. All Dostoevsky—his favorite author. I reached the bottom shelf, they weren't here.

The wood filing cabinets spanned the back wall. I pulled the first drawer, it moved half an inch and stopped abruptly. Locked. I hadn't thought of this. The thought of first stealing Emerick's keys and then breaking into his office sent fresh waves of anxiety rushing through me. I tried every drawer, not one opened.

Emerick's desktop was a blank slate. No files, no photos, not a single scrap of paper cluttered the highly polished wood. Only his slim monitor stood blank faced keeping guard. The keyboard and mouse lay hidden on a sliding drawer under the desk front.

I took a breath.

Moving his chair just enough, I slid the keyboard out and cupped the mouse in my hand, shaking it across the pad a few times. Emerick's screen woke up, bright white light radiated from the monitor and reflected off the desktop.

He had left his email account open.

I glanced at the door and then scoured the subject list of his in-box.

Halfway down the first page, one title marked urgent caught my attention.

Press Release. It was from Edge Water Public Relations.

Dear Mr. Wriothesley:

Attached is the press release draft announcing your candidacy for the upcoming Shadow Cabinet election. Please review and send any revisions...

I clicked the attachment. Emerick was running for some political appointment but I had no idea what the Shadow Cabinet was.

My eyes ran down the other subject titles while I scrolled farther and farther down.

E.S. Surveillance Photos. It was from a company named Hancock.

E.S.? As in, Elizabeth Stevens? I clicked the email.

"What are you doing?

I jumped and fell against the office chair, sending it flying into the bookshelf. A girl stood at the door scowling. "Who are you? Does my father know you're in here?"

My mind flew. This was Diana, Hayden's little sister. "I..." my mind raced to find a legitimate excuse for me to be snooping around Emerick's office. "I'm sorry," I got up off my knees. "I'm Charlotte...Hayden's girlfriend."

Her expression relaxed a little.

I looked at the computer. "I'm staying with my uncle for the summer, but I'm not allowed to use his computer."

Her face was suddenly sympathetic.

I had found a way. "I know, right? I have no cell, no computer, I'm completely cut off."

Her shoulders actually drooped with empathy, "How horrible."

"Yes!" My eyes pleaded with her, "I know I shouldn't be in here," I paused and bit my lip for effect. "If my uncle finds out, he'll kill me."

"I won't say anything," she touched her chest. "But really, Hayden has a computer in his room."

"Really?" I reached for the mouse but kept my eyes glued to hers. "I don't remember seeing it." I closed the email. "But your brother..." I rolled my eyes hoping she would infer some meaning, anything other than I was trying to back out of her father's personal email without getting caught.

"Oh! Don't get me started," she threw her hands up in exasperation.

I smiled, quickly rolled the screen back to where it had been and stood up. "So I'm really sorry, I was just *desperate*. I'll be sure to use Hayden's from now on...now that I know."

"You could use mine."

We walked back to the party together, Diana promised she wouldn't tell and I nodded, smiled, cringed, and made appropriate single phrase responses. *"No!" "Really?" "Oh my God."* While she talked like lightening.

When we reached the doors leading back to the grounds, she stopped. I opened the door, but she didn't move.

"Aren't you coming?"

Diana looked out the large glass doors for a second before taking a step back. She shook her head, "No, maybe later."

Hayden had seen us and was heading towards us.

"I actually have some stuff to do."

"You're sure?" Although I was kind of relieved I wouldn't have to listen to her anymore. Hayden met us and gathered me into his arms.

"I'll see you later," she backed away while her brother ate my neck.

"Okay," I whispered back.

I watched her leave and turn down a hall I didn't know.

"Where were you?" Hayden kissed my neck and tried to shove my bathing suit strap off my shoulder.

"In the bathroom," I yanked the strap back up.

"What took you so long?"

"Do you have to know my every *movement*?"

"Yes, especially the bathroom ones," he bit my earlobe, shivers ran through my body.

"You're disgusting," I pushed him but he sprang back.

"Let's go to my room."

"What for?"

His hand slid down my back and rested on my butt. "Guess," he whispered.

I wiggled out and away from him. "My God. Your parents..." but when I looked to the bar area, I could see that all the adults had left.

"No," he shook his head. "I don't want them to come. That's just weird Charlotte."

I ignored him and walked back towards the pool. Hayden *might* control himself more in a crowd.

Halfway to the pool, I felt his hand on my arm. "Charlotte."

I turned, "What?"

"I'm sorry."

I flinched with shock. "For what?" He actually hadn't done anything *that* bad.

His face was completely serious. His hand reached up and tucked a strand of my hair behind my ear and then held my chin. His thumb brushed my lips. "I'm glad you came today."

He leaned down and kissed me gently on the lips.

I couldn't help it, I kissed him back. My mouth fell open and his tongue lightly brushed mine. His hands slipped down my sides but this time held the small of my back.

When he was like this, it was impossible. I reached up and held his face in my hands, his tongue pressed harder against mine. My legs shook, but he held me.

Please, don't let him ask me to go to his room now.

I would.

I opened my eyes but Hayden's were already open, he was staring over my shoulder while we kissed.

I pulled away and turned.

Caleb.

Caleb and Sophie were standing on the other side of the lawn. Caleb's eyes burned into mine while Sophie tried to pull him away. He shook her off.

I stumbled out of Hayden's arms.

Caleb glared at Hayden. Hayden smirked, his chin high, he snapped his head slightly, daring Caleb.

Caleb charged across the lawn.

No.

Hayden widened his stance, preparing for Caleb's impact.

I rushed up to him and grabbed his arm, "No!

He kept his eyes centered on Caleb "Go Charlotte," he shoved me off him and I fell backwards, my tailbone hitting the concrete.

Caleb hit Hayden running, his whole body slammed into Hayden's chest and abdomen.

It was his only hit.

Hayden recovered from the blow quickly, pulled back his fist and punched Caleb in the face.

The blow shocked Caleb, his body buckled.

Hayden punched him again with his other fist.

Caleb fell to the ground,

Hayden's nostrils flared, his lip raised up off his teeth. "Get up! You want to fight for her, get up you piece of shit!"

Caleb rolled onto his side, his face was covered in blood.

Hayden hovered over Caleb and lifted his leg.

"Stop," I cried.

Hayden stomped Caleb's ribs forcing the air out of him.

I watched Caleb gasping, trying to breath.

Where were the adults? I searched the grounds, and then I remembered they'd all gone inside.

But then, I saw her. Emerick's mother was standing next to the door to the house.

Hayden kicked Caleb's face.

Mrs. Wriothesley didn't move. She only stood, expressionless, watching her son kill Caleb.

I scrambled to my feet, pain shot down my spine from my own fall. I threw myself on top of Caleb. "Stop it!" I screamed.

"Move Charlotte."

"No!"

Hayden looked like he was about to grab me, but Monster stepped between us. "Hey man," he put his arms out, put his own face in front of Hayden's.

Hayden glared at him. "Move!"

Monster was calm, he moved slightly one way and then the next, like a snake charmer, he kept Hayden's eyes on him. "Let's not have a repeat," he said.

Hayden eyes flicked. Monster had his full attention.

"I think he gets the point," Monster continued.

Hayden stood seething a moment longer before he turned, kicked a chair and stormed into the house.

Caleb laid gasping and bleeding beneath me. He needed help.

Everyone just stared, paralyzed by what just happened. I

looked back towards the door, searching for Margot—she was gone.

TWENTY SIX

HURTING YOU, HURTING ME

Monster helped Sophie and me carry Caleb to his car. His eyes were swelling and turning purple, his mouth and teeth were stained in blood. We helped him into the back seat and he cried out when Monster touched his torso.

"His ribs might be broken," Monster said.

"They're not broken," Caleb mumbled through his swollen lips.

"Thank you I said." I wanted to ask him what he'd meant when he told Hayden 'Let's not have a repeat,' but he was already walking away and Caleb probably needed to get to a doctor.

I closed the back door and got behind the wheel while Sophie climbed into the passenger seat. She had been crying since watching her brother get his head kicked in.

The car started and I steered us down the drive. I couldn't speak, I didn't dare.

It was all my fault.

When my uncle saw us, his eyes swept over Caleb before narrowing on me. After Ms. Steward and Sophie rushed Caleb to the hospital my uncle stood, like a statue, holding me with his stare. "Were you hurt?" only his lips moved.

"No."

"What exactly is your relationship with Hayden Wriothesley?"

I bit my lip, hesitating. My uncle waited in stony silence. "He's my boyfriend."

His brow furrowed. "And what does Caleb have to do with this?"

I took a breath and wished I could escape to my room. "Caleb and I were seeing each other."

"Were?"

"Yes."

"But not now."

I rolled both my lips between my teeth and stared at the floor. My throat felt stretched and my eyes blurred with tears that threatened to overflow and fall any second. "Except," I started to cry. "Except I hadn't told him."

My uncle sighed. "And Caleb showed up..."

"He saw us."

"And the boys fought."

"It wasn't a fight."

My uncle turned and looked out the window. Minutes passed while we stood in silence.

I finally asked, "May I go to my room?"

My uncle turned back to me as if surprised to find me still there. "Yes...and I want you to stay there." He returned his attention to the window. "I have business tonight Charlotte. I don't want to have to be second guessing your safety."

"Yes sir," I turned and left.

In my room, I turned on my bedside lamp. The small light warmed the area around the bed but was not powerful enough to stretch to the chaise or the large armoire in the far corner. The sun was setting and the small library was growing darker. Soft evening light from the window washed the room in diffused light. The picture out the window pulled me to it and standing there, I could see to the east a large moon rising on the horizon.

The image of Caleb, swollen and bloodied would not leave my mind. But as agonizing as the physical images of Hayden breaking Caleb's body were, there was one worse.

Before Caleb was angry, he was hurt. In my mind, I turned, my mouth still wet, my blood still warm from Hayden's kiss. And there was Caleb, across the lawn, watching in agony. Physical pain, shock—betrayal, in that split second, all fighting for space.

And then he did the only thing he could do.

But Hayden was much better at that.

I laid down on the sofa with my arm over my face and cried.

I wanted to go home. Now that Caleb knew what I had done, how hurtful and horrible I could be, I couldn't face him. No apology could ever make my betrayal easier.

And I had wanted Hayden. Welcomed his hands on me, relished the press of his body against mine. Caleb saw all of that.

A fresh wave of tears escaped between my eyes and my arm. I rolled on my side and pulled my knees to my chest.

My body felt drained, lifeless. Unmoving, I watched the light change from soft gray to blue as the moon beamed brightly through the window.

I had no idea how long I'd been there, awake, numb. Car lights suddenly illuminated the wall behind me, traveling in a slow arc.

They were home.

I stood and went to the window. I expected to see Ms. Steward and Sophie helping Caleb into the house. But the car was still rolling to a stop when the passenger door flew open.

Caleb ran across the drive and into the house.

My stomach twisted. He was coming to yell at me, throw it all in my face. I imagined him at the hospital, realizing the cruelty of what I'd done and hating me for it. I faced the door and waited. Whatever he was going to say, I deserved it.

Seconds passed, any moment he'd be through the door. I heard him turn the handle and closed my eyes, steeling myself for his anger.

Even though I didn't look, I knew he was standing in the door, I could feel his eyes searching the room, soon, he would see me.

His feet fell hard and fast across the wood floor and were muffled when he crossed a rug.

I felt him getting closer and then, right in front of me.

He took my hand.

His touch surprised me. I opened my eyes. He was kneeling on the rug in front of me, holding my hand in both of his. He looked up into my eyes, his face looked worse. The skin around his eyes had turned black and his nose and lips were swollen and purple.

Tears filled his eyes, "Please Charlotte."

My breath caught in my throat.

"Please," he begged. "Not him..." he shook his head. His tears ran down his face. "I'm sorry...so sorry."

I couldn't bear him apologizing to me. "*I'm* sorry..." but he got quickly to his feet and pressed my head to his chest. His heart thundered next to my ear.

He pulled away and held both sides of my head in his hands. He looked into my eyes, his mouth quivered as he cried.

"I don't understand,"

He shook his head and pulled my hand, leading me from the room. I followed him down the dark hall to his bedroom. He paused for a moment at the door, his eyes closed, fresh tears spilled down.

"I love you Charlotte," he whispered and opened the door. We walked inside and he flipped on the light.

At first I didn't understand what I was looking at, there was a mud-encrusted crate lying in the middle of Caleb's floor.

"What…" I started but Caleb pulled me closer. He stood next to it, watching me closely.

I looked down. It wasn't locked, only a small metal latch secured the lid to the box. Bending down I reached for the latch.

"I tried to tell you yesterday," he mumbled miserably.

I flipped the latch and pushed the lid up.

The overhead light illuminated the crate's insides. I stared, trying to make sense of what I was seeing, how Caleb was acting, how all those pieces didn't fit together with what I had been thinking.

"I don't understand," I pulled one from the box, held it in my hand, opened the cover to her words. "How?" I looked up at Caleb. His eyes were closed.

"I took them," he said.

I ran my hands over them, felt the leather, the raised symbols. It didn't make sense, how could they be here? Emerick had them stolen, the man in the dark trench coat, he had stolen them—Emerick had them.

But he didn't.

Caleb knelt next to me, "I tried to tell you…"

"Why?" All this time. All my rambling, searching, fretting.

"Your uncle asked me to. That first day Hayden picked you up. Your uncle called and asked me to collect some books from the armoire in your room and box them up. He told me to bury them. In the garden, there's a secret storage area, he told me how to find it."

"All this time," I whispered. "You knew all this time."

"I didn't know what they were," he tried to defend himself.

"Not at first!" I remembered noticing Caleb's dirty nails that night at the kitchen table. "You didn't know at first. But for weeks now..."

"I'm sorry Charlotte, you have to believe me. I didn't do it to hurt you. Your uncle, he's trying to protect you I think."

"You think! No that's exactly what you didn't do! Did it ever occur to you that my uncle, your oh so generous *benefactor*, that maybe he has something to hide? Something about my mother! Think Caleb! Why was he so swift to bury my mother without a shred of evidence? She's still out there somewhere and he doesn't want her to come back. The last thing you did Caleb was think!" My voice turned to ice, "At least not for yourself."

"Charlotte," he begged. "Please. I never meant for this to happen. I never dreamed you would think the Wriothesley's would have them. And now..." he choked.

"And now I'm Hayden Wriothesley's girlfriend," I hoped his heart burst. "And it's nobody's fault except yours."

Caleb's keys were on the nightstand. I stood, grabbed them and left his room.

"Charlotte," he called down the hall. "Where are you going?"

He wasn't chasing me so I stopped at the staircase. "I'm going to Hayden."

He shook his head. "Don't. I'm begging you. Be mad at

me, hate me...never speak to me again. Please don't go to him Charlotte. He's dangerous," his voice cracked. "He'll hurt you Charlotte."

"Really? That's actually ridiculous coming from you. Hayden hasn't ever hurt me. But you," I started down the stairs. "You've been hurting me for weeks."

CHAPTER TWENTY SEVEN

RUN

The moon was full and hung just above the treetops as I pushed Caleb's decrepit car past its limit. It complained every half-mile with a violent shudder and I thought for sure it was going to die any minute. I worried his crappy car was going to leave me stranded in the middle of a dark country road so I eased off the gas a bit. The shudder grew more desperate and added a loud clacking to its death knell.

"Don't die," I begged.

I concentrated on the short strip of road illuminated by the headlights and counted the seconds between shudders. I couldn't think about Caleb.

Caleb was so worried about losing my uncle's favor, and so grateful for his help getting in to Cambridge, he was blind to my uncle's motives. Caleb didn't want to believe my uncle might not have the best of intentions for me—that would mean he would have to make a choice. Cambridge or Charlotte.

Keeping my mother's diaries from me, even after he knew how much they meant to me—he made his choice.

I rolled through the Wriothesley's main gates relieved to have made it. Even if the car wheezed to a stop now, I could run the rest of the way. There was enough light from the moon to keep my panic in check.

When I reached the drive, I finally let the car stop but it shook for so long after I removed the key, I wondered if it would ever have the energy to start up again.

I didn't care. Gaersum Aern was the last place I wanted to go. Hayden would let me spend the night.

A number of cars and SUVs were parked on the driveway. I ran past them, up the stairs and rang the doorbell. I waited, staring at the square and compass symbol etched into the entrance floor.

No one answered.

I pushed the bell again. With all the cars parked, they probably still had guests from the earlier pool party. I imagined Emerick and Margot talking and drinking with friends, maybe no one could hear.

Nothing. I tried the door handle, it was locked.

I backtracked down the steps and walked past the topiary gardens. Everyone might be in the back garden around the pool. I followed the path that led around the side of the mansion to the back gates.

When I was closer, I strained to hear voices, music, something to indicate I wasn't alone. The full moon illuminated the sky and the grounds around me—but it was still dark.

I turned the corner and passed through the wrought iron gates. I couldn't hear anything. When I came around the last corner, the pool deck and bar were empty. The pool light was on and the water shimmered brightly against the night sky.

But I was alone.

I hurried past the pool—the back door might still be open. I pushed against the heavy glass door and was relieved when it drifted, soundless, to the other side.

It was so quiet.

The Wriothesley's mansion was enormous but still, with all the cars parked out front, I had thought there would be some noise, even a distant mummer of collective voices from a far room. I headed down the hallways leading to Hayden's bedroom. It wasn't just that the house was quiet, it felt empty.

Hayden's door was closed.

I knocked gently and waited. When he didn't answer I opened the door a crack and peeked my head in, "Hello?"

He wasn't here. He might be in the theater room. In all the commotion throughout the day it hadn't really occurred to me that Hayden might be mad at me. After all, I had thrown myself on Caleb to try and protect him. But I would do that again. Hayden needed to learn to control his temper.

On the way to the theater, I kept listening for the sound of someone else in the house. Where was everyone?

I pulled the door to the theatre, the screen was blank and

the red velvet seats were all vacant.

I didn't know what to do. Margot had welcomed me as family, in her flat, emotionless way, but I wasn't sure the invitation extended to lurking around the house when it didn't look like anyone was home. The thought of driving all the way back to Gaersum Aern and dealing with Caleb was not at all what I wanted to do right now.

I decided to go wait in Hayden's room.

I turned to leave the theatre when white light caught my attention. I stopped. Up over the entrance, white light glowed behind a tinted window. I stepped further into the room and looked up. The other times I had been in the theater, I hadn't really thought about how their giant screen worked. I'd never noticed the window but now that I saw it, it reminded me of a commercial theater, where the projector would be. I realized now that the Wriothesley theatre was the same, only Hayden could have the projector show movies or TV—Hayden could have it show whatever he wanted.

The white light was coming from the projector room up there.

I looked, there was a door, designed to look just like the wall. In the corner near the theater entrance—a thin brass handle gave it away.

The door was heavy so I pulled hard. A narrow set of black stairs led directly to the room above. The walls on both sides of the stairwell were carpeted, when I reached the top, I saw right away what was creating the glow.

The projector was positioned at the front of the room. It looked like a complex computer with a giant lens. But that wasn't where the light was coming from.

All along the back wall, a series of tiny flat screen monitors projected images from all over the house.

It was the video surveillance system. Standing in front of the video patchwork, I could see the kitchen, the entrance-way, the pool deck, the theatre room I had just been in—it seemed like every room in the house. I gasped, there was an image of Hayden's empty room. Somewhere, there was tape of me lying on his bed half naked, tape of what we had done together.

I groaned, *Oh God.*

And then I saw Diana. She was sitting in her room on her computer. Emerick spied on his own children.

I continued to scan the screens, looking for more people. My eyes stopped. One image held lots of people all in one room. They were standing in a thick circle around a checker-board floor with a sunburst in the middle. One person stood in the center next to the white stone pedestal. It was the room attached to Emerick's workroom.

They were all dressed in long robes making it difficult to at first tell who was who. But then I saw Emerick, he stood at the top of the circle and next to him was Margot's pinched face.

Everyone seemed to be speaking at once, their lips moved in unison. I couldn't hear what they were saying but I didn't dare touch the complex looking digital board in front of me.

The person in the center of the room raised their arms into a T and began turning in a slow circle. Their face moved into the camera's view—a small click escaped my throat. It was Hayden.

I stared as he moved first to his mother. Standing in front of her, she made some motion with her arm and Hayden bowed to her. He moved in front of his father. Emerick made the same motion as Margot had, Hayden bowed. When Hayden stood in front of the third person, a man I didn't recognize with jet-black hair, I was able to distinguish what they were doing. Hayden stood in front of each person standing on the inner wall of the circle, each person held out their arm, drew an invisible five pointed star and then circled it. Hayden bowed to each one.

A quarter way around the circle, Hayden stood in front of my uncle.

Surprised, I fell back half a step.

I watched my uncle make the sign in front of Hayden, this was the *business* he had to attend tonight. What looked like Hayden's initiation.

Everyone's lips continued to move, to chant, but it looked like they were getting faster, their expressions more intense. Hayden was rounding the last quarter of the circle.

I noticed the man standing next to Emerick, the man with the black hair. My eyes were drawn to him. His lips had stopped moving.

Slowly, his head turned and then his eyes, until he stared

directly into the camera. It felt like he was staring directly at me.

My blood began to rush and I felt it pulse in my neck.

I waited for him to look away, *he only noticed the camera, that's all.* He couldn't *know* someone was watching.

And then I knew who he was. The man from the driveway, the man deep in the woods, the man who I thought had broken into Gaersum Aern, and stolen my mother's diaries—vandalized the library.

The man who was obviously involved with both Emerick and my uncle.

His eyes burned into the camera, burned into me. And then I heard it, as clearly as if it had been whispered into my ear, only, he whispered into my brain.

"He knows Charlotte. Emerick knows you took Elizabeth's diary. He wants it back."

His black eyes held me. His lips started to move again and now, I clearly read his message.

Run.

CHAPTER TWENTY EIGHT

HIDING

I slammed my door and locked the bolt. I turned, bashed my shin into something hard and fell sprawling onto the floor.

Caleb had brought the crate of diaries and left them in my room—in the middle of the doorway.

I rolled myself into a sitting position and inspected the gash on my shin. The wood had grazed off a few layers of skin right over the bone. I kicked the box with the sole of my other foot. *Stupid Caleb.*

I started to cry, like a kid waiting for a band-aid. I held my shin and cried. I wanted to go home, right now, I wanted to pack my bag, drive to the airport and grab the first flight back to LA. I didn't care anymore. That man's voice inside my head had terrified me. The entire wretched drive home I had wondered—worried, if I was losing my mind.

No one was bringing me a band-aid.

I got up off the floor, stumbled up the step stool and fell

across the bed. I crawled under the covers and shut my eyes. I didn't want to see anyone, anyone except my father.

But—the thought brought a fresh wave of tears—*he was gone too.*

It broke over me like a wave and pulled me under. The truth of Camilla's warning was so clear. *'Trust no one Charlotte, no one.'*

I didn't have anyone.

When I opened my eyes, they felt swollen and scratchy. I rubbed them hard with my knuckles and looked for the clock.

The sun blazed through the large windows—nine-twelve. I had actually fallen asleep, eventually.

I rolled on my side and saw the crate still lying where I'd tripped over it last night. Next to it, on the floor near the door, someone had shoved what looked like a folded note through the crack.

It was from Caleb, I knew it. I ignored it.

If I had to, I would stay in this room until my father was found and I could go home.

But what if Susan doesn't find him? I pushed the thought from my mind. There was no way I could deal with that possibility right now.

I laid back against the pillows with my hands on my head. I didn't know what to do.

I sat up and rolled all the way out of bed this time, careful to land with both feet squarely on the floor. In one movement

I swiped the note off the floor and flicked it open.

Breakfast?

I slid the bolt open and I cracked the door, a tray sat outside my door. It was probably cold, I didn't care. My foot caught the outside of the tray and pulled it inside. I grabbed a piece of toast and locked the door again. Whoever had made it, put the tea in a travel mug, it was still hot.

On my way back to bed, I stopped by the crate and grabbed one of the diaries from the top. I placed the tea and toast on my bedside table, crawled back under the blankets and read for three days.

CHAPTER TWENTY NINE

BEFORE

Many of the journals were from before, before Emerick and his obsessions entered her life. In the before journals, my mother wrote of school and a terrible teacher, her friends, Margot and Emma, her annoyances with her younger brother, Nigel, her frustrations over her parents' restrictions over her life. She wrote about her life as a teenager. After reading all of the before journals, I found it rather easy to follow the narrative flow of her life and place them in a chronological order that started with her receiving the first journal on her twelfth birthday and finished with Emma and Adam beginning to date, a great upset to the Elizabeth, Margot, and Emma friendship, sometime after her seventeenth birthday.

Through them all, my mother loved her parents even though she was "longing to be free from their overbearing controls." She loved her brother, though he, "drove her crazy" on a regular basis. She even "felt fortunate to have the two best friends in the entire world," regardless of the fact that, "Emma has clearly chosen Adam over Margot and me."

And while it was true that a great many passages were about receiving, "a new, gorgeous, custom designed dress by..." an apparently famous designer, I realized that her life, while immensely privileged, was overwhelming typical.

Until she met Emerick.

It was like her entire life, her whole personality even, changed in the after journals. The after Emerick journals. It was the most obvious in the books dated after the one I had retrieved from Emerick's workroom.

I've lost a day. A whole day. I have no idea what I've done since yesterday morning. Emerick said I spent the afternoon with him, that we had lunch. He assures me that we met at The Glaring Goose, I ordered fish and chips.

My mind cannot find this.

Mother called me today. She sounded strange on the phone, as if she were trying to sound normal but found it impossible. When I asked her what is wrong she insisted it was nothing. "Nothing at all dear." But then informed me that she and father were coming out. Tomorrow! When I asked her why she floundered for several seconds before saying that they simply, "missed me terribly" and they, "want to ensure that you are quite all right there at school."

I promised her I was fine. School was fine. I had everything I could ever need. But she would not be swayed. So I am to have a visit with the parents tomorrow afternoon. Regardless of what they say, I know something is up. I have only a handful of weeks left before my final exams for the year and then I would be back home at Gaersum Aern.

I can't help but feel it has something to do with Emerick.

I was right! So right! They have forbidden me from seeing Emerick. The whole while we sat eating lunch they smiled and nodded, asked me benign questions about school, instructors, what marks I expect to receive for the semester. But their eyes, their eyes scrutinized my every movement, I could see that they were weighing my every response—looking for something. While we waited for the check I found I could take no more and just asked them straight out, "What is going on?"

They tried to smile and shake their heads, "Whatever was I talking about?" When I wouldn't let it go and insisted that I wasn't stupid and knew something was going on, that there was absolutely no reason whatsoever for them to make the trip all the way from Somerset when I was to be home in less than a month, they both finally dropped their smiles.

They didn't want to speak of it in the restaurant and would rather wait until we were all back at my room.

Essentially, they have heard it on good account that Emerick is, "delving into dangerous waters." And that I have become, or may become, "irrevocably compromised by my continued involvement with him."

I said I had no idea what they were talking about (although I knew perfectly well) and that I was greatly upset that they should choose to trust a "good account" rather than speaking to and asking me directly.

It was then that my mother came forward, placed her finger on the sapphire cross at my throat and said, "Then let's be clear, Elizabeth. We speak of this. We speak of Alchemy and Emerick's attempts to master the art unguided. Our good account is a man that I believe both you and Emerick have become familiar with, a man that had offered to teach Emerick the art and science, the same man who had the great misfortune to experience Emerick's rage first hand when he attempted to reign him in. Plainly, we are speaking of the secrets Elizabeth."

Franzen! Franzen has run to my parents and told them everything.

They said the secret is my birthright. Nigel's birthright, and they were to begin introducing me to the basic tenants of their organization, The Eastern Star, when I arrived home this summer.

The words caught me and the memory of Camilla's whispered warnings, her tattoo, her body tumbling over the roof of the speeding black Land Rover that killed her—Camilla had been a member of The Eastern Star.

"But who is to teach Emerick?" I boldly asked. The injustice of his circumstances, the betrayal of his own family, his predictions that he was to be left out of the circles of influence all cartwheeling through my thoughts at once.

363

This caught them off guard because they knew perfectly well that if Emerick's own family would not support and guide him, would not even publicly acknowledge his existence, there was little hope that members of The Eastern Star would open the doors to him against the wishes of their most powerful members.

"What of Emerick's birthright?" I asked. "This is why he sought to learn on his own, for us all to learn together."

This surprised them—"All?" my father asked.

I told them of our members, mostly my friends, and of our progress. In a rush to convince, I told them how much we have already learned, how far we had come—I told them I alone had managed to cross into the astral plane.

They both went white as ash. My father grabbed my shoulders, "What do you mean? You have left your body? You have crossed?"

I have never seen my father angry, not truly angry. His eyes burned into me and when I couldn't immediately answer him he shook me and shouted, "Answer me Elizabeth!"

"Yes, yes."

With that he let me go and turned from me to look directly at my mother. They were quiet for so long, as if communicating with their eyes alone. Finally, my mother spoke.

"You are never to see Emerick again. Do you understand me," my mother's voice shook. "You have no idea what you are messing with, what irrevocable damage you could cause."

"But, if I spoke with Emerick, explained to him..."

"NO," my father erupted. "That boy is dangerous and you

will do as I say."

I started to cry.

My mother placed her hand on his arm in an attempt to calm him, but he continued.

"This is not some game, some parlor trick. You are messing with powers you don't comprehend. I have half a mind to pull you from school and take you home with us this instant."

His anger had stunned me into silence. I only stood, waiting for them to decide if I would be allowed to finish out the year. Eventually, my mother calmed him. When I promised that I would do nothing more than attend class and return to my rooms for the remaining month, they agreed to let me stay. I am not to see Emerick, I am not to take calls from Emerick, I am not to write to Emerick.

I am not even supposed to speak with Margot or Emma until this summer and my parents have had the opportunity to share with other members of Eastern Star what has been going on in our group meetings.

I have broken the promise of silence. And now, we will all pay for my betrayal.

My parents have returned to Gaersum Aern without seeming to realize that what they have forced me to promise is impossible.

How am I supposed to just ignore Emerick for a month? He would beat the door down. So, I'm going to his flat tonight. I need to at least explain what has happened. Try to make him understand my parents' fears. I will tell him that they want to help (although it is only the sliver of a hope that I have created) that they will speak to the other members of The Eastern Star.

I am going to his flat tonight to try and explain everything.

For all the times Emerick has lost his temper I should have thought that tonight, given what I had to share with him, would have been one of the worst episodes ever.

He never even raised his voice.

After I told him of my parents' sudden visit, their questions, worries, and my new restrictions from seeing him, he only stood still as a statue staring out at the night sky visible through his window. "It was unwise of me to make an enemy of Franzen. A man with so much influence should be kept close." He turned and looked into my eyes. "It is a lesson I will not forget."

He then moved across the room towards the stereo. "What are you doing?" I asked.

"Just once more."

The sounds of Moonlight Sonata began rippling through the room. "No, you said before it was the last time you needed me."

"I'm almost there Elizabeth. I can almost cross all on my own. I feel myself on the brink."

The notes wove through my mind and I felt the connections happening, the pull of letting go. I moved to leave before I slipped farther under its influence but Emerick grabbed my hand and swept me into his arms.

His lips brushed my ears, "Please Elizabeth. If they manage to keep us apart," he kissed my lips so gently, "I might never be able to accomplish the crossing again. You know as well as I do that The Eastern Star will not go against my family's wishes. The other members will not expose them, they are too powerful, too influential. I need to be able to do it alone. Just this once more. If I can learn the art for myself, then I can continue to practice with whatever members of our group will stay loyal...even if you are not able to guide us there." His words were spoken softly, but his meaning stung—I had betrayed them all by confirming Franzen's reports to my parents.

His arms held me close while his mouth traced a line of warmth down my neck. His body pressed so close, he hadn't held me, touched me like that in so long, I held his face while his lips found mine again, a slow burn building between us. Like the longing of lovers saying goodbye.

The music swept me away. We crossed again, together, and when I could feel us both inside that veiled reality I heard his voice echo through my mind, "Thank you Elizabeth. This was all I needed."

I looked for the shadow, its slinking dark presence like a residue of a diseased emotion. It was always here, watching us, watching me, but not tonight. Tonight it was gone.

I have just awoken from the darkest of dreams. Every light in my room is burning brightly but my heart is still exploding in my chest. In the dream, I was in a house unlike any I have ever seen and yet I knew it. Knew its walls and floor, the layout of rooms around and above me. I stood in the foyer. I roamed the halls, passing through room after room, a bedroom, the ad-

joining bath, a dressing room. Like a maze, I wove farther and farther through connecting rooms with strange doors of varying sizes and shapes, some cut right into the middle of walls, like a cupboard door I would have to crawl through. Until I was deep into the center of the house, unsure of how I came to be there, unsure how to wind my way out. The only way was to go through the entire house, through the next door set in front of me. Blood red with fiercely cut uneven edges. This door paralyzed me. I only stood in front of it, staring, hoping some other way out would present itself until, slowly, I reached for the knob that felt soft and fleshy in my hand and squeezed it. A wet plasma oozed between my fingers and the door swung open.

It was a cave. Its close walls, the few feet that were visible from the light of the room behind me, looked stony and jagged and I could see the beginning decent of a rough-hewn staircase beckoning me into the depths of this place. I shook, wanting nothing but to escape when a cold flow, like an icy breath, whispered up and surrounded me.

If I wished to leave, I would have to follow the way down into the dark.

I took a breath and stepped over the threshold. The red door slammed shut behind me. Plunged into the dark, panic erupted through my body. Something was coming up from the deep. I lunged back for the red door, my hands frantically searching for what my eyes couldn't see, but there is no knob on this side of the door.

I could feel it at my back, raising the hairs on my neck. The coldness crept up from the bowels below. Closer, I knew it was closer. I banged on the door, tried to scream. I am alone, alone with the deep, with the cold, with the something coming.

It is running, leaping, it lunges for me. Its razor sharp claws pierce the flesh on my back and the weight of the creature forces me to the floor. My face pressed into the cold, damp stone, it thrashes at my back, shreds my flesh. I feel it working its way inside me. Tunneling through my body until it has an iron grip on my spine.

That is when I woke up. The dream was so real, even now I'm still shaking and jumping at every creak. I am too scared to go back to sleep, I can't even close my eyes without reliving the sensation of that beast on my back. I don't feel alone, it's like the thick presence of something else, someone else, is charging the room with its electricity. As if the air was breathing around me.

I wish I had gone home with mother and father.

The next entry had a date above it.

June 10

I am terrified. I must keep the date ever in front of me. Days, weeks even, have now slipped from my knowing awareness. I have attended classes I do not recall, conversed with people I do not remember, I have even purchased a new dress, custom tailored, without even the slightest trace of a memory for the actions. At this moment, I am sitting on my bed with the tailor's box and the beaded gown it contains.

My own hand written instructions are scrawled across the purchase receipt: Sapphire blue, plunging back, beaded pentagram just above the tailbone.

This is my writing. The dress undoubtedly will fit with perfection. But I have not done these things! I went to see Emerick, he said he has seen me nearly every day for the past two weeks. He said he hasn't noticed anything different about me, suggests that I am merely overtired. When I asked him about the dress he said that I had it made for the summer solstice ritual the group has planned.

"What ritual," I asked him.

He smiled and shook his head. "You really are tired love. It was your own idea. Since your parents' meddling, you said we all needed to bond more formally together. On the night of the summer solstice, we will cross into the astral plane together and bond our souls to one another.

But we had never all crossed together I said. Emerick then told me that I have been instructing the others with amazing success over the past two weeks! I have managed to help them all over, one at a time and, just yesterday, we crossed as a group. "It's no wonder you're over tired."

"And this was my idea?" I asked him.

He nodded his head. "Why don't you lie down, I'm sure you'll feel much better after some rest."

I shouted at him them. "Stop saying that! I am not tired, something is wrong. I can feel it. There is something wrong with me. People don't just forget two weeks of their life because they *are tired!" I told Emerick that I didn't want to see him again. I told him to stay away from me, that I was going home, telling my family everything.*

It was then that he changed. His expression turned to pure hatred as his rage swept away all pretense. It was then that he grabbed my arm with such violence, he left finger shaped bruises in his wake. He yanked me close and brought his lips to my ear, "I wouldn't if I were you," he whispered. "Do not make an enemy of me, Elizabeth. You will regret it."

I pulled free of his grasp and ran from his flat.

I am calling mother and father immediately, telling them everything. There is nothing more clear to me than the fact that I can not handle whatever is happening alone. I need to go home.

Even now, my mind feels borrowed, it's as if it only holds broken pieces of a mirrored life. Glimpses in a fleeting light. I'm losing myself. Everyday, I slip further away from reality.

My life is being stolen from within.

I turned the page to find the next entry, but it was blank. This was the last book, her last words. I flipped back to the beginning of the dated entry, *June 10*. A thought occurred to me that stopped the breath in my chest.

I put the book down and slid off the side of the bed. Grabbing a cardigan from the back of a nearby chair, I unlocked the door and slipped quietly into the hall.

Downstairs, alone in the kitchen, I opened the cupboard where Ms. Steward kept all the keys to the house neatly labeled in hooked rows. Adrenaline surged through my body as I quickly scanned the key tags, sure that someone would round the corner at any minute and catch me. There it was, *Mr. Spencer's study*, I grabbed the key and closed the door.

"Charlotte!"

I jumped and almost screamed. The key fell from my hand and clattered loudly on the wood floor near my feet. Sophie bent down and picked it up. "What are you up to?"

"You scared me to death!"

Sophie read the tag then looked at me. "Well if you're up to this," she held the key like it was evidence, "you're going to need someone to be a lookout." A wicked smile spread across her face.

I sighed and considered what she was offering. "If *I* get caught, only *I* get into trouble. But if *we* get caught...your mother might lose her job."

"Then *we* don't get caught."

I sighed again, "Fine, but you stay outside the door."

"Deal!" she agreed, thrilled by the excitement of espionage. It wasn't until we were standing outside my uncle's office that she thought to ask, "What exactly are we up to anyway?"

I turned the key in the lock and cracked the door, "His scrapbook," I pushed the door open and slipped inside. "Filled with old newspaper clippings. I need it."

"What for?"

"A date," I whispered getting annoyed with her questions. "Wait here," I instructed and turned to begin my search.

"Wait," she hissed.

I stopped and turned back. I might have already had the book if I'd just come alone. "What?"

"What should I do if someone comes?"

I didn't know. "Make some noise or something," I shrugged. "But don't be obvious."

She nodded.

I turned back to the office. The first time I'd seen the scrapbook, it had been lying on the table near the window. No such luck this time, the table's bare, highly polished top gleamed in the sunshine. Where would he keep it? I scanned the bookshelves for the irregularly shaped large book. Nothing stood out.

His desk had a small pile of papers layered with a few folders. The shelves behind his chair had more books but not the scrapbook. Glancing at the door I could see Sophie's back through the crack, I moved around his desk. It had to be in one of the drawers.

The top drawer slipped open silently along its smooth rolling casters but was only filled with pens, scissors, and a stapler. I glanced again at Sophie's back and pulled the second drawer, there was stationary, a few opened letters. When I pulled the third and largest drawer on the bottom, my heart leapt almost immediately when I caught sight of the large leather book's binding. I'd found it.

I pulled the book from the drawer and hugged it to my chest. I would have to sneak it back upstairs to my rooms and find a way to return it later, it would be too risky spending any more time here investigating the many pages. I started to push the drawer closed but stopped. At the bottom, pushed to the back of the drawer was a black lacquered box.

I placed the book on top of the desk and pulled the box forward. On the top, etched in gold, was the symbol of the ouroboros. I lifted the lid. Inside, on a red velvet liner were two highly polished sliver objects. One was the twin to the necklace in my mother's emerald puzzle box, the pentagram necklace. The other was a dagger. I picked it up and could see that the handle was covered in symbols. Some I recognized from my readings with Caleb, but the largest one, in the center of the handle was the Egyptian ankh. The sign for eternal life.

The blade caught the light. I ran my thumb over the edge, it didn't seem dull but I couldn't feel a sharpness. It was only a decorative piece.

The door to the office closed.

I looked up and saw the door now flush with the wall, heard the sound of the key turning, the lock's tumblers trapping me inside. A deep flood of panic coursed through my body. Sophie closed the door, someone must be coming.

I placed the dagger back in the lacquered box, closed the lid and the drawer, and scanned the room for somewhere to hide. The room was all bookshelves and rugs. There was an armchair in the corner I could crouch behind that might delay the eventual finding of me but getting caught hiding like a seven year old might be worse than just standing here and confronting my uncle head on. If the connection I was making between my mother's journal and the newspaper clippings in this scrapbook were correct, I would have to face my uncle eventually anyway.

Closing my eyes, I took a deep breath and steadied my shaking body by holding the desk's edge in front of me. There would be no hiding. I had a right to know the truth and no matter who came through that door, I would stand my ground and demand to know.

The tumblers in the lock clicked as someone turned the key on the other side. I squared my shoulders and tried to stand as straight as possible. The handle turned and I steeled myself to face the onslaught of questions about my presence in this room.

The door pushed open and Sophie's head popped through, "Are you about done?"

My breath left me and my shoulders slumped, it was only Sophie. I picked the scrapbook up off the desk and headed for the door, "Yes. Why'd you close the door?" I slipped through the crack and watched while she closed and locked the door behind us.

"Caleb came down the hall. I figured you didn't want him to know what you were doing."

I sighed and shook my head. "No." Caleb's actions clearly indicated where his allegiance lay. With my uncle. I knew he was sorry for keeping my mother's diaries from me, but only because it meant me spending so much time at the Wriothesley's and losing me to Hayden. If Caleb was truly on my side, if he really did love me the way he professed, he would have come to me the minute my uncle asked him to hide my mother's words from me.

At the bottom of the staircase, I stopped for a moment. The sound of the piano, the sweet and haunting melody of Moonlight Sonata drifted from the library. The same piece of music that my mother and Emerick used to help trigger their crossings into the astral plane. Caleb would be sitting there, his body and fingers pressing out those simple, single notes. But the collective force of the melody pulled at the core of my being. Connected me to his sadness.

I wanted to go to him. Wished I could share my mother's words, the newspaper articles, everything I was thinking with him.

"I know he didn't mean to hurt you," Sophie whispered.

I looked into her eyes, the conflict I felt must have been written all over my face. "But he did," I whispered back.

Wanting to trust Caleb wasn't the same as being able to.

"Come on," I said starting up the stairs. "I want to show you something."

"Wait," she grabbed my hand. "You're bleeding."

Blood dripped from the razor thin cut across the pad of my thumb. It wasn't decorative at all. The dagger had been so sharp, I hadn't even felt how deep it cut.

CHAPTER THIRTY

THE GIFT OF TRUTH

I couldn't quite believe it. I stood staring at my reflection in the wardrobe mirror. I twisted one way and then the other trying to see what it looked like from every angle. My mother's dress fit me perfectly. The only flaw was a stain that ran down the front of the dress. Because it was beaded all over, I hadn't even noticed it until I put the dress on and could see the discolored fabric on the inside, as if my mother had spilled a drink down her front the last time she wore it. I turned again and inspected the dress in the light, you couldn't even see the stain from the outside. I looked over my shoulder at my reflection from the back, this dress had been made following my mother's instructions: *Sapphire blue, plunging back, beaded pentagram just above the tailbone.*

It was the dress she wore to Midsummer eighteen years ago. The night she, against her will, bound herself to Emerick and the other members of their new order.

Sophie straightened my hem, she was the only person I'd let in since my self-imposed quarantine. She had agreed wholeheartedly that Caleb was an idiot not to have told me about the diaries. Ms. Steward and my uncle had given me my space. "Mum is hoping that your going to this ball means you're coming round."

"What did she say?"

"She thinks you and Caleb had a falling out."

"We did!"

"Yes, but she thinks that's all it is and that you're both just depressed about it. When she makes you or him some food for me to run up she mumbles to herself, 'give it some time, give it some time.' I haven't told her anything else."

"And what about Hayden almost killing him? Did she say anything about that?"

"Jealous rage?"

"Close enough."

"And your uncle promised her he would speak to the Wriothesley's about *Hayden's behavior.*"

I didn't say anything. I hadn't told Sophie what I had seen that night on the security camera at the Wriothesley's house. Partly because I didn't know how to explain the man's voice, clearly, speaking into my mind. And I didn't really know what they had all been doing. Some ritual, and Hayden looked like their newest member. But I doubted my uncle would be saying anything to the Wriothesley's about *Hayden's behavior.*

Hayden was one of them.

I watched my reflection bite her lip, her eyes nervously searched her face. The beaded indigo dress followed the curves of my body, the weight of thousands of tiny, hand stitched beads, pressed against my skin.

"It's heavy," I said.

Sophie admired the intricate scrollwork design. "It must be worth a fortune," she pulled a pair of black high heels from a brown paper sack. "Here," she placed them on the floor in front of me. "They don't fit me...yet."

Sophie had smuggled them up from her clothing stash in the garage. I slipped my feet into the sleek shoes making myself instantly three inches taller. They were maybe half a size too big and left a small gap at my heel, but seeing as my only other options were tennis shoes or flip-flops, I figured I could make it work.

Tonight, the Wriothesley's Midsummer Ball was my chance to get back into Emerick's office, back into his email. What was *E.S. Surveillance*? I needed to know.

"It's beautiful," Sophie gasped. "You're beautiful." Her expression turned dark. "I'm not sure this is a good idea Charlotte."

Sophie knew my suspicions, and my plans. I looked her in the eye, "Well then I suppose it's too bad it's the only idea."

"I'm not joking, Charlotte," she turned from me and picked up the scrapbook lying on the table near the window. "The Wriothesleys are powerful people. Connected to even more powerful people. If Emerick really did what you say, if he..." she stopped, unable to say the words.

"If he abducted my mother," I turned and watched myself say the words in the mirror. As if the practice could force them to lose their stab. "If he killed my grandparents eighteen years ago."

"Yes," Sophie sighed. "What's to stop him from doing the same to you?"

I turned to her and met her questioning stare, "I don't know, Sophie...myself I suppose." I took a breath. "Myself is all I seem to have."

A sound by the door made us both look. Caleb stood in the doorway, hands in his pockets, looking up at us from his hung head. He looked miserable.

For a half a second, I felt bad for him. Felt the instinctual pull to go to him, lift his head and look into his eyes.

I squashed the feeling and gave him a stony glare. Caleb had lied to me. He helped my uncle keep my mother's words from me.

I pretended to adjust the cabinet door and ignore him.

"Charlotte?" he asked.

"What?"

"...I'm sorry...I'm so sorry."

"Great! I'm glad you're sorry Caleb," I felt small throwing words in his face. But it was easier, safer than thinking about how I had hurt him too. "Hey, and I wanted to thank you. Thank you sooo much for finally giving me my mother's diaries." I shook my head sarcastically. "That was just...so great."

He stood and took it. There were so many words he could spear me with. So many ways I'd hurt him too. He stood and let me break his heart even more.

And I promise to love you forever and ever and ever and be your wife forever and ever until I die Amen.

I slipped off the shoes and turned my back to Sophie, "Can you get the zipper?"

Caleb turned and left.

Sophie looked sadly after her brother, it made me feel worse.

In his tuxedo, Hayden would have looked amazing, except for his pouty scowl.

"Why haven't you taken my calls?" he grabbed my arm on the drive as we headed for his car.

"I haven't been well."

"Don't give me that," I felt his hand tighten, his fingers digging uncomfortably into my flesh. "I've been going insane. I actually thought you might have crawled back to that drudge," his mouth was close to my ear. "Next time, I'll knock the damn door down," he threatened.

I yanked my arm from his grasp and tried to ignore him. But having watched him beat up Caleb, his words didn't feel like idle threats anymore. As I slipped into the Aston Martin, my eyes caught movement in the upstairs window.

I didn't think it was Sophie.

The Wriothesley's had an actual ballroom.

The wide staircase curled into the room already swarming in a mixture of brightly colored sequins and silk contrasted by full forms in black and white. The brilliant crystal chandelier hanging high over everyone aided the hundreds of candles that flickered throughout the room and the orchestra at the far end filled the room with a classical song that seemed familiar to me.

Unsure of myself in Sophie's heels, I clutched Hayden's arm as we rounded the staircase into the crowd. Halfway down, out the corner of my eyesight, I felt Emerick Wriothesley's eyes on me. Would he recognize this dress? I remembered my mother's words.

On the night of the summer solstice, we will cross into the astral plane together and bond our souls to one another.

When I had chosen the dress from her collection, I had hesitated, my hand shaking over the memories attached to it. The memories not written in her diary. I turned my head and looked right at Emerick. He met my eyes for a second.

I know, I know what you did.

He turned and continued his conversation with the man next to him.

My body trembled. The night my mother wore this gown, Emerick Wriothesley had gotten rid of the biggest obstacle standing between him and my mother. Emerick killed my grandparents.

I wondered, should they be made public, what my mother's diaries would mean for Emerick's political aspirations? For his current position at World One Bank?

If the message I'd heard in my head the other night was right, and not just me losing my mind, Emerick knew I'd taken the diary back—the most incriminating one.

He would come for it. He would come for me.

Just like he'd come for my mother four years ago. He couldn't afford to have her just floating around out in the world, not with first hand knowledge that would destroy him.

Tonight, while he and every servant that worked for him were busy with their guests, I would find the evidence I needed. I would find out what happened to my mother and hopefully, how to get her back.

Hayden led me into the crowd. I would wait, wait and watch for my opportunity to slip away undetected.

We snaked our way through clusters of conversations. Hayden obviously had a specific destination in mind. "Where are we going?"

He looked back over his shoulder, "The bar's in the back."

Of course.

Someone clasped my trailing arm. I turned to see who it was while pulling Hayden to a stop.

"Charlotte?" a short woman with a round face asked. She looked familiar but I didn't know why.

"Yes?" I shook my head puzzled.

"Charlotte Stevens?"

"Yes."

Her face beamed and she held her hand to her chest as if containing her happiness. "Oh I can't believe it, Adam," she turned and grabbed the coat sleeve of the man behind her until he stopped his conversation and came to stand next to her, "Adam, *this* is Charlotte Stevens."

His eyes widened and he looked me up and down. "I don't believe it. It's like looking at Elizabeth...except darker."

Seeing them together, I suddenly realized where I recognized them from. At the meeting the other night, they were there, drawing the invisible pentagram in front of Hayden and then accepting his bow.

The woman extended her hand smiling, "I'm sorry, it's just,"

I took her hand.

"You look so much like your mother," she gasped.

"You knew her?"

They both nodded. "She was one of our dearest friends when we were your age."

"I'm sorry, your name..." Hayden tugged lightly on my hand.

The woman laughed at herself, "I'm sooo sorry, of course. I'm Emma Shepherd and this," she gestured to the man, "is my husband Adam."

Emma and Adam. From the diary. "You introduced my mother and father," I blurted.

They both looked surprised. Adam looked to Emma, "I guess we did. I haven't thought of that in a long time. But yes," he looked back at me smiling. "We did pluck Simon from that bookstore in Bath and sort of make him one of our own...sort of."

"I'm surprised they would have remembered to tell you that," Emma added.

They didn't. "Yes, well..." I shrugged and smiled.

"Strange business that was," Adam said and finished off his drink.

Emma glared at him.

"Strange?" I asked ignoring Hayden's impatience.

"Well," Emma interjected. "Not strange."

"It was strange," Adam insisted looking around for somewhere to deposit his empty glass.

"Unexpected," Emma corrected eying me and smiling in the way adults do when they are trying to communicate over your head.

I wasn't a child. "How so?"

"Well," she looked around nervously.

"Bloody *well* strange."

"It was just that none of us knew they were even involved with each other...not like *that*."

"She was dating *Franzen*," Adam scoffed.

"Franzen?" I couldn't hide my surprise. "I thought she used to date Emerick?"

Now they both looked around, "She did...how did we even end up talking about this?" Emma gave Adam a dirty look but he didn't see her. "It was so long ago, I'm sure there's a lot we don't remember quite right." Emma nodded her head enthu-siastically encouraging Adam to follow.

"I remember just fine," he plucked another tumbler off a passing tray and took a drink. "No one knew they were seeing each other and we all thought Franzen was going to bash Si-mon's skull in."

Emma stopped trying to give him subtle hints and hit her husband across his arm. "She doesn't need to know all that!"

Adam looked at me as if it just occurred to him that I was Elizabeth and Simon's daughter, not just some other party guest. "Oh...right." He turned on Emma, "Why'd you let me go on like that."

Hayden leaned in, "Sorry folks, another time maybe," and pulled me away.

Emma and Adam quickly covered their surprise with big smiles and waved while Hayden led me through the throng of people.

"I was *talking* to them."

"*They* will never shut up and I'm thirsty."

Once we made it to the other side of the room, I stood waiting for Hayden to order his beer. It actually might be bet-ter if he drank a lot, it would be easier for me to slip away.

Hayden came back with both his hands full. "I guess you are thirsty."

"This is for you," he held out the frosty glass.

I made a face and waved my hands in front of me, "I don't like beer."

"Take it," he pushed the glass at me.

"I don't *want* it."

"Take it!"

I took the glass and held it away from my body, like I was holding it for someone else. It felt weird holding a glass of alcohol openly in front of so many adults. Not one of them even gave me a second look.

Hayden took a long drink from his and then eyed my uncomfortable position. "Bloody hell Charlotte. Not a single person here would dare say anything to you...they know you're with me."

"Great! I still don't like the *taste*." A waiter came by with an empty tray and I handed him the full glass.

"Well don't waste it!" Hayden plucked the glass off the tray. "Hang on," he told the waiter and chugged the rest of his other glass before giving the guy back his empty.

Monster appeared out of nowhere and slapped Hayden on the back, "Fantastic party." He had some kind of blue mixed drink with a slice of orange floating on top. "Charlotte," he nodded at me and took a sip. "Your friend lived I assume."

"Yes," I smiled sarcastically. "Thank you for asking."

Hayden scowled at the mention of Caleb and took another long swig from his glass.

Monster and Hayden started talking rugby. I floated on the edge of their conversation—just a little longer.

After a few minutes, I leaned in, "I'm going to run to the restroom," I whispered to Hayden.

He rolled his eyes at me and nodded.

After I had excused my way past enough people for Hayden to lose sight of me, I checked my watch. Twenty minutes. If I could get to Emerick's office and back in twenty minutes, Hayden would not have time to wonder if I wasn't taking too long. As I got closer to the grand staircase, I noticed that all the wait staff were coming and going into the room from double doors at the back of the room. I changed direction and headed for those. The staircase was designed to draw attention, I didn't want to risk Emerick or Margot seeing me leave and then wondering where I was going.

I scanned the room once, just to make sure and slipped through the doors into the kitchen.

I found my way back to the main part of the mansion, the part I was familiar with. When I checked my watch I couldn't believe it, I'd wasted eight minutes just getting here.

This time, I didn't hesitate. I rushed into Emerick's study and through the portrait hall. I knew exactly what I was looking for—*E.S. Surveillance.*

When I reached the door to his office I paused and knocked twice. When no one answered, I pushed the door.

I hurried, as quickly as I could in Sophie's heels, across the room to the other side of his desk. Reaching under his desk, I pulled the drawer out and shook his mouse. Like last time, Emerick's screen lit up.

I snatched my hand away from the mouse and stood up.

My brain was struggling with what my eyes were sending

it. Last time, Emerick had left his email open and I had considered that I might not be as lucky this time, that I might end up locked out of his personal email and staring at his desktop.

But not this.

His desktop was an image, a picture.

It was my mother, she was smiling, her head tilted back slightly as if the image had been captured while she laughed. Laughed with the smiling toddler she held in her arms. Tiny hands grasped my mother's cheeks.

The little girl looked exactly like me.

But she wasn't.

"Can I help you Charlotte?"

Shocked, I looked up into Emerick's cold eyes.

"I..."

"Please, don't insult yourself. I've watched your every move since I discovered you'd reclaimed your lost property."

I stared at him. The threat lingering on my lips, "I know what you did."

His eyes burned into me, "Do you? What do you think you know?"

"You killed them."

Emerick raised an eyebrow and smirked, "Killed whom?"

"My grandparents."

"A serious, and incorrect, accusation."

"She wrote about it, in her diary...that's why you took it. If...if it got out..."

"Just so we're clear...if it got out that I killed your grandparents?"

I nodded my head but his tone of voice and self-possessed demeanor was making me unsure. Was there something I was missing?

"I took it, because I was curious. And I didn't at first understand why my maid would have it. One might assume she would want to use it against me, might try to hold it over my head. But, as I've said before, I don't make a habit of speaking ill of the dead."

"You killed her as well. Had her run down in the street."

"Another very serious accusation. I think you'll find Charlotte that, in this world, few people, people with any power that is, care much about listening to seemingly random accusations made by a child...with no evidence."

"I have the diaries."

Emerick smiled, "The diaries? So there are more. I had no idea your mother was such a prolific writer. I think I should like to read the rest of that story. But these diaries say what exactly? Did I miss the part where I am accused of a crime I didn't commit?" he moved across the room, removed a key from his pocket and unlocked one of the cabinets along the wall. While his back was turned, I ran for the door.

My hand slipped on the door handle, *open the door*, any minute I would feel Emerick's hands grabbing me. The handle turned and I flung the door open.

My body ran into something, someone.

"I think you should join us now Charles," Emerick said.

"Our guest appears to be agitated."

I had run into Charles. I stepped backwards into the room and then ran back to the other side of the desk. My mother's smiling face still illuminated the computer screen.

Emerick removed a file from the cabinet in front of him.

"Where is my mother?"

He closed the doors, "You don't know?" and locked the cabinet.

I didn't say anything.

"Oh dear, that is disappointing. You're not quite as smart as I gave you credit for. Do you like the photo I left for you?" he asked nodding at his computer screen. "I mean, I only assumed you would come snooping back around. You know, I've heard it said that the best predictor of future behavior is past behavior. We are creatures of habit."

"You have her," I nodded my head. "You had her kidnapped."

Emerick smirked. "Is that what you think? And why would I do that?"

"Because," my eyes flicked to the photo of her smiling. "Because you were obsessed with her...you never got over her."

Emerick seemed to consider this and then slowly, he shook his head, "No. I would say, at most, I experienced an, how would I say it, an adolescent preoccupation with Elizabeth." He leveled his eyes at me. "But I was soon over it."

"She left you. She left you for my father."

"I left her for Margot. You really should be careful where

you get your information Charlotte, personal journals are hardly comprehensive historical documents. Don't they teach you anything in those American schools?"

"You hated him, hated my father for getting her pregnant. So they ran away to America, only, you couldn't let her go."

Emerick didn't say anything. He stared at me, silent, his eyes narrowed. He glanced at Charles and then back at me. "You say," he smiled. "I was mad with jealousy because your father got Elizabeth pregnant...before they left for America," he whispered. His smile grew, "Of course."

"Your mother was nothing. A vapid stupid girl with dull doll eyes before I showed her the light. Transfixed by the superficial glut of this material existence, incapable of seeing beyond this," he rubbed his fingers together, "flesh. And I see you have inherited her ignorance. You look, but you don't see. You study, but you don't learn. Like the vast majority of the blind drifting through the greatest gift ever bestowed on them, they shackle and starve themselves with their own short sightedness. Those who don't seek knowledge don't deserve it. But I have to thank you Charlotte," he shook his head. "Thank you because in your own stupidity you have shown me what I missed...what was right in front of me, but that I did not see. You are a more useful pawn than I could have even hoped for and I plan to play my next move to take full advantage. But first, allow me to give you a gift Charlotte. A gift that neither your mother or father felt fit to bestow upon you. I shall give you the gift of truth."

He opened the file in his hands, pulled out a stack of large photographs and tossed them onto the desk top in front of me. The glossy papers slid across one another creating a series of shuttered images. Images of my mother. I stared at them, so many. Laughing, smiling, drinking from a mug outside a cafe. Pushing a toddler on a swing.

Emerick walked to Charles and reached inside the other man's coat pocket. I couldn't see what he had.

"You might be curious to know," he strode across the room towards me. "I've recently learned that your mother is living quite happily in Germany. You would like to believe your mother was taken from you Charlotte when in fact, she simply walked out of your life. Those images before you were all taken within the last six months." He nodded at them.

"She wouldn't just leave me," I whispered.

"But clearly she would because she did."

There was movement near the door. I looked up, Hayden was standing in the doorway. He saw me then looked to his father and Charles, "What's going on?" He looked nervously at me, as if I could somehow give him a signal, let him know how to proceed in front of his father. He came into the room carefully, trying to read the situation he'd found us in.

Emerick pursed his lips and shook his head, "Hayden, join us. Charlotte has been snooping around the estate, but I'm afraid she's not very pleased with what she has learned."

Hayden stood, speechless, he held my eyes intently with his. There was an emotion there I had never seen in Hayden—

fear.

I was in trouble.

He began walking towards me, "I'm sure she didn't mean anything by it. I'll just take her home."

Emerick grasped his son's arm. When Hayden turned to face his father, Emerick's expression was one of quiet control. "That won't be necessary."

I looked down at the desktop in front of me, stared at those photos. It couldn't be true—what was I looking at? My mother with another child, another daughter?

Emerick released Hayden's arm and watched me closely, gauged the reactions, emotions I was powerless to control. "That is her other daughter," he offered. "She's two and her name is Grace. There are no photographs of who she's living with, who the father is. My people haven't been able to figure that piece out yet."

He came towards me.

"Please," I heard Hayden say. "Don't...don't hurt her."

Emerick opened his hand, the needle flashed in the overhead light. I backed up but Charles moved around the other side trapping me behind the desk.

"But thanks to you," Emerick said. "I know who he is now."

It was fast, I barely registered what they were doing. Charles grabbed my arms and Emerick made a stabbing motion at my neck, the thin needle pierced my soft flesh.

"Since I met you, I've often wondered over your lovely dark hair."

I could feel whatever they'd injected into me running hot through my veins, slowing my heart to a sluggish *boom...boom*. I looked up into Emerick's eyes, unable to help myself, I had to know. "But why?"

Emerick held me in his arms while my legs began to fail. "When I saw you arrive tonight, I marveled at your choice in evening wear. Wondered if you could possible know what you were doing. I see now that you don't. He flicked one last photograph, a small one, an old one, into my line of sight. My brain did not understand it.

"Why, you ask. Why would your mother leave you? She left because she had to. She left because she was finally going to be caught. Because the man who has been protecting her for so many years is losing his powers to continue."

In the picture, it was me. Me in the very dress I had on right now. Only my hair was blond and hung in tangled clumps. *But I don't have blond hair.* My arms were streaked in blood.

I shook my head. Everything was slow, too slow. My brain.

Emerick leaned close, I could feel his whisper on my ear. "She killed them herself."

I shook my head. Tried to speak. My tongue, limp and thick, filled my mouth. I shook my head.

Emerick smiled down at me and nodded, "I was there." he brushed my hair from my face. "Only the guilty run, Charlotte."

CHAPTER THIRTY ONE

IN THE DEEP

Hands grab me, roughly, I am moved and shoved. I can't move. I can't see. I am so little, small, tiny enough to fit in a pocket. But then I am forgotten. Left alone, bumping along, lost in a pocket. I am there a very long time...forgotten.

I can't move.

I can't see.

I can't scream.

My brain cracks into a thousand pieces and I feel them float away, on a gentle breeze. Each piece is searching. Each piece is calling.

Mom. Help me.

They stole me. Please, come get me.

Don't forget me.

I'm afraid...I'm afraid you'll never find me.

You forgot me.

The weight of my eyelids was overwhelming. They refused

to open. Someone had fastened them shut.

That's stupid.

That was stupid. *Why won't my eyes open?* The effort was exhausting; my body had never felt so heavy. *Am I on my back? I think I'm on my back.* I couldn't even roll over.

What happened?

I knew for sure my eyes were open. I felt my lids dragging across them like rough cloth. But they weren't working because I couldn't see anything. My arms, they had no feeling, dead flesh. I manage to get them up off the floor but they were hard to control and they fell back and hit me in the face.

I moved, rolled onto my side. *What's happened?*

My eyes were both open.

But it's black.

I was waking up from death. My body fought my every effort to wake up. My heart felt sluggish, unwilling to pump fast enough. I sat up, pain exploded through my head, white lights flashed behind my eyes. I held my head in my hand, trying to press the pain back.

Where was I?

It's dark.

Oh God.

It wasn't dark, it was black—I couldn't see my own hands, any part of me. My heart, I felt it, the effort it took to speed up. It was preparing, picking up, I heard the beat....beat... beat...beat pounding through my head, pulsing my brain.

Not this, not the dark. Tears ran down my face. I didn't

know what was happening. How had I gotten here? It felt like a bad dream but it was so real. The darkness stretched forever in every direction, it folded over me, blanketed me. I didn't know how to get out.

Run, Charlotte. You have to run.

My chest, it felt like a clamp was squeezing it, I couldn't breathe. My throat was closing, swelling, cutting off the air.

I didn't know where I was.

Charlotte!

My breath came in explosive gasps, it wasn't enough. I couldn't get enough air.

The darkness had caught me, swallowed me. I was lost.

I'm never going to get out.

Move!

I can't. I can't.

Something was out there, surrounding me. Waiting for me to make the smallest movement.

I could hear it breathing.

There is nothing Charlotte. No one but you. You have to move, you have to get out.

No.

Honey, you have to...I can't come this time.

"Mom?" Her voice. I heard it clearly but not with my ears. Like when I was little and I believed I heard her words running through my mind.

You can do this.

"Where are you?" I sobbed.

Only the sound of my own heart thundered through my head.

I tipped my head back and tried to take one breath and then another. I got on my hands and knees. My arms trembled beneath me, my whole body was racked by violent shaking.

I crawled a few inches and waved one arm blindly in front of me. The tiles were cold on my palms and the tiny beads from my dress dug into my knees. I forced myself to move a few inches at a time, my breath came in sharp bursts that echoed through the darkness around me.

Something, something sat in the darkness and waited for me. Any moment it would grab me. *I can't.* I stopped crawling and sobbed, shrinking as close to the floor as I could, I pulled my knees to my chest, hid my head within my arms.

I had been this way before. When I was four and lost in Mrs. Grayden's basement.

But Mrs. Grayden didn't have a basement.

Yes she did, I was lost during a game of hide and seek. And Mom was so angry she never had anyone babysit me ever again.

Mrs. Grayden didn't have a basement.

Mrs. Grayden, lived on the third floor of our beachfront condo. There were thirty-three steps and I would count every one as my short legs pushed me up to her pink front door.

We had played hide and seek that day. But that was before, before the people grabbed me.

I was four, curled in a ball, in the dark. I had wet my pants. I kept wetting them because I couldn't move. My ankles and hands had thick tape around them. I couldn't yell because that gray tape was over my mouth. I cried, but the crying scared me because my nose got stuffy and then I couldn't breathe.

I was all by myself and I was scared. I worried that no one was coming. I didn't think my mom knew where I was. I had never seen her drive this way before.

I had been there a long time.

I was not at Mrs. Grayden's. I was stolen from Mrs. Grayden's.

Mrs. Grayden didn't have a basement.

I was down there so long. My tummy had stopped hurting from being hungry but my throat, it burned and my mouth kept swallowing and swallowing behind the tape even though I didn't have any water.

It was hard to stay awake and I fell over. It felt like my brain cracked into a thousand pieces and I felt them float away, on a gentle breeze. Each piece was searching. Each piece was calling.

Mommy. Help me.

They stole me. Please, come get me.

Don't forget me.

I'm afraid...I'm afraid you'll never find me.

Did you forget me?

She didn't come. Not at first. She couldn't, she didn't know where to find me. I felt her, in my mind. She was looking, I kept seeing the front of the house with the basement. The numbers, the numbers—she needed the numbers.

Later, she was on the stairs, rushing, grabbing me. Squeezing me so hard it was like she was trying to put me inside her.

Upstairs, police were everywhere and the ambulance and a fire truck. My dad looked over me while someone pushed me on a rolling bed.

I was so thirsty.

And then—I made myself forget.

Mom helped me. "Hide and seek," she would often repeat. "Remember, you got lost playing hide and seek."

"In Mrs. Grayden's basement?"

"Yes, that's right. Now let's not worry about it anymore."

Emerick had put me here. I remembered Charles holding me and Emerick injecting something into my neck. I reached and felt the swollen and tender flesh on my neck.

Get up Charlotte.

I made my body uncurl and got back up onto my hands and knees. Wherever I was, I needed to get out. My arms shook as I crawled forward, uncertain if I was moving out or further into my dark cell.

I pulled my mother's evening gown up from under my knees to keep the beads from digging into them, my feet were already bare. I'd lost Sophie's shoes somewhere between Emerick's study and wherever he and Charles had put me.

I had never been anywhere this dark. My eyes kept trying but there was not even a speck of light. In the dark, my ears stretched and searched trying to help me make sense of what was happening.

I was not in a vast void of emptiness, I could hear water trickling, through a pipe behind a wall.

My hands felt every spec of dirt on the floor beneath me. Tiles. I could feel the thin grout lines separating the tiles of the floor. They weren't regular, square tiles. I stopped crawling and pushed my finger along one line. It stopped at a point where it met another line. I crawled over a few inches and sat on my knees while both of my hands traced the two lines away from the point.

Shuffling back, I continued to trace the lines. They kept going and I pushed myself back further until both lines were intersected by another arced line. A triangle with a curved bottom line. I followed the arc around until it met with another line moving up—another triangle with a curved bottom line. I stopped and sat up. I knew where I was. I turned to face the exact opposite direction and moved slowly forward sweeping my arms gently in front of me.

My finger brushed the stone. I reached and grabbed the cold white alter with both hands. I was on the sunburst tile in Emerick's ritual room.

My hands were my eyes and they felt the cloth that was draped over the alter top and down the sides. I felt the pedestal—it wasn't on this side. While I held the stone, I guided myself around to the other side to look. My hands ran down the pedestal's other side, I felt it. The metal square and cross symbol I had seen attached to the front.

I stood up and, holding the altar for reference, turned ninety degrees to my right. The wall with the door leading to Emerick's workroom would be right in front of me. Get to the wall and I would be able to feel along it until I found the door. Through the door to the model platform, from the platform to the ladder, turn on the light and get out the door in the floor.

Let go of the altar.

I gripped the edge of the solid stone. With it next to me, I knew exactly where I was.

Let go.

My fingers slid from the altar's edge but I could still feel the reassuring press of it against my hip.

Now, go.

CHAPTER THIRTY TWO

GOING THROUGH

My bare feet ran through the maze of halls leading to the exit. Any minute, Emerick would grab me, his hands would hold me and drag me back—back to the dark. This time, I would fight. I wouldn't go back without a fight.

The house was dark. When I passed windows, moonlight cast bright white beams across the marble floor. But I had no idea how long I'd been down in the subfloor. Had I been out a day, a week? Was it still the night of the Midsummer Ball? I had no idea.

I stopped running and froze. Something had made a sound in the hallway ahead of me. Instinctively, I shrank back against the wall, into the shadows.

I heard footsteps falling. Coming closer.

"I saw you Charlotte," Emerick called out. "I know you're here. You've seen the surveillance system, you know there's no hiding from me." His footsteps slowed, he was close to finding me and he knew it. "You think I'm the bad person. You're wrong Charlotte," he whispered. "I am trying to keep this world turning just the way it already is. There is order to this world Charlotte. A necessary hierarchy. Systems are in place."

I pressed myself as far into the shadow as I could. *Please, please don't let him see me. Please God, help me get away.*

He was so close now, I could smell his cologne, "What do you suppose would happen, Charlotte, if everyone in the world knew they could do, have, or be anything they wanted in this life?" He whispered. "Do you trust your fellow man enough to hand them that kind of power? The criminals, the psychotics...religious zealots? Imagine if they knew, if they understood their universal powers...it would be chaos."

He stood right in front of me.

I closed my eyes, waited for his grasp. *Please God.* I imagined myself covered in an invisible blanket.

He took a step, and then another. "Charlotte, I saw you Charlotte. I know you're here." He moved up the hall, away from me.

I didn't move. I didn't breathe.

"You think I'm a bad person..." I heard him moving further away. When he reached the end of the hall and turned, I allowed a single ragged breath to escape. When I could no longer hear his words, I slipped from my shadow and around the corner nearest me.

I felt the press of someone else up against me, stopping me immediately. I had run into someone, Charles, Emerick. My scream rose up my throat when a small hand clamped over my mouth muffling my voice.

Diana. I had run into Diana. She looked into my eyes, "They'll hear you," she whispered. Her hand slid slowly away from my mouth like she wasn't certain I wouldn't still lose it. After a second more, she nodded down the hall, "Hayden couldn't come, but he sent me to help you. This way, follow right behind me...I know how to stay out of the cameras."

I followed her as she zigged and zagged down the hall, a few places we pressed ourselves hard against walls opposite expensive pieces of art. When we reached the door to the atrium, she cracked it enough for us to slip through and then closed it gently behind us.

The hot, tropical mugginess enveloped me and made the liner of my dress cling to my legs.

"There are no cameras in here,"

"But why help me?"

"I'm not like him Charlotte," she shook her head. "One day, I'll run as far away from here as possible." She pointed to the opposite side, "Stay on the straight path all the way through. It leads to the exterior door on the other side," she looked into my eyes. "Remember this, seven, two, eight, five, nine. On the wall, behind the trumpet vine, there's a keypad for the door security. That code will shut it off."

"Wait, what was it again?"

Diana stared into my eyes, "Seven."

"Seven," I whispered to myself, repeating all five numbers

after her.

"When you get outside, try to stay as close to the wall as possible until you're ready to run."

"Wait, where should I go?"

Diana shook her head, "I don't know. The closest other house is seven kilometers away...but that's the first place he'll look."

I shook my head. I'd worry about that once I was out. "Thank you."

She nodded, "Go."

I started quickly down the path into the dense tropical foliage that hung all around and over my head but after only a few steps, my bare feel slipped on the wet yellow tiles and I nearly fell.

"Be careful," Diana hissed behind me.

I steadied myself and kept going, slower, making sure each foot pressed through the thin film of water that coated every surface in this room. I gathered the long fabric of my dress up in my hands to keep the now damp liner from tangling in my legs.

The wide leafed trees and plants closed in around me as the smell of earthy growth and rot infiltrated my senses. As I moved, gaps in the trees allowed moonlight from the glass ceiling above to illuminate the path immediately in front of me. But when I turned to search for Diana at the door, the growth and darkness kept her from me.

Go.

My feet kept moving, sliding beneath me—I could see the other side, my pace quickened as much as I dared.

There was the door and I could see the trumpet vine guarding the keypad. I pushed the heavy vine to the side releasing it's sweet honey scent into the air and flipped the small door down on the front of the pad.

I pressed the first rubber numbers, *seven, two*...I stopped, I stared at the pad in front of me. *Seven, two...five, nine. What was the middle number?* I dug my fingernails into my palms and tried to remember Diana's words. *Seven, two...five, nine. Seven, two...What?*

The keypad beeped softly and reset because I was taking too long.

*Charlotte, think! Seven, two.... Seven, two....*It was no use, it was gone. I looked back across the path behind me and considered going back to find Diana. But she wouldn't still be standing there, I would have to find her in the house.

I was not going back. Without Diana to guide me past the cameras, Emerick would catch me for sure.

I didn't think. I pressed the large door handle and ran into the night.

Spotlights illuminated the grounds all around, the loud blare of the alarm reverberated through the night air. I ran. My legs pumped hard beneath me across the grass around the house to the gravel drive. I would cut through the fields on the east side of the property.

I didn't feel the small stones on the drive digging into the bare flesh of my feet, I only heard them shifting and scattering behind me as I ran. I needed to get off the property. I was pushing myself, using everything I had to fuel my body. *Run Charlotte.*

But it felt like I was moving in slow motion.

At the end of the drive in front of me, headlights suddenly threw me into their bright beams and blinded me.

No. I heard the doors open. They had been waiting for me. I heard their shoes moving fast across the gravel towards me and I fell to my knees.

"No," I begged. "Please."

A man appeared in front of me, the light from the headlights made him hard to see. He stepped closer and reached for me.

I screamed and hit him with my fists.

He lifted me into his arms and I kicked and screamed. I saw his face. It wasn't Emerick or Charles, it was the man from the woods, the man I'd seen through the security camera. The man who had whispered into my brain. I arched my back and clawed at his face.

He held me tight and hurried back to the car.

"Charlotte!"

"Charlotte, we're here!"

Someone was running along side us. Someone was touching my hair, my face. "Charlotte, it's okay, it's okay."

I looked into Sophie's frightened eyes.

"It's okay," she cried. "We've got you. We've got you."

The car door opened and the man put me in the backseat. Sophie climbed in behind me and held me in her arms.

Caleb got in the other side.

"They're coming," he called into the front seat.

I looked through the windshield and could see three figures racing towards us.

The man got behind the steering wheel, shifted the car into reverse and looked back over his shoulder.

Sophie, Caleb and I slammed into the seats in front of us as the car lunged beneath us.

"Hang on," the man shouted.

We pushed ourselves back onto the seat while the car sped backwards up the drive and through the Wriothesley's front gates. When we reached the main road, the man spun the wheel, flipped the car around, and we rocketed away into the night.

CHAPTER THIRTY THREE

BLINDED BY THE LIGHT

The tea Ms. Steward gave me warmed my hands. Curled in my mother's chair in the main library, I waited while Sophie, Caleb, Ms. Steward and my uncle left the room.

The man, the man who had been following me, keeping an eye on me, the man who had raced to find me when I didn't show up after the Midsummer Ball, stood at a bookcase nearby waiting too.

When they were gone, I took a sip. My body felt hollow with exhaustion. The clock on the mantle read four-twenty. The sun would be coming up in a couple hours. "Where is she?" I asked.

Franzen came over and crouched in front of me. "Germany. She's been living in Germany with me for the last four years."

I avoided his eyes and took another sip. I felt the tears starting to rise behind my eyes.

"She loves you Charlotte. We bo..." he trailed off.

The tears ran hot down my face. "If she loved me...if she loved me why would she leave me? Why would she leave us?"

Franzen reached for me and held my hands in his. "She left because of me Charlotte. Not you," he shook his head. "Not you. It's hard to explain—"

"Try," I snapped suddenly angry.

He sighed and closed his eyes. "I imagined this happening a thousand different ways over the last sixteen years." He looked at me. "But I never imagined it like this. We wanted to wait, until you were older. But we didn't know."

"Know what?"

"We didn't know that I would start dying." He stood up and walked to the window. "We didn't know that I would not be able to protect her."

I stared at his back. "I don't understand what you're talking about. Just tell me what is going on. Where is my mother? Why did she leave me? Why isn't she here?" The photograph of my mother, bedraggled and bloodied, filled my mind. "Is what Emerick said true?" I cried. "Did she do what he said?"

He turned and faced me, his eyes burned into mine. He took a breath. "Yes and no."

Yes and no? I stared at him. I didn't say anything. I considered throwing something at him but I was too tired, too overwhelmed. I looked out the window and took a sip from my tea. Maybe if I ignored him he would go away.

"Her body committed those acts, not her. Not her mind, not her soul...it wasn't her intention or will that killed her parents, stabbed her little brother or burned down Saint Mary's."

His words were a cold flood of awareness trickling through my mind. Yes, he said. Yes your mother killed her own parents. And more. The questions formed outside of my ability to ask them. I stared, slack and white faced at this man before me.

"You should know everything Charlotte," he whispered.

My mind flashed to the scrapbook kept in my uncle's office, the articles cut and pasted into that book. The ones about the fire, the one about the over eight hundred people who were inexplicably trapped inside the building, all of them burned to death. Doctors, nurses…patients. Patients of Saint Mary's.

Saint Mary's asylum. There was also the letter from Emerick to my mother. The letter explaining about how Emerick had learned of his mother, Lilith Brewster. His mother committed to Saint Mary's asylum.

"I don't understand," I whispered, my mind circling around the how of it.

Franzen turned back to face the scene outside the library window. The morning mist stretched and thinned across the grounds illuminated by the slow creep of first light. "There is so much Charlotte, it is difficult to know where to start. There are the mysteries themselves, which take a lifetime to understand, and there is your place among those mysteries. Your history, your family. Your mother…" he hesitated. "And me."

"Lilith, start with Lilith Brewster," I breathed.

Franzen turned from the window to face me. He nodded his head once and moved across the library to one of the worktables nearby. For the first time, I noticed that all of my mother's journals were stacked there along with the stone puzzle box. A single journal sat alone on the edge, he picked it up and brought it over to where I sat. I recognized it immediately, a hard shard of dread settled near my heart.

The black diary.

"This," Franzen held up the book. "Is Lilith Brewster."

I shook my head. "It's my mother's handwriting."

"And Lilith's mind. What little there is left of it."

"How is that possible?" I asked incredulous.

"You've read her diaries?"

I nodded.

"She wrote of a shadow in the astral plane. She could feel and see it when she crossed. That shadow, was Lilith Brewster. When Elizabeth continued to cross into the astral plane unaware, unprotected, she left herself open. Made herself vulnerable. Lilith," he shook the diary, "moved into your mother's physical being while she was in the plane."

"That's not possible."

He placed the black book back on the table and sighed. "It is possible," he whispered. "Lilith's soul took over Elizabeth's body. She killed Elizabeth's parents, tried to kill Nigel, all so she would be free to rage against her true mark, Saint Mary's asylum."

I can only see my mother quiet and curled on her chaise back home with a book open before her. The blood drenched murderous image of her from Emerick's photo makes no sense

414

with my memories of her. "My mother wouldn't do those things."

Franzen nodded his head in quiet agreement. "Your mother wouldn't...but her body did."

I glared at him, "So what you're saying," my voice bitter with sarcasm. "Is that she was possessed?"

His eyes left mine and lifted high above my head. They bore into the case of books behind me, as if the answer he needed was buried among the titles. He closed his eyes and grief settled into the lines around his mouth. "No Charlotte. What I'm saying is that your mother is possessed."

"What?" My tea sloshed in my cup, threatening to slide over the china's edge.

Franzen rubbed his forehead before dragging his hand over his exhausted expression. "Lilith's soul still resides inside her. You mother struggles every day to keep her back, wages a constant and seemingly quiet war inside herself just to maintain control of herself, her life. But Lilith is relentless."

I shook my head, it wasn't true. "You don't know her. This is insane. You're insane!"

He sighed and nodded. "If only that were true. I would trade my sanity in a moment if I thought it would release your mother from Lilith's ironclad grip. If Elizabeth were here, if she could be here, she would tell you herself." He sat in the window seat, his hands clutching his knees. "I wish your mother were here," he spoke to himself.

I couldn't stand hearing another word, "So do I!" I yelled.

Rage surged through my veins and begged for release. Without thinking, I grabbed the nearest book off the shelf and threw it at him.

He moved faster than I could have imagined and easily snatched the book from the air. I watched as he took a deep breath, closed it gently, and read the cover. He stared at whatever was printed there for a long time before speaking again. "There are no accidents Charlotte."

I looked at the shelf I had grabbed the book from—it was a Shakespeare. He tossed the book back to me and I read the cover. *Richard II.*

"Charlotte, I know this is hard for you, but everything I'm telling you is true. And I realize you're not likely to believe me right now, and maybe not even in the near future, but soon, very soon you're going to have to really think about what I'm telling you. There is more. So much more. You're going to have to start listening to what I have to teach you."

I threw the book on the floor. "Why should I believe anything you say?" I spat. "You're crazy and you've obviously brainwashed my mother. Made her believe she's done things she would never do. I read about you in her diaries and she may not realize it but I know exactly what you're doing. You've got her roped into your...your cult. She got away with my father but you've somehow reeled her back in. I don't believe anything you say, how could I? It's ridiculous!"

He sat with his elbows resting on his knees, his hands clasped in front of his mouth. He nodded his head. "Okay

Charlotte. For now—"

"No! Don't condescend to me! I will not be taken in. I am not staying in this house a minute longer! I won't give you the time you need to *groom me.* I'm not going to listen to anything you have to *teach me.* I'm going home. To my father!"

Despite my ravings, his voice was calm. "You're not Charlotte. You're in too much danger now for me to allow that."

"So you say! Not once have you said why any of this has anything to do with me."

He stood and looked me directly in the face, "Because you are *my* daughter Charlotte."

I flinched with shock. His words were like an object between us, they took up room, filled space. They grew larger with every second and the possibility of them pushed on my brain until the memory they needed dislodged and fell before my eyes. The image was of Adam and Emma at the Midsummer ball, *"She was dating Franzen,"*

"Liar!" I shouted.

He sat and stared at an invisible spot in front of him, "I'm sorry Charlotte. Your mother and I only ever wanted to protect you."

It felt like my mind was tearing in two, "Stop it!" I begged. Exhaustion and confusion took over and I couldn't help the sobs that erupted. "Stop lying!" I screamed, my voice reverberated through the room.

Franzen rushed to me, he tried to take me in his arms but I shrank as far away from him as I could. "Get away from me!"

I screamed.

His hands fell to his sides, "Please Charlotte." His eyes filled with anguish. "I know this is hard..."

"You don't know anything about me!"

"I know," he said miserably.

I buried my face in my hands, "Please, just leave me alone. I want to go home. I want to see my father."

He stood for a moment silently staring at me, as if considering my request then he knelt down in front of me. "Charlotte," he whispered. "You don't have to believe me, not right now, but please listen. We are all going to have to work together...and soon. I don't have the power I once had, I won't be able to keep the authorities away from Elizabeth forever. They are looking, reinvestigating the murder. Emerick will see to that now more than ever."

I felt his hand tenuously rest at the side of my face. "When your mother told me she was pregnant I was overjoyed...and then terrified. There are people in this world Charlotte who know who I am, powerful people who do not want me to continue my work. Who would stop at nothing to either stop me or control me. They have never held power over me, there was no threat they could bring against me that could ever deter me from my work...until you."

"Work? And what work is that?"

"Influence."

"What does that even mean?"

"I am the whispered words of reason that fill the ears of

power. A guiding mark, a gentle hand, an alchemist of the highest order. My life's work is to continue the mission set forth by one of the greatest men in history. My ancestor, and yours Charlotte, Sir Francis Bacon."

"A.K.A. Shakespeare," I said more to myself than to him.

He looked at me, his eyes questioning how much I had already learned. "Among other things, yes." He got up and walked to the worktable. Standing beside the puzzle box, he began dialing the ouroboros. "His whole life he worked to bring knowledge to the world. Education, resources, new ways of thinking. When he was very young, he had his mind opened, opened to the universal knowledge, the possibilities inherent in every man woman and child on this planet. His soul's purpose, since that time, was to oversee the advancement of mankind."

My hands slid from my face. "What could I possible have to do with it?"

He shook his head and smiled. "More than you can yet realize. But right now, you make me vulnerable. They could use you against me...and they would win every time. They have used you Charlotte."

The memory of being taken, taped and left alone in a dark basement. "When I was four..." the words escaped in a whisper.

He turned the snake's center and opened the puzzle's top. "Luckily, it was one small group. They hoped to use you as leverage to get me to influence decision makers in America to release a number of their political prisoners. They discovered who you were by gaining employment here," he pointed his finger at the ground, "as a housekeeper. They found and read your mother's diaries and pieced together the truth." Franzen reached into the small compartment and removed the pentagram wrapped in black silk and my mother's note.

"And what about my dad? How does he fit in to all of this?"

He brought the items to me and looked carefully into my eyes. "He's not your real father," he whispered.

All I could think of was dad's soft ruddy face, his gentle hands brushing hair from my face every night of my life before kissing my forehead, *"Goodnight Tot."* Every night of my life he was there. Even after mom disappeared.

Left. Even after mom left he was always there.

"Does he know?" I asked.

Franzen shook his head. "It's true, we used him Charlotte. Your mother and I used him to keep you safe. We needed everyone to believe that you were his child. I knew the minute I met him that he was madly in love with your mother. And he was her friend. But your mother and I...we share the same soul Charlotte."

"Twin flames," I whispered.

He looked at me. "You know?"

"No," I said, still not wanting to believe him. But, in my heart, I knew what he said about my mother and father was true. It had been in her every movement, her every glance. She was a woman who had known what it meant to be bound, mind, body, and soul to the other half of her being and then be forced to set up house with her best friend.

To protect me.

Franzen pulled a chair close and sat in front of me. He handed me my mother's words.

What is the above is from the below and the below is from the above.

I closed my eyes and shook my head. "What does it mean?"

"That is what I have to teach you. It's what I'm trying to teach the world...the secrets. But I'm running out of time."

I refolded the paper and handed it back to him. It was all too much, a crushing weight pressing in from every side. My brain couldn't take any more. "I'm tired."

Franzen nodded. "Of course. You've been through so much...you should rest now. I'll be here when you wake up, we can talk more then."

I pushed myself from the chair and headed for the door. Before I got there, I stopped and turned back to him. "You said earlier you were dying."

Franzen nodded his head.

"Why, are you sick?"

He smiled at me, "No...just very old."

"You don't look very old."

He nodded his head like he understood what I was saying and took a deep breath. He held it, suspended in his chest for a moment before he let it rush from his deflating lungs. "Looks can be very deceiving."

Upstairs, I stopped at my door. I didn't want to go in there, in her room. I didn't want to sleep in her bed surrounded by her things, haunted by her past.

I walked down the hall and knocked.

Caleb opened his door. His bruised face looked much worse now that the black and purple had changed to a sickly yellow.

"I don't want to be alone. Can I sleep with you?"

He took me into his arms and buried his face in my hair.

It felt good. It felt safe.

CHAPTER THIRTY FOUR

KEEPING SECRETS

They found my father. My uncle had hired an investigator to help Susan. It took them half a day to find him passed out and drunk in a hotel in San Francisco. He had completed his first manuscript since my mother's disappearance.

"It's good," Susan shared excitedly over the phone. "It's probably his best in twenty years."

"Can I talk to him?"

I heard her give my dad the phone. He didn't say anything.

"Dad?"

"I'm sorry Charlotte," he blurted. "I couldn't stay there."

"What happened? Why didn't you call?"

"Everything was going okay...at first. And don't misunderstand me, I'm not drinking, that much I did get. But all the therapy, and listening to all those other people...Charlotte I'm not like them. They gave us these journals to write down our feelings so we could share at group but after a few pages of that mine started turning into a book idea. Well once that started, I was so excited Charlotte, I couldn't stop, I mean...I was *writing* again!"

"But why leave? If you were doing so well..."

"I couldn't think right in there. All those people, and it was so depressing. I didn't want to lose the flow, it felt so good to be writing again. I needed to go somewhere, be alone and just get that book out of me. I'm sorry I didn't call, I figured everyone would just assume I was still at Oasis. But I don't want you to think I didn't get what they were teaching me. I did Charlotte and it's going to be different when you get home. You'll see."

I could hear the sincerity in his voice, he believed what he was telling me. I wanted to believe him too, "When they found you," I whispered. "You'd been drinking dad."

Silence stretched between us on the line and I began to wonder if the call had dropped, "Dad?"

"It was a slip," he said. "A mistake. When I finished the first draft, I was so excited I thought I could celebrate with one glass of champagne."

"You couldn't stop," I said flatly.

"No. But now I know Charlotte. It won't happen again."

"I'm coming home," I said.

"Maybe there's a do-it-yourself thing I could try. Like on-line."

"We'll see. I love you."

"I love you too Charlotte."

424

I was packing my bag when Franzen walked in. "I won't allow it Charlotte. It's too dangerous. Now that Emerick knows that you're my daughter he will absolutely come after you again. The only reason you escaped was because he was unprepared. He didn't intend to or have a plan in place for taking you and keeping you Charlotte. But I can promise you, he won't make that mistake again. The next time he comes for you he won't be hiding you in his basement until he can think up something better. If he gets you again...it will be as if you never existed. Your uncle has been tracking Emerick's political involvements for years and he is no longer aiming to join the ranks of The Eastern Star...he is a member of the Bilderbergs."

My hands froze inside my duffel. I had heard that name before—no I'd read about the Bilderbergs. "At the café," I whispered to myself.

"What's cafe?" Franzen asked.

I continued packing. "The Bilderbergs, I read something about them, something about an annual conference of world leaders."

Franzen nodded his head, "Yes, a conference where the future is decided and planned by people who have knowledge, who know how to use that knowledge and the power it brings to rule over those who do not."

I stuffed a t-shirt into my duffel bag.

"Imagine every powerful political figure that has held a major world leadership position in the last fifty years. They are world shapers, controlling and guiding the futures of entire nations. Emerick knows who you are now, he knows you are my daughter...they know too. The descendants of Francis Bacon have worked for four hundred years trying to help lift man out of the mud and there are some, like Emerick, that believe man has come far enough. It is enough that those who live in the wealthiest nations have access to general education. They don't believe the ultimate truth should be taught, they don't believe people deserve to know what they don't seek on their own."

I didn't stop packing, "And what is the *ultimate truth*? Why do they care if people *know*?"

Franzen reached out. He stopped my hands and turned me towards him. It felt like electricity swept through my body as he stared intently into my eyes, "The truth, Charlotte, is that we are all, every one of us connected. We are one thing. And being a part of that one thing, that is also this one universe, we have access to all the energy and power possessed within it. Every one of us can access it, harness it, use it...if only we have the knowledge of how to go about it. Imagine the end to suffering as we know it. There are many people who already know how, and they use that power in their daily lives. Some try to help others, and some only try to help themselves...but there are some, like Emerick, who use it over others."

I pulled my hands from his grasp and, like a dimmer on a light switch, I felt the connection between us fade. "Alchemy," I said.

"Is one way," he corrected.

"And this is what you want to teach me? How to access universal power?"

He sighed. "Yes. When you're ready."

I turned back to my bag and continued packing. "I'm going home. We'll get a security system."

"To make it easier for them to watch your every move? They are controlling the world Charlotte, you think it's anything for them to control a security system, control the police who show up at your door."

"I have to go home. My father needs me."

"We'll bring him here. He should know, he's in danger as well."

"No," I dropped my jeans on the bag and turned around. "I don't want him to ever know the truth. How you both used him, that I'm not his daughter. It would kill him. He adores my mother and I'm all he has in this whole world." I turned back around and shoved my jeans down the side of the bag. "He has been there for me my whole life. I won't do that to him. Not now, not ever."

"They'll be watching your every move."

"I'll keep an eye out."

"You don't understand Charlotte. They will pluck you right off the street."

I picked my mother's diary up off the bed and held it in my hand. "I have a bit of insurance."

"What?"

I wondered how the public would view Emerick's involvement in secret orders, astral plane crossings...the occult. What effect might that information have on his political aspirations? "I have Emerick's past to hang over his head."

Caleb and Sophie drove me to the airport.

"Don't go Charlotte," Sophie begged.

I hugged her in the back seat, "I have to."

"What are we supposed to do without you?" she wailed.

My eyes met Caleb's in the rearview mirror.

When he pulled up to passenger drop off, Sophie stayed in the backseat crying while Caleb helped me with my bag. He placed it on the rolling dolly while I gave my flight information to the porter. When I was done, I turned to him to say goodbye.

He closed his eyes.

I moved closer and leaned my forehead against his chest. There was so much we hadn't resolved. What had happened with Hayden, my own lies, so much hadn't been said. I knew in my heart I was running away.

"I'm sorry," I whispered.

He smiled, but I saw the tears escape beneath his lashes. "Don't," he said and put his arms around me. He lowered his head and rested his lips near my ear. "Just this is hard enough. I don't want to think about anything else right now." He kissed me softy. "I love you Charlotte, I always have."

I leaned back and brushed a tear from his cheek with

my thumb. I couldn't say it back. Too much had happened, I didn't have any idea what I felt. I kissed the corner of his mouth. "Goodbye Caleb."

I turned and left. I didn't look back.

I bought a Coke and waited for my flight to board. When I unscrewed the top, I caught a man staring at me from behind his mobile phone.

His eyes darted away but somehow I knew—he had taken my picture.

I thought of Franzen's words. *They will be watching your every move.*

The doors to the gate next to mine opened, a private jet was parked at the end of the jet bridge. A woman walked out.

It was her. She wore jeans and a t-shirt with a lavender cardigan, her face was masked with large black sunglasses, but her elegance was unmistakable. On her hip, the pudgy toddler girl with jet-black hair slept with her head on her mother's shoulder.

My sister, baby Grace.

I didn't move. My heart squeezed so tight in my chest I knew it would burst. She stood, watching me too, not daring to move. I saw her body tremble from the strain of it. Her lips rolled between her teeth holding back the same sobs that pulled at my chest. Her wet face glistened in the terminal light.

My eyes flashed to the man who had taken my picture.

I love you, I heard her clearly even though her lips never moved. I watched her face crumple and she took a step towards me.

No! I tried to call back to her but I had no idea if she could hear me.

Franzen appeared as if from nowhere and put his arm around her. They both stared at me for a moment more.

I love you too, I mouthed back my lips quivering.

She choked on a silent sob. And they walked back down the jet bridge.

Without me.

"Dad, I have to finish this." It was the third time he'd interrupted me. I was trying to rewrite my *Richard II* paper—in my own words.

"It's not my fault this time. It's the package you've been waiting for." He pushed past my door with the dolly and placed the rectangular shipping crate on the floor next to my bed.

I got up out of my office chair.

"What is it?" he asked.

I looked at him, there was so much I couldn't say. "It's a stone puzzle box that used to belong to mom."

He scoffed, "Why such a big box?"

The crate was much bigger than the puzzle, "I'm not sure."

"You need help opening it?"

"Actually, I'll do it later. I've almost finished my paper and

I don't want to get distracted."

"Well, let me know. You'll probably need a hammer."

Later that night, after he had gone to bed, I did need a hammer. When I pried off the lid and pulled the bubble packing out, I gasped. It was my mother's diaries. There was a piece of paper sticking out the top of one journal. I pulled it out and read the note.

I thought you'd like them back.

Love, Caleb

"Thank you," I whispered to the room running my hand over the covers. My father couldn't ever know about them. If he ever read them he would learn the truth for himself. Quietly, I ferried the journals across the hall and hid them amongst the books already on her shelves. He would never notice them.

I carried the puzzle box to my mother's chaise in her tiny library. My finger traced the ouroboros from mouth to tail and I turned the inner circle to open the first compartment. I pulled out the black silk that contained the pentagram, something slipped out and landed in my lap.

I picked it up and held it in front of me.

It was my sapphire cross. I unfastened the clasp on the new chain and slipped it around my neck. I closed my eyes and pressed it against my neck.

I lifted the note from inside the box.

What is the above is from the below and the below is from the above.

I flipped it over and read the new message, my breath caught in my chest—it was from my mother.

Franzen forgot to return this before you left. When you are ready, the truth will unfold to you. You're going to need this. All My Love, Mom.

I closed the lid and hid the puzzle box on the bottom shelf behind her chaise.

The End

Acknowledgments

Thank you to my husband Rod and our two children.

About Rebecca Taylor:

Rebecca Taylor is the author of Ascendant (winner of the 2014 Colorado Book Award), Midheaven and The Exquisite & Immaculate Grace of Carmen Espinoza.

She lives in Colorado with her husband and two children. In addition to writing, she works as a school psychologist and teaches creative writing at Regis University.

You can find more information about her and her work at:

Web: www.rebeccataylorbooks.com

Charlotte's story continues in

MIDHEAVEN

Book Two in the Ascendant Trilogy

Available May 2015

Midheaven

Chapter One

I wasn't paranoid, I had seen the man before. Not just browsing shelves in the library or scanning bar codes at the self-checker, last week he'd been behind the wheel of a brown Camry in the lane next to mine. He was following me.

I shut the book balanced on my knee and checked the small digital clock on the computer in front of me. Five minutes before I was off.

"Aaron?" I turned to the middle-aged man perched over the computer terminal next to mine.

"Hum?" he didn't look up from his library book.

"Do you mind if I take off early?"

He glanced briefly at his own digital computer clock before he returned to his reading and shooed me away with his hand.

"Thanks."

"Yeah," he said, already lost again in the library's brand new copy of *Resurrections Test,* my dad's latest installment of his Devin Kruger series.

The guy was down the hall across from us fingering books displayed on the New Arrivals table. I avoided looking at him, tucked my book, The Lives of the Kings and Queens of England, into my bag and slid off the stool.

"Bye," I whispered sliding my strap over my shoulder and rounding the counter.

Completely absorbed, Aaron didn't say anything. I wondered what he would say if I ever decided to tell him who my father was. A woman pushing a double stroller and balancing a tower of children's books navigated through the retractable black straps meant to control the lines of people, when there was more than one, checking out books.

"Sarah, give the man the books. He's going to check them out to us, but just for borrowing."

Aaron closed his book and sighed loudly. The woman didn't register his annoyed glare; she was too busy trying to pull the picture books from her toddler's hands without dropping her own stack. When the mom finally pried them away, Sarah started to scream and the baby in the backseat of the stroller started to cry.

Aaron's eyes bulged while he silently watched the scene in front of him. I bit my lip and slipped quickly towards the electric doors. I wanted to get away before he changed his mind and decided to call me back to deal with the mess.

As the electric doors slid shut behind me, I dared a glance at the man near the New Arrivals. The children's crying and screaming didn't appear to even register to him, his attention was perfectly captured by the book in his hands—until his eyes slid over the top of his book and met mine.

I turned away and started to walk quickly across the parking lot. Fear trickled through my body making my legs feel weak. As soon as I was out of his direct eyesight, I ran to my car. My heart raced while I fumbled through my bag looking for my keys, any minute the sliding doors would open again and I would see the man come out. Franzen's warning had echoed through my ears for the last ten months, *Charlotte, they will pluck you right off the street.*

I couldn't find my keys. For one horrible moment I realized I must have left them inside. But I shook my bag and heard them jingle from somewhere deep within. I glanced up at the doors and shuffled all the contents of the bag once more. My fingers felt the sharp metal edge of a key just as the doors slid open.

My heart thundered in my ears as I pulled the keys from their hiding place and fumbled through them for the fob to unlock my door. I yanked the door handle and slid onto the driver's seat of my Jeep just as Sarah, the screaming toddler, came darting out the library doors. A moment later her mother struggled to keep up while balancing the baby on her hip and pushing their enormous stroller piled with books.

The man was still inside. I turned the key in the Jeep's ignition and shifted into reverse. The Jeep lurched and sped backwards, I slammed on the brake at the last second barely missing a lamppost anchored in a block of concrete. I pulled the gearshift into drive and accelerated out of the parking lot. I was driving too fast and the mother, now gripping Sarah's arm, yelled something after me as I sped past them.

I looked apologetically into my rearview mirror—*stupid Charlotte you could have run that little girl over.* But there he was. Standing in front of the library doors, staring after me. I could feel his eyes long after I made the turn and raced up Venice Boulevard.

I felt their eyes everywhere.

My arms were shaking. I looked up at the last minute and slammed on my brakes for a red light. The Jeep's front end traveled too far past the crosswalk and into the intersection. Cars crossing in front of me honked and took the time to roll down their windows to yell.

My whole body felt like it was shaking loose now—I needed to get home. It was the closest I ever felt to safe now, sitting in my room, surrounded by my four walls. But lately, even there, I had started to believe they watched. Their eyes had infiltrated every corner of my life.

The Bilderbergs.

I wasn't paranoid. At least, I didn't think I was.

The light changed and I gently pressed the accelerator trying to control the movement. Cars behind me began honking—I was now driving too slow. I could feel the pressure in my face building and I tried to swallow down the tears. *Come on Charlotte, just get yourself home.* I sped up a little but the tears still ran down my cheeks.

I was so alone.

I had thought, hoped, that after finding my mother, we

would eventually be together again. For weeks after seeing her in the Heathrow Airport, I had waited for a phone call, or a letter—any word from her that indicated she and Franzen were finding a way for her to be with me, at least in regular contact with me again. But weeks morphed into months and, other than the quick note she had sent locked inside the stone puzzle box, there had been no word.

I had no idea where she was, if she was okay, when or if we would ever see each other again. All I had received was a brown envelope with no address stuffed between the pages of my economics book during the first week back at school. How it got there I had no idea, but when I looked around my classroom to see if anyone was watching, waiting for my reaction, all I saw were thirty-two other kids doodling, texting under their desks, or staring out the windows while Mrs. Harris droned through her lecture on Division of Labor and Specialization. I tore away the envelope's edge and pulled out a piece of plain printer paper. In the center was typed:

You are being watched. Phone, email, computer. Zero contact.

U.N.

When I had fist read it, I was shocked—*The United Nations?* Until I realized, U.N. was Uncle Nigel. But did he mean zero contact with my mother? With him? When I had first returned home from Gaersum Aern, Caleb and Sophie had emailed me almost every day since their mother, Ms. Steward, had lifted their computer and cell phone embargo. But after receiving the note in my book, I didn't hear anything from either of them. Not a single reply to any of the many, "What's up with you guys?" had been answered either. So I guessed *Zero contact* meant zero so I stopped trying.

That was nine months ago.

I pulled my jeep, my father's seventeenth birthday present to me, into the garage beneath our bungalow. His truck was gone. Since the release of *Resurrections Test*, and the huge sales success it had been, my father had been gone a lot. There had been signings, interviews, guest lecture spots—my father, at least, was alive again. But seeing as how my only friends lived over five thousand miles away, his success meant I was alone most of the time.

I opened my door and got out. When I looked up and over my shoulder, I saw the flick of the blinds in the window of the second story condo that shared our alley. Whoever lived there had moved in nine months ago and I had never seen anyone come or go from the condo except that first day when the movers parked a small truck in the alley and lifted furniture up the stairs. Since then, the movement of the blinds every time I came home had been the only indication that anyone lived there.

You are being watched.

I grabbed my bag off the passenger seat and hurried inside.

The voice mail light was blinking on the phone. I dumped my bag and keys on the kitchen table and grabbed a microwave dinner from the freezer. "Yum, turkey in gravy," I whispered sarcastically to myself. Not that it mattered, I hardly tasted anything I ate anymore and probably only remembered to actually eat when my stomach demanded I put something in it. I checked the directions then tossed the frozen food block into the microwave and pushed the four-minute button.

While my dinner rotated, I turned to the message light. I already knew what it was—West Christian Academy's automated attendance line *with a message for the parents and/ or guardians of Charlotte Stevens. This message is to inform you that your son or daughter accrued one or more absences from school today. Please call West Christian Academy at...* Before I went to my job at the Venice Beach Library this afternoon, I had, again, ditched all my afternoon classes.

It was at the beginning of the second semester that I had started to slide. There had been one missed assignment, and then a missed day, then four missed days. Lately school felt like nothing more than time consuming busy work that kept me from what I wanted to be doing—researching everything I could about the Masons, alchemy, the Bilderbergs, and my biological father, Sir Francis Bacon a.k.a. Shakespeare, the man my mother and I knew as Franzen.

Dad knew I had missed some school—but he had no idea how bad the last month had been. Luckily, I could almost always catch the messages before he heard them—I leaned over the counter and pushed the delete button without even listening to the latest one. For the last couple of weeks, Ms. Carney had been giving me doleful looks whenever she did spot me in the halls. The only thing probably stopping her from hauling me into her office again was the fact that summer break was only a week away.

Ironically, I usually ditched my afternoon classes only to sit in the West Christian computer lab because I was too paranoid to use my own computer for my personal research. I didn't trust any of the communication devices in our home any more, they all felt like large eyes trying to capture my private world and share it with Emerick. Emerick Wriothesley, the man who wanted to know what I was up to, how much I knew, and if I planned to take up Franzen's four hundred year old mission in the world—sharing the secrets of alchemy with all of mankind.

I wondered if Emerick realized he had nothing to worry about. In the ten months since I had returned from Gaersum Aern, in the hours I had spent crawling the Internet, searching the library shelves, I still didn't understand anymore about alchemy then I had before. Sure, I knew dates, names, important figures throughout history who had believed in and practiced alchemy—but I still didn't know *what* alchemy was.

The microwave beeped loudly and I pulled out my turkey in gravy dinner. I peeled back the plastic film and stared at the lumpy mess. The directions had said something about stirring it or letting it sit but suddenly, I wasn't hungry at all.

The door to the garage opened and I heard my dad come in. "Charlotte!" he yelled before bothering to look up and see me standing five feet away.

"I'm right here."

"Oh," he looked up surprised and his face broke into a huge smile.

Something wonderful had obviously happened. "What?" I asked.

"How would you like to spend the summer touring with your number one," he held up his index finger, "bestselling father?"

"The New York Times?"

He nodded his head, "The New York Times. I've got tour dates set up for the whole summer."

My brain was processing all of this and I ended up staring at him too long without the expression he was looking for.

"Aren't you thrilled?"

"Yes."

"You don't look thrilled."

"No, I am...really. Where are you touring again?"

"The U.S."

I nodded my head and tried to figure out how I was going to say what I was about to say. "How many cities?"

"Twenty-three! Can you believe it?" he opened the fridge and peered inside. "They're begging for me."

Twenty-three cities in three months? The idea of following him in and out of hotels while we jumped from bookstore to bookstore for the entire summer was the opposite of thrilling.

He turned to me and noticed my turkey in gravy, "Are you going to eat that?"

I looked at the now gelatinous thing sitting in the plastic tray in front of me and shook my head.

"Good," he grabbed a fork from the drawer. "I haven't eaten all day." He speared a slice of turkey and took a bite.

"Dad?"

"Hum?"

"If I didn't go..."

He looked at me wide eyed, his mouth was too full to protest. He chewed a few more times then swallowed hard. "What do you mean? I thought this would be great. You and me, traveling, touring...seeing the sights."

Sights? What sights did he think we were going to have time to see in twenty-three cities in just three months? "Dad, you're going to be really busy."

"Not *that* busy."

"Yes dad, *that* busy."

He shoveled another mouthful of processed turkey into his mouth. "Well..." he swallowed. "I can't just leave you here. I mean, I know you're not a kid anymore but three months is too long."

I already had an answer to this. "I don't have to stay here. I could go to Somerset for the summer."

He wrinkled his nose while he chewed, "With your Uncle Nigel?"

"With Caleb and Sophie," I corrected.

He raised his eyebrows and seemed to consider this but then shook his head. "I'd really rather you came with me. It's an entire summer Tot, and probably the last summer I'll really have with you before you leave for college."

A hot flame of annoyance ignited in my chest. "What are you talking about? I only just finished my junior year...I'll still be here next summer."

"Physically, maybe. But the summer after your senior year? You'll never be home. There'll be parties with your friends, and saying goodbye, packing and getting ready for college. You'll be too busy for me then."

I stared at him. *Parties with my friends*? The closest person I had to a friend in Venice Beach was Aaron, my middle-aged coworker at the library and all he ever did was grunt at me from behind books. The magnitude of what my dad didn't know about me was astounding. "I can promise you, there will be no parties. I will have plenty of time to sit and wait for you," I snapped.

He concentrated on the last piece of turkey coagulating in the now cold gravy. Neither of us was used to this. His sobriety had come with an unanticipated side effect—parental awareness. It hadn't come up much in the last year, only once when I hadn't been able to erase the auto absence message before he got home. We had exchanged a few rapid-fire verbal shots before I stormed off to my room with the more damaging artillery burning on my lips. *You're not even my real father!* But I didn't say it. I locked myself in my room until I calmed down.

I had been running my own show since I was twelve...I

didn't know how to deal with a participating parent.

He carefully cut the last piece of turkey with his fork and then pushed it around the tray.

I could already tell he wasn't going to rise and do battle with me.

"I worry Tot," he whispered.

I closed my eyes and took a breath. *I worry too*, I thought. *I have worried for the last five years. I've worried about my missing mother, about you drinking yourself numb, about taking care of everything! Now I worry about things you can't even imagine.*

"I worry that it's my fault you are the way you are."

My eyes flew open and I glared at him, "The way I am?"

"You don't have any friends," he pleaded. "And what about a boyfriend? Please tell me there is someone you sneak around with because that would be fine by me. At least I would know you had *someone.*"

"No dad, there isn't anyone I sneak around with. You're right, I don't have any friends," I pointed at the ground for emphasis, "here." "Is that your fault? I don't know. Maybe it's mine, maybe it's mom's!"

His head snapped back in surprise. We never spoke of my mother and my flip comment shocked him.

"But I do have two friends dad, it's just unfortunate that they happen to live five thousand miles away. So forgive me if I would rather spend my summer-break with them, with my friends, than following you around twenty-three cities." I pushed past him and headed for my room.

"Charlotte."

It was the sadness in his voice that stopped me.

"Okay," he said. "Go to England, be with your friends. I know I've been a terrible father Charlotte. I know it every day. But I still want nothing more than for you to be happy. I just don't know how to give you that happiness."

I knew he was crying—I could hear it in his voice. But a small ember of anger still burned inside my chest and I didn't turn around. "You can't give me happiness dad." I shook my head. "You couldn't give it to mom either," I whispered. "And that's not your fault."

I walked away and shut my door.

CPSIA information can be obtained at www.ICGtesting.com
Printed in the USA
BVOW08s2251211015

423036BV00020B/100/P